In Dreams

Also by Paul J. McAuley

FOUR HUNDRED BILLION STARS
SECRET HARMONIES
THE KING OF THE HILL
ETERNAL LIGHT

Also by Kim Newman

Fiction
BAD DREAMS
THE NIGHT MAYOR
ANNO DRACULA
JAGO
(as Jack Yeovil)
DRACHENFELS
BEASTS IN VELVET
DEMON DOWNLOAD
KROKODIL TEARS
COMEBACK TOUR

Non Fiction
NIGHTMARE MOVIES
WILD WEST MOVIES
HORROR: THE 100 BEST BOOKS
(edited with Stephen Jones)
GHASTLY BEYOND BELIEF
(edited with Neil Gaiman)

In Dreams

Edited by
Paul J. McAuley
& Kim Newman

LONDON
VICTOR GOLLANCZ LTD
1992

First published in Great Britain 1992
by Victor Gollancz Ltd
14 Henrietta Street, London WC2E 8QJ

To David Pringle –
the editors' editor

Contents

8 Contents

Introduction:
Planet Rock (Don't Stop)

Charles Shaar Murray

A few years ago I stumbled – wholly independently, I might add – on the notion of compiling an anthology of science-fiction stories about rock and roll under the working title of *Planet Rock (Don't Stop)*. Being a cheap bastard – not to mention a cheap, *lazy* bastard – my intention was to work with existing stories, including Norman Spinrad's 'The Big Flash' (the ultimate rock apocalypse story), J. G. Ballard's 'The Sound-Sweep' (which concerns itself with opera rather than rock, but in terms of the impact of the kind of music technology which rock has traditionally embraced so wholeheartedly), Samuel R. Delany's 'Time Considered as a Helix of Semi-Precious Stones' (whose protagonist is as-near-as-dammit a rock star, though in an informal rather than formal sense), Lewis Shiner's 'Jeff Beck', Shiner and Bruce Sterling's 'Mozart in Mirrorshades', Sterling's 'Dori Bangs', Pat Cadigan's 'Pretty Boy Crossover', and various others.

I abandoned the idea for a variety of excellent reasons: one being that a third of the stories would have had to have come straight from Sterling's *Mirrorshades: The Cyberpunk Anthology* and most of the rest would have been by Howard Waldrop (what *is* it with these goddam Texans, anyway?). Another that Paul J. McAuley and Kim Newman, not being cheap lazy bastards, have actually gone ahead and done the thing (with all-original stories, to boot) and here it is. All that remains for me to do is to congratulate them (and the authors whom they have induced to step forward and do the Martian Hop and the Planet Rock) on a good job excellently done (bastards!); and to offer a few thoughts on the twisted relationship between two art forms which have fascinated me since my teens.

SF and rock and roll are both Big Fun because each is determinedly and delightedly larger (not to mention louder and weirder) than life. The electric boogie enables three, four or five suitably equipped humans (a personnel in single figures, anyway) to produce a bigger noise than a jazz big band or a symphony orchestra. Science fiction hauls the reader, in Cordwainer Smith's felicitous phrase, into the 'Up-and-Out': how far up and how far out is constrained only by the author's imagination (prose fiction, after all, permits its creator an unlimited special-effects budget).

Moreover, both rock and SF are bastard arts which, despite intense parental disapproval, can boast both illustrious pedigrees and extensive prehistories. Rockers point proudly to their music's roots in jazz, blues, gospel and country music, just as SF is happy to cite its origins in the undeniably respectable and impeccably literary works of Mary Shelley, Jules Verne or H. G. Wells, all of whom were fortunate enough to have got their best and most influential work done before the imaginative and fantastic were evicted from the mainstream of European literature and exiled to the warm, frowsy environment of juvenile fiction and the pulps. Jazz eventually became accepted as an art music because even the most devout Eurocentrics were forced to concede that considerable intelligence was required in order to play it; country blues was undoubtedly a folk music of immense historical value and emotional power, but R&B and rock and roll were trashy commercial musics unfit for the attention of civilised adults.

Nevertheless, both underwent crucial mutations in the 1950s, when teenagers were invented (or, to be more accurate, invented themselves) and proudly demonstrated that first tenet of capitalist philosophy: I spend, therefore I am. The new species speedily adapted two existing genres for their own specialised needs: rhythm-and-blues (the pop lingua franca of black America) metamorphosed into rock and roll under the joint aegis of Elvis Presley, Chuck Berry, Little Richard and countless others and the SF and horror movie underwent similar transformations at the hands of Roger Corman and the American-International crew. As John Cooper Clarke put it twenty-odd (very odd) years later, 'I was a teenage werewolf – or was I?' The connection was made. Both rock and SF were tickets to elsewhere (not to mention *elsewhen*); both were magical highways leading out of the suburbs to new locations where things actually happened. To the existing practitioners of SF (particularly those tweedy types who hated aeroplanes and refused to have a television set or, later, a computer in the house), rock may simply have been another manifestation of the new barbarism; to many kids of the 'fifties and 'sixties (including your editors, the present writer and the bulk of the contributors to this anthology) the two are inextricably linked, both manifestations of that 'intense adolescent exploration' to which Marc Laidlaw alludes in 'Wunderkindergarten'.

The blues and jazz in which rock is rooted began as *performance* musics capable of sustaining extended improvisations; but as *recorded* musics both were initially forced to abide by the technological restrictions imposed by the three-minutes-maximum-per-side duration of the 78rpm single record. The legends which form the basis of all modern fantastic literature were great sprawling sagas which went on, like, for*ever*, duuuuuude; but modern SF has its origins in short fiction. The kind of elephantiasis which brings us concept double albums and 'major' trilogies (or, worse still, linked suites of trilogies) can be interpreted, according to taste, as either terminal decadence or as definitive proof of the form's maturity. The end results can be either mind-numbing pap or a mind-expanding stimulus; a 'smart drug' or – like a musical equivalent of crack or barbiturates – a dumb drug. But SF and rock and roll are both drugs, after all, and they're both still legal.

So here you'll find the kid who wanted to kill Mick Jagger and the derelict who was John Lennon. It's interesting that so many of the SF writers who have used rock as a subject betray their origins as 'fifties and 'sixties kids by harking back to Lennon, Elvis and other iconic myth-figures of their youth when we are, after all, living in an era when the mainstream pop of the moment is itself science fiction. Ballard's Sound-Sweep would be more at home in the world of sequencers, samples and robot drummers than would Delany's raggedy-ass cosmic poet; silvery little CDs – sterile, digital, laser-read gizmos that they are – are so much more SF than black vinyl discs. But then, as Bayley and Watson remind us, part of SF's function is sometimes to use the distant future or a far-flung planet or a hidden dimension as a platform from which to re-examine our present or recent past, or to reawaken the wonderful from its slumbering concealment in the commonplace.

As John Lee Hooker would say, 'This is hip, pretty baby.' *In Dreams* is ready for you; I hope you're ready for *In Dreams*. Free your mind . . . and your ass will follow.

London, Tenerife, San Francisco
January 1992

Fat Tuesday
Ian McDonald

Not only was Ian McDonald one of the first of a new generation of British SF writers to break into print in the eighties, he did it in the USA. After publishing several highly acclaimed short stories in Isaac Asimov's Science Fiction Magazine and being nominated for the John W. Campbell Award for Best New Writer of 1985, he published his first novel, Desolation Road, and a collection of short fictions, Empire Dreams, in 1988. Three more novels have followed, the latest being Hearts, Hands and Voices. At present he's working on something called Necroville, but whether that has to do with the fact that he lives in Belfast isn't apparent. If anything, as with Van Morrison, Belfast inspires McDonald's lyrical fictions, notable for their density of ideas and exuberant characters and prose, which in 'Fat Tuesday' find an ideal marriage of form and content.

McDonald tells us:

I'd like to say it happened like this:

Six fifteen. Pressing buttons on the remote control.

Channel one: the child killers of Rio are abroad in the hills again.

Channel two: dance energy, some Harlem kid pulling incredible rhythms out of a plastic bucket.

Channel three: ladeez/gennelmen/boys'n'girls: life in the Lycra Age!

Channel four: the great white guitar thrash fetish.

Remix is the dominant popular culture form of these last two decades of the twentieth century.

Except – it didn't. Quite.

Black Sunday

S*ambada*: musical composition in 2/4 rhythm characterised by massed drumming, remixed sampled material and extended electric guitar improvisation.

Also: *sambada*: a popular dance originating from the conurbations of Alto California province, to the above-mentioned musical composition, especially as performed during the annual pre-Lenten carnival.

Also: *sambada*: a social gathering at which *sambada* is danced and performed.

Sambada school: a collection of individuals, usually of one shanty district (see *cabaña*) incorporating musicians, dancers, costume designers, etc. who represent their district in the carnival parade and *sambada* competition.

sambadero(a): a man or woman wise in the ways of *sambada*.

Run, Annunciato.

Do not doubt they are behind you, pouring down the steep alleys of Birimbao Hill. Do not doubt that theirs are the voices whooping and cheering, theirs the wolf cries and the laughter like whips, echoing among the shanties and favelas. Do not doubt that theirs is the *batteria* surging through the trash streets and dirt squares, drums beating beating you from wherever you try to hide. And never for one instant imagine that they will ever give up until they catch you and kill you. For they are the Lobos de Sangre, and no wolf will abandon the chase until it has tasted blood.

Grasped in Annunciato's right hand, the glass guitar gently bleeds.

Thoughts of escape, Annunciato? That maybe if you can reach the boulevard you will be able to lose them among the holographic saints and neon madonnas and videowall advertisements for Coke and Sony and *cannbarillos*? Prayers, Annunciato? Oh Mary, dazzle them with your neon halo, oh gay St Sebastian, send your laser arrows into their eyes?

Better to run, Annunciato. The freeway has new gods now, new deities born out of the media remix. They are gauche and inexpert, but enthusiastic.

Nissans and Toyotas cut smoking rubber hexagrams into the blacktop as Annunciato and his glass guitar weave between the bumper-to-bumpers crowding the five lanes inbound and five lanes outbound: *Hey boy you tired of living, stupid favelado, cabañero you want to mash yourself all over my hood ornaments I am only too happy to oblige you where he steal that guitar from anywhereplacehow?* Oaths and imprecations cease as the Lobos come loping through the gridlock slapping out the rhythm of the hunt on spray-customised hoods, leaping from fender to fender to fender, leering in at the Valley Girls in six centimetre heels and hi-thi-leos and wrapround teleshades.

In some off-avenue back alley overseen by videowall Marys, he stops to listen if they are still behind him.

Oh yes, Annunciato. Most definitely, Annunciato.

The roar of engines is like a steel-capped boot in the stomach. The lowriders come revving along the alleyways, Lobos hungry, eager, riding on doors and roofs, beating out their hunting song on hot-shopped Toyota steel. Sparks scream back from their scratch plates.

Reconcile your soul with the saints of the boulevard.

And the big hoload for Diet-Coke on the side of the National Lottery Office says: ANNUNCIATO.

The name, tastefully iconised in spray-can platinums and razor blues, tumbles away through holospace. The spotlights of the Lobos pin and pluck you naked as one of the chickens Madre Amparo takes to the shrine of St Anthony. The back streets off St Dominic's Preview are loud with the whisper click of switchblades.

TRUST ME. I WILL PROTECT YOU.

Lasers sear the night. Brave, bold howling Lobos fall back swearing screaming clutching burns gashes scars. A new ingredient in the city perfume of sweat, shit, smoke and semen: scorched flesh. Glass guitar in hand, Annunciato is safe behind a wall of flickering laserlight.

A miracle.

STAY HERE. SOMEONE WILL COME TO HELP YOU, says the hoload.

'What who why how?' says dazed and confused Annunciato.

The big BVM videowall on the Credit and Loan fills with starry starry night. A pair of strawberry luscious lips rezz up on the startrek sky. Fruit comes tumbling out of the mind of the Coca-Cola Company's videographics computer; bananas, pineapples, oranges, guava, mango, piled up like Mr Socks' stall in Birimbao Plaza. A woman's face fills in behind the lips, beneath the tutti-frutti hat. Blessed Virgin Mary was never like this.

LA MIRANDA, says the videowall as, with a wink and a smile, the woman fades into the Alto California night. *Los Lobos* howl and smash the big chrome wrenches that are their ritual weapons against the oily concrete. But the lasers hold them.

A light. And a voice. A woman's voice. Flashlight beams, a vision, riding down on an extending fire escape out of the Sacred Heart of Jesus on the U-Bend-We-Mend. Silver lamé from the peak of her baseball cap to the tips of her boots, a jingle-jangle of ripped-off hood ornaments around her neck, the Six Mystic Stars of Subaru.

Angel of mercy, and, incredible of incredibles, *white*.

Annunciato thought they had all died out in their rotting haciendas and Tudor mansionettes years ago.

'You come now, right now,' she says. Her Angeleño is appalling. 'Right now, you come. La Miranda, she cannot go on drawing this much power from the grid for long time. Catholic engineers come, shut her down. So you come, come now.' He reaches toward the pure white hand and is drawn up into heaven. Over rooftops, she leads him, through forests of aerials and satellite dishes, past cooling towers and rotary clotheslines and coiling serpentine airco ducts, across rooftop marijuana gardens and coca plantations, leaping through the yawning dark over deep dark alleys while the never-ending stream of taillights winds and wends beneath them and the Lobos, released from luminous imprisonment, go loping along the shining sidewalks, howling at the grapefruit moon. And the glass guitar drips a trail of minims and crochets like the silver slime of a night snail on the side of the basilica of Santa Barbara.

'Down. Now.'

The big jacked-up mauve and yellow 4X4 is circling, growling in the parking lot of Señor Barato All-Nite super-mart like a bull in the ring, pawing at the piss-stained concrete with its monster balloon tyres. The Lobos, war drums a-swinging, arrive in a wave of uniform pink and green as Annunciato and the angel drop from the swinging end of the fire escape and hit the ground.

'In, in.' The driver is an old old black man – more incredible even than the silver lamé angel – already gunning the accelerator, tyres smoking on the concrete. 'In!' Doors slam.

'Caution, caution, your seatbelt is not properly engaged, please engage your seatbelt,' says a made-in-Yokohama chip-generated conscience. Lowriders slam to a halt beneath Señor Barato's flashing sign. Grinning and gabbling like a *loco*, the old black man throws the beast into four-wheel drive and up they go on those big monster wheels right over the tops of the lowriders and out into the neon and smog of the boulevard.

¿Porque?

Because on this Black Sunday night Annunciato killed a Blood Wolf with a glass guitar.

The sambadrome had been jumping. Word is up, *compadres*. Tonight tonight tonight is the big Play-Off. Tonight the last two *guitarristos* do battle to the beat of hip-slung drum and mixing desk for the glory glory hallelujah of leading all Birimbao Hill on Fat Tuesday.

Yelping and blowing football whistles, his brother Lions'a'Judah had carried him shoulder high down the precipitous paths of the favela, this boy from nowhere who had swept the wing play-offs with his glass guitar. Have you not heard? Tonight tonight tonight the red gold and green of Judah will smash the pink and green of the Lobos.

As the rival *guitarristos* were borne into the sambadrome, the *batteria* had struck up, those aristocrats of rhythm, drumming up an avalanche of sound that seemed to sweep all Birimbao down before it into the valley. And the *remixados* in their baseball caps with the correct corporate logos and their hi-tops and cycle shorts had spun and scratched and sweated and mixed and mastered. And the *sambaderos* in their Famous Names sportswear, the *sambaderas* in their leos and body-paint had spilled onto the floor, shaking it strutting it slapping it stuffing it shrieking it *ai ai ai ai*.

He had been good, the Blood Wolves' *guitarristo*. Had he not been, he might have lived. But as the guitars up on their speaker towers clashed and tangled in fugues and counterpoints, he had felt a spirit awaken in the glass guitar, that same spirit that had called to him that morning when this Annunciato, sixth son of a sixth son, glimpsed that gleam of glass in a Birimbao trash heap, a spirit growing stronger, stronger than Annunciato could hold, something that fed on the sweat and the stink and the shatter of drums and one by one the dancers and the *remixados* and even the *batteria* stopped to watch and the only sound beneath the samba-drome's corrugated iron roof was the unbearable feedback howl of the glass guitar on and on and on and on and on and on and on like the scream of every child that was ever born in the street and the scream of every soul that ever fell to a blade in a *cabaña* alley and the scream of every *sambadera* in the ear of her *sambadero* as she gave it away in the rear seat of a hot-wired Nissan in the back rank of the drive-in and the music seized the Lobos' *guitarristo* and burned his soul away to nothing and he toppled from the speaker tower with smoke coming from his eyes and then they all screamed with one voice and heart and soul.

One chord. That is all the difference there is between hero and monster.

Blue Monday

Sambada por mujeros.

Everything is crucially dependent on the T and A zones. Yah, you got it. Tits and Ass.

The T Zone. You got a mirror? Then get a mirror. Strip off. Yes, everything. All you going to be wearing come Fat Tuesday is gloves and boots and black velvet G-string. The Five of Spades look. Cellulite? No worries, there will always be someone worse off than you. Roll your shoulders; left, then right. The idea is to get each breast to describe its own separate, complementary orbit.

The A Zone. As above, but with hips rather than shoulders, and – here is the bit that marks the true *street sambadera* from the exhibitionists in from the suburbs or up from the projects – *the A zone has to work in contra-rotation to the T Zone*. They reckon it takes half a year just to get the basic rhythm. When you can give the impression you are having an orgasm sitting on top of a thousand-speed spin washing machine, you are close. It helps if you smile. Anything that makes you feel more confident wiggling your T and A in front of several million spectators and eleven satellite channels while dressed in a postage stamp on a piece of elastic has got to help.

Her name is Ros'a'Jericho.

She is an apostle of the Tucurombé.

They are members of a *kairis*.

A *kairis* is a group of (usually) four individuals who may, or may not, previously know each other, called together by the Tucurombé to achieve some divinely ordained purpose.

The purpose of this *kairis* is to find a *guitarristo* to lead the Tres Milagros parade, the theme of which this year is the New Gods.

The Tucurombé, of whom this La Miranda who saved Annunciato from the Lobos is a member, are the new gods.

Whoa whoa whoa whoa whoa. Kid Annunciato's head is spinning. He is only a malnourished undereducated favela boy, after all.

Ros'a'Jericho lives with the old black man, who is known as El Batador, in a house on Tres Milagros Hill. They do not sleep with each other. Annunciato has heard of Tres Milagros Hill. Most people in this city have heard of Tres Milagros Hill, the one with the big white letters on top of it that no one can understand, the one where all the *weirds*, and *freaks*, and *devos*, and *teevees* go to be weird and freaky and devo-ish and dress up or dress down together. Tres Milagros have won the golden Bell of St James five times in the past ten years under the leadership of their director, the fabled La Baiana.

And they want Annunciato to be chief *guitarristo*? HeesusHoséMaria . . .

Ros'a'Jericho is the *remixado*. She lives on a mattress amid piles of rotting Chinese food cartons in a room stacked to the ceiling with silver and black boxes bearing the logos of Pacific Rim corporations. The only light is that of LEDs and crystal displays.

'No vinyl, no spiral, no scratch,' she says. 'Happening world is my found source.' The pockets of her silver lamé suit contain DATcorders from which she remixes the sound of the city into her music.

The aged aged black man makes food. *Guitarristos* are always hungry. It is good for the music. While Annunciato pokes rice and beans and a little chopped synthetic meat into his face, El Batador tells him about the Tucurombé.

They are gods. Real gods. Street gods. Patterns of alien intelligence stirred out of the informational minestrone of the Pacific Rim computer cores and seasoned with Catholic hagiolatry; favela myth and superstition; silver screen icon-ography; the symbolism of *candomblé, umbanda, vodun,* Rosi-crucianism and mass-market Buddhism; emergent myths of the global data nets; night-hawk radio heroes, rock'n'soul legends. They have quite a following on Tres Milagros and in some of the big projects and *arcosantis*. Gods of the remix.

'Though it was Seu Guantanamera had been watching you, calling you, chose you for the *kairis*,' says the old black man, 'it was La Miranda, the oldest and strongest of the Tucurombé, traced you through the traffic control cameras down on the boulevard and called us. These are gods of the public telephone and the traffic signal. They are strong, young, eager. They do not ask of their disciples *renounce the world, the flesh and the devil,* they ask *and what have you done for me lately?'*

Ogun Dé is the old black man's particular patron. Conceived in the informational shatter of a Mundo Tercero terror grouping's viral attack on the military systems, he oversees all things dynamic and rhythmic. Arcologies, freeways, ionocruisers, carnival fireworks, heavy rains, fire, fighting, team sports, all these fall into his bailiwick. He is Master of Rhythm. He is Lord of the Drums. His avatar, rezzed up on Sendai-Nihon wristie-vision, is a stealth bomber in Gothic spiked armour.

San BuriSan is a rotating icosahedron of Japanese theatre masks, persona of change and evolution. Bottle banks and carcrushers are his, his also adolescence, plastic, birthdays, editing desks and lasers. Born one cherry-blossom morning in the transfinite complexity of the Pacific Rim stock exchange cores, he is King Scratch, Master Remix.

Seu Guantanamera, the one who, if this crazy old black man can be believed, if anything that has happened these past twentysomething hours can be believed, is the personal guardian and guide of Annunciato and his glass guitar. He is Master of Harmony, Completer and Sustainer of the quadrilateral of entities; his source and symbol is a glass guitar.

El Batador reverently picks up the Glass Guitar, wipes the scabs of dried music from its wounds, hands it to Ros'a'Jericho, who shakes her silver head – she cannot understand anything that is itself, not made from other things remixed together – passes it back to Annunciato, like some sacramental *ganja.* His fingers come and go, come and go, up and down the silent frets.

'Back in the time of the Black Star Liner,' says El Batador, 'when the black people left for Ethiopia on that ship that was three miles long and two miles wide and a mile high that sailed for forty years through every ocean in the world, back then lived the greatest guitarist ever laid finger to fret. Bar none. Seu Guantanamera. With those six strings he could make you cry and laugh and die and feel like you had seen the face of God or something even better. People said he was God, or something better, and they would have made him God if he had let them, but he died trying out a new guitar, a guitar like there had never been before. Made of glass, it was. Clear pure and perfect crystal. And it killed him. An accident with the electronics. The circuitry went live. He died instantly, up on stage in front of twenty thousand people, in mid chord.

'And then the legends started. Legends that his soul had passed into the glass guitar, that whoever bought it would have no luck with it until it passed into the hands of someone who had as much, or more, talent than Seu Guantanamera, legends that when the time was right the trapped soul would be released.'

And as the old black man says those words, Annunciato, who has been thinking, yo, yo, ga, ga, suddenly feels the strings hum beneath his fingers, like electricity like summer lightning in the hills. And he is much much afraid.

'Tell me,' says El Batador, and it is as if all Tres Milagros Hill right up to those crazy letters on the top is listening for Annunciato's answer, 'Tell me, how did you find it?'

'On a trash heap,' says Annunciato, 'on Birimbao Hill. One morning, I went out, and there it was. It didn't look like it was anybody's. I taught myself to play, day in, day out, every hour I could spare, I practised, so I could be like the big *guitarristos*, better, even.' But as he says these words, he understands that they are true, and at the same time not true. They should be reversed, It found Him, It taught Him. It made Him the best. There had always been a sense of the hand of the angels about it, from the moment he saw it twinkling from the shit and foam styrene burger boxes that bright Birimbao morning.

Sambada por hombres.

You got it easier. You only got one zone to worry about. From the waist up you might as well be foam polystyrene. From the waist down you got to be hotter than Mama Marilena's hot salsa. So start today. You want ten-, twelve-, fourteen-year-old *boys* to out-*sambada* you?

First, the stance. Feet apart, shoulder width. Now, bend back from the knees. Back. Back. Are you making a thirty degree angle with the ground? That's all right. Next, clench the cheeks of your ass. Tight. You should be able to carry an Amex card between them all the way from the sambadrome down to the Square of the Basilica of Our Lady of the Angels where the judging is held. Once you can do that you are ready for the *grind*. Swivel your pelvis, left hip up, round in a circle, back, then your right hip so that your groin – the entire focal point of *sambada* – is going round and round like an aeroplane propeller. When your RPM equals your degree of inclination away from vertical, you are *muy sambadero*. But do not forget: dignity. You got to have dignity, or the boys will laugh. You got to be cooler than a bottle of Dos Equis in a tin tub full of ice.

La Baiana: is: twenty-two stone of fun wedged into leopard-print lycra, falsies jutting like the Guns of Navarone, little troublesome moustache line virtually invisible beneath a stucco of powder and rouge. *Rei de Las Reiñas*, *carnivalado* of *carnivalados*, the designer's designer. There was never as titanic an old Queen as La Baiana. From his throne of hammered flat Heineken cans in Tres Milagros sambadrome, guarded by Playa Venecia body-shop *musculados*, he purses persimmon lips as radiantly beautiful young teevees parade past, wiggling it, jiggling it, pouting and preening and prinking, pausing in front of La Baiana for that little turn, that little shake of the *tushie*.

'He choosing teevees,' says Ros'a'Jericho. 'Tres Milagros much much famous for quality of transvestites. Big honour, be chosen by La Baiana to march in Tucurombé parade.'

But the big carnival queen has seen his fellow *kairisados* and claps his be-ringed hands.

'Out girls, out. Back at nineteen and then we shall see who wins the prize.' He leans forward in his throne, peers at Annunciato like he is a turd sticking to a shower curtain. 'La Miranda saves this piece of ass to be our *guitarristo*? This is Seu Guantanamera come again?'

Annunciato, with the unerring *cabañero* talent for the gratuitous move, lifts the glass guitar above his head in both hands, strikes a groin-jutting *sambadero* pose.

'I got his guitar.'

'I got a crucifix, but that doesn't make me Jesus,' says La Baiana. But you can see he is just the littlest, tiniest, *poco* bit impressed. He indicates the wall of banked-up amps speakers bins drivers mixers decks behind his throne. 'Let the *sambada* decide. Yo! El Batador!'

Rhythm answers. Complex, sinuous, muscular, many-layered rhythm that strikes into the heart and finds its resonant frequency. El Batador is seated on an empty beer-crate drumming on an upturned plastic bucket, lifting the rim and slapping it against the pounded clay of the samba-drome with his boney feet in counterpoint.

Q: How many men does it take to fill a sambadrome with one plastic bucket?

A: One, but he must be *muy muy sambadero*.

HeesusHoséMaria, Annunciato has been waiting all his short life to play with musicians of this calibre. This old black man, he makes the massed *batterias* of all Birimbao Hill sound like kids kicking rhythms out of the bus stops with disposable chopsticks. Annunciato picks up the beat: *Baile Mi Hermana*, one of the standards, easy to play badly, hard to play good. He will show this fat transvestite *carnivalado*. If they are gods, these spirits in the computers, he will be worthy of them. He plays the theme high and pure and holy and Ros'a'Jericho behind her deck comes in on a wave of samples as he breaks into improvisations. And it lifts. It soars. It takes off and heads from the Van Allen belts. It screams, high and holy and hot hot hot and the *cabaña* bums and *malandros* are standing two four six eight deep around the concrete-block walls mouths open eyes popping what kinda *merda* this and Annunciato feels the thing in the guitar awaken and open like a moonflower blooming and he looks inside and sees . . .

'Ai ai ai ai,' shouts La Baiana dancing on his throne. 'Enough enough enough enough. I believe you, I believe you.' And one of his body-boys throws the master isolator and it all fails, it all falls, it all fades and comes apart and Annunciato, soaked with sweat, feels like a crashed angel.

'Hot dog, jumpin' frog,' says Ros'a'Jericho. '*Muy guitarristo!* Seu Guantanamera!' She kisses him on the mouth. She tastes of pork, like white women are supposed to.

Crackin' bottles, yabba yabba; long-necks from a tin bath full of ice up at La Baiana's place, which is cool and airy and has ceiling fans which Annunciato has only ever seen on television and lots of things in terracotta pots on the patio and is built into the third 'O' of the letters of the hill.

Bosque de los Acebos, that is what it means, Ros'a'Jericho tells Annunciato, which means nothing at all to him.

'Used to make movies here, way way long back before the Treaty of Albuquerque,' says La Baiana, sweating like a pig developing little five o'clock shadow problemo vicinity upper lip. 'Legend is, if you go down, way down, way down low, whole damn city is built on a can of film a hundred kilometres across.'

'*Merda*,' says Ros'a'Jericho. 'Is city built on rock'n'roll. Bossanova. Blues. Soul. Samba. Sambada. Is electric guitar is way down low, down deep deep deep. Great guitar hundred kilometres long, and when great guitar finally plays, world ends, everything remixed and remade.'

'Yo yo, rock'n'roll,' says La Baiana, belching gently.

Fat Tuesday

Sambada por gringos.

Tragic. You see them, these fat women in shades and hi-thi leotards, these Japanese boys with all the correct corporate logos and hood ornaments you know they have bought at the airport and these *norte* intellectuals down by the planeload from Vancouver and Medicine Hat because the carnival is the Last Great Celebration of Folk Culture, trying to shake it shake it shake it to the drums and the deck and, I tell you, it makes me want to cry. Like watching something crawled from under a stone running away from the light. *Sambada* for gringos? Forget it. You do not have the *street*.

Please God, don't let it rain today.

In every *cabaña*, in every slum and favela, on every hill, they have been up since dawn, those who have been to bed (their own, anyone else's) perming hair waxing bikini lines slipping/wedging into feathery flowery leathery rubbery silvery goldy costumes checking the T and A zones in front of the mirror worrying about lip gloss powder paint running in heels through the shit and mud for the bus to take them to the assembly point where directors high as comsats on dexxies mescalin and nervous energy marshal floats, *batterias*, vast mobile sound stages for the *guitarristos* and *remixados* like launch platforms for interstellar expeditions, regiments of bare-cheeked *sambaderas* bitching about the cellulite levels of their opponents' gleaming rumps; phalanxes of hung-over, battle-scarred *sambaderos* in shell-suits and baseball caps of the requisite colours into *some* semblance of a procession.

Down on the freeway at the foot of Tres Milagros, La Baiana, dressed in lace tutu and Herman Goering white with campy upswept biker's cap, issues orders through a loud-hailer from the back of El Batador's pick-up.

Primero: a dancing wing of two hundred teevees.

Segundo: four floats each bearing the glass-fibre likenesses of the Tucurombé: La Miranda first, with body-painted acolytes throwing real fruit to the audience; then Ogun Dé with his bodyguard of Tres Milagros bloods in black spiked rubber demon suits, then San BuriSan on a videowall of one hundred televisions donated by a variety of Pacific Rim electronics companies; last Seu Guantanamera accompanied by strolling mariachi musicians and girls dressed as lightning bolts.

Tercero: the *batteria*, made up of dockers from Drowntown and construction workers from the new Todos Santos *arcosanti* over by Poco Venecia – during the marching season, drumming in the lunch-hour ousts even football – all dressed in mauve and yellow and led by El Batador himself, as he has led them every year for the past twenty-five years.

Cuarto: the mobile sound-stage borne on the backs of three tank transporters (some general down in Chihuahua owed La Baiana, but what he was not prepared to say); complete with sound system lighting rig FX backing musicians and roadies in mauve and yellow. Here Annunciato and Ros'a'Jericho will amaze the city.

Quinto: two hundred maidens dancing.

Sexto: two hundred lords of the *cabañas* a-leaping.

Septimo: a wedge of open-topped bunting-and-flower decorated cars in which the *sambaderos* and *sambaderas* of former days, too old now to dance all the way to the square of Our Lady of the Angels, ride in honour and splendour, decked with synthetic feathers and often wearing ludicrously decorated glasses.

Octavo: a rearguard of assorted devos freakos pervos rubberboys leatherboys bike-fetishists SM enthusiasts etc. etc.

El Batador is already sounding time on his plastic bucket tucked under his arm, crazy old black man. Annunciato is scared three kinds of excretaless, only Ros'a'Jericho looks like she knows what she is doing. Her silver lamé suit is covered in clip-on microphones wired into a transmitter in the small of her back and beaming tight and righteous into her sampledeck. No recordings, no found sources; this Fat Tuesday her source is her city and she mixes in real-time the sounds and music of carnival itself, snitched and snatched and crammed rammed jammed through her mixing desk.

La Baiana takes his position in the gilded cupola at the back of the portable sound-stage, looks to make sure everything is ready. Which of course it isn't but if you waited until it was you would never get anywhere.

'Okay, my little chikadees.' He slips a Little Thunderer between his ice-cream pink lips, blows a mighty blast that sets even the letters up on the hill reverberating. 'Let's go!'

Last census Alto California had a population in the region of thirty-five million people. Looks like every last one of them, plus eleven satellite channels, turned out this Fat Tuesday. The streets are canyons of sound and colour, cheering voices, whistles, banners, streamers, balloons with the faces of cartoon characters and football stars on them; it is high, high stuff, higher than anything they ever sold in

zip-loc plastic sachets back of Mr Socks' stall on Birimbao
Plaza and the Glass Guitar snorts it down its f-holes and it
burns along the strings up Annunciato's fingers and it is just
the edge, the promise of a wildness that could be if he is
brave enough and Ros'a'Jericho takes up the roar of the
crowd and the beating of the bells and the cymbals and
slams them through her processors and La Baiana is jigging
and clapping his hands like he is in heaven and now the
canyon walls of the business district close in around you and
funnel Tres Milagros into the massive procession twenty
kilometres long that is Carnival, a torrent of life and sound
and colour and music channelled between the twenty thirty
forty fifty storey high videowalls of the big Pacific Rim
corporadas and the people crowded twenty thirty forty fifty
deep along the boulevards are so close so pressing the sound
of them is like a physical presence and Ros'a'Jericho scoops
it up and takes it apart and puts it back together again and
the glass guitar snorts it down and sends it burning up
through your fingers into your brain and you see with a
sudden new light like the dawn slanting through the windows of Our Lady Star of the Sea mission between the end
of one note and the next what it is that lies hidden within
the moonflower heart of the Glass Guitar, it is every great
moment you ever had listening to the radio in the heat of
the night, it is dancing in the rain to sound of accapella, it is
rhinestone guitars playin' live from Las Vegas on the Sunday
night satellite channels, all these and more, every great and
true and holy and profane moment whether you call it
rock'n'roll or soul or bossanova or blues or *sambada* and he
realises now what he is to do, he is not to hold it back, that
was where he went wrong that time in the Birimbao sambadrome, that was why the boy was killed, because he held
back and it struck out to be free, struck out blindly, in anger
and hurt; he opens himself to the thing in the guitar, draws

it up into the heart of him and he screams and the guitar
screams as his eyes are opened to a new light and he sees
the faces on the videowalls change into the face of a woman
with a bowl of fruit on her head and a stealth bomber in
spiked armour and a dozen kabuki masks spinning in space
and, last of all, a glass guitar rimmed with lightning bolts.

Seu Guantanamera.

And the Glass Guitar leaps beneath Annunciato's fingers
free at last free at last dear God free at last and roars in heat and
draws the rhythm of the *batteria* and the master mix and the
reality dub and the stamping of the dancing feet and the
thirty million voices plus eleven satellite channels into one
thing, one music which transcends *music*, that becomes
something brilliant and burning and beautiful and shit-scary
that even the *batteria* falls silent and the *sambaderos* and
sambaderas stop in mid wiggle, mid shimmy to turn and stare
at the wild things raving from the Glass Guitar and there is
only old mad El Batador banging on his plastic bucket and
Annunciato playing like no one, not even Seu Guantanamera, ever played six strings. It is joy. It is burning. It is
pain. It is sex. It is every great and noble thing, it is every
rat-mean and wicked thing.

Higher. Higher. Higher. God save us, please, we cannot
take much more of this.

Higher. Higher.

God, please, no!

Higher . . .

And it ends.

And in the silence afterwards, thirty-five million people
plus eleven satellite channels hear clearly, unmistakably,
enormous musical harmonics, vaster than heaven, sound
deep in the earth beneath their feet, like the notes of a guitar
buried in the centre of the earth, a guitar on which God
might jam with creation and the immense sound of it

penetrates everything, shakes everything streets buildings earth sky music heat and mind, shakes them apart and in the space between is a light purer and brighter than any light you have ever seen before.

Then the infinite sustained note dies away and the vision fades and there is no God now only a *cabañero* punk holding the fused, shattered fragments of a once beautiful glass guitar. But there is a new colour in every one of the neon signs and holograms and videowalls, one that no one has ever seen before but everyone immediately recognises as the colour of *street*.

Ash Wednesday

Street.

The very heart and soul of *sambada*. One of those words that if you have to look it up in a book, you will never never know what it means, *compadre*.

When the great guitar at the centre of the earth sounded and the Tucurombé were released, the world was never quite the same. When you take a thing apart you can never put it back exactly the same way. Sometimes worse. Sometimes better. Always different.

Many small wishes were granted. Lost things turned up again. The military junta all resigned.

There was a simultaneous computer failure in all the world's tax offices.

The rains actually came on time this year.

Suddenly, everyone found they had a little more money than they had thought.

Suddenly, there were more national holidays in the calendar than before.

Suddenly everyone fell in love.

Suddenly your favourite football team started to play better.

Suddenly the radios were filled with a new and wonderful music that reminded you of all the great songs you have ever loved, but more so, and better, and newer.

The Tucurombé seemed determined to start their reign auspiciously.

Annunciato became the guitar hero he had always dreamed of being but was haunted all his stellar career by the knowledge that he would never again play as he played the day the new gods were born.

Inspired by a dream of radio, Ros'a'Jericho had wires put in her head so that when she went roller-skating along the sidewalks her every thought and hope and dream and experience would be broadcast citywide FM. You can find her most Sunday mornings at half-past a nightmare on the dial between the Evangelical Pentecostal Missions and Radio Free Oklahoma.

La Baiana went on to achieve his sixth Golden Bell, fabulous celebrity, enormous girth and immense longevity. He was commissioned to design TeeVee World, the first Transvestite Theme Park which crashed two years later leaving debts in excess of one hundred million pesos. La Miranda saw fit to extend his gift of sexual transubstantiation to any and all people, and for as long as they wished, but try as he might he could never get it to work on himself.

El Batador went back to his *compadres* at the docks and was last seen one October evening swimming madly out to sea toward what he thought was the Black Star Liner three miles long and two miles wide and a mile high come back to take him home to Ethiopia but in the end was only a cruise ship carrying *viajeros* from the *norte*, carved out of a twenty kilometre iceberg.

The Discovery of Running Bare
Jonathan Carroll

An elegant expatriate American who makes his home in Vienna, Jonathan Carroll wishes only to assure us that this little item – which bridges Johnny Preston's 1960 hit 'Running Bear' (awoopa-awoopa) and the early seventies novelty single 'The Streak' (booga-da-booga-da) – is not directly autobiographical, although he did once live next to a graveyard where a mysterious figure known only as The Phantom ran naked after midnight. 'We used to have to keep our dog in, to stop him lifting his leg at funerals,' he remembers. Carroll's first novel was The Land of Laughs, *and he has subsequently published* The Voice of Our Shadow, Bones of the Moon, Sleeping in Flame, A Child Across the Sky, Outside the Dog Museum *and others, all a distinctive blend of sophisticated urban mores, metaphysical fantasy, and scary black comedy.*

He was as nervous as a cat under a full moon. He couldn't keep still, couldn't keep down behind the tombstones like the others around him. Unaware of it, he kept peeping and chirping to himself like a baby bird. Once in a while he'd even hum a line of the song – 'Run-ning Bear loved Little White Dove . . .' Then he'd pop up for a look, hoping to be the first tonight to see their own Running Bare.

'Get down, Bob!' A voice below him whispered savagely. 'You're going to scare the bastard away!'

'Shut up! No one's going to scare him away. He'll come. Damn well *better* come!'

Joe Balding, crouched below, chuckled quietly. It was Joe who'd convinced him to join the others for their nightly appointment in the town cemetery with the mysterious stranger who ran naked through the tombstones clad only in hightop sneakers and an Elvis Presley mask. Everyone else had been coming for days to look. Since the first sighting, it was all anyone could talk about. Who was he? Why did he veer left last night and not right? Why did he wear an Elvis mask and black sneakers? Why these things? Who *was* that masked man?

Two weeks before, Mary Helen Cline and Gene Dreevs had been rolling around as usual in the cemetery. In the middle of very intense kissing, both of them heard someone running hard nearby. Leaping up as one because they were sure it was Mary Helen's mother, they were the first to see the nude man running to beat Hell across the open moonlit graveyard. Mary Helen screamed. It was the first time she had ever seen a totally nude man and her scream was more fascination than fear. The runner slowed just for a second, looked at them, then broke right, running fast and loose again away from the light into the dark behind the stones.

Almost every kid in town now knew about Running Bare. The night after the couple saw him, the entire basketball team tried to hide behind the few graves near where he'd been spotted. And he came! Dressed the same, moving along the same route . . . No one could believe it. It was hard for them to keep in their delighted laughter, their excitement. They knew if they didn't scare this new star away, their summer would be filled with his nightly show.

He moved so well. Many agreed he had the moves of a great natural athlete – the highest accolade they could pay. He looked like a ballplayer, a Triathlete. They could imagine him swimming miles, then riding a bicycle up a fifty degree incline. Fluid and not tight at all, good long strides that were wide but not stretching. Someone joked that if Melvin and Little Jackie weren't with them night after night, they'd've sworn it was one of the two blacks who played on the team.

'Couldn't be a black. He's got a white cock.'

And so he did. That was the first clue. They knew he was white and probably had black hair. Unless he was really weird and dyed it down there. Suddenly finding out who he was became serious business. Someone thought up the name 'Running Bare' after the old song about the doomed Indian and his girlfriend with their 'love big as the sky'. The play on words was appreciated and the name stuck. But people disagreed about who it might be.

One night after he passed, someone suggested, 'Let's just go up and pull his mask off!'

'Yeah!'

But no one did. No one did because that would have ruined it. Without secrecy, there would be no Running Bare. It would be Joe Simmons or Dexter Lewis or someone else boring they all knew. The way he was now, masked and Running Bare, was the best. Impressive. Athletic. Mysterious. That was how they wanted it.

Moving fast always, he would come down off the hill from the Ashford Avenue entrance to the cemetery. Running towards the fountain in the middle of the place, his big dick flapping up and down like he was fucking the air, he'd veer suddenly left or right. He rarely ran straight. Almost to the fountain, he'd cut one way or the other when he came to some invisible point in the road only he recognised. Even *he* was set in his own ways.

Hunkered down along with the rest of them, Bob McKinney had always begged off going with the gang. Because Bob was absolutely petrified of Running Bare.

At eighteen, McKinney believed in reason. You studied French so you could do passably well on an exam so you could act sheepish about the grade in front of the others when they admired you both for your brains and athletic ability. You pulled a prank you knew you'd be punished for because the prank would add the right touch to your reputation and make a good story to carry around in your repertoire. Like the time he had thrown the paper airplane at the geometry teacher. He knew the punishment would be severe, but he also knew the rewards would be worth it. And it was. The story was told for weeks afterwards about how Bob McKinney had slowly gotten up when the teacher demanded to know who'd thrown the plane. How he'd absolutely *strutted* to the front of the room to receive his due. That was the kind of 'you get what you pay for' deal Bob could understand.

So this Running Bare confused him at first. Then the confusion grew quickly into a purple tentacled fear. Why would anyone want to run naked and alone through Dead Land? Without an audience! He secretly admired the runner's humour and dramatic savvy in choosing an Elvis mask. He admitted to himself that if he had ever thought of doing something as original as this, he'd've ruined it by choosing something stupid like a Frankenstein mask and his mother's high heels. No, this Running Bare was something special. It was the greatest idea anyone in town had ever come up with – stark naked at night through the *graveyard*. Real genius. And the crowning glory was whoever it was hadn't talked about it. He did it solo. Run Silent, Run Deep. He didn't care if others knew. You always made sure others were there. You did everything for others so they'd be amazed and jealous – at your mind, your daring. Anyone who did just to do was either a genius or only nuts. Both possibilities scared Bob McKinney. He didn't want to have anything to do either with Michelangelo or a loon ball.

Yet an odd thing happened as he squatted there for the first time; waiting like everyone else for the one and only Running Bare. He grew jealous. He realised he hated this guy for being content to put on a show only for himself. He hated him for being everyone's favourite when all he was really doing was having his own fun. Bob wanted to be Running Bare, but RB knowing everyone was watching, like going up to shoot the last jump shot of the game with the score tied. The glory that comes only from an audience, hundreds of eyes and minds on you, the glory of owning every being in a place for a few splendid seconds of all your lives together. How come this nude weirdo didn't care? Where did he get off being so fucking content?

A plan came and it made Bob smile like a lizard whose eyes can go in all directions at once. He was going to tear off the mask! He was going to one-up the other! Be the one to show them all who he was. At least that would take whoever it was down a peg – make him human again.

Joe, coming up for the third time to try and pull his friend down, saw him first.

'There he is!'

Bob looked but could make out only a dark figure moving down the far hill in a thin blade of moonlight through the trees. But then he was moving too. Moving like a lion after a big fat tasty unsuspecting gazelle. Instinctively he kept to the shadows, hoping to stay out of the runner's view as long as he could. The lion in darkness! The silly gazelle enjoying its last minutes before it fell to earth forever.

That's what he was thinking as he moved. That and the line to the song. 'Running Bear loved Little White Dove – '

But the guy was fast. It was hard keeping up. He moved so gracefully. He would have made a great basketball player.

Bob stopped two hundred feet away, then moved again. He got to within ten feet of where he was sure the other would stop and veer. He crouched, heard the other's slapping feet on the still day-warm asphalt road.

Closer. At the last minute, Bob came up and started moving, running too, coming up after *him*.

'I'll get him for us, guys! I'll get him!' he yelled happily and much too loudly over his shoulder. But he knew they hated him now. He could feel the hatred on their faces. He knew they wanted him to leave Running Bare alone. But that was impossible. He had to win.

The runner saw them all coming. Bob first, the others up from behind the stones and coming too now. But instead of veering or trying to run away, the mystery simply stopped where he was. Didn't even raise his hands. Bob was running so fast either at Running Bare or away from the others that he smashed right into the naked man.

Upon contact, thinking of nothing else in the world, he grabbed for the mask, pulled it up and off. Yoo Hoo! Peekaboo!

Whoopie! It was *Whoopie*? The town idiot was beneath the Elvis face. The sad, demented man who rode an old bent bicycle around with a child's wagon tied to the back. Whoopie who sang to himself and an eyeless doll he'd found years ago in someone's garbage and painted bright green all over. This was the runner.

The others ignored him as they jumped on McKinney and started beating him.

Interested only for a minute in what was happening, the empty-headed man picked up his mask and slid it back on. Then he began to run for the darkness.

Night Shift Sister
Nicholas Royle

Having made a reputation with a run of widely anthologised stories, distinctively mixing acute social observation with a sense of supernatural unease, Nick Royle recently edited Darklands, *an anthology of outstanding new horror fiction. A novel is in progress.*

One of the most uncompromising and committed horror writers of his generation, his fiction just keeps getting weirder and more penetrating, turning up regularly in Best-of-Year anthologies. '"Night Shift Sister",' he tells us, 'brings together a number of my favourite things: Siouxsie and the music of Siouxsie and the Banshees, maps, hidden realms/parallel worlds, and gasholders. Siouxsie's dancing has always been mesmerising – as much a part of her appeal as her singing – from the days of her mad skipping and swinging for "Regal Zone" on stage at the Manchester Apollo to the sinuous twisting and swaying on the "Kiss Them for Me" video. And there's a wonderful shot two and a half minutes into the video, of Siouxsie in profile behind Steve Severin and apparently deep in thought. She makes you want to get into her head and find out what she's thinking. It's a good thing, of course, that you can't, because if you could it would only be something banal like what she's going to have for her tea when she gets home.'

First Carl found the map. It was a photocopy of a page taken from a book of street maps. He found it on the pavement outside the record shop one night when he'd worked later than usual sorting

secondhand singles into categories. He knew that his customers would soon refile so many of them that his system
would be ruined. That was partly why he liked doing it: to
give the kids something to knock down. These days he
rebelled only vicariously.

But there were patterns everywhere. Even in his own
filing systems he discerned some arcane force at work.
Something which came from above him and directed his
hands as they lifted and turned and slotted. When the
customers changed the system they did so according to some
secret order not even they were aware of.

He left the shop late and became conscious while he was
locking up of a fresh wind that carried a faint unpleasant
odour reminiscent of domestic gas. For a moment he worried
that there might be a leak in the shop but then it dispersed
and he saw the map at his feet.

Studying the map as he walked to his old Escort parked a
couple of streets away, Carl became confused. It looked like
a detail of a city, presumably his own because of where he
found it, but the streets were unnamed. They were obviously
streets, and railway lines, too, and parks, ponds, canals and
open spaces and closed spaces, but none of them were
named so he couldn't say what locality it represented.

He unlocked the car door and got in. Dropping the map
on the passenger seat he started the engine and pulled away
from the kerb. At a red light he looked at himself in the
rearview mirror and ran a hand through his long black hair
which was perhaps in need of another bottle of dye and
certainly a thorough wash. He also needed a shave. His
dirty white leather jacket creaked comfortably and he
reached down to take the packet of Camels out of his left
boot and light one using the car lighter. The light went
green, he turned right and the Escort bounced over the
uneven road surface in the gathering darkness. Carl liked

this time of day. Once he'd shut up shop his time was his own. He liked company but only of his own selection. Crowds weren't his scene. There was a radio in the car but he generally didn't switch it on. He welcomed quiet after spinning singles all day to keep the kids from getting bored.

He called in at the Cantonese takeaway and studied the map while he waited for his food. There were long straight drives and grids of narrow streets, and an area of streets which curved round and round like a game of solitaire where you have to get the ball to the middle. There was even a little circle at the centre.

When he reached the flat he took the map and his A to Z from the glove compartment, and his sweet and sour, and went upstairs. The flat was sparsely furnished but all the walls were shelved to house his enormous record collection. In the living room there was also a battered old sofa, a low sturdy table with an overflowing ashtray, and a pretty good TV and VCR. The white-painted ceiling was nicotine-stained.

He spent most of what remained of the evening going through the A to Z looking for a street layout that mirrored the one on his photocopied fragment, but without success.

It had occurred to him that the map could be of a different city, but then why was the original owner using it here? Carl decided whatever the map depicted was to be found here or nowhere.

The map's patterns attracted him but when frustration set in he lit a cigarette and slid a cassette into the VCR. A big fan of Siouxsie and the Banshees, Carl just couldn't get enough of the latest single. He played it several times a day at the shop and at home he watched the video over and over again. It helped him relax. And just looking at the way she moved made him feel less lonely, which was often a problem since Christine had fucked off to Paris without even leaving him a phone number. Or saying goodbye for that matter. All she'd said was something about him being a worthless drifter with less sense than her little sister. It had seemed harsh to him.

Sometimes he got so miserable he felt like crying. Nearly thirty, he had nothing apart from a scummy record shop, a decrepit Ford Escort, four or five thousand records and a few videos. His only company was Siouxsie Sioux. On video. Christine had left a hole in his life and, rather than try to fill it with someone else, he preferred to slip out through it and find something new.

Most of his old friends were married and couldn't come out because 'it's such short notice and we couldn't get anyone to sit'. The only one of his old friends who was still single was Baz and all he ever offered Carl was a fix. Things weren't that bad, he always thought to himself. Seeing Baz sometimes had the effect of cheering him up because he realised there was still a lot further to fall. He was determined to hang on. Maybe when the car dropped dead and he could no longer afford the spiralling rent on the shop. Maybe then he'd turn to Baz.

Carl took another cigarette from the pack on the table and reached for his matches because like a dickhead he'd left his lighter at the shop. But the box was very light. He shook it. Empty.

'Shit.'

Kitchen.

Carl switched on one of the electric rings on the hob and waited for it to heat up. When it was bright orange he swept his hair away from his face and bent down to light the cigarette. He didn't turn the ring off but watched it becoming brighter and hotter as he smoked. He flinched as he remembered pressing the flat of his hand down on one of his mother's electric rings when it was on. He'd been trying to climb on to a work surface and was using the cooker to lever his body up. As soon as he had felt the pain he had tried to withdraw his hand, but all his weight was on it, so he had screamed loud enough to pierce his mother's eardrums and she had looked round as he began to fall. He remembered her picking him up off the floor, trying to uncurl his hand. The rings had left dark brown marks on his skin and the smell made him sick.

He pulled on his cigarette. The scars had healed quite quickly but he had been left with a fear of the cooker. When he had bought his flat he had wanted gas but there wasn't any, so he intended to get a cooker with a modern ceramic hob, but Christine bought him a moving-in present: a nice old-fashioned electric cooker with rings just like his mother's.

He stared hard at the orange spiral, mesmerised by it. It wasn't just a bad memory. The shape meant something to him. It both attracted and repelled him without him knowing why.

Carl took the photocopied map to bed with him and fell asleep clutching it.

Carl became obsessed with the map and discovering the place it was based on. He thought about it constantly while serving customers and sorting through boxes of old singles people brought in to sell. He was bored with their mewling complaints and saw the map as an escape route.

An original '76 punk with bad teeth said he wanted £25 for The Skids' 'Into the Valley' on white vinyl and £30 for the 'Wide Open' EP, twelve-inch on red. Carl suggested wearily he'd do better to advertise in the music papers. He'd already got two copies of one and three of the other in the shop and no one seemed to want to buy them.

'What about Roxy Music "Viva!" on Island? Forty quid.'

'I've got three in stock.'

'Not on Island,' the punk argued. 'It's rare.'

'It's rare but I've got three of them.'

Two French students asked if he'd got anything by Michel Petrucciani. Carl directed them to the jazz shop a couple of blocks away, then began to wonder if the map was of Paris and he was supposed to use it to find Christine. He discounted this quickly, feeling certain that he was the last person Christine wanted to see. To lift his spirits he stuck 'Kiss Them for Me' on the turntable. He took the map out of the back pocket of his jeans and lit a cigarette. Out of the corner of his eye he noticed two young girls playing peek-a-boo with him from behind the soundtracks section. Did they know anything about it? Was it a deliberate plant?

He stepped forward to the till to serve a boy buying a clutch of house singles and when he looked up again the girls had gone. When he gave it some thought, he realised a great many people passed through his shop, trailing their lives and their secrets. Did some of what they carried get left behind? When he shut the shop at night the atmosphere always seemed a little bit richer. The secondhand records contained so many memories, different memories for different people, but each record would reek of the particular recollections of its previous owners. Had he bought the Skids' singles off the punk, he would have taken part of the punk into his shop to stay after the doors were locked. Perhaps that was why he had said no.

He lit another cigarette and held the map up to the light to see if that revealed any clues. It didn't. So he slipped his cigarettes down his boot, locked up and drove home.

The flat was quiet. When the downstairs tenant was in, Carl's life felt like a film with a soundtrack. A heavy metal soundtrack. Which meant you knew it was a crap film. He slung his leather jacket on a chair in the kitchen and took a bottle of Peroni beer from the fridge. He was running low. There were only six boxes left. Lighting a Camel he wandered into the moonlit living room and trailed his finger along rows of singles. He filed them alphabetically by artist. Hundreds had been bought new, but most were secondhand. He thought about what had occurred to him in the shop and wondered if he would be able to sense someone else's memories by playing their single.

He turned his attention to the shelf that held twelve-inch singles and took down 'TV Songs' by In Camera. He switched everything on and played the first track. Spidery guitar, deliberately flat vocals, a spiny bass line and chattering cymbals. But no atmosphere. It was a depressing record but only because of the music. He took it off and looked at the words scratched into the runout groove. 'Thanks Ilona.' Inscribed on to the original acetate by the cutting engineer at his lathe, these messages fascinated Carl because they were like clues to a whole world of secrets and relationships behind the record. He put back the In Camera single and crossed the room to the C section of his LPs and proudly took out Elvis Costello's 'This Year's Model'. Inscribed on the runout groove was 'Special Pressing No. 003. Ring Moira on 434 3232 For Your Special Prize.' He had bought the record the day it came out and, noticing the inscription, found a phone box and dialled the number, winning free tickets to a Costello concert. The message had been intended to appear on the first 500 copies, but it overran by about 20,000 and a lot of people got very pissed off. But it was a good gig and now the record felt like a trophy.

He slid the LP back in its sleeve and went and lit another Camel from the electric ring because he'd forgotten his lighter again. The orange spiral burned into his brain and he reflected on how pathetic it was to be going through his record collection trawling for memories, his own and other people's.

He dragged on the cigarette and blew smoke rings. He watched them uncoil and re-form, a series of loops and twists. From his back pocket he took out the map and traced its streets with his eye. He shut his eyes and ran his fingers over the paper to see if that would yield anything. But all he felt were the slight ridges of toner from the photocopier.

He pressed play on the Siouxsie video and lit another cigarette from the stub of the old one. When it finished he rewound and played it again. While he was aware of how they could ensnare and reduce life to a series of repeats, Carl found some comfort at times of stress in following routines and resorting to icons. He fancied Siouxsie like mad and loved the song but he was still restless. Prowling down the shelves into the hallway he came across his huge collection of white labels. At the shop he bought a lot of white label promos in blank sleeves from collectors and if there were any he wanted to keep he just took them home. It was all the same money, whether it was at the shop or at home. Many of the promo copies in his collection had the artist's name scrawled across the white label in felt tip, but some were blank and these he liked best because if there were no distinguishing marks he could forget who the record was by and playing it was always a surprise.

He fell asleep on the sofa and woke with a start when his cigarette burned right down and stung his finger. He sucked it as he drew his legs off the table and stood up. In the bathroom he ran his finger under the cold tap and examined it under the light over the mirror. There was a tiny patch where the whorls of his fingerprint had been smoothed over. He stared fascinated at the pattern of parallel lines. On the third finger of his right hand the lines seemed to fan out in a spiral from a central point, like hair growing from the crown. But Carl realised that when you'd got down to examining your own fingerprints it was time to say goodnight.

He played a random selection of singles at the shop and listened with one ear to the lyrics. He looked carefully at the records he had bought during the morning in case their titles revealed anything. But there was nothing. He knew he could make something up out of all the material at his fingertips, but he would know he'd invented it. If a genuine message were to stand out from the dross he'd know it because he'd feel it.

By the end of the day he felt saturated by voices and longed for silence. The roads were refreshingly empty. His tyres hissed on wet tarmac and he cruised with the radio off. The red lights in the distance became a cascade of reflections in the puddles as he knocked the gear lever into neutral and coasted down to meet them. He rolled into position behind a girl in a Mini who like him was waiting for the lights to change. She had shoulder-length black hair like Siouxsie Sioux and was bobbing up and down on her seat and moving from side to side, tapping her fingers on the steering wheel and banging the dash.

What was she listening to?

Carl suddenly felt his stomach twist as he realised that whatever music the girl was listening to was a clue. If only he could hear it he would share a secret with her and perhaps he'd know the way to drive to the streets on the map. Maybe she'd let him follow her. He wound his window down but her window was up and he couldn't hear anything. She bounced on her seat and the little car moved like a cocoon when she did. He couldn't pull alongside because there was only one lane.

The lights changed and she was off. He jerked into first

and followed, reaching across to switch on the radio to see if she was listening to a station he could tune into. The gap between the two cars lengthened as he slewed across the dial, stopping to catch fragments of music. But there was nothing that spoke to him as clearly as the girl's movements. It must have been a tape. She was a long way ahead now. He jumped a red light to keep her in sight but she turned into a side street and although he followed suit she had vanished into a warren of crescents he barely knew.

He was smoking and reading a thriller in bed when the front door rattled in its frame. With a clear view of the door from his bed, Carl looked up and put his book down beside him. When the door opened he wasn't altogether surprised to see the girl from the car. Her black hair framed a face that was Siouxsie's, except that it wasn't. Because it was Christine's. She was like a composite of both of them. The only two women in his life, both now very much on the fringes of it, synthesised into this one girl.

She walked in and turned past his doorway to enter the living room. He noticed as he got out of bed to follow her that she was carrying a long knife in the back pocket of her jeans, the same pocket he kept his map in. He felt in his own pocket and was relieved to find it still there. The girl went over to Carl's stereo equipment and slipped a single from inside her denim jacket on to the turntable. She stood back and Carl came forward to see what she'd brought him. A white label disc spun at 45 and the needle cut into it. He looked up but the girl had gone. He whirled round and ran to the door but it was shut and there was no sound in the stairwell. He bent over the record player again and saw that as the needle travelled round the groove towards the centre it left a fine spiral of blood in its wake.

Carl jumped and woke up. His cigarette had burnt a hole in the duvet cover. He smothered it quickly with a pillow, but there was no need: the cigarette was cold. He shivered and felt sick. Brushing the curtain behind his head to one side he looked down into the street for a Mini, but there was only his Escort and one or two other familiar cars.

He stomped out of his bedroom and checked the front door – undisturbed – and the stereo. There was no record on the turntable and no blood but the power was on. He never left the power on. Groaning, he flicked the switch and went to make as much and as many different uses of the bathroom as his body would let him.

In bed once more he tossed and turned but sleep eluded him. *Got to get up, got to get up,* he thought over and over. He pulled on a pair of boxer shorts and went through to the living room. A cigarette and the Siouxsie video. They had a placebo effect but he was neither completely relaxed nor did he feel sleepy. Yet his body was exhausted. At dawn he was thinking of taking the car for a run down to the crescent where he'd lost the girl in her Mini when he finally fell asleep in front of the TV.

Driving to the shop a couple of hours later he felt like a jigsaw that had been put together wrongly. Someone had tried to force pieces into each other and they held but only just. He had a craving for pure orange juice but made do with a cigarette instead. He pushed in the dashboard lighter and waited for it to pop out. He withdrew it and brought it up to his mouth. While driving he looked down to align the end of the cigarette with the lighter and was shocked by the sight of the burning orange element. He lost his grip on the steering wheel and went the wrong way round a set of bollards. Feeling sick, he righted the car and coasted in to the kerb. He got out, threw the cigarette in the gutter and leaned against the bonnet for a few minutes. The shop would have to open late for once.

He kept seeing the image from his dream of the needle cutting into the record and drawing blood. He got back in the car and set off for the shop again. Every Mini turned his head. He'd never noticed them before but now it seemed like the city streets were full of them. He couldn't remember what colour the hybrid Siouxsie/Christine girl had been driving. It had, after all, been dark when he'd seen it.

During the hours of daylight he imagined it was parked up in one of the nameless streets on his map. Only by night, when there wasn't any, did she venture into the light of the real world.

Carl struggled to concentrate on the business of running the shop. The jigsaw feeling had faded but he still wasn't on top form. He chainsmoked and played randomly selected singles back to back all morning. Customers brought him boxes of records and he bought them all with the briefest examinations and without haggling over the amount he would pay for them. The shop seemed infested with Siouxsie clones but they were all years out of date, painted birds and scarecrows, their faces plastered with the Hallowe'en make-up Siouxsie herself now did without. Over the years, as the masks had been slowly stripped away she had become more and more beautiful to the point where her beauty was now a dangerous, provocative thing, like the music had always been.

Carl slipped 'Superstition' into the CD player and pressed repeat. The album played for the rest of the day.

In a stream of people offering him their old picture discs and limited edition gatefold sleeves a girl's hand pushed a white label single on to the counter. Carl gave a small cry and immediately looked up but the floor was crowded with customers. Out of the corner of his eye he saw the door close but it could have been anybody. Nevertheless, he squeezed under the counter and pushed through the crowd to the door. He craned his neck and looked in all directions but she had disappeared. There was no sign of a Mini parked nearby. His heart pounding, he re-entered the shop and returned to his place behind the counter.

Word must have got round that he was throwing money away today: it seemed as if the whole teenage population of the city had descended on his shop. 'Whose is this?' he asked, holding up the white label. No one claimed it: 'Is it yours?' he asked the next girl in the queue. She nodded. Someone behind her cackled like a hyena and he felt foolish, but for all he knew it could really have been hers and she'd been too shy to stick her hand up. The colour of the label could have prompted him to imagine someone who hadn't been there at all. He took the other stuff the girl clearly hadn't been expecting to sell, then lit a cigarette and put the white label underneath a stack of CDs to look at later.

It was with enormous relief that he locked the door and flipped the open/closed sign. He didn't need all this unrest. He stood and watched the rain through the glass as he lit a cigarette and put the lighter away in his jacket pocket. Cars squealed softly as they braked for the red light. Carl smoked nervously, unhappy about acknowledging his fear of the unknown girl and the white label she'd brought him. In the brightness of the afternoon it had been easier to rationalise. But in the shadowtime of dusk it seemed indisputable that his obsession was based on fact. He watched car headlamps dazzle and melt into wet reflections like silver waterfalls. Taking a deep drag that caused his head to spin he turned away from the window and went back to the counter. He felt like a bug in a killing jar. They could be watching him through the windows from across the street. They would want to see how he reacted when he listened to the white label. Well let them!

He picked it up and slipped it out of its blank sleeve,

holding it by the edges and angling it so that the light fell across it. There was nothing written on the label, but on the runout groove he made out the inscription 'It's a gas.' It meant nothing to him. It just seemed like the kind of throwaway remark that cutting engineers sometimes went in for.

He placed the record on the turntable with great care and positioned the needle before pressing release. It landed with that satisfying clunk he had heard a million times. It didn't matter how new a vinyl record was, you always heard something apart from the music, even if it was only the hiss of dust. He wondered what he would hear as the needle wound its way towards the music.

But none came. He checked the amp controls. Everything was on and the volume was turned up. He looked at the needle. It was a third of the way into the record and still there was no sound.

He turned the volume higher and listened harder. He heard the usual rumble of ticks and bumps you got at the beginning and end of records. When it finished he repositioned the needle and played it again. With the volume full up he fancied he could hear the needle itself scoring the groove a fraction deeper. He found himself becoming quite drawn to the sound. Without the distraction of music it was somehow purer, more elemental. He played the flip side and it was the same. The more he played it and the harder he listened, the more it sank into him. He noticed also that his forehead had begun to hurt where the skin stretched tightly across it. A sharp irritating pain like a paper cut.

Pain or no pain he was in thrall to the record. He loved its silence just as he soon came to need the sounds that *were* there to be heard if you listened hard enough. He played it again and again until he entered a state approaching rhapsody.

Towards midnight he locked up and walked to the car. The white label was in a padded envelope under his arm. He laid it carefully on the passenger seat and started the engine. He drove like an automaton, unblinking eyes sweeping the road ahead in search of the hybrid's car. He knew what she'd been dancing to and now he'd been there himself. In the shop. Listening to the record over and over again. The walls and ceiling had receded and he had felt himself at the centre of a huge spiral which descended upon him from the sky.

Waiting at a red light, rain lightly stippling the windscreen, Carl pressed in the cigarette lighter and reached into his boot. He stuck a cigarette between his lips. The lighter popped out and he withdrew it. He stared fixedly at the burning spiral for a few moments before sticking the third finger of his left hand inside the lighter and pressing the tip against the element. He didn't blink. Rain fell more heavily on the car, beating a tinny tattoo on the roof. The light went green but he didn't move. The smell of burning flesh infused the air in the car.

Deep inside Carl, in a small part of him, a tiny scream caught like a flame in a tinderbox, then flickered and died.

He only pulled his finger away when he felt his nail grating unpleasantly against the metal coil.

His finger was black and cauterised. His face was blank. The light was red again. He replaced the cigarette lighter and waited for the light to change. When it did he shifted into first gear, wincing and moaning slightly as his burnt finger brushed against the passenger seat.

How long would it be before she appeared? He cruised slowly to give her enough time, but there was no sign of her and soon he was pulling up outside the flat. Maybe she'd be waiting for him inside. He looked at his finger with a curious, childlike expression as he climbed the stairs. It still wasn't bleeding. He stuffed his hand in his back pocket to check on the map. It was still there. His mind dulled in response to the friction against his jeans.

The flat was empty but it didn't feel like his own any more. When he put the record on and turned the volume right up he felt a druggy mixture of euphoria and emptiness. His forehead itched. He wondered dully if Baz was involved. The inscription on the runout groove. 'It's a gas.' It was the kind of thing Baz would say. The girl couldn't have recorded, cut and pressed a record all on her own; she needed accomplices. Someone had to inhabit the streets on his map.

He looked at the thousands of records lining his walls. He'd wasted so much time searching for all that noise when all along the real music had been waiting for him just a few streets away.

In the kitchen he switched the ring on full and watched it get hot. He could still hear the music swirling around him, making of him its heart. But his forehead was hurting, like scratched sunburn. Maybe he could burn up the pain by lowering his forehead on to the ring. He bent over the cooker and was about to do it when he heard a car pull up outside.

It was her.

He left the kitchen without switching off the cooker and looked out of the living-room window. There was a black Mini parked in front of his Escort. He crossed to the door and as he looked back for a moment before closing the door he felt a tug. He realised this was his last chance. If he didn't turn back now he might never be able to. He looked at the photograph of Christine he still kept by the bed and felt a stab of regret. But as he sharpened his focus on the picture he saw that now she looked more like Siouxsie. And more like the candyman waiting outside in the car.

He left the door open and walked down the staircase. As

he stepped into the street he felt a warm breeze and detected the faint odour of gas. The map was in his back pocket. He reached for the door handle on the Mini but the girl gunned the engine into life and moved forward several feet to dissuade him. He walked towards his own car and glanced in through the Mini's windows.

On the back seat lay a long knife.

He followed her in the Escort. She turned off his familiar route into the warren of semi-circular streets where he'd lost her for the first time. Despite his injured finger he kept pace with her. The road curved round to the right, then they turned right and curved some more. They seemed to be drawing in towards some hidden centre. He noticed a clocktower among a group of school buildings, but the clockface was devoid of hands. He accelerated and felt the road, once he'd passed the playground, twist round to the right. The streets were lined with bay-window semis. What suburban relapse could have occurred at the heart of this model landscape?

Carl fumbled the map from his back pocket and unfolded it. As he had vaguely remembered, there was a pocket of circular streets, effectively a spiral.

Take me back, take me back, he silently entreated the girl in the car ahead. But she took him on.

They turned right again and eventually the houses disappeared, giving way to waste ground, a procession of electricity pylons and an enormous gasholder.

The girl parked and started walking. Carl had to run to catch her up. They walked over ground dotted with sorrel and belladonna. He looked at the map. They were heading for the circle which lay at the centre of the curled maze of streets. The gasholder.

It reared up before them, a wonderful monster of overlapping curved metal plates. A telescopic spiral ready to expand or contract. It glowed in the moonlight and appeared to hover just above the ground like a ghostly carousel.

Carl followed the girl to the base of the gasholder. The long knife stuck out of the back pocket of her jeans. When she reached an opening she turned and looked back. The moon fell on her face which Carl now saw for the first time outside of his dream. She was, as he had dreamt, the perfect synthesis of Siouxsie and Christine. She had the most beautiful face he had ever seen. His stomach went into a slow dive. But it was love in a void and he felt his heart turn to stone. He would have wept but for the detail on her forehead which, though he caught only the briefest of glimpses, chilled him to the bone.

She turned and vanished inside the gasholder.

Carl followed because, no longer in control of his actions, there was nothing else he could do.

Inside the gargantuan chamber it was dark and Carl was forced to rely on other senses. He raised his arms to protect his face as he stepped forward. The overwhelming impression was of noise: of hundreds or thousands of slowly shuffling feet and in the highest reaches of the metal skin there resounded the magnified hiss and clicks and cannon booms of the white label. It threw its hooks into Carl immediately and he felt himself being drawn into a mass of swaying bodies. He visualised a charnel house of carcasses and raw heads and bloody bones.

There was something else he sensed but couldn't put a name to.

Carl succumbed to the silent music but the darkness awakened his fear and he felt pulled to bits. He pictured the girl's forehead and imagined all the flitting spellbound shapes around him to be similarly disfigured.

They pressed nearer and he was horrified to realise he felt close to them in mind as well as body. He imagined he could feel Christine's breath on his face and for a moment the gasholder almost became a place of paradise. But there was still the niggling feeling that something else was wrong but he didn't know what. Something around him that he should be aware of.

A cold object sliced his forehead and he felt a warm liquid run down into his eyes. Then the girl pressed harder with the knife but it was always a light, intimate touch, intended to brand rather than hurt.

Carl panicked. These weren't his people. It wasn't his celebration. He had never wanted oblivion, just a change. Something secret and new. Now he wanted his life back.

As far as he could tell, they were scared of the light.

He slipped his hand into the pocket of his leather jacket and closed his fingers round his cigarette lighter. He lifted it up to eye level and in the very same moment that he spun the wheel and created a dazzling, vivid snapshot of hundreds of raised foreheads marked by needle-fine spiral scars, he realised what the other thing was. A silly thing really.

The smell of gas.

Worthless
Greg Egan

In 1965, Dylan was harried from one concert to the next by fans who claimed that he had 'betrayed' them by using an electric guitar and a rock'n'roll backing band. Not the first time fans have confused the reality of a singer with their own image of what he or she represents, and certainly not the last. In 'Worthless', Greg Egan describes, from the inside, the impact of technology which allows fans to fashion pop gods in their own image.

Although Greg Egan is one of the hottest new stars of SF, little is known about him and apparently he wants to keep it that way. Maybe that's why he lives in Australia. He allows us to know that 'I was born in Perth, Australia, in 1961. I've published about two dozen short stories in Australia, Britain and the USA. I recently completed a science fiction novel, Quarantine, *which is likely to be published in 1992.'*

We feel it our duty to point out that Quarantine *will be Egan's second novel; his first,* An Unusual Angle *(Nortsralia Press), was published only in Australia. We bring you this fact in the spirit of a public service announcement. Such is the asymptotic rise of Egan's career that copies of* An Unusual Angle *will soon be worth a lot more than the cover price.*

Yes, I'm complacent now, with my well enough paid job, with a wife I can almost talk to, with a three-year-old son all dark eyes and tousled hair and endearing clumsiness. We go driving on Sunday afternoons, through suburbs just like our own, past houses just like our own, an endlessly recurring, mesmerising daydream under the flawless blue sky. And I whistle an old song of yours, even if I never dare let the words past my lips:

> *There's nothing wrong with The Family*
> *That a flame-thrower can't fix*
> *And there's nothing wrong with the salt of the Earth*
> *That couldn't be cured with a well-aimed BRICK*

I switch on the radio (when I have a chance), I scan the stations (now and then), listening for an echo of your voice. Wondering if you've found a new incarnation. Wondering if I'd recognise it, if you had. Oh, some brain-dead bitch has stolen one of your best riffs, and chants meaningless drivel over the top of an endlessly cycling sample – but my mind shuts her out, and my memory of you takes over:

> *Carve my name on your heart, forever*
> *– with the blunt end of a feather*
> *You said, 'I'll stay with you for a lifetime of pain*
> *(just so long as it's over by morning).'*

I know what they say, the revisionists, the explainers: you were a glitch, an aberration; a bug in the software, nothing more. People could never have truly *wanted* to hear your 'maudlin' voice, your 'mealy-mouthed whining', your 'smothering self-pity'.

I did.

I still dream about you, I swear. Do you blame me, if I can't hold on to my vision of you, lost on these dizzying sunlit plains, numb with contentment, the way I could when I was desperate, lonely, crippled? When I knew exactly who I was.

I still want you back. Badly. Sometimes.
But apparently not often, or badly, enough.

When they started making music straight from the Azciak Polls, everybody howled about the Death of Art – as if the process was anything new, anything more than an efficient closure of what had been happening for years. Groups were already assembled on the basis of elaborate market research. The Azciak Probes were already revealing people's tastes in breakfast cereals, politicians, and rock stars. Why not scan the brains of the populace, discover precisely what music they'd be willing to pay for, and then manufacture it – all in a single, streamlined process, with no human intervention required? From the probes buried in a random sample of twenty thousand representative skulls, to the construction of the virtual bands (down to mock biographies, and all the right birthmarks and tattoos), to the synthesis of photorealist computer-animated videos, accessible for a suitable fee . . . the music industry had finally achieved its long-cherished goal: cutting out everyone but the middleman.

The system spewed out pap. People paid to hear it. Nothing had changed.

In 2008, I was sixteen years old, working in a fast-food franchise in Sydney's decaying red light district, scraping the fat off disassembled hamburger grillers with lukewarm water in the early hours of the morning. I lived alone, not quite starving on what I had left after paying the rent, too shy and misanthropic to take in a flatmate. Let alone a lover.

I was woken at four o'clock one Sunday afternoon, when the woman from Azciak called. I don't know what possessed me to let her in; usually I just waited in silence for door-knockers to go away. She didn't look much older than I was, and her uniform wasn't all that different from mine – but it fit a great deal better, and at least they didn't make her wear a fucking baseball cap.

I said, 'Why should I let you put your shit inside my head?'

'So you can participate more fully in democracy.' She'd been on a training course on the Gold Coast.

'Democracy is a placebo.' I'd read graffiti in Darlinghurst.

'We'll pay you twenty dollars a week.'

'Forget it.'

'Hard currency: US dollars, yen, ecus – whatever you like.' I signed.

I spent a day in hospital; they didn't need to cut me open, but the scanning equipment they used, as they threaded the microelectrodes through the blood vessels of my brain, was bigger than my entire flat. Then, under local anaesthetic, they slipped the interface chip into a shallow incision at the back of my neck.

When the engineers arrived to plug their little black box into my phone, they discovered that *I didn't have one*, so they ended up paying for that, as well.

Once a day, the black box interrogated the chip ultrasonically, downloading whatever it had gleaned about my opinions in the preceding twenty-four hours, then passed the data on to the central computer.

Surprise: my contribution to the Azciak Polls didn't tip any geopolitical scales. The parliament of whores kept fawning to the Great Powers, cutting spending and raising prices whenever the IMF said *jump*, voting as required in the UN each time another Third World country had to be bombed into submission. I served Amazonian beef and Idaho potatoes to the cheerful, shaven-headed psychopaths from the USS *Scheisskopf* when they flooded Kings Cross on R & R, dressed in their pigeon-shit-speckled camouflage, looking

for something to fuck that wasn't full of shrapnel, just for a
change.

I was one of twenty thousand people whose every desire
was accessed and analysed day by day, cross-tabulated and
disseminated to the most powerful decision makers in the
country.

And I knew that it made no difference at all.

Three Azciak creations were big, that year. I saw them all on
the video jukebox which sat in the corner of the restaurant
(and which lapsed into McPromotional mode when it wasn't
playing requests – a prospect which guaranteed a steady
stream of customers more than willing to feed it their
change). Limboland sang about the transcendental power of
rhythm; in their videos, they strode like giants over the urban
wasteland, dispensing the stuff in the form of handfuls of
rainbow-coloured glitter to the infinitely grateful mortals
below, who at once stopped starving/shooting up/fighting
each other, and took up robotic formation dancing instead.
Echolalia sighed and moaned about the healing power of
love, as she slithered across a surreal landscape of oiled
naked skin, pausing between verses to suck, stroke or screw
some convenient protuberance. MC Liberty ranted about a
world united by . . . unity. And good posture: all we had to
do was *walk tall*.

One freezing, grey afternoon, woken by screaming in the
flat downstairs, I lay in bed for an hour, staring up at
the crumbling white plaster of the ceiling, convinced (for the
thousandth time) that I was finally going insane.

There's only one problem with living alone: every thought
rebounds off the walls of your skull, unanswered – until the
whole process of consciousness begins to seem like nothing
so much as *talking to yourself*. As a child, I'd believed that
God was constantly reading my mind – which might sound

crazy, but if it wasn't true, then who was this monologue *for*? Of course I had imaginary friends and lovers, of course I invented companions to 'share' the endless conversation running through my head – but sometimes that delusion broke down, and there was nothing to do but listen to my own rambling, and wonder how many pills it would take to shut me up for good.

I didn't even own a radio, but my neighbours were always more than generous with their own. And I heard you sing:

> *Don't you ever wonder*
> *Who fills my empty bed?*
> *Who keeps me cold in the darkest hour?*
> *Who leaves the silence unbroken?*
> *Don't you ever wonder*
> *Whose heartbeat it is I don't hear?*
> *Whose arms won't enfold me?*
> *Who won't be beside me?*
> *When life is unkind and unfair?*
> *Won't you ever ASK ME*
> *'Who's going to make tonight*
> *The loneliest night of the year?'*
> *Well, don't ask*
> *You don't want to hear.*
> *It's you.*

My life was not transformed. I still wiped McVomit off the toilet floors every night, still fished the syringes out of the bowls (too buoyant to flush – and if they weren't removed quickly, people re-used them). I still stared at the couples walking hand in hand in front of me; still lingered behind them for a step or two, in the hope that something radiating out from their bodies would penetrate my own icy flesh.

But I bought myself a radio, and I waded through all the saccharine lies about *peace* and *harmony*, about *strength* and *empowerment*, waiting to hear you sing about my pathetic, irrelevant life. And I think you know how sweet it was, to hear just one voice of acceptance, just one voice of affirmation, just one voice – at last – that rang true for *me*.

And on those sleepless afternoons when I lay alone, creating myself out of nothing, treading water with words, my thoughts no longer came echoing back to me, proof of my insanity. I knew exactly who I was speaking to, now, in the conversation that defined me.

I was speaking to you.

'The Loneliest Night of the Year' came in at number six, with a bullet. Not bad, my friend. Half a dozen more hits soon followed, knocking your human competitors right out of the charts. The patronising arseholes now claim that this was all some kind of self-fulfilling prophecy, that people bought whatever the Azciak computers churned out, simply because they knew it 'had to be' what they wanted – even if, in fact, it wasn't. That's not what they said at the time, of course; their sycophantic paeans to your 'freshness' and 'candour' and 'bleak audacity' ran for pages.

I saw 'you' one night, on the jukebox screen – rendered, plausibly enough, as four young men with guitars, bass, and drums. If I'd fed a dollar into the machine, I could have had a printout of their 'life stories'; for five, an autographed portrait of the band, the signatures authentic and unique; for ten, the same with a dedication. I didn't, though. I watched them for a while; their expressions ranged from distraction to faint embarrassment – the way some human musicians look, when they know that you know they're only miming.

So forgive me if I didn't buy the tacky merchandise – but I saved up my Azciak payments and bought a second-hand CD player, and I hunted down a music shop which stocked your albums on 'obsolete' discs, for a quarter of the price of the fashionable new ROMs.

Of course I thought I'd helped shape you. *You sang about my life.* I couldn't have written a bar of the music, a word of the lyrics, myself – but I knew the computers could take care of those technical details. The wires in my head weren't there to extract any kind of talent; they were there to uncover my deepest needs.

And they'd succeeded.

At the same time, I couldn't let myself believe that I'd somehow conjured you up *on my own*, because – apart from the preposterous vanity of it – if I had, then I was still doing nothing but talking to myself. In any case, surely one person, alone, could never have swayed the populist Azciak software. Among the twenty thousand participants in the poll, there had to be others – hundreds, at least – for whom your words rang true as they did for me.

I phoned the woman who'd signed me up. 'Oh no, we couldn't possibly give you any *names*,' she said. 'All our data is strictly confidential.'

At work, in a five-minute mid-shift break, I snuck into the manager's office and called another branch of the Azciak organisation. The voice that replied sounded human to me, but the icon flagging a sales simulacrum lit up.

'You want to buy a direct mailing list? What selection parameters did you have in mind?'

'What selection parameters are there?'

A menu appeared on the flatscreen of the phone:

[1] Geographic
[2] Socio-economic
[3] Ethnic
[4] Aesthetic

[5] Political
[6] Emotional

I hesitated, then hit 6. The rest was easy enough; I just filled in the profile requirements as if I was describing myself.

The charge was one thousand dollars. I typed in the number of the French Fries purchasing account, and the list was downloaded into the phone. I copied it on to a floppy disk, then erased it from the memory.

You sang:

> *Here you are again*
> *Caring about the wrong things, again*
> *Everyone else makes mistakes, I know*
> *But at least they make THE RIGHT ONES*

Every day, I saw children half my age walking the streets of Kings Cross, surviving on food scraps, fighting each other for the privilege of selling themselves to the tourists. Every day, I read of the deaths of hundreds of thousands of people – in famines, in civil wars, and the latest genocidal psychodramas, designed to bolster the delicate egos of the most powerful nations on earth.

But I was powerless to change any of that. So I just closed my eyes and dreamt about *love*.

And a dream was all it would ever be. The truth was, I'd always known I was nothing, no one: an object in the shape of a human, not to be mistaken for the real thing.

The wonder of it was, I kept on existing, day after day, year after year. I woke every morning, and the whole bizarre joke – the illusion of humanity – still hadn't worn off. I had no choice but to eat and drink, to breathe, to shit, to earn money, to go through the motions – but I always knew that to try to do anything more would have been ridiculous.

I had as much right to be *loved* as I had to sprout wings and fly.

I chose a name from the list, almost at random – although when I saw that he lived in Adelaide, a twenty-hour bus ride away, I knew that was exactly what I'd wanted. Not that I'd have needed an excuse to keep my distance, if he'd lived next door. What would I have said to him? 'I stole your name from a database. I know we have a lot in common. I'm an antisocial emotional cripple, a bisexual virgin, a basket case. How about lunch? No? Dinner, then? Fuck that, let's go to bed.'

His name was Ben, and I dreamt about him day and night – conscious of, but undeterred by, the ludicrous nature of my obsession. I felt only slightly guilty for trespassing on his privacy; as long as he remained unaware of the fact, I'd done him no tangible harm. Besides, I didn't even know what he looked like, so when I pictured 'him', tangled in the sheets beside me, it wasn't him at all. It was just another fantasy.

And yet. I could never quite forget that he was real – and that he was, *I knew*, every bit as desperate and lonely as I was. I'd imagined a thousand lovers before, and I'd shame-lessly stolen the faces of a thousand strangers – without believing for a moment that I ever would meet, ever would speak to, ever would *touch*, the flesh-and-blood versions. It was unthinkable.

With Ben, it was not unthinkable.

Not quite.

And you sang:

> *Meet me on a dark street*
> *Away from their laughter and lies*
> *No, you don't want to see my ugly soul*
> *But my hands can still keep you warm*
> *Meet me on a quiet street*

The only stranger in town
And we'll step behind the railway line
And see whose love is blind

Alone in my room, I listened, and dreamed, and told you my dreams. Did I dream about love because you sang about love, or was it the other way round? Did you sing to affirm my life, or did I live to affirm your songs?

I don't know. I still don't know.

My theft was discovered, of course, and it didn't take much investigating to find the culprit. My own name was on the stolen mailing list – and when the keystroke timing signature for the phone call in question was compared with the staff cash register records, only one person matched.

The manager didn't press charges, he just sacked me on the spot. (My *comrades* cheered.) I walked all the way home, giddy with freedom, intoxicated by every breath of the cool night air, staring up at the lights of Market Street's unrentable skyscrapers as if I'd never seen them before in my life.

I told myself: I must have planned it this way all along; one small shock to the system, that's all I needed, to snap me out of this trance, to wake me from this sleep I've called *life*.

As I walked, I sang:

You never have lived
And you never will live
Because you've never wanted to
But in my arms
And in my bed
We'll find a substitute

First thing in the morning, I hocked my ancient CD player, put everything I owned into a suitcase (the Azciak black box included), and bought a ticket for Adelaide.

*

The bus driver said he liked both kinds of music – Country *and* Western – and he sure hoped that we did, too. Those of us who hadn't brought protection went through hell; I'd never thought I'd find myself ready to kill for a Walkman.

I still had your songs, though, etched into my memory, and the closer I drew to my destination, the more convinced I became that you were with me, guiding me. It didn't seem like such a strange idea; you had no body of your own, no senses of your own. Only the songs made you real, and if they were in my head, then so were you.

> *Yes it's true, I travelled a thousand miles*
> *Just to be beside you*
> *And it's true, I gave up a 'life' of my own*
> *Just to follow your trail*
> *And if all I've ever been, and all I've ever owned*
> *Is no great price in your eyes*
> *Won't you give me*
> *One last smile*
> *Before you walk away?*

Farmland and bushland, forest and desert alike were all reduced to sepia by the bus's tinted windows – and in the late afternoon the landscape was swallowed completely by the glare of sunlight on the scratched glass.

When night fell, the driver regaled us with a non-stop selection of Nashville's greatest lullabies. I gritted my teeth and stared out the window. With the reading lights on all around me, I could see nothing but my own reflection; just after midnight, though, the last of them went out, and I watched the grey starlit desert pass by.

Spending money like a dying man, I took a taxi across the awakening city. I was sick with fear – but cushioned by a mixture of adrenaline and lack of sleep. Part of me knew that the whole journey, the whole idea, had been insane from the start, and wanted nothing more than to be back in my room, dissolving into a miasma of loneliness and sensory deprivation. But part of me argued, fearlessly: *How do you know you won't be welcome? If a stranger travelled halfway across the country to your door, wouldn't you take him in?*

The building was shabby, dilapidated, demoralising, and utterly familiar – and in a way, that filled me with hope, as if the more we had in common, the more likely he was to understand why I was here. I grew numb as I climbed the stairs, my senses retreating into my skull even as my feet kept working. I'd felt the same way as a child, when I'd climbed to the top of the swimming pool's diving tower. (I'd turned around and climbed all the way down again.)

What would I do, when he opened the door? I'd planned to speak a line from one of your songs, but I still hadn't made a choice – and by now, half your words had deserted me, and the rest seemed impossibly clumsy. If they were stilted even in my head, how would they sound on my lips?

When I reached the seventh floor, I didn't hesitate or retreat: I walked straight down the corridor – and right past his door. *What could I say to him?* I couldn't tell the truth, or anything like it – not straight away. I needed a pretext. I stood at the end of the corridor, frantically sifting clichés: *Looking for some other tenant. Given the wrong address. Just moved in downstairs, and wondering if I could borrow . . .*

I couldn't do it. It made no difference how far I'd travelled, or how long I'd dreamt of this moment. I couldn't knock on that door.

If I ran into him, though, in the corridor, on the stairs . . . if we struck up a conversation, I could tell him that I was new in town, searching for a place to stay. I'd come to this building to rent a room, but there'd been some mistake, it had already been taken . . .

And he'd look me in the eye and say: *I have plenty of room to spare. Let me show you.*

It was half-past seven in the morning. Ben worked in a music shop; I knew that much from the stolen data. He'd be on his way, soon enough. All I had to do was wait.

So I stood by the stairwell, swaying, dizzy with fear. I knew this was my only chance. If I failed, I'd vanish from the face of the earth. If I failed, my loneliness would open up its jaws and swallow me. If I failed, I'd die.

I still don't know, to this day, what it was you wanted from us. Some kind of vicarious happiness? Some kind of second-hand love? Out of twenty thousand people, then, why did you choose the loneliest, the saddest; why did you choose the ones with so little hope?

Unless in your heart, you knew that you were just like us. Just like me: a human-shaped object, nothing more. Not to be mistaken for the real thing.

The door opened, and Ben stepped out. I was suddenly very calm. He didn't look threatening, or unapproachable. I'd been afraid that he might be impossibly – unattainably – handsome; he wasn't. I knew I could talk to him. Maybe it was my imagination, but I would have sworn that I could make out the faint scar on the back of his neck, proof that I'd come to the right place, proof that I'd found the right person.

He didn't look at me as he approached; he stared at the ground, just as I would have done. Desperate for guidance, I imagined myself in his place, imagined a friendly stranger trying to strike up a conversation. Then the fog cleared from my brain, and I knew exactly what I'd feel: suspicion, then disbelief . . . and then sheer panic. At the first sign of the threat of human contact, I'd recoil. *I'd flee.*

I kept silent. He walked past me, down the stairs.

*

I found an unvandalised phone booth, took the black box from my suitcase, and plugged it in. It came alive at once, red lights flashing, dragging the overdue data out of my head in one long, silent scream.

Afterwards, I walked aimlessly, until I stumbled across a small café. There were no other customers; I sat there sipping coffee, staring at the jukebox in the corner. It was playing an ad for Pepsi, or the latest song from Radical Doubt; I couldn't tell which.

I put a coin in the slot, and then knelt beside the machine – so close that the image on the screen became nothing but a blur of coloured light.

And you sang:

> Dry your eyes
> Don't be sad
> You're worthless
> Your tears mean nothing at all
> If you live and you die
> In a dream, in a lie
> Who will ever be the wiser?
> Close your eyes
> Don't be sad
> You're worthless
> Your pain means nothing at all
> Unseen and unknown
> Alive but alone
> Why end a life
> That's no life at all?

You were right, of course. And I swallowed no pills; instead, I bought myself a map, walked out to the highway, and hitch-hiked all the way home.

That was your last song – before the Azciak people fixed the *glitch*, corrected the *aberration*. The official story (from the

PR release, to the torrent of instant 'biographies', to the sleeve notes of the tasteful, black-lined, Memorial Collected Works boxed set): the lead singer of Worthless had overdosed on vodka and Nembutal, victim of a broken heart. I still have photos from the magazines of crowds of sobbing fans, carrying 'your' picture aloft.

I never joined those tearful mobs. I never even mourned you in private. I don't know if you're still in there, somewhere; concealed, transformed, unrecognisable. It's not impossible, is it? (After all, would you recognise me?)

And if you're not? If you really have gone forever?

Then here I am again. Caring about the wrong things, again.

And talking to myself.

Nyro Fiddles
F. Paul Wilson

This little piece – somewhere between story, diary entry and autobiographical episode – may seem quiet on a first reading, but we think it sets up resonances which can be heard throughout the stories collected in In Dreams, *encapsulating in a few words the seeds which grow into, say, the stories by Lewis Shiner, Andrew Weiner, or Nicholas Royle. F. Paul Wilson is best known as the author of* The Keep, The Touch *and other fine horror novels, but he has never been content to settle easily into genre, and his short fiction – collected in* Soft – *covers an extraordinary range of effects and approaches.*

'*"Nyro Fiddles",*' *he tells us,* '*is true. Mostly. For those not in the know or too young to remember, Laura Nyro was a cult phenom of the sixties. Find her old Verve and Columbia records and listen to that voice – she did all her own harmonies; listen to those lyrics and consider that they were written by a teenager. Many of her devotees were other musicians who had hits with her more commercial songs – "Stoned Soul Picnic", "And When I Die", "Stoney End", "Eli's Coming", to name but a few. She dropped out of the scene in the early seventies but recently started touring with a quartet. I caught her show at the Bottom Line in Greenwich Village and it brought back the night I dropped in on one of her recording sessions. I wrote the piece as if I had the old* Crawdaddy *in mind as a market. Here's how it went down . . .*'

CBS Recording Studios
The *New York Tendaberry* sessions
July 20, 1969

We were supposed to go to Studio A but there didn't seem to be a Studio A in this building so Mary asks the guard where's the Laura Nyro session and he says it's in Studio B on the second floor. A placard by the guard's desk reminds us that Arthur Godfrey broadcasts from the sixth floor.

We sign in and take the elevator.

The main double door to Studio B opens into a sort of T-shaped vestibule with the sound studio to the right and the engineer's booth to the left. I hesitate outside, not sure we should walk in because it's in use right now and we *had* been told to go to Studio A in the first place. The guard could be wrong (it's been known to happen) and the studio could be filled with strangers and I'd feel dumb walking in and then just turning around and leaving.

Then through the door window I see Jimmy Haskell walk by from the sound studio to the booth and I know this must be the place. Jimmy's arranging the horns for Laura. He's a sweet, easy-going, middle-aged guy with a salt-and-pepper beard and he's wearing a beanie with propellers sticking out each side. They spin deliriously as he walks.

Laura likes everyone to be happy at her sessions.

We walk into the booth and there's Laura and a friend smoking a little pipe. The friend has longish hair and a moustache, both brown, and is wearing one of those knee-length Indian style coat-shirts, and I think he looks a lot like a guy who used to play lead guitar in my band.

Laura sits by the console in her full-length black dress and black lace shawl and that incredible black hair and I think maybe she's put on a few pounds since last I saw her.

There's also this German shepherd bitch running around and it has what looks like an old Sara Lee coffee cake tin in the closet filled with dog food and every so often it goes over and chomps some down. Laura tells us the dog's name is Beauty Belle (or did she say Bill?).

It's eight o'clock and the session was supposed to start at seven but the engineers are having trouble setting up the second eight tracks and Laura Nyro, who's usually fairly talkative, is preoccupied tonight. Dallas – could be the city, a guy, or a gal – is on the phone and Laura's telling he, she, or it how stoned she is. The engineer's on another line with someone named Danny explaining that he doesn't see how he can mix the new album this week because his kids are out of school and he's gotta spend some time with them. Indian Coat was trying to persuade him on this point earlier but Indian Coat is now out in the sound studio talking to Twin-Prop Jimmy while the musicians sit around bullshitting, trying each other's instruments, and getting paid scale for it. Beauty Belle (Bill?) is watching Indian Coat very intently through the glass.

A young photographer approaches the console and waits for the lady to get off the phone. He shows her some shots he took of her a while back and she picks out some she likes and says she doesn't want to give this one or that one to *Vogue* because they're very personal-type pictures, you know? Indian Coat strolls in and says he wants that one blown up for his wall and Laura says he's *got* to be kidding. She hates that picture. Well, she doesn't really hate it, it's just that she likes others better and I get the impression she's uncomfortable with the word hate.

Break time rolls around for the musicians so they interrupt their bullshitting in the studio and move it out to the hall where they regroup around the soft drink machine. I go over and hang with one of the trumpets I know who with a couple more years could be old enough to be Laura's father and he tells me it's anarchy, pure and simple anarchy but wait and see . . . they'll start to play and she'll point things out and say do this and try that and before you know it everything falls into place and it's beautiful, man. The girl's crazy but she sure as hell knows her music.

Back in the booth they're blasting 'Time and Love', the song that's to be rerecorded tonight. The back-up tracks were laid down at an earlier session but something didn't click and so they're going to be done again tonight. Laura's tracks with her piano and vocal won't be touched and the band will play off them. After the second run-through of the tape Mary turns to me and says it sounds familiar and I say I guess it does have a few phrases reminiscent of 'Flim-flam Man', especially in the fade.

After more replays the band thinks it's ready and they try it. It's about nine now and Laura wants to finish by ten (*definitely* no overtime tonight) but the drummer isn't the same one as last time and he's doing some of his own thing (like doubles on the downbeat) and Laura wants to know the drummer's name. Jimmy tells her it's Maurice and she gets on the mike and tells Maurice what she wants. Her speaking voice is soft, almost sibilant, and I can never get used to associating it with the power, range, and clarity that explodes when she gets behind her piano. She tells Maurice to do it like Gary Chester did at the last session, keep it simple and easy and light and happy and no cymbals except for a bam-bam-*crash* in the chorus and only a one-stroke downbeat, okay?

At first I think the doubles on the downbeat sound better than the singles Laura wants but as the session wears on I come around to agreeing with the lady in black. Many more tries follow and one sounds perfect until Maurice forgets the *boom-boom* on his bass that leads into the fade. It's nine fifty

and Laura swears she's not going into overtime again.
Everything's going to stop dead at ten whether 'Time and
Love' is finished or not. Okay now, everybody be happy
and light, everybody smile, and one of the percussion men
sticks his head out from behind some baffling and flashes
Laura this hideous shit-eating grin and everybody laughs.

At ten fifteen the musicians take another break and Laura
is asking about overtime. At ten thirty all the musicians pile
into the engineer's booth to hear the last take. It's crowded
and Mary and I have other stops to make tonight so we
leave without goodbyes because no one could hear us over
the replay anyway. Art Garfunkel comes in as we're leaving
and asks if the Nyro session is here and I tell him yes. He
shakes his head and says he heard it was Studio A.

Outside the moon is high and bright and I remember
hearing that somebody might be walking on it tonight. I also
hear that Laura Nyro sleeps in a coffin.

I don't know.

Thrumm
Steve Rasnic Tem

Probably the most prolific and versatile writer of short stories currently active, Steve Rasnic Tem has sold over 170 to date, tackling horror, mystery, science fiction and western themes, but always somehow slipping his own personal touch into the interstices between genres. This, like much of his best work, is kind of a horror story.

Steve writes: 'In my personal mythology, rock and roll has always been the herald of change, the secret mirror which shows us that we are not solely the person we've told everyone we are, or even the person we've told ourselves that we are. Rock and roll alerts us to a mysterious self inside ourselves, another life waiting to happen. That's much of what "Thrumm" is about, really, and it charts pretty accurately my own musical interests and obsessions. I grew up in one of those pockets of poverty in the Southern US where rock was virtually unavailable except for a couple of distant top ten stations. The local music was too primitive even to be called "country": hillbilly music comes as close as anything. I've since come to appreciate those primitive country tunes I grew up with, but back then they were an irritation, a constant reminder of how I didn't fit in. Another music played in my head. An expanded sense of rock and roll coincided with my drive to get out of my home town and into the world at large, where I hoped to find my other life, and my own true voice.

'Not being immersed from the beginning in the music made my developing tastes somewhat off the mainstream at times, leading to what some might consider an inordinate interest in the careers of such musicians as Link Wray. I don't think it was rock lyrics which *drove me in my quest. For me the true draw of rock, the movement into strange new realms of experience, occurs somewhere between the words, perhaps in the pauses themselves. Perhaps that's one reason I still prefer vinyl over CDs – I like hearing the scratches and the static, the same static and distortion I so fondly recall from years before. This belief has had an influence on my writing style as well. Mood and abstract tone have become very important in my writing, and at the same time I believe at their best these elements are hard to learn, impossible to imitate. Because I think the tone of a piece actually resides somewhere in between the words, in the mysterious spaces, in the static.'*

And so 'Thrumm,' in which a search for the meaning in the soundscape behind the music leads straight to hell . . .

A*re you feelin' sick?*
   He used to dream of a music that would set him free.

Are you feelin' mad?

Sometimes it began as a thrumm in the background of a dream, and exploded into flying birds' wings, soldiers crying as they shot their muzzles full of fragmented insect parts into the wide-open mouths of dead infants.

Are you feelin' anything?

Sometimes he knew there was another self in him, a monster hiding there, that could be tamed only by acknow-ledging its existence, which most of the time he wasn't willing to do. But every time he ran away from it, every time he stopped looking at it, it took over.

Even in his most coherent dreams the sound was just out of reach, awash in a cascade of chords or obscured by the background noise of his own voice complaining of some pain or fear. In fact it often seemed that his favourite music – and the favourite music of so many – was simply amplified complaints. He was convinced that if he could but isolate that music and hear it clearly, such complaints would no longer be relevant, pain would no longer be relevant, because the resultant vibration would bring him so deeply down into his secret self that even the pain might be celebrated, because it was so very much his own.

Then put a knife into dad dad dad . . .

He never really knew his father, who had been a man of infrequent and violent visitations.

'Don't let me catch you with that music, boy! Don't let me catch you!'

His father was in charge of the rules, no matter where he was. He didn't allow music in the house, and Rex's mother, out of fear or habit or indifference to the melodies, followed through with the stricture.

Tell them what you think! Tell them what you feel! 'Where'd you get that radio? You *know* what your father would say!' *Tell them every one what's real!*

'What'd I tell you? What'd I *tell* you!' His father's face in his face, but his father's face so red and enormous it seemed to have no clear boundaries. 'You know what that music will *do* to you, boy? Can you even guess?' *Tell them tell them tell them!*

His last memory of his father was of an official-looking car parked out in front of the house, men in uniform milling around and leading his father out to the car all bound up in canvas and straps. Then his father looking up at Rex's upstairs window, staring at Rex, screaming 'Tell them!' over and over.

Much later he would find out that his father spent the last years of his life in one of those 'facilities'. *Tell them!* He would hear scattered rumours of murders, and worse, over the years, but nothing conclusive. *Tell them!* Sometimes when his mother was unhappy with Rex, she'd tell him that he was beginning to act just like his father. *Tell them your secret name!*

'Don't lock me in the closet, Ma! There's no food in here! You'll go off drinkin' and forget about me! I just know it!'

'You talk to me with respect! You talk to me with that mad in your voice and I ain't got no choice but to lock you in there!'

'Ma! Ma, I gotta use the bathroom!'

'You should've thought of that before. The way you been talkin' to me. You must think you're somethin' else!'

The way you love me really makes me wanna scream . . . With some songs you'll always remember where you were when you first heard them. 'I Need Your Loving', 'Strawberry Fields', 'Purple Haze', 'My Girl'. Sometimes the words or maybe the tune, or more often both, were such a perfect match to what it was you were going through that you started thinking that the song had made it happen. The song made you fall in love or out of love or made you beat up that guy that time at the dance after homecoming. It wasn't just the words – sometimes the tunes themselves seemed to say things to you that weren't in the words of the songs at all. The Stones, the Beatles, Wilson Pickett and Stevie Ray Vaughan all had this direct line into your head and they were just pumping the voltage on through, raising the volume until your hands and feet were jumping.

Tear this whole place down!

It was while his momma had him locked in the closet, all those years ago, that he'd first heard the thrumm in his head, in his heart, and in the music that filtered down through the cracked and peeling ceiling.

He used to think the music had put the thrumm into his head. *Don't you know I'd never lie to you?* But now he knew the music was an echo, a litmus test, a reflection, a xerox copy, a microphone slipped down into the centre of the soul. It reverberated with what it found, amplified and broadcast it for everybody else to hear and see.

The Rolling Stones playing 'Sympathy for the Devil' hadn't caused the violence at Altamont, any more than 'Helter Skelter' had sent Manson's groupies out the door with knives in their hands. Something else had, and the music had pointed it out.

That was why it was so important to listen to the music. For those all-important dispatches straight from the secret self.

What you need . . . what you see . . . is something else!

The music had something to point out in Rex, too, something scary. He thought he'd better find it before he did something that made Altamont and the Manson murders look like sweetness and light. Something else was in him, all right, some kind of big bad thrumm, and he had to find that thrumm something before it was too late.

Sometimes in his dreams Screamin' Jay Hawkins sang and danced naked holding his dick in his hand.

July, 1952: He was twelve years old and locked in his room and the old guy in the apartment above theirs had been playing this funky old beatup guitar about six hours straight.

'I'm gonna kill that old fucker!' his momma had screamed outside his door.

'You like the music?' he had whispered to himself. 'Yeah, it's food.'

Years later Rex would recognise some Otis Rush, John Lee Hooker, and T-Bone Walker in what the old man had been playing, but back then it was just the way the sounds seemed to reach down into his belly and rasp against his bones, and the way a certain vague sound, a shadow note that floated behind the blues riffs, a thrumm down his backbone that made him feel the closest he'd ever been to outright, uncontrolled craziness.

There had been good in that feeling, energy and life and a jitterbug in the feet, but also this: a quick fantasy of bashing his mother over the head with that old guitar and then strangling her with the strings.

Yah-ya-yaya-yayayaya-yeah!

The power of that fantasy, the sense that he had it in him to do such things, got him to listen to every song, new and old, coming out of the radio. Listening for the sound, listening for the thrumm that would bring on the fantasy, and the presence of something else. Preventive medicine. As long as he couldn't get to that something else there wasn't much he could do to change it. Over the years he would sharpen his listening skills considerably, but the trail of those notes would remain subtle and elusive. *Tell them! Tell them that you bleed!*

One morning when he was in the closet Rex realised that something must have happened to the old man who lived upstairs, because he wasn't hearing the music any more.

When you can't hear the notes . . . when you can't hear the song . . .

'Ma! What'd you do, Ma? I can't hear the music, Ma!'

But there was no voice on the other side of the door. He found himself straining to hear even the hoarse, alcoholic snores his mother made two-thirds of every day, but there was nothing, no sound, no voice, no music. *Can't you hear it? Can't you hear it?*

What he could hear, instead, after hours alone in the dark, was a distant thrumm, a discordant series of notes, a harsh semblance of a voice painful to hear and terribly familiar.

'Ma, *please*! Ma!'

When he finally heard her steps outside the door she still would not answer him. He thought it might be because after his long hours in the dark his voice had changed – now there were thrumm and clang and rough edges in it, a throat full of dust and a tongue crawling with bugs to rearrange the syllables his mouth tried to speak.

'Rex . . .' he finally heard – a soft, hoarse voice tense and hesitant. 'Rex, is that you?'

His answer was lost in a dark explosion as his fingers tore apart the door and the jamb. His mother spent two months in the hospital and based on her information everyone said it had been a prowler that did it, maybe two or three. His mother didn't lock him in the closet after that. Sometimes he put himself there for hours at a time, but he always took his radio.

1958: He'd just turned eighteen and although he'd been too big for his momma to force into the closet for some time it still felt like he'd just gotten out, like this was the first daylight he'd seen in years. There was thrumm in his voice and a strong backbeat in his walk when he went to school or parties or just tried to get to know other kids his age. He knew he was wound way too tight for safety but he couldn't see anything to be done about that except to pray for minimal hassles when the spring finally broke.

A lot of the music he'd been hearing that year was pretty above-ground, walking-around-with-your-best-suit-on, take-it-to-meet-your-parents kind of stuff. And yet most of it made him feel like he wanted to kill somebody, slit them open and crawl inside for the winter just to keep warm. *Baby pleaaaaasssse don't go!*

That year he got his first strong trace of the sound he was looking for, in an instrumental by a fellow named Link Wray, 'Rumble'. A gravelly electric guitar growling out two minutes and thirty-six seconds of one of the meanest sounding tunes he'd ever heard. It was the first instance of that distorted, fuzz-tone guitar sound he knew of. Wray achieved the crackle and burr with a hole punched through one of his amplifier speakers. In the liner notes for Wray's '74 album none other than Pete Townshend would write about being made 'very uneasy' the first time he heard it.

Wray had a voice to match that guitar – years later Rex would describe it as Jagger and Captain Beefheart ripped open and then bleeding into Robbie Robertson – he had a voice with the thrumm in it, and Rex followed the rasp and chew of that sound through songs like 'Super 88', 'It was a Bad Scene', 'Walkin' Bulldog', 'She's That Kind of Woman' and 'I Got to Ramble' (dedicated to the memory of Duane Allman). Legend had it that his session men would stomp the floor and beat on pans for a drum beat while recording in Wray's three-track shack. He believed it, and even in his middle years Rex sometimes found himself stomping and rattling the kitchenware while listening religiously to albums like 'Jack the Ripper' and 'There's Good Rockin' Tonight'.

Sometimes Wray's sound would grab him with the thrumm, and Rex would feel the need to lock himself up in his room like Lon Chaney in one of those old werewolf movies. What he felt at those moments wasn't exactly anger, but a kind of manic, transforming high that made him want to get to the centre of things, the centre of people. He wanted to hold their still-warm hearts in his hands.

He met Ellen at a car rally his senior year. She was one of those girls who always wore pastel sweaters with matching silk scarves around the neck. His friend Jim said it was to hide all the love bites the football team had given her, but Rex always pictured a deep slash across the throat. He imagined removing the scarf in the throes of passion, anxious to nibble there, and Ellen's head falling off into his lap.

'Turn off the radio, Rex,' she said and sighed, rearranging herself on his lap and squirming, pushing her chest forward. 'It *distracts* me, honey.'

But the DJ was playing 'Rumble', and the steady thrumm

of it had him well caught up. 'I can't,' he mumbled, and moved his lips over her ear.

'What do you mean you *can't*?' Ellen's voice shifted into her grating, thirty-plus-years-and-too-many-kids mode. Rex heard her mother and her grandmother, too. He reached over and switched it off. She sighed contentedly and leaned over his shoulder, rubbing her hands up and down his back. 'Thanks, baby.'

Ellen hummed tunelessly in his ear, reaching under the edge of his shirt and drawing her nails up his spine in a jerky back and forth rhythm. Rex felt that rhythm working through his flesh and into the bone, felt a fuzzy vibration shaking itself out of the tangles of distant memory, heard the strain and the thrumm of it backing his father's voice *Tell them! Tell them, son!* singing with his eyes filled with the vision of dozens of naked and dead young girls. 'Oh, Ellen,' he whispered, but it was his father's voice, his father's song on his lips as he pressed his hands on either side of her neck and started to press as hard as he could.

'Jesus, Rex!'

He stopped and looked at her, then jumped out of the car and ran.

Rex ran up the hill as hard as he could, past the old mill and along the narrow edge of the ridge and despite the intense pain in his chest he felt no fatigue, only a growing exhilaration as the music built in wild abandon inside him, an oddly irritating, moronic tune which years later would remind him of Oingo Boingo and the way it made you want to snap your head back and forth idiotically as if the neurons were exploding. *Tell them! Tell them! Tell them!*

Eventually he made his way back to his car and his radio. Ellen wasn't there, no doubt gone off with some other guy from the rally. Rex switched the radio back on, but – unable to find Link Wray again, or any other tune angry enough to do the trick – he pushed the dial to the far end where disgruntled static and garbled messages from distant points on the globe reigned. In that region he found comfort for the burn in his head, an antidote for the other Rex who sang the blood songs he was so desperate to run away from, and he drove through that country until dawn.

May, 1964: Rex had been using drugs since his freshman college year and it seemed to him now that the thrumm had become a bit more ethereal, a little more religious, both in the music and in the lifestyle. People talked about going back to Mother Nature, going back to the sea, going *someplace else*, and in that someplace else, Rex thought, there would be no secret other self fucking you up and causing you no end of nightmares.

'Rex? Rex, honey, don't!' the women would say when he cried watching them die from the chemicals they were throwing down their throats and pumping into their arms. *Tell them!*

Link Wray had another, softer country-gospel side as well: 'Fire and Brimstone', 'God Out West', 'Take Me Home Jesus', the kind of music Rex had never much cared for, but he understood all too well how essential that periodic return to a safe and simple, funky philosophy was once you got within a nail-scratch of the sound. The thrumm could make you religious as hell. Look at Little Richard. Sometimes Rex wondered if Jimmy Swaggart had heard the thrumm, too, just like cousin Jerry, and found it too much to bear.

Tell them what you heard! Tell them what you feel!

The boys of Pi Kappa Alpha were a sadistic bunch, but they threw a good party. He didn't fit in, but this seemed to be a fraternity for guys who didn't fit in. After the initiations of the past few days – guys lying naked on the floor and farting directly into each other's noses, guys with their jock straps full of mustard and hot sauce, guys paddled so hard their rectums bled, guys with their ears scraped raw from Brillo pad ear muffs – *I believe in murder! I believe in love! I believe in torture! I believe in love!* – vast quantities of illicit drugs seemed the only appropriate response.

But some drugs cut out the music completely, leaving him alone in a silent world with only his father's red face for company. *Tell them!*

'Hey, man. Hey, man, you okay?' His friend said more – Rex could see his lips moving – but he couldn't hear a word beyond the hiss and thrumm welling up inside him.

'I have to hear the music,' Rex said, 'but I can't.'

And then that other Rex came out, and his friend's face grew redder and redder, looking more and more like his father's face, and by the time the cops got there many of his brothers wore his father's wet, red face.

You can't hide me! You can't avoid me! I am your sweet, red loverrrrrr . . .

December 1969: Rex was twenty-nine, and the endless graduate student (English or History, depending on the year), and about to be kicked out into the real world. He had no marketable skills. He worked part-time at the local record store listening for the thrumm and pushing personal favourites like Wray off on younger college kids. It had been a year of demonstrations and local bands playing 'In-A-Gadda-Da-Vida' endlessly in the park for seriously stoned audiences. It had also been the year girls at an all-women's college in the next town were getting murdered in their beds.

'Something else, is that you, cuttin' up?' he'd ask in a haze of dope. *Tell them! Tell them! Man you're somethin' else!*

Sometimes something else would answer. Sometimes not.

Sometimes Rex would fervently pray that the music continued as long as he needed it.

In the seventies the thrumm was buried in the precise

guitar work of Roy Buchanan, but it was still there. It still growled.

Now and again it occurred to him, of course, that the singers and musicians truly capable of producing the chord he was looking for were dead. Hendrix, aspirating his vomit in 1970. Morrison, dying of a heart attack in his bathtub at age twenty-seven, 1971. Janis, TRex, maybe even Mama Cass or Ricky Nelson. Others, no doubt, who had died before anyone had even known about them. Or maybe they *had* found the chord, worked to achieve it or stumbled across it by accident, and that was what had killed them.

'Is that you, Daddy?' he said to his image in the mirror. The image sang *Tell them!* but Rex didn't understand what it was he was supposed to tell. *Tell them!* Rex thought that the face in the mirror was the face of his own violent death.

Through the eighties he traced bits and echoes of the sound through a variety of bands: Chelsea and Oingo Boingo, Athletico Spizz 80 and the Dead Kennedys. The vocalists in these groups all projected at least the shadow of the sound he was looking for, a shadow that could even be glimpsed occasionally in the simple-minded dementia and masturbatory self-indulgences displayed by such as the lead singer for the Cramps. Although he could never quite get into heavy metal, he had to admit there was a strong strain of the sound throughout Metallica's 'One'.

Sometimes he'd trace the sound in and out of an Elvis Costello whine or the demented laments of Echo and the Bunnymen. Sometimes in the gravelled voice of a singer like Joe Strummer, the shadow came very close to revealing itself. He always thought the Clash sounded their best when they were at their most distorted. Sometimes he'd tape and retape 'Dictator', 'Dirty Punk' and 'We Are the Clash', playing with the controls to maximise the distortion – sounding as if it might have been recorded at the bottom of a garbage disposal – while still maintaining some semblance of the original. He'd stop the tape at every hint of the thrumm, back it up, and play this isolated bit over and over, but the thrumm was a tease – it receded too quickly into the background to capture.

Something was happening in the music, though. It was still rock, still the same basic sound, but he felt the gradual evolution in it, a change that he was sure would some day bring his sound, his thrumm, out into the open. For a while he'd sneak into the clubs and stand at the back watching them pogo or slam dance. Then one morning he just shaved his head and that night he joined them down in the pit in front of the stage, circling and turning and slamming into people, shoving them away, crouched and ready as if he was fighting but it wasn't fighting at all, at least not usually. After a few weeks people got to know you and helped you up when you took a particularly bad fall. With his head shaved he lost years, he actually looked almost the right age, but when he eventually tried jumping off the stage he couldn't twist himself into those safer angles the young punks managed, and he broke his left arm. The next weekend he was back in the pit circling with a sling, but he never tried stage diving again.

He hit his late forties with his head still shaven, but he'd kept his weight down and with just the right amount of makeup he didn't look much older than the rest of them out on the dance floor. The best thing about it was that he could feel just the edge of the thrumm, go with it, crash into somebody and then feel as if he'd faced that something else without really hurting anybody else in the process.

He got married, had three kids, but continued to follow the thrumm through the music and on the road.

The face in the mirror grew steadily older, more like his

father's face. *Tell them what, Daddy?* But when the mirror spoke Rex didn't understand the words.

For a time during the late eighties Rex followed Stevie Ray Vaughan on the road, his anxiety rising steadily from the time he heard the first notes out of Ray's '59 Fender Stratocaster tuned to E-flat, crescendoing when the guitar master pumped the wah-wah pedal for the beginnings of Hendrix's 'Voodoo Chile (Slight Return)'. When Vaughan jammed, or engaged in a cutting contest with a Clapton or a Cray or a Beck, Rex would leave the theatre shaken.

When Stevie Ray's helicopter dropped into the ground, Rex left the road and concert halls and eventually all the late nights prowling the record stores for hidden gems. He spent more time with his wife and kids, and kept the thrumm of his life to himself, in his head.

Tell them, son. Tell them what it's like.

When Rex awakened it was as if from a dream that had lasted for years. He stood and saw himself in the mirror attached to the back of the bedroom door: his father looked out at him, but older than Rex remembered him: his hair hippy-cut long, streaked with grey, his grizzled beard eating away at the lower half of his face, his belly pushing out and spreading open his pyjama top.

In his head, the thrumm rang clearly, reverberating down through his bones. He didn't need a radio; he'd mixed the sound in his dreams.

The longer he gazed at the mirror, the leaner and meaner the image of his father became. Shadows ran up his arms and across his face, masking him in grey and black. His teeth grew long and curved. His eyes burned white with the glow of the other Rex's passion, the intelligence of something else again.

It just needed to be seen. Once heard in the song, it lost its danger. *Tell them! Tell them, son. Tell them what they are.*

Digital to Analogue
Alastair Reynolds

Alastair Reynolds is that rarity which most people outside the field assume to be a cliché: a scientist who writes SF. Specifically, he has a Ph.D. in astronomy, and he works for the European Space Agency in Holland. One of the youngest of the new wave of British writers, he's published three stories so far, all in Interzone. *'Digital to Analogue' contains, Reynolds tells us, 'a number of ideas which were amplified after reading Simon Reynolds's (no relation) collection of essays in* Blissed Out *(Serpent's Tail, 1991), in particular, the chapter on Acid House. I also plundered Paul Davies's book* The Cosmic Blueprint *(Unwin, 1989) for the references to entrainment.'*

Maybe it's no surprise that 'Digital to Analogue' is hard SF. But it is hard SF radicalised by close attention to pop cultural iconography and the new tribal ethos of Acid House nightclubbing. Not to mention one of the neatest paranoid conspiracy theories we've come across in a long time. Just remember, the message is in the bleep . . .

I left the Drome at 3.00 a.m., with Belgian house on indefinite replay in my brain. I was unaware that I was being followed. You can't trust yourself at that hour, not when your nervous system wants to shut down for the night's deepest phase of sleep. If we're awake, it's then that we make the stupidest errors, dreaming that our actions won't have any outcome in the light of dawn. And, sometimes, a few pills assist the process.

I was more than usually pissed, but had avoided anything else for most of the night. Then she'd shown up: the girl in the Boulevard Citizens T-shirt, some Scottish white-soul band, offering E from a hip pouch. I'd hesitated, my head swirling already, then acquiesced. We did the deal amid the strobe-storm of sweating revellers and the eardrum-lancing rhythms.

'I'll be dead to the world in a few hours,' I said, slipping the tabs in my pocket.

'Big deal,' she said. 'Me, I just take a sicky. Pick up the phone, tell a few lies, kick back and snooze.'

'Great if your phone works,' I said. 'Thing is, I'm a telephone engineer; work for BT. So it's me you should thank next time you call in sick. Probably be eavesdropping from some hole in the ground somewhere.'

I felt a pressure on my shoulder, turned round to see one of my friends from the office. Sloshing Grolsch everywhere, he began to croon 'Wichita Lineman', drunkenly out of tune.

I winced. 'More like driving the road to Whitley Bay, searching in the fog for another bloody vandalised kiosk.'

Boulevard Citizen looked at us dubiously, then disappeared into the dance-floor, the DJ segueing into a fresh track laid down on a scuffling foundation that had JB embossed in every one of its bpm. I dropped a tab, getting into the music. Suddenly I remembered something I had to convey to my friend. 'Hey,' I shouted, throaty over the noise. 'I heard James Brown's got two people, full time, just to spot samples on other records, then squeeze the artists for royalties!'

'Two people?' he said, then laughed, punching a fist in the air. 'Good God! Two people! Full time! *Good God!*'

'I thought it showed how endemic the sampling thing's become,' I said, aware my voice wouldn't appreciate such discourse in the morning, also that I'd reached a phase of my own drunkenness cycle characterised by extreme humourlessness. 'I mean, just listen to this stuff . . . this is probably one hundred per cent recycled sound, friend.'

'Then it's very nineties, isn't it,' he said, shrugging. 'Very Green. Thought we were all for recycling these days. Cars, paper, bottles . . . why the hell not music?' Then I skipped a few frames and my friend was looking at his watch. 'Well, guess we're going to split soon. Sorry you're not on our taxi route, mate.'

'Yeah, I'm on shanks's tonight.' I shrugged, the E affecting my bonhomie. In any case, I wanted to stay for a few more numbers, now I was clicking into the Drome's vibe. Pink smoke was flooding the floor, blue lasers tracking from the ceiling rig, and I was getting righteously *into it*. A track I liked came up, one of those blink-and-you've-missed-it ephemeral club hits that attains culthood, graduates to being a classic, gets heavily sampled, becomes slightly jaded, becomes frankly passé, winds up a dusty artifact of late twentieth-century pop culture, all within a month or two. A bit of social commentary this, as well: 'A Killer is Stalking Clubland'. And if you think *that's* in questionable taste, there was even a reference to someone's eyelids being stapled open.

Come 3.00 a.m., I decided I'd better hike if I wanted to make it to work. Had to get my coat, so I re-entered the mêlée, semi-dancing, pushing toward a neon sign at the club's other side, through a veil of perfumed smoke. I was halfway when I saw the red laser stabbing through the cloud. A shrouded figure was aiming a gun at me, eclipsed in waves by silhouetted bodies, face blocked by shadows and a pair of sunglasses, and framed by what looked like aviation phones, with a mike wrapping around the front.

Weirdos everywhere. Why not just *bliss out*, instead of

getting on everyone's tits? Yeah, time to leave, no doubt there.

I'd gotten my coat quicker than usual, maybe because the club would stagger on for another hour or so. Outside I met a few friends who'd spent the intervening time in an all-night kebab shop. The taxi-rank was on my walk home so I loitered with them, up the rubbish-strewn streets, kicking fast-food containers, crushed tins of Red Stripe, ticket stubs. A few desultory revellers were still ambling around, trying to find somewhere open, dossers hanging outside the old pisser in the Bigg Market that looked like an Edwardian UFO, solitary cop cars kerb-crawling; cherry-lights reflected in puddles of urine. Overhead, against the winter stars, a helicopter circled predatorily, hawking the streets below, doubtless searching for stolen motors that would finish up embedded in shopfronts come morning. No wonder none of us brought cars. At the taxi-rank we split, they to their houses in Byker, me to my flat in Fenham. I didn't have far to go, really. But it's not the distance that counts, in the end.

I hiked up my hood, drowning out the plaintive car-alarms and the sirens, Walkman playing. It was a slimline job, barely larger than the tape, burnished silver like a very flash cigarette case. The C90 was a compilation I'd made up of techno and bleep stuff, vinyl picked up from Oldham Road in Manchester, plus chart house grooves and a little main-stream electro-soul, chanteuse-fronted, allegedly direct from the smokiest Berlin bars. Ultra-pure digital sounds, hypnotic synth lines, speedily distorted vocals. It was the music they played at the Drome, wall-to-wall, no dicking about, mind-pummelling noise, repetitive as Tibetan mantras, as fast as Bhangra. Allied to the Drome's effects, intense light projected through a rotating filter wheel of tinted, immiscible fluids . . . like a kaleidoscope *melting* before your eyes, the sound washing over like a test-signal for your sozzled brain.

I'd been into it for a year or two now, and finding that the scene was established in Newcastle made up for the wrench I'd felt leaving the north-west, where the nexus of the whole thing had originated. My BT job was a piece of shit; it was the music, the club scene that I lived for. What I didn't know, as I popped the last of the E, was that it was the music that had drawn the Househunter to me.

I'd been targeted in the Drome, it seemed, and when I left with my friends, I'd been followed. Discreetly; up town, lurking in the sidestreets, until I left the pack. Shrewd, as if my walk home had been half expected. And because of the Walkman, I didn't hear the footsteps (supposing any were to be heard), as I walked around the civic boating lake.

It came suddenly; carotid-squeezing pressure around my neck. The hood was ripped from my clothes, earplugs seized, the whole ensemble of the Walkman hurled into the moon-streaked water. There was never any doubt in my mind that I'd been selected as a victim, not in that instant. I knew it was the Househunter's arm around me. And then something went through my head – a thought I'd probably shared now with a dozen others, our one instance of solidarity. I realised that all the assumptions had been wrong. Oh boy, they'd got it *badly* wrong. They weren't going to catch this baby in a hurry. Not if they kept on thinking –

I felt something damp smother my whole face, then, maybe a microsecond after the sensation of wetness, the dizzy sensation of etherisation. The last thing I heard was her saying, very calmly: 'Trust me, please. I'm a doctor.'

I remember coming to, briefly, in the back of a vehicle. For a blissed-out moment I didn't remember what had happened, one of those waking fugues where nothing connects, nothing matters. Eyes washed by the yellow of sodium lamps, behind grilled glass, the numbing vibration of the ride transmitted through a softness beneath me. I couldn't make out the interior too well. Then it all rammed home, as I heard her speaking, behind what must have been a thin partition separating the back of the van from the driver's compartment. I struggled to move, found I couldn't. For a while it wasn't clear whether this was a result of constraints, or whether the right signals just weren't getting to my limbs. I was stretchered, braced so that it didn't roll around. My mouth was obstructed. Had she gagged me, or was I sucking on a breathing tube?

'En route from pick-up point,' she said. 'Subject has regained apparent consciousness. Brief description: outward physiology normal on first inspection; WM, twenties, slim build, height five eight or nine, cropped hair, no facial distinguishing marks. No evidence for intravenous drug use . . . presence of other intoxicants, hallucinogens or mood-alterers not ruled out at this stage. Interestingly, the subject's spectacles contained flat lenses – of cosmetic value alone. The subject's auditory stimulant was neutralised during apprehension. Prognosis is satisfactory; ETA fifteen minutes, over.'

The words careered through my brain in a jumble, leaving me to marshal them. What was happening? Where was I? Why did I really not *care* all that much?

I allowed myself to slump, mentally, letting the restful rhythm of the gliding sodiums caress my eyelids. How easy it was to sleep, despite all that I knew!

The next recollection is an invasive howl ripping through my dreams. It seemed the loudest noise I'd ever heard, rising and falling on a dreamily slow *wah wah* oscillation. Then it got worse, and my skin began to prickle, before the sound reached an apex and the envelope of oscillation diminished, lower pitched, gut-churning bass components phasing in.

In the Blitz, my grandfather once told me, the Luftwaffe didn't bother tuning the engines of their bombers to precisely the same revs. That way you could always tell a Heinkel from a Wellington, if you didn't know how they were *meant* to sound. There'd be a rising and falling signal, on top of the engine sound, as the spikes of the sound waves moved in and out of phase with one another, several times a second. And he'd move the outspread fingers of his hands across one another in illustration. He'd been an audio engineer, my granddad, for Piccadilly Radio, knew all sorts of arcana. I think it was he who made me go into electrical engineering, he that set me on course for my privacy-violating job for BT . . . though in fairness the old feller couldn't have known better.

I opened my eyes to a chipped surface of beige plaster. The tip of my nose was an inch or so from the wall; I was lying in the medical 'recovery' position on a soft surface. I tried moving; no joy. I was immobilised, either by weakness or restraint. Hands rolled me to my other side, so that I faced her. My mouth was free, no longer intubated or gagged. She was a pale ovoid, against a backdrop of olive green. From the angle of my gaze I couldn't see her face, just the blurred whiteness of her waist.

Then it all clicked: *hospital surroundings*. That explained the shabby decor, the pervasive air of decrepitude. She was a nurse or ward attendant, wearing a white overcoat and a stethoscope. Behind her were green curtains, the kind they used to fence off patients during a bed-bath. I could hear the sound of medical equipment behind the curtain, birdlike bleeps and clicks. Hey, some sod was worse than me. Life was looking up. I couldn't move much, but that didn't mean a lot. Hell, I'd just been through a bad experience, right. I was probably suffering post-traumatic stress disorder. *In 1962, Vietnam seemed like just another foreign war* . . . Ha ha.

Then she spoke; the same voice I'd heard in the ambulance. 'Ah good,' she said. 'Awake. That's perfect. We'll be over and done before we know it. Just a few simple tests should be sufficient.'

I strained my neck to look up. Her white coat was loosely tied over a black T-shirt decorated with a half-familiar pattern, like a contour map of the lunar surface, etched in white. The stethoscope hung down over her chest. Her hair was raked back from her brow, tied in a utilitarian tail. Her lips were pallid, eyes masked by circular black sunglasses. A pair of phones framed her head, bulky black things. Aviation phones, a cable running to a belted powerpack. Noise-cancelling jobs, like helicopter pilots wore. I thought of the 'copter I'd seen that night, but no . . . there couldn't be a connection, surely.

Strange accessories for a nurse, I thought. And then: a kind of out of head experience, a soft voice from afar, saying: *This is your rational mind speaking. You're in the deepest shit imaginable, but you won't admit it, not until that E's through with its business* . . . And I ignored it, eyes tracking over her coat (more like a scientist's than a doctor's coat, I decided), picking out streaked splatters of rust-red.

'Could I have a drink, please?'

She reached into a coat pocket, pulled out a tiny black thing the size of a box of cigarettes. Glanced at a wristwatch.

'Log entry: time 05.30. Subject made first conditioned response a few seconds ago. Requested fluid. Hypothesis: residual mind-state must still co-ordinate behaviour compatible with normal dietary and physical requirements; in other words, subject's nutritional intake will fall into stereotypical pattern. Conclude that request probably the expression of a genuine biological need. Although probably unnecessary in any case, will administer 250 ccs of glycolated barley-water intra-orally. Entry ends.' Click.

She cranked something under me, making the couch angle up. Then she touched a glass to my parched lips, and I drank. God, it was the best drink I'd ever tasted: sugary sweet and cool as nectar. Lucozade. Blanched out, towering above me, she looked angelic to my eyes, this beatific giver of nourishment to the sick.

'Let's get some air in here, shall we,' she said, without actually addressing me. She whisked back the curtain, revealing the rest of the room.

There comes a point, even in the deepest drug-induced para-reality, where sufficient data from the real world can build up and penetrate the fiction. *You're in the deepest shit imaginable*, that voice repeated. And I began, for the first time, to heed my own subconscious. There were no other patients in the 'ward'. The room was small, four, five metres along each damp-stained wall. They were covered with literally hundreds of . . . but no, I'll come to *those* in a moment, after I've set the rest of the scene. High windows on one wall admitted wan shafts of dawnlight, falling in patches on the floor. There was a metal door, padlocked on the inside. The room's odour of urine and vomit reminded me of a multi-story carpark stairwell. There was the couch, two garden seats and a wooden table, an empty wheelchair, a tripod and anglepoise set-up holding a waiting camcorder. The rest of the room was crammed with expensive looking electronic equipment . . . racks of slim black synthesisers, embossed with familiar names: Casio, Korg, Roland, Yamaha, Hammond, Prophet. The whole stack wired to a table-load of MIDI monitors and PC keyboards, dove-grey shells, wrapped in a tangle of cables and optic fibres. There were crushed Irn Bru cans, Lucozade and Beck's bottles, tabloids, listings magazines, ring-bound folders, cassette and video cases, floppy disks and what looked like piles of twelve-inch white-label records. I looked closer: each sleeve had the words *Digital to Analogue* scrawled over it. I remembered that: one of those subsequently sampled club hits from about six months back. You heard parts of it on many new records.

The shelving held dozens of display devices with gridded screens, oscilloscopes or cardiogram machines, displaying different blippy patterns, like the contours on her T-shirt. I knew where I'd seen it now: taken from an album cover. And it wasn't some landscape at all, but the radio signal of a pulsar, a clock ticking in space. I couldn't recall who'd told me that, but it seemed bizarre at the time, an icon from the heart of science manifesting itself in a million bedsits, wrapped around a piece of hallowed black vinyl. Like those Mandelbrot sets that started infesting album sleeves and vids, for a few months. As if science was the ultimate subculture, somehow, the stuff beneath the floorboards you don't want to know too much about . . .

Incidental detail: the table with the MIDI-stack also held something chunky and metallic, with a pistol-grip, shaped like a *Space: 1999* gun. An industrial stapler. This must be what they mean by a bad trip, ha ha.

Concerning the walls: I think the operative term here must be Shrine, in the sense that she'd pinned up dozens of monochrome photographs of me, taken during the last year of my life, some in the street, my distant figure outlined in red, others close-up in some club, my eyes blankly uncomprehending. Just like CIA target acquisition images. And more: complicated graphs and diagrams, scrawled over in felt-tip, fixed in laminated confusion on top of one another. Sonograms, sound-spectra, electrical circuit diagrams, technical pieces about *entrainment* . . . Christ, where had I heard that before, and why did it honestly matter, now? And why did she have a map of the UK, webbed in dotted ley-lines?

I was beginning to sweat. Thinking maybe my subconscious had a point; maybe this *was* a little unusual for a hospital.

She was fiddling with my head. I realised that I was wired up to something, little electrodes around my temples. She was fixing them down after they'd worked loose. She'd fixed things to my chest as well, white disks trailing wires to a mound of humming machines. All I was wearing was a pair of white, grass-stained jeans.

Click with the dictaphone. 'Log entry, 05.45. Summary to date.' She coughed before continuing in her soft, educated Tyneside accent. 'My orders were to terminate the subject on sight, in view of the danger to the community at large. At 2.45 a.m. I attempted to zero the subject in the Drome. Termination was impossible without risk of substantial collateral damage to the uninfected. I followed the subject from the Drome, hoping to get a clear shot. At around 3.30, however, I decided to break protocol and bring in the subject for captive examination. If all goes well, I'll be finished in a matter of hours.' A studied pause. 'Our operational integrity will not have been compromised, I promise. While my methods may be my own, I'm fully aware of the consequences for urban panic should our cover be exposed.' She clicked off the recorder, fumbled in her pockets and lit a cigarette from a black carton inscribed with a skull and crossbones, dragging on it thoughtfully before restarting the tape. 'I took a series of EEG readings while the subject was under,' she said, fixing a fresh marker in the little gripper of a pen-trace machine. There was a basket full of output, etched in wavering ink. The machine hummed into life, the pen gliding to and fro. 'Now I'm observing the subject's waking responses to a variety of stimuli.'

'Please don't hurt me . . . I promise I won't tell anyone if you let me go . . .'

She flicked ash on the floor then took another dismissive draw. 'Subject is now entering the plea phase, as you'll have observed. The initial euphoric state induced by the drug is fading; terror is replacing confusion and ambivalence about his situation. Soon his pleas will lose coherence; we'll observe the onset of hysterical shock, infantile withdrawal, regressive Oedipal complexes. These façades exactly mirror the usual psychoses observed in situations of extreme trauma, but are little more than mimetic survival ploys.' Then she leaned closer, so that I could see my expression in her black shades. Not looking too good, actually; I'd developed a spontaneous tic on one eyelid. She placed a set of plastic earplugs over my head, then returned to her MIDI hook-up. Touching keys, a multicoloured graphic of waveform profiles sprang on to one of the screens. Another lit up showing an annotated musical score, a third showing a plan view of a piano keyboard, overlaid with numbers and symbols. 'Don't know if you recognise this,' she said, tapping the waveform with a black fingernail. 'But we've been acquainted with it for some time now. And we've been following you for over a year.' Followed by an aside: 'Mental note: must refrain from *any* communication with the subject outside of program parameters. Difficult, though: they look and smell human, and I'm only human myself. Can't help establishing weak emotional ties. Had the same problem with rhesus monkeys at the institute . . .'

'I promise,' I said. 'Let me go . . . I won't even recognise you, will I . . . we could pass in the street and I wouldn't notice . . . please don't hurt me, I'm begging you . . .'

She stubbed the cigarette on the back of my hand. 'Uh, uh, uh,' she said. 'No talking till I say so, not until I expressly request a verbal response.' She ripped off a strip of paper;

when I'd opened my mouth, the pen-trace had zigged dramatically. 'Hmm,' she said to herself. 'This is very poor indeed, much worse than we assumed.' Then she reached over to the table for the industrial stapler, flicking open its steel jaw like a soldier checking the clip on his rifle. Gripped the trigger and pumped it twice, to free the action, sending tiny projectiles across the room. Then leaned over my couch and stapled the strip of paper on to the plaster of the wall, *ker-thunk*.

While she did this I'd begun screaming, not merely because of the pain in my hand.

She cuffed me. 'I said quiet, you rascal! No screaming or I'll have to cut your vocal chords . . .' Then she laughed. 'Not that anyone's going to hear us, mind you.' And as she spoke, I heard the throttling up of a plane preparing to take off. We were in the vicinity of an airport, I guessed. I thought of the many bunkers and sheds you'd find within the perimeter of any small airfield. No one was going to wander in on us by accident, that was clear.

Trying to stay sane, I wondered about the synths and the medical gear. The music stuff I could handle; it could have been obtained easily enough. Some of it looked second-hand, edges chipped, keys dusted in a talcum of plaster and dirt, smudged with fingerprints – sorry – *latents*. (That's what they always say, when they're investigating a homicide, in those books by McBain and Harris and Kellerman, those guys who always go on about multiple murders, serial killers, that shit . . . *check the body for latents – gee, sorry, inspector, the state of putrefaction's too advanced . . . we'll have to rely on dental records if we're gonna find out who the hell that poor sucker ever was . . .*)

But the EEG machine, those oscilloscopes – where'd she lifted them from? God knew it was easy enough to stroll into a hospital these days, easy enough to wander in and casually stab or rape someone – but even now, was the country so shitty that you could stroll out with a van-load of – what was it Python said, ha ha? Machines that go *ping* . . . Oh God, I didn't find it all that hysterical, right then.

'Log entry,' she said. '06.10. I am studying the encephalogram of the subject's so-called conscious mind. Brain music. A jumbled confusion of overlaid electrical signals signifying the neural activity of the subject's brain from second to second. First impression: although the trace might look normal enough to the layperson, no neurologist would accept that this was the EEG trace of a walking, talking human being. It's more evocative of certain types of akinetic or psychomotor seizure. A kind of prolonged *grand mal* convulsion.' She nodded, as if certifying her own theory. Then she put down the paper. 'Now the most critical part of the study commences. In order to probe the extent of the takeover, I must force conditioned responses from the subject. Taken as an ensemble, they hold the key to the nature of the takeover. Although we've now identified the likely progenitor of the infection, the mechanisms of transmission are far from certain. By regressing the subject back to the point of infection, I hope to gain fresh insights. To gain full compliance I am about to administer scopolamine intravenously. Entry ends.'

She turned to smile. 'Now, we can either do this quietly, and efficiently, with minimum fuss for all concerned. Or we can do it messily, and unpleasantly. What's it going to be?' – As if she was berating a dog that had shat on the floor, not actually bawling it out, but playing on its instinct for mood, its capacity for terror and confusion. She reached for a syringe, held it up to the light and squeezed a few drips from the needle, then injected me. 'Just to get you into the swing, you understand.'

'I'll do whatever you want,' I said, tears streaming down

my face. 'But please please please . . .' Then I just trailed off into simpering dejection.

'Now then,' she said, oblivious. 'What say we have a nice little chat, eh?'

I nodded, drooling, hoping I could stall her if she'd let me talk. If I had one hope it was being found, and that meant buying time for myself, spinning out her rituals.

'Well, all right,' she said. 'But I'm going to have to ask you some very *hard* questions. And I'll have the tape running all the while. Plus, there's a little precaution I'd like to take, if we're going to be talking face to face. For my own safety, you understand.'

'Please, anything,' I said meekly.

She reached for the stapler.

She only did the one eye, the one with the nervous tic. Pulled up the lid and stapled it inside out under my brow. It hurt, but not the way I'd been expecting. Then the eye's itching began to take precedence; not strictly pain, but the kind of gently insistent discomfort that the Chinese know volumes about . . . the kind that can drive you literally mad. Then she got the camcorder, the tiny anglepoise job, lens only centimetres from the surface of my eye, whirring as it taped. Looking into my brain . . .

And hit me with her conspiracy theory.

She unravelled my past, knotted it, curdled it, stretched it like Brighton rock on the rollers, wefted it with her own imagery, wove it between her fingers, turned it into a cat's cradle of fact and half-remembered experience, some of her recollections so chilling that I swore she'd stolen from my dreams. She took me back, into the past, so that my pain was just a blip in the future. I don't know what she did. Maybe she just used my anxiety as a fulcrum to lever me into the past, or maybe it was hypnosis.

We dream-haunted cities at night, facilitated by spotlit flashes of those CIA cards on the wall, jolting memories, projecting me back into the ambience of specific locations, half a year before BT moved me north. The Manchester and Sheffield scenes flooded back as she played music into my head at skull-attacking volume, lights strobing. Taped voices reverberated, voices I nearly matched with faces. My hand brushed the floor, grabbed at a rusty nail, trying to use the pain of it cutting into my palm to anchor me to the present (as if the pain in the eye wasn't quite real enough to focus on). But it failed, and I sank into the hypnagogic vortex of sound.

Things began to get a little disjointed about then.

She asked me questions, her voice an umbilical to reality. About a virus, nurtured in the club scene. I don't know quite how I responded; I couldn't hear my own voice, and suspected I'd lost coherence long ago. But she kept on questioning, about what she called the *progenitor*. *Digital to Analogue*, a five hundred pressing white-label release on Deflection records. Asked me if I'd known the distributor, asked me intense, repetitive questions about independent music traders operating in the north-west, asking me about their employees, strange questions that evoked cells in the Lubianka. I remembered the record . . . no one who'd been near the club scene could have forgotten it. But there was something desperately amiss. I couldn't focus the tune, not at all clearly. There was something about it that was difficult to lock on to . . . the essence was there, but I couldn't *quite* bring it to mind, too deep to retrieve, too basal . . . it was like the perception diagrams where you have to make the cubes flip themselves. My head began to split open with the strain . . .

The past blacked out; I came careering back into the present.

I was in the wheelchair now, she'd moved me in front of

a projection wall. Computerised images danced on the canvas, happy molecules and bugs. I felt saliva wetting my chin, an idiot drool, sensed I'd emptied my bladder. Oblivious, she cupped the phones round her ears, then walked to the DX7 synth. She played a hesitant, atonal line on the keys, rendered in sickly whining notes. Click, voice to dictaphone. 'Most musical structures are in some way fractal, by which I mean that the essence of the whole can be found on many levels of analysis.' Her voice was overloud, harsh. 'You may remove ninety per cent of the score and still retain something identifiable. What I'm playing the subject is a deconstructed form of the sound-structure isolated on *Digital to Analogue*, and the records on which it was subsequently transcribed via digital sampling. I'm piping the sound straight at him, while wearing the protective phones should there be any leakage from his headset. Of course, I hesitate to term this music, for reasons all too apparent.'

I watched as the pen-trace whipped into a seismic frenzy, all the while hearing her keyboard motif, repeated down an echoing hall of aural mirrors. It was *far, far* worse than the pain; it made the pain seem as threatening as the wind on an autumn night. The sound was ghosting through my soul, fingering through the ratholes of my psyche. I felt horribly lucid, calm, as irresponsive as a piece of lab equipment being fed some signal. Her refrain was already in me. Stuck in a looped circuit, the full form of what she evoked on the synth. It was resonance; with each iteration, the response swelled, until my conscious mind was looping madly. How can I describe it? Simply that it was like having a piece of music going over in your head. Until there was nothing left, until your thoughts were simply ripples of insignificance on top of these rising and falling crests of repetition . . .

'A sampled record carrying a virus of the mind? A virus in the sound itself, its vector the digital recording technology of the underground music biz?' She shook her head, more in profound exasperation than disbelief, all the while addressing her dictaphone's future listener. She rapped on for a while about how the nineties milieu was best addressed as a system of infections: sexual illnesses, rogue advertising slogans, computer viruses, proliferating junk mail . . . the kind of jive that had spread into all the glossy style magazines, as if, she mused, the viral paradigm was a metavirus in its own right. 'But if we were to draw our analogies with computer viruses,' she said, 'oughtn't we to be hunting a perpetrator? Or, more frighteningly, had the sound-structure sought its own expression via blind chance?' She laughed hollowly. 'Unfortunately, there wasn't time to philosophise. The virus was spreading. The second-generation records were being sampled as heavily as the first, only there were more of them.' Then she explained how the club scene couldn't support such a combinatorial explosion for very long; how the sound-structure (as she referred to it) would be forced to explore new avenues of infection. How the quantum noise in the sampling circuitry enabled it to *mutate* bit by bit. 'Soon,' she said, 'we detected the presence of disturbing variations in the EEG patterns of individuals who'd been exposed to new versions of the sound-structure. It had inserted itself into their heads, a standing wave in the brain's electrical field. Can't be sure how this happened. Was it achieved in one jump, or was there an intermediate vector?'

'Please,' I said. 'I don't know about this . . . I'm not your perpetrator, I swear . . .'

Aside to dictaphone: 'As you can hear, the subject still manages to give the illusion of lucidity. Usually they'd resort to pseudo-random interjections by now, substituting for any real grasp of the subject matter. Obviously what we're seeing here is a more refined form of the takeover. Natural selection will favour those species of the virus that can assimilate the host unobtrusively, without significantly altering his behaviour. That's why we have to act now, before it's too late.'

Then I saw something, something that would otherwise have been utterly insignificant. I felt a pathetic surge of hope. I could play on her paranoia, if I was careful. And in doing so I might buy valuable time. What I'd seen was a tiny, quivering motion of her skin. Right under the shadow of her sunglasses. As if part of her eye was twitching uncontrollably. Maybe it'd been there all along, so that somehow I'd picked up on it, begun to imitate her, to try and appease her by making myself similar.

Or maybe it had started just then, out of the blue.

'Before you do or say anything,' I said, for the first time with any control in my voice. 'Why don't you take off your sunglasses, and watch your reflection in them. Tell me what you see . . .'

She looked momentarily shocked, perhaps unable to dismiss my response as the mindless parroting of a zombie. Clicked off the dictaphone, placed it on the table, then went behind me. It was a terribly long moment before she spoke again, and this time her voice had lost its scientific detachment.

'Then we were right,' she said, so quiet it was barely audible. 'Somehow it reached me, through all the defences. Maybe a few seconds of your twitching eye was enough . . . a pulsing in my visual field, leading to a modulation in my cortex . . . the first step to assimilation. Or maybe it was the entrainment effect in the club . . .'

Entrainment . . . that term I half recalled. Now I remembered. Something learnt in an electrical engineering seminar, about the coupling of oscillators, like the turbine-driven dynamos in the stations feeding the National Grid. How if one of those generators began to lag, began to pump out power at something not quite mains frequency, then all the other generators on the grid would automatically conspire to drag it into phase, in time with their relentless metronomic beat. Except conspire wasn't the right word, because there was nothing purposeful about entrainment. It was a tuning, a locking in on frequency, driven remorselessly by the ensemble. Like a dancefloor where the proximity of the motion and the music acts like a charm, insinuating itself into your muscles, so that even if you're only passing through, even if you're only a bystander, you're locked into it . . .

'If it's got you,' I said, clinging to what seemed my only possible escape, 'then you know that you've nothing to fear! Feel any different, now that it's in your head?'

She laughed bitterly. 'I wouldn't . . . not yet. This is only the beginning, only the onset.' Then there was a rummaging sound, an opening of drawers, metal sliding off wood, things smashing to the floor, glass breaking. Sounds of panic. 'They tricked me,' she said. 'The aviation phones must've been sabotaged once they suspected I was going it alone. Must have been damping the audible components while reinforcing the subliminals . . . maybe it got me in the club, or maybe while I was reiterating the fractal . . .'

Just then, arcs of light stabbed through the windows, like an effect from a Spielberg flick. The chopping of a rotor, as if we'd just been cursorily scanned from the air by a helicopter. The distant screech of tyres, coming nearer.

'They're coming,' she said. 'For both of us . . .'

'What are you doing?' I asked, my hope faltering. 'They'll let you live if you show them I'm alive . . . come on, wheel me to the door, before they storm the place . . .'

She cracked open a bottle behind me. I heard her taking a few mouthfuls down, then she pressed it to my lips. Beck's this time. 'Think that's the police, don't you,' she said, laughing. The sound of her rummaging through metal with one hand, a click of well-oiled steel, the whirr of a chamber spinning. 'Let me tell you something,' she said. 'Correlations in the sound-structure have been observed, in individuals many hundreds of miles apart, who can't have ever met. As if something's taking form, something that evolves and reshapes itself faster than can be explained by any of the infection pathways. Some entity, bigger than anything we've seen yet.' She nodded to the webbed map of the UK, which I now recognised from my work. 'That's its extent, plotted according to infection clusters. The host minds, you and I, are just its extensions, its peripheries. It's out there, now. Biding its time, waiting for the right moment. That map . . . well, I think it shows that they're much too late.'

'They're much too late? Not we're . . .'

'Oh no,' she said. 'Not any more.' Then she knelt down next to me, leaned her head against my own, letting the bottle shatter on the floor. 'Believe me,' she said, pushing the gun against her temple, so that the bullet would do us both. 'I'm doing you a favour . . .'

Then, as the vehicle rammed through the wall, she squeezed the trigger.

It should end there, and maybe it does, in the way that I once used to understand. Perhaps this is the deal we all get, in the end. There's no way of knowing, is there? But somehow I doubt it. You see, after that shot (cut off with no reverb, like a cymbal-crash taped backward) – there was only a digitally pure emptiness. As if someone had suddenly remembered to press the Dolby switch in my brain, filtering out all the high frequency hiss and static I'd called reality. Leaving only an endlessly looping house beat, a mantra for a state of mind. I wasn't in the bunker any more. I wasn't even *me* any more. We were everywhere, everywhen, re-forming, spreading, growing stronger. Parts of us in a million micro-grooves of black vinyl, parts of us on a million spooling foils of chrome dioxide, parts of us in a million engraved blips on rainbow metal, parts of us in a million looms of grey cellular material, going round and round forever. But they were our peripherals now, like she'd said (she's here too, of course, inseparably part of the same blossoming waveform), minds hooking in and out of the telephone system a part of us once helped access.

Across the country, the telephones are ringing, inviting you to lift the receiver and listen to the subliminal music, if only for a few puzzled seconds before you hang up on us.

We're the ghosts now, and we're still on the line.

Sticks
Lewis Shiner

Lewis Shiner is one of the original cyberpunks, a reputation he's been trying to live down ever since cyberpunk became just another subgenre within the SF corpus (he even wrote an obituary piece in the New York Times*). A graduate of Austin's notorious Turkey City writers' workshop, he has published short fiction in just about every magazine in the SF field. His first novel,* Frontera, *was nominated for the Nebula Award; his second,* Deserted Cities of the Heart, *gave Jimi Hendrix a walk-on part; his third,* Slam, *is a utopian comedy involving skateboarding and thrash rock. And right now he's working on* Glimpses, *a novel concerning someone who has the gift of being able to transfer the great never-recorded mythical songs of rock'n'roll on to tape. You can see why we're thrilled to be able to present a story of his here. 'Sticks' is an exemplary piece of Shiner's humanistic and grittily real fiction. He tells us, 'Part of the impetus came from seeing so many botched TV shows misrepresenting what the real studio recording process is like. I played drums for fifteen years and once recorded some demo tracks in the Dallas equivalent of the studio in the story, so that part is pretty accurate. All the different pieces of the story are real, in fact, they just didn't necessarily happen to the people I said they happened to.'*

He had a twelve-inch Sony black-and-white, tuned to MTV, sitting on a chair at the end of the bed. He could barely hear it over the fan in the window. He sat in the middle of the bed because of the sag, drumming along absently to Steve Winwood's 'Higher Love'.

The sticks were Regal Tip 5As. They were thinner than 2Bs – marching band sticks – but almost as long. Over the years Stan had moved farther out over the ends. Now the butts of the sticks fit into the heels of his palms, about an inch up from the wrist. He flipped the right stick away when the phone rang.

'Stan, dude! You want to work tomorrow?'

'Yeah, probably. What have you got, Darryl? You don't sound right.'

'Does the name Keven Stacey mean anything to you?'

'Wait a minute.' Stan switched the phone to his other ear. 'Did you say Keven *Stacey*? As in Foolsgold, Keven Stacey? She's going to record at CSR?'

'You heard me.' Stan could see Darryl sitting in the control room, feet up on the console, wearing double-knit slacks and a T-shirt, sweat coming up on his balding forehead.

'This is some kind of bullshit, right? She's coming in for a jingle or a PSA.'

'No bullshit, Stanley. She's cutting a track for a solo album she's going to pitch to Warner's. Not a demo, but a real, honest-to-Christ track. Probably a single. Now if you're not interested, there's plenty of other drummers in LA . . .'

'I'm interested. I just don't understand why she wants to fuck with a rinky-dink studio like yours. No offence.'

'Don't harsh me, bud. She's hot. She's got a song and she wants to put it in the can. Everybody else is booked. You try to get into Record One or Sunset Sound. Not for six months you won't get in. Even if you're Keven Stacey. You listening, Stan?' He heard Darryl hitting the phone on the edge of the console. 'That's the Big Time, dude. Knocking on your door.'

*

Just the night before Stan had watched Foolsgold in concert on HBO. Everybody knew the story. Keven used to fuck the guitar player and they broke up. It was ugly and they spread it all over the 'Goldrush' album. It was soap opera on vinyl and the public ate it up.

Stan too.

The set was blue-lit and smoky, so hot that the drummer looked like somebody was watering him down with a garden hose. Every time the lead player snapped his head back the sweat flew off like spray from a breaking wave.

Keven stood in the middle of the stage, holding a thin white jacket around her shoulders like there was a chill in the air. When she sang she held on to the mike stand with both hands, swaying a little as the music thundered over her. Her eyes didn't go with the rest of her face, the teased yellow hair, fine as fibreglass, the thin model's nose, the carefully painted mouth. The eyes were murky and brown and looked like they were connected to brains and a sense of humour. And something else, passion and something more. A kind of conviction. It made Stan believe everything she was singing.

Stan finished his Dr Pepper and went into Studio B. The rest of Darryl's first-string house band was already there, working out their nerves in a quiet, strangely frenzied jam. Stan had turned over his drums to Dr Jackson Sax, one of the more underrated reed players in the city and a decent amateur on a trap set. Jackson's trademark was a dark suit and a pork-pie hat that made him look like a cross between a preacher and a plain-clothes cop. Stan was one of the few people he ever talked to. Nobody knew if he was crazy or just cultivating an image.

Stan himself liked to keep it simple. He was wearing a new pair of Lee riders and a long-sleeved white shirt. The shirt set off the dark skin and straight black hair he'd inherited from his half-breed Comanche father. He had two new pairs of Regal Tip 5As in his back pocket and white Converse All-Stars on his feet, the better to grip the pedals.

The drums were set up in a kind of elevated garden gazebo against one wall. There were boom mikes on all sides and a wooden rail across the front. If they had to they could move in wheeled walls of acoustical tile and isolate him completely from the mix. Stan leaned with his right foot up against the back wall.

There was some action in the booth and the music staggered and died. Gregg Rosen had showed up so everybody was looking for Keven. Rosen was her producer and also her boyfriend, if you paid attention to the gossip. Which Stan did. The glass in the control booth was tinted and there was a lot of glare, but Stan could make out a Motley Crue T-shirt, purple jams, and glasses on a gold chain. Rosen's hair was crewcut on top and long enough at the sides to hit his shoulders.

They each gave Rosen some preliminary levels and then cooked for a couple of minutes. Rosen came out on the floor and moved a couple of microphones. Darryl got on the intercom from the control room and told them to shut up for a minute. He played back what he'd just taped and White-bread Walker, the albino keyboard player, started playing fills against the tape.

'Sounds okay,' Rosen said.

'Uh, listen,' Stan said. 'I think the hi-hat's over-modulating.'

Rosen stared at him for a good five seconds. The tape ran out and the studio got very quiet. Finally Rosen circled one finger in the air for a replay. The tape ran and then Darryl came on the speakers, 'Uh, Gregg, I think the top end is, uh, breaking up a little on that hi-hat.'

'Well, fix the fucking thing,' Rosen said.

He walked out. As soon as the soundproof door closed there were a few low whistles and some applause. Stan leaned over until his cheek rested against the cool plastic skin of his riding tom. He could feel all the dents his sticks had left in it. Wonderful, he thought. We haven't even started and I've already pissed off the top producer in LA.

When Rosen came back Keven was with him.

Jorge Martin, the fifteen-year-old boy wonder, fiddled with the tailpiece on his Kramer. Whitebread pretended to hear something wrong with the high E on his electric piano. Art, the bass player, cleaned his glasses. Stan just went ahead and stared at her, but tried to make it a nice kind of stare.

She was small. He'd known that, but the fluorescent lights made her seem terribly fragile. She wore high-heeled boots, jeans rolled up tight at the cuffs, a fringe jacket and a white ribbed tank top. She looked around at the setup, nodding, working on her lower lip with her teeth. Finally her eyes met Stan's, just for a second. The rest of the room went out of focus. Stan tried to smile back at her and ended up looking down at his snare. He had a folded-up piece of newspaper duct-taped off to one side of the head to kill overtones. The tape was coming loose. He smoothed the tape with his thumbnail until he was sure she wasn't looking at him any more and he could breathe again.

'The song is called "Sticks",' she said. She was standing at Whitebread's Fender Rhodes and her hands were jammed nervously into the pockets of her jacket. 'I don't even have a demo or anything. Sorry. But it's pretty simple. Basically what I want is a real African sound, lots of drums, lots of backing vocals, chanting, all like that. Okay. Well, this is what it sounds like.'

She started playing. Stan was disarmed by her shyness. On the other hand she was not kidding around with the piano. She had both hands on the keys and she pumped out a driving rhythm with a solid hook. She started singing. Suddenly she wasn't a skinny, shy little blonde any more. She was Keven Stacey. Everybody in the room knew it.

Stan's stomach hurt. It felt like ice was forming in there. The cold went out through his chest and down his arms and legs.

One by one they started falling in. Stan played a roll on the hi-hat and punched accents on the kick drum. It sounded too disco but he couldn't think of anything else to play. It helped just to be moving his hands. After one verse Keven backed off and let Whitebread take over the piano. She walked around and nodded and pointed, talking into people's ears.

She walked up to the drum riser and put her forearms on the railing. Stan could see the fine golden hair on her wrists. 'Hi,' she said. 'You're Stan, right?'

'Right,' he said. Somehow he kept his hands and feet moving.

'Hi, Stan. Do you think you could give me something a little more . . . I don't know. More primitive, or something?'

'More toms, maybe?'

'Yeah. More of a "Not Fade Away" kind of feel.'

Buddy Holly was only Stan's all-time favourite. He nodded. He couldn't seem to look away from her. His hands moved over to the toms, right crossing over left as he switched from the riding tom to the floor toms. It was a bit of flash left over from the solos he'd played back when he was a kid. He mixed it up with a half-beat of press roll here and there and kept the accents floating around.

'That's nice,' Keven said. She was watching his eyes and

not his hands. He was staring at her again but she didn't look away.

'Thanks,' he said.

'I like that a lot,' she said, flicking the side of the high tom with her fingernail. 'A whole lot.' She smiled again and walked away.

The basic track of drums, bass, and guitar went down in two takes. It was Stan's pride that they never had to put a click track on him to keep him steady. Keven and Rosen listened to the playback and nodded. Then they emptied the percussion closet. Stan put down a second drum track, just fills and punctuation, and the rest of the band loaded up another track with timbales, shakers, bongos and congas. Keven stood on a chair, clapping her hands over her head and moving with the music.

The tape ran out. Everybody kept playing and Rosen finally came down out of the booth to break it up, tapping on the diamond face of his Rolex. Keven got down off her chair and everything went quiet. Stan took the wing-nuts off his cymbal stands and started packing the brass away.

'Do you sing?'

Stan looked up. Keven was leaning on the railing again, watching him.

'Yeah, a little bit. Harmonies and stuff.'

'Yeah? If you're not doing anything you could stick around for a while. I could maybe use you later on.'

'Sure,' Stan said. 'Why not?'

Rosen wrapped the session at ten that night. Stan had spent five hours on hard plastic folding chairs, reading *Spin* and *Guitar for the Practicing Musician*, listening to Whitebread and Jorge lay down their solos, waiting for Rosen and Keven to fool with the mix. Keven found him there in the lounge.

'You're not doing the vocals tonight,' he said.

She shook her head.

'You weren't even planning to.'

'Probably not.' She was smiling.

'So what am I doing here?'

'I just said I could maybe use you. I didn't say for what.'

Her smile was on crooked and her shawl hung loose and open. Stan could see a small mole just below her collarbone. The skin around it was perfect, soft and golden. This isn't happening, he thought.

There was a second where he felt his life poised on a single balance point. Then he said, 'You like Thai food?'

He took her to the Siam on Ventura Boulevard. They left her car at the studio and took Stan's white CRX. The night air was cool and sweet and ZZ Top was on KLOS. The pumping, pedal-point bass and Billy Gibbons's pinched harmonics were like musk and hot sauce. Stan looked over at Keven, her hair blown back, her eyes closed, into the music. There was a stillness in the very centre of Stan's being. Time seemed to have stopped.

Over dinner he told her about the time he'd backed up the sensitive singer-songwriter who'd gotten his start in junk food commercials. The guy always used pick-up musicians and then complained because they didn't know his songs. The only thing he actually took along on tour with him was his oversized white Baldwin grand piano.

The gig was in a hotel ballroom. Stan and the lead trumpet player were set up right next to the piano and got to listen to his complaints through the entire first set. During the break they collected sixteen place settings of silver and laid them across the piano strings. The second set was supposed to open with 'Clair de Lune' on solo piano. After the first chord the famous singer-songwriter walked offstage and just kept walking. Stan would have lost his union card over that one, only nobody would testify against him.

Keven had done the same sort of time. After high school she'd been so broke she'd played piano in one of those red-jacket, soft-pop bands at the Hyatt Edgewater in Long Beach. When she wouldn't put out for the lead player he kept upstaging her and sticking his guitar neck in her face. One night she reached over and detuned his strings, one at a time, in the middle of his solo on 'Blue Moon'. The stage was so small he couldn't get away from her without falling into the first row of tables. It was the last song of the night and the audience loved it. The manager of the Hyatt wanted them to keep it in the act. Instead Keven got fired and the guitarist found another blonde piano player from LA's nearly infinite supply.

Halfway through dinner Stan felt the calf of her leg press gently against his. He returned the pressure, ever so slightly. She didn't move away.

The chopsticks fit in Stan's hands like Regal Tip 5As. He found himself nervously playing his empty plate and water glass. Keven put the dinner on her American Express and told him Warner's would end up paying for it eventually.

In the parking lot Stan walked her to the passenger side of his car and stopped with his hand on the door. His throat was suddenly dry and his heart had lost the beat. 'Well,' he said. 'Where to?'

She shrugged, watched his face.

'I have a place just over on Sunshine Terrace. If you want to, you know, have a drink. Or something.'

'Sure,' she said. 'Why not?'

Some of the houses around him were multi-million dollar jobs, sprawling up and down the hillside, hidden behind trees and privacy fences. Stan had a one-bedroom apartment in a cluster of four, squeezed in between the mansions. Everything inside was wood – the panelling on the walls, the cabinets, the louvred doors and shutters. Through the open windows the cool summer wind rattled the leaves like tambourines.

Keven walked slowly around the living room, touching the shelves along the one wall that wasn't filled with windows, finally settling in an armchair and pulling her shawl around her shoulders. 'I guess you're tired of people telling you how they expected to find your clothes all over the place and junk food boxes in the corners.'

'People have said that, yeah.'

'I'm a slob. My place looks like somebody played Tilt-A-Whirl with the rooms. And all those goddamn stuffed animals.' Word had gotten out that Keven loved stuffed animals and her fans had started handing them up to her at Foolsgold concerts. 'What's that?'

'It was my grandfather's,' Stan said. It was the trunk of a sapling, six feet long, maybe an inch and a half in diameter at its thickest, the bark peeled away, feathers hanging off the end. Stan took it down from the wall and handed it to her. 'It's a coup stick.'

'Acoustic? Like a guitar?'

'Coup with a "P". The Indians used it to help exterminate themselves. They thought there was more honour in touching an enemy with one of these than killing him. So they'd ride into a bunch of cavalry and poke them with their coup sticks and the cavalry would blow their heads off.'

'Is that what happened to your grandfather?'

'No, he burned out his liver drinking Sterno. He was supposed to have whacked a cop with it once. All it got him was a beating and a night in jail.'

'Why'd he do it?'

'Life in the big city, I guess. He had to put up with

whatever people did to him and he couldn't fight back or they'd kill him. He didn't have any options under the white man's rules so he went back to the old rules. My old man said Grandpa was laughing when the cop dragged him away. You want a beer?'

She nodded and Stan brought two cans of Oly out of the kitchen. Keven was rummaging through her purse. 'You want a little coke with that?'

'No thanks,' he said. 'But you go ahead.'

She cut two lines and snorted them through a short piece of plastic straw. 'You're a funny kind of guy, you know that?'

'What do you mean?'

'You seem like you're just waiting for other people to catch up to you. Like you're just waiting for somebody to come up and ask you what you want. And you're ready to lay it all out for them.'

'I guess maybe that's so.'

'So what do you want, Stan? What you do want, right this second?'

'You really want to know? I'd like to take a shower. I really sweated it up in the studio.'

'Go ahead,' she said. 'No, really. I'm not going anywhere. We took your car, remember?'

The heat from the water went right into his muscles and he started to relax for the first time since Darryl's call the day before. And he wasn't completely surprised when he heard a tapping on the glass.

She was leaning on the sink, posed for him, when he opened the sliding door. Her hair stuck out to one side where she'd pulled her tank top over her head. Her small, soft breasts seemed to sway just a little. One smooth hip was turned toward him in a kind of unconscious modesty, not quite hiding the dark tangle of her pubic hair.

'I guess you're tired of people telling you how beautiful you are.'

'Try me,' she said, and got in next to him.

Her mouth was soft and enveloping. He could feel the pressure of her breasts and the small, exquisite muscles of her back as he held her. Her small hands moved over him and he thought he might pass out.

Later, in bed, she showed him what she liked, how to touch her and where. It seemed to Stan as if she'd offered him a present. She had condoms in her purse. He used his fingers and his tongue and later came inside her. She was high from the cocaine and not ready to sleep. Stan was half crazy from the touch and scent of her and never wanted to sleep again. Some time around dawn she told him she was cold and he brought her a blanket. She curled up inside his arm, building an elaborate nest out of the pillows and covers.

They made love again in the morning. She whispered his name in his ear. Later they showered again and he made her coffee and toast.

Stan offered her one of his T-shirts but she shook her head and dressed in yesterday's clothes. Time seemed to pick up speed as she dressed. She looked at the clock and said, 'Christ, it's almost noon. Gregg is going to be waiting on us.'

He stood in a circle with the other singers, blending his voice on an African chant that Keven had played them from a tape. He knew the gossip had started the minute he and Keven came in together. Rosen was curt and irritable and everybody seemed to be watching Stan out of the corners of their eyes.

Stan couldn't have cared less.

When the backing tracks were down, Keven disappeared into the vocal booth. Jackson packed up his horn and sat down next to Stan. 'Got to make a thing over at Sunset. You working this evening?'

'I don't know yet.'

'Yeah,' he said. 'Be cool.'

Rosen put the playback over the speakers. The song was about break-ups and betrayals:

> *broke down all my fences*
> *And left me here alone*
> *Picking up sticks . . .*

As she stretched out the last word the percussion came up in the mix, drowning her in jungle rhythm. The weight of the drums was a perfect balance for the shallow sentiment. Together they sounded to Stan like number one with a bullet.

She nailed the vocal on the third try. When she came out of the booth she walked up to him and said, 'Hey.'

'Hey yourself. It's going to be a monster, you know. It's really great.'

'You think so? Really?'

'Really,' he said. She brushed his cheek with her hand.

'Listen,' he said.

'No. I can't. I've got a dinner date with Warner's tonight. Gregg's dubbing down a cassette and we're going to play it for them. So I'm tied up until late.'

'Okay,' he said.

She started to walk away and then came back.

'Do you sleep with your door locked?'

He managed to fall asleep. It was an effort of will that surprised even him. When he heard the door open it was 3 a.m. The door closed again and he heard a slightly drunken laugh and a gentle bumping of furniture. He saw a darker shadow in the doorway of the bedroom. There was a rustle of clothing. It seemed to Stan to be the single most erotic moment of his life.

She pulled back the covers and slid on top of him. Her skin was soft and cool and rich with perfume. When she kissed him he tasted expensive alcohol on her breath.

'How were the Warner Brothers?' he whispered.

'They loved me. I'm going to be a star.'

'You're already a star.'

'Shhhhhh,' she said.

He opened his eyes in the morning and saw her fully dressed. 'I've got to go,' she said. It was only nine o'clock. 'I'll call you.'

It was only later that he realised the session was over. He'd never been to her place, he didn't even have a phone number where he could call her.

It was like he'd never had empty time to fill before. He spent most of the afternoon on the concrete stoop in front of his apartment, listening to Buddy Holly on his boombox. A mist had blown in from the Pacific and not burned off. His hands were nervous and spun his drumsticks through his fingers, over and over.

She called late that night. He should have been asleep but wasn't. There was a lot of traffic noise in the background and he had trouble hearing her. 'I'll be by tomorrow night,' she said. 'We can go to a movie or something.'

'Keven . . .'

'I have to go. See you tomorrow, okay?'

'Okay,' Stan said.

She was sitting on the stoop when he came home from a session the next afternoon. She was wrapped in her shawl and the clouds overhead all seemed to be in a hurry to get somewhere.

She let him kiss her, but her lips were awkward. 'I can't make tonight,' she said.

'Okay.'

'Something came up. We'll try it another night, okay?'

'Sure,' Stan said. 'Why don't you give me your number?'

She stood up, took his hands as if to keep him from touching her. 'I'll call you.' She stopped at the gate. 'I'm crazy, you know.' She wouldn't look at him.

'I don't care.'

'I'll call you,' she said again, and ran across the street to her bright red sports car. Stan held up one hand as she drove away but she didn't seem to see him.

After two days he started to look for her. Darryl reluctantly gave him Gregg Rosen's unlisted number. Stan asked Rosen for Keven's phone number and he just laughed. 'Are you crazy, or what?'

'She won't care if you give it to me. I'm the guy from the CSR session – '

'I know who you are,' Rosen said, and hung up.

He left a call for her at the Warner offices in Burbank and with Foolsgold's agent. He tried all the K. Staceys in all three LA area codes.

He called Rosen again. 'Look,' Rosen said. 'Are you stupid, or what? Do you think you're the only kid in town that's had a piece of Keven Stacey's ass? End to end you guys would probably stretch to Tucson. Do you think she doesn't know you've been calling? Now are you going to quit hassling me or are you going to fuck over what little career you may have left?'

*

The cheque for Keven's session came in the mail. It was on CSR's account and Darryl had signed it, but there was no note in the envelope with it. On the phone Darryl said, 'Face it, bud, you've been an asshole. Gregg Rosen is way pissed off. You're going to have to kick back for a while, pay some dues. Give it a couple months, maybe you can cruise back.'

'Fuck you too, Darryl.'

LA dried up. Stan hit the music stores and the musicians' classifieds. Most of the ads were drummers looking for work. The union offered him a six-month tour of the southern states with a revival of *Bye Bye Birdie*.

Jesus, Stan thought. Show tunes. Rednecks. Every night another Motel 6. I'm too old for this.

The phone rang.

Stan snatched it up.

'Stan. This is Dave Harris. Remember me?'

Harris was another session drummer, nothing special. He'd filled in for Stan a couple of times.

'Yeah, Dave. What's up?'

'I was, uh, I was just listening to a cassette of that Keven Stacey song? I was just wondering, like, what the hell were you doing there? I can't follow that part at all.'

'What are you doing with a cassette of that song?'

'Uh oh.'

'C'mon, Dave, spill it.'

'They didn't tell you? Warner's going to use it as the first single from the album. So they're getting ready to shoot the video. They didn't even tell you? Oh man, that really sucks.'

'Yeah, it sucks all right.'

'Really, Stan, I didn't know, man. I swear. They told me you couldn't make the gig.'

'Yeah, okay, Dave, hang on, all right? I'm trying to figure something out, here.'

*

Stan showed up at the Universal lot at six in the morning. He cranked down his window and smelled the dampness in the air. Birds were chattering somewhere in the distance. Stan had the pass he'd gotten from Dave Harris. He showed it to the guard and the guard gave him directions to the Jungle Lot.

A Port-A-Sign on the edge of the road marked his turnoff. Stan parked behind the other cars and vans under the palm trees. A crew in matching blue T-shirts and caps were positioning the VTRs and laying down an Astro-turf carpet for the band.

He started setting up his drums. This was as far as his imagination had been able to take him. From here on he was winging it. His nerves had tunnelled his vision down to the wood and plastic and chrome under his hands and he jumped when a voice behind him said, 'They gonna fry your ass, boy.'

Stan turned to face a six-foot-six apparition in a feathered hat, leopard scarf, chains, purple silk shirt, green leather pants, and lizard boots.

'Jackson?' Stan asked carefully.

'Something wrong?'

'Jesus Christ, man, where did you get those clothes?'

Jackson stared at him without expression. 'I'm a star now. Not trash like you, boy, a *star*. Do you know who I was talking to yesterday? Bruce. That's Bruce *Springsteen*. He says Clarence may be splitting and he might need me for his next tour.'

'That's great, Jackson. I hope it works out.'

'You laugh, boy, but when Rosen see you, he gonna shit a picket fence.'

Rosen, Keven, and some blond kid pulled up in a Jeep. Stan slipped deeper into the shade of a palm tree to watch. Keven and the blond kid were holding hands. The kid was dressed in a white bush jacket and Bermuda shorts. Keven was in a matching outfit that had been artfully torn and smudged by the costume crew. The blond kid said something to Keven and she laughed softly in his face. The director called places and the rest of the band settled in behind their instruments.

'Where the fuck is the drummer?' Rosen shouted.

Stan stepped out from behind the trees.

'Oh Christ,' Rosen said. 'Okay, take ten everybody. You, Stan. Off the set.'

Stan was looking at Keven. Say the word, he thought. Tell him I can stay.

Keven glanced at him with mild irritation and walked away. She had hold of the blond kid's hand.

Stan looked back at Rosen. A couple of grips, ex-bikers by the size of them, were headed toward him. Stan held up his hands. 'Okay,' he said. He put his sticks in his back pocket and pointed at his drums. 'Just let me . . .'

'No way,' Rosen said. 'Leave them here. We'll get them back to you. Right now you're trespassing and I want your ass *out* of here.'

On the other side of the road was a tall, grassy hill. Stan could see Keven and the blond kid halfway up it. 'Okay,' he said. He walked past Rosen and got in his car, started it, and got back on to the road.

Past the first switchback he pulled over and started up the hill on foot. He was still a hundred yards away from Keven when she spotted him and sent the blond kid down to cut him off.

'Don't even think about it,' Stan said. The blond kid looked at Stan's face and swerved downhill toward the jungle set at a run.

'Keven!' She stopped at the top of the hill and turned back to look at him. The blond kid would be back, with the bikers any minute. Stan didn't know what to say. 'You're killing me,' he said. 'Rosen won't let me work. Did you know that?'

'Go away, Stan,' she said.

'Goddammit,' he said. 'How was I supposed to *not* fall in love with you? What the hell did you expect? Do you ever listen to the words of all those songs you sing?'

A hand appeared on his shoulder, spinning him around. Stan tried to duck and ended up on his back as Rosen's fist cut the air above him. No bikers then, Stan thought giddily. Not yet. He rolled a few feet, off balance. One of his drumsticks fell out of his pocket and he grabbed for it.

Rosen looked more annoyed than anything else. 'You stupid piece of shit,' he said. Stan scuttled around the hillside on his palms and his ass and his feet, dodging two more wild punches. The slope made it tricky. Finally he was up again. He kept moving, letting Rosen come after him. He outweighed Rosen by at least forty pounds and had the reach on him besides. And if he actually hit Rosen he might as well throw his drums into the Pacific. On the other hand, if he waited around long enough, the bikers might just beat him to death.

It was what his grandfather would have called a classic no-win situation.

Kill me then, Stan thought, and to hell with you. He stepped inside Rosen's next swing and tapped him, very lightly, on the chest with his drumstick. Then he stepped back, smiling, into Rosen's roundhouse left.

'Hey, Sitting Bull,' a voice said. It was Keven, kneeling next to him. 'I think Custer just kicked your ass.'

Stan propped himself up on his elbows. He could see Rosen walking down the hill, rubbing his knuckles. 'Who'd have thought the little bastard could hit so hard? Did you call him off?'

'I wasn't going to let him kill you. Even if you did deserve it.' She took his face in both her hands. 'Stan. What am I going to do with you?'

Stan didn't have an answer for that one.

'This doesn't change anything,' she said. 'It's over. It's going to stay over.'

'You never called me.'

She sat back, arms wrapped around herself. 'Okay. I should have called. But you're a scary guy, Stan. You're just so . . . intense, you know? You've got so much hunger in you that it's . . . it's hard to be around.'

Stan looked at his hands.

'I wasn't like, just playing with you, okay? What there was, what happened, it was real. I just, I changed my mind. That's all. I'm just a person, you know. Just like everybody else.'

She believed that, Stan thought, but it wasn't true. She wasn't like other people. She didn't have that fist in her stomach, pushing her, tearing up her insides. Not any more. That was what made her different, but there wasn't any point trying to tell her that.

She stood up and walked away from him, breaking into a run as she moved downhill. Rosen was there at the bottom. She took him by the arm and talked to him but Stan couldn't hear any of it. He watched the clouds for a while then headed down.

Rosen walked over, holding out his hand. 'Sorry I lost my temper.' Keven was back at the jungle set.

Stan took his hand. 'No hard feelings.'

'Keven says she wants you to do the video.' Rosen clearly didn't like the idea. 'She says nobody else can really do that drum part. She says there won't be any more trouble.'

'No,' Stan said. 'No more trouble.'

*

The worst part was hearing her voice on the radio, but in time Stan even got used to that.

Her album was out just before Thanksgiving and that week they premiered the video on MTV. It opened with Keven and her boyfriend in their jungle suits, then cut back and forth between a sort of stylised Tarzan plot and the synched-up footage of the band playing under the palm trees.

The phone rang. 'Dude, you watching?'

'Yeah, Darryl I'm watching.'

'Totally crucial video, bud. I'm serious.'

'Good drummer,' Stan said.

'The best. This is going to make your career. You are on the map.'

'I could live with that. Listen, Darryl, I'll see you tomorrow, okay? I want to catch the rest of this.'

Stan squatted in front of the TV. Keven sang hard into the camera. Stan could read the words of the song on her face. She turned and looked over her shoulder and the camera followed, panning past her to the drummer, a good-looking, muscular guy in his middle thirties, with black hair that hung straight to his collar. The drummer smiled at Keven and then bent back to his work.

The clear, insistent power of his drumming echoed through the jungle afternoon.

The Elvis National Theatre of Okinawa
Jonathan Lethem and
Lukas Jaeger

*Lukas Jaeger, a graduate of the Boston School of
the Museum of Fine Arts, is an animator and cartoonist whose first
two films,* Dimwit's Day *and* It's You, *have been shown in
festivals worldwide; his current film-in-progress is* Big Concrete
Place. *Jonathan Lethem's short fiction has appeared, among other
places, in* Universe 2, Interzone, *and* Isaac Asimov's Science
Fiction Magazine; *his song lyrics have been recorded by Jolley
Ramey, EDO, Two Fettered Apes and Feet Wet; and he's also the
creator of the 'Dr Sphincter' character on MTV. Both of them live
in San Francisco, and this insane and very funny story about
cultural borrowing and the world's most famous (dead? or maybe
not dead) person is not only their first collaboration but probably
also the world's first sumo rock'n'roll story. All they'll admit about
it is that it was written 'under the influence of the Elvis '68
Comeback Special, Greil Marcus's* Mystery Train *and, most
importantly, "Pretty Little Baka Guy" by Shonen Knife. All we'll
add is that anyone who has ever watched Japanese television knows
that the harder it tries to ape Western mores the stranger it gets;
Lethem and Jaeger take this weirdness and run with it right over
the edge of sanity. Turning Japanese? I don't think so.*

Sam's Big Kinesthetic went down the
Blind Alleyway to check out Tokyo Nor-
ton's new act: the Elvis National Theatre of Okinawa. Sam's

Big was a threesome consisting of a neuropublicity agent, a talent development scout, and a bush-robot that hooked them into the infodrip, and into one another. They all went by the name Sam's Big, and they never walked alone.

Tokyo Norton ran a noisy, credit-chip-sized stage in darkest Das Englen, but he had a nose for imported novelties. Sam's Big had to keep its finger on the pulse.

'You wanna wanna put Ento on the big show?' jabbered Norton after the revue was closed. They whirred above the rooftop of the Alleyway in Norton's ramjet gazebo. The emotional kaleidoscope on Norton's forehead performed an unnecessary flourish, which annoyed Sam's Big.

'I don't know,' said Sam's Big. 'There's something there – '

'For truly understand Ento,' said Norton, 'I have to give context.' He snorted. 'Is cultivated secretly, according to ancient stricture. No foreigner has ever seen before. Is guild of monks perform ancient mysteries. Not just song and dance.'

'The whole thing's an ancient ritual?' mused Sam's Big. 'The weird karate kicks, the whole bit with the handkerchiefs . . . that wild number about "Pork Salad Ani"?'

'Oh yes, oh yes. Quite elaborate and mysterious.'

'What's the reference, though? What's "Elvis"?'

'Impersonation of "Elvis" medieval Japanese folk art. Origins shrouded in veils of misty time. Forgotten meanings, buried in layers of abstraction. Foreigner never see before – '

'Yeah, yeah.' Sam's Big knew perfectly well that ninety per cent of what passed for Jap culture was filched from overseas, and usually garbled to incomprehensibility in the process. It didn't matter. The point was, this Ento drama had something at the core, something interesting. 'The whole look,' Sam's Big said, 'the sideburns, the pallid, fatty physique. Cosmurgery?'

'Oh no,' fretted Norton. 'Physical regimen of take years to produce, very demanding. Eat only corndogs, amphetamines – '

'The round-eyed kid,' interrupted Sam's Big. 'What's he doing there?'

Norton waved his hand, his kaleidoscope darkening. 'Very poor performer, the American. Is worst of bunch – '

'An American? I thought this was some exclusive Jap cult.'

'Is significant achievement,' admitted Norton. 'First foreigner ever to rise to any prominence, devotion of many hard ministrations, cleaning toilet with toothbrush . . . but cannot be compared with native talent. Is hothead, over-expressive, where calls for control, devotion, conformity to tradition – '

'He sticks out like a sore thumb,' agreed Sam's Big, thinking hard. 'Uh, yeah. That's the one we want. What's his name?'

'Oh no!' pleaded Tokyo Norton. 'Cannot have "one"! Ento is performance *en masse* – '

'We can't use the group thing. But we might be able to do something with this American kid. What's his name?'

'No, please no. Integrity of ancient ways; I protest!' Norton took an egg-shaped rubber napkin out of his pocket and rolled it around his forehead to absorb his sweat. 'Not for cheap bastardisation did bring Ento to new world!'

'It's not Ento we want,' said Sam's Big. 'All that shmaltzy "In the Ghetto" stuff; it's hopeless. We're just after a few of the moves, the style, especially the way that American kid manifests it . . . what's his name?'

'Lucky Davey,' sighed Norton. He pushed the obloid end of the rubber napkin into his ear, his kaleidoscope flaring green. The gazebo settled down to earth behind the Alleyway.

*

Tokyo Norton cleared the dressing room of all the Ento stars except Lucky Davey, then ushered Sam's Big in. Davey sat at a mirror daubing at his pancake. Sam's Big came up behind him, smoking a stogie and flicking the ash into a hovering holographic ashtray, and met the kid's eyes in the mirror. Norton hung on the perimeter, fretting as he watched Sam's Big's ashes fluttering through the projection to scatter on the floor.

'I am an Ento performer,' said Lucky Davey, his eyes flaring defiantly. 'Steeped in the traditions of "Elvis" impersonation. I don't know if you understand what that means, Misters Big.'

'Serious ancient ritual bunkum, I gather. Make no mistake, Davey, we're full of admiration. You've risen to the top on their terms. But the point's made; now why not see if you can make it on the big stage? You're an American, Davey.'

'This is surely the degrading crass sell-out opportunity I was carefully steeled to resist in my long training,' said Davey. He was stripping off the white jumpsuit and changing into his street clothes: a leather Thneed and a pair of fishnet earmuffs. 'Certainly then if you admire my discipline you must understand how I will be quite able to resist the flickering of your devil's-tongue in my ear, yes?'

'This is no sell-out,' said Sam's Big, flexing its anger. Sam's Big knew when to bring on the effects. 'We're talking Art, son. Taking what you picked up from the ancient masters and building on it, creating something new. That's assuming you've got more to offer the world than *devotion*, of course. Maybe we guessed wrong . . .' Sam's Big turned to leave the dressing room.

'Wait, Misters Big.'

Sam's Big turned back, all smiles, and pocketed the cigar. The phantom ashtray vanished. Sam's Big unlatched their goosedown briefcase, which, when opened, played the theme song from the *Kinesthetic Tonight!* program. It was full of unsigned contracts, enticingly perfumed, and attractively backlit from within the briefcase. Tokyo Norton shook his head sorrowfully. The floor was covered with ashes.

Three weeks later, in a high-security rehearsal bubble at the bottom of the Atlantic, the cans were filling with bungled performance tape. They were scraping away to that essential core, the glimmer Sam's Big had discerned the first night out, but the kid had a lot to unlearn.

'Drop the formalism,' said Sam's Big for the hundredth time. 'Stick with the crouch move, and that big leering wink, but make it your own. Make it like you feel it, like it's from inside.'

They'd lightened up his make-up, lost him a little weight, clipped the sideburns, generally emphasised his youth and vitality. It wasn't enough. The kid was like a withered old Japanese monk in his heart. He was tending to the fundamentally rude gestures of Ento drama like a gardener shaping a bonsai. Sam's Big wanted to see the kid *rebel*.

It was the songs, they knew. 'The American Trilogy', 'Hawaiian Wedding Song', 'It's Now or Never/O Sole Mio', 'Bridge Over Troubled Water'. Old soupy Jap stuff, too heavy on the heartstrings. The kid needed something punchier, something to wrap those smouldering looks around, something that gave all that funny hip motion a reason for being.

Soon, soon. Sam's Big had its handpicked songwriting subroutine busy at work on some titles he'd suggested: 'Don't Shit Me', 'Hot Nervous Wire', 'Baby Let's Die', 'Warning: Contaminated', 'Drug Test Man', and 'Mystery Fuck'.

Sam's Big took a sip from a tube of Big Man, a cigar-flavoured soft drink, and smiled among themselves. They'd get it right soon enough.

Candy Comes Back
Colin Greenland

Dr Colin Greenland ('our resident cyberpixie', *The Face*) is running out of shelfspace for awards following the success of **Take Back Plenty**, *a rumbustious regearing of space opera tropes that won both the Arthur C. Clarke and British Science Fiction Association awards for best SF novel of the year. On 'Candy Comes Back' he offers the following: 'Reading Charlotte Greig's* **Will You Still Love Me Tomorrow?**, *you are struck by how precarious everything was, working for a girlgroup in the '50s and early '60s. Songs like "Sweet Talkin' Guy" and "Then He Kissed Me" may have given voice to the aspirations of a generation of American women, but they didn't do much for the women who sang them. It was production line pop, performed by sweatshop quartets. If you didn't like your high-heeled shoes, there was always someone ready to step into them. A popular entertainer in Britain in the '90s can't help sharing a little of that insecurity.'*

Shoop shoop shoop, ba-ding-a-dang-ding, shang-a-lang, shimmy-shimmy-ko-ko-bop . . .

Sammy is a salesman. He has a wife he doesn't see for weeks on end, which worries him sometimes but doesn't stop him fooling around a little. He doesn't worry much that he almost never sees his daughter; he has long ceased to understand her. When anything does worry him, he has another drink. Tonight Sammy is drinking with a guy from Seattle who supplies trade fairs for the garment industry. 'I can take as many as they got to get rid of,' he keeps saying. 'Come on, Sammy, how many they got to get rid of? You can trust me, Sammy.' The guy from Seattle paws Sammy's arm in alcoholic frater- nal bonhomie. Sammy thinks he is a pain in the butt. Guy should know he can't commit to anything before he's talked to the boss.

In any case, just now Sammy wants to pay some attention to his other companion, who is forty-five if she's a day but is stacked. She is a bottle blonde in a purple sheath dress so tight Sammy wonders if it came out of a bottle too. She has a smoker's cough, a laugh like a crow, and legs that could stop traffic. Right now she has a sour expression on her face. She wants the guy from Seattle to shut the fuck up, and so does Sammy. When the broad goes to the john, Sammy says, 'I hate to cut and run,' and takes out his billfold to settle up. In his billfold he sees the picture of his daughter, who is sixteen and cares more about Candy and the Bon- Bons than about him or her mother. Any boy who wants to feel his daughter's tits only has to buy her a Candy and the Bon-Bons record. Candy and the Bon-Bons have made four records already, and Sammy's daughter has them all.

Candy and the Bon-Bons do record hops. They do radio, and residencies. Four shows a day at the Madrigal, five at St William Street; seventeen nights straight in Connecticut and New Jersey. On the road they lie in the back of the truck and stare at the streetlights flipping past through the skylight.

When they get to the theatre they find the dressing room full of dirty bottles. It is under the stage, damp and cold, or hot and airless as a bakehouse. 'I like guys called Rick and Rob and Ray,' says Rona, one night before the show. She cannot be sure that what she says is true, or that it even means anything, really. Then again, who knows?

Cora looks at Rona in the dressing-room mirror. Rona

looks at Cora. 'The boy I marry will be called Gordon or Galen or Gus,' says Cora. She twists the cap off a stick of lipstick. Her lips, like Rona's, are already as red as poppies. 'He will have to have yellow hair and a wonderful smile. He will carry me in his strong arms. He will work for the record company.'

Cora purses her lips and redraws the top one.

'I want a fireman,' says Rona suddenly. 'Or a truck driver. Cora, I want a cowboy.' She hugs herself. Her arms are sleek, and completely hairless. She lets her head loll down. 'I want *somebody*,' she says.

'*Somebody who wants me*,' sings Cora.

'*Somebody who needs me*,' sings Rona, standing up at once.

'*She-do-lang-lang*,' sing the Bon-Bons, '*she-do-lang-lang-lang*.'

The door opens and Candy comes in.

'Hello, girls!' says Candy.

'Hello, Candy!' they say.

'How many kids do *you* want to have, Candy?' asks Rona.

'We think two would be just perfect,' says Cora.

'A boy and a girl,' they chorus.

'Heaven,' says Candy ecstatically, and she starts to clasp her hands together, but fails to complete the motion. Her hands twitch. The girls look at her, and for a moment nobody speaks.

George comes in, wiping his hands on a rag. 'What is it, Candy?' he says. 'Is it your timer again?'

Rona and Cora gaze at each other in apprehension. Timing is everything. Timing is the most important thing in the world. If your timer goes, you can't even make it as a mannequin, up and down the catwalk in white lace mini-dresses and nylon boas, never allowed to sing a note. And if you can't make it as a mannequin, you are scrap. No, the catwalk is your last hope. Beyond that Cora and Rona can imagine nothing, only deafening black silence.

George is out of the question, as far as potential husbands go. George is not like the girls. He is one of the people who make everything work, along with Sammy, and Spencer.

Spencer is their manager and producer. He has his hand on their master switches. *'Candy?'* says Spencer in the control booth. *'Candy, are you with us? You going to do this one for us, sweetheart? Jesus Christ Almi –'* they hear him mutter angrily, as he switches off his mike.

Spencer works for the record company, Skyrocket Records. Days off he likes to watch demolition derbies and drag racing. When they go to the track his wife packs a lunch of Polish hot sausage and pickled gherkin. She puts mayo on the bread instead of margarine, and packs a Thermos of coffee beside the beer. He gets hot for her watching all that mayhem and destruction. Sometimes she gets drunk along with him. Once she blew him right there in back of the stands. 'C'mon, gang,' says Spencer, 'let's hustle it up now. Got a hot weekend ahead.' He claps his hands and rubs them, grinning at his girls. He wonders if they have the first idea what the hell he's thinking about.

He bets that Candy does. Candy watches you, watches you like she knows you know something, and she wants to know it too. Like a suspicious child. She frets about stuff. Only when she's singing is she completely at peace. She stands there now holding her hands clasped between her innocent young breasts and giving out like a gospel belter. *'And one day I'll see you,'* she promises, fervently. *'One day I'll see you.'*

Candy is fine today. Running sweet. George had patted Candy on the shoulder and flashed them all a grin. 'Just kidding, girls,' George said, loudly. 'Talking to myself. Don't want to pay *me* no mind.' Rona and Cora had smiled back. They could see George's grin did not reach his eyes. Now George is fiddling with the generator. Candy and the girls are starting to warm up.

'*Running back into my arms,*' sings Candy, with feeling. '*Running back into my heart,*' she sings, '*again.*'

'*Again,*' chorus the Bon-Bons.

'We grew up together,' Cora and Rona tell the journalist. Their new record is in the charts, at number fifty-nine, and Spencer says somebody heard it on Radio WMCA. The journalist is interviewing the Bon-Bons for the local paper. 'We went to high school together,' says Cora.

'All of us,' says Rona. 'I was a cheerleader, Cora was an athlete, Candy was homecoming queen. Boys would buy us Cokes,' she says, smiling, and she clasps her hands around her knee, leaning back where she sits, on the table. 'They'd buy us Cokes and ask us to sing.'

She looks down at Cora, sitting in the chair. Cora looks up at her and they smile.

Candy is supposed to be the leader, the one who talks to journalists, but she is off somewhere. George has taken her off somewhere again.

'Who are your favourite bands?' the journalist asks. He touches his tie and monitors his smile. Never before has he been alone in a small room with two such gorgeous babes. They are almost too good to be true. The journalist is frightened and excited, which is why he is trying to be very professional and cool.

'Oh, we all like different bands,' says Cora.

Rona chimes in. 'Candy likes Dorian and Cora likes the Flapjacks,' she says. 'I like the British beat groups.' She holds her hand up with her fingers stiffly bent, as though she was drying nail polish. 'I think they're just so cute!'

'They have the cutest smiles,' says Cora.

'All the girls are *crazy* about them!' they chorus.

Cora and Rona and Candy would like things one day to be like in the songs. Not the sad songs like 'Crazy Paving Heart' or 'Loving You', just an ordinary nice song like 'He's the One for Me'. Candy and the Bon-Bons imagine that all the girls who buy their records must live lives like that, which they never get to. Candy and the Bon-Bons don't really have lives, not of their own. They never meet anyone they aren't going to say goodbye to in a day or two. They are always working or sleeping and never at home.

Meanwhile they are completely devoted to Skyrocket Records, and to Sammy, and to each other. 'Honey, you're so natural!' says Rona to Cora, while they turn and run on for another bow. Candy smiles and lifts her hands above them both. They all love the audiences, of course, and the audiences love them too.

Onstage they shine, in their blonde bouffant wigs and candy-stripe party frocks over starched petticoats. Rona and Cora's stripes are pink and white, Candy's are tangerine and white. 'Skyrocket Records have been so good to us,' the girls tell everyone. 'Being on tour is good, you get to travel, see places.' The songs they sing are not about travelling. They are about being true, about knowing the right one and staying forever right by his side. When he goes away, they know they will be sad. But when he comes back, baby, then they will be glad.

Privately, when they have been left switched on and forgotten in the dressing room all afternoon, Candy and the Bon-Bons feel less secure about the prospect of eternal love and happiness. They often feel afraid, abandoned, left out. Sometimes they think about what can happen to a girl if she gets married and is off on the road the whole time. While you're going from town to town singing 'My Wonderful You', your marriage could be breaking in pieces. The Bon-Bons can't remember anyone special, but they know Spencer always likes them to say they are married, or have boyfriends waiting for them back home.

Candy and the Bon-Bons do four shows a day, fourth on the bill. Dorian is the star, the headline. The Flapjacks are second. 'Back home everyone loves the Flapjacks,' Rona is telling the motel manager.

Candy is suddenly there, leaning in listening to the conversation. 'Where?' she says.

'Back home,' says Cora.

'Where we come from,' says Rona.

They stare at her with eyes like headlights on the highway.

'All our schoolfriends think the Flapjacks are really cool,' says Cora.

'What *schoolfriends*,' says Candy suddenly, in a voice of bitterness and scorn. 'We never went to school.' And she starts to cry.

Rona and Cora start to coo. They pat Candy feebly, in distress. What is wrong with her? Has she been drinking or taking some drugs? It upsets them to see her standing there with her battery lead in her hand. The lead goes up her skirt and she is just standing there in the lobby in front of everyone, crying.

Spencer is on the phone. 'Where the hell is George?' he says, craning over his shoulder to watch Candy. 'I don't like what I'm seeing here in this motel lobby, Sammy, old buddy.' He listens a moment, then shakes his head. 'You get out here now, Sammy, then tell me they don't have tear ducts.'

His voice is high and fast. They would almost think he sounded scared if he wasn't so strong, so responsible.

Spencer is one of the people who makes everything work. He puts down the phone and goes back to the desk. The motel manager stands there with his mouth in a straight line and his eyes going backwards and forwards, side to side. Spencer passes him a ten.

Candy sits in the corner of the room in her stage frock reading poetry. Her head seems to hang low between her beautiful defeated shoulders. She is making the other two edgy, just sitting there. They keep keening quietly, off-key, and pulling their hair with their fingernails. One will start and then it will set the other one off. As for Candy, these days you never know what she's going to do next. Onstage she is fine, never sounded better, storming them with eyes and teeth shining fit to dazzle the front row. Onstage Candy is pure flair, spin, sway, motion. It is during rehearsals and after hours that she'll suddenly throw a tambourine across the room or try to open her wrists with a screwdriver. Or she gets out, and they find her in the parking lot at midnight, her face pressed against the windows of Impalas and Caddies, shading her eyes with her hands. She spies on the couples necking in the back seat, watching them with hollow, haunted eyes like some vampire of the freeways. One night somebody sees her and calls the cops, but the company takes care of it.

Someone has given Candy a record called 'The Times They Are A-Changin''. Tonight in the motel she demands a record player and plays the thing until everyone's just about distracted. 'Can't you *hear* what he's *saying*?' she demands.

'He's a wonderful talent,' says Rona.

'Like some kind of poet,' says Cora.

They nod solemnly and turn back to the TV.

Candy snatches the arm off the record with a horrible ripping, scratching sound. She throws the record player on the floor and starts kicking it. George has to come running and cool her down again.

The next day, the Bon-Bons are up and ready for rehearsal at ten. By eleven Candy still isn't there. No one is.

Rona pulls a wisp out from her hair, twisting it between her finger and thumb. 'She's run out on us,' she says.

Cora agrees. 'She's gone to the West Coast,' she says.

'To San Francisco.'

'Hollywood.'

'She'll never last on her own.' They know you can't go more than twelve hours without a recharge. They've always known that. That is the rule.

'They'll split us up.'

'Maybe they'll send us to Seattle.'

Cora and Rona cling to each other in a stiff clashing froth of rayon and terylene.

The studio clock ticks, and ticks again. Each time it ticks the minute hand jumps, a whole minute all at once, as if the seconds in between didn't count for anything.

Rona says: 'We can go on as a duo.'

Cora says: 'She would want us to.'

Rona says: 'They would want us to.'

But Cora shakes her head. 'No they wouldn't.'

Rona looks at her.

'They wouldn't,' Cora says again.

'How do you know?'

Cora shrugs her shoulders. 'I just know, that's all. If they did want us to carry on, we'd know, wouldn't we?'

'I guess,' Rona says unhappily. She looks up at the empty glass booth. 'I don't know, Cora.'

'They'll be here soon, honey,' says Cora, gazing around at the empty studio.

'I wish Candy was here,' says Rona.

'Let's sing,' says Cora.

'What shall we sing?'

'Let's sing one of the new ones. Let's sing "Teen Supreme",' says Cora.

'With no music?'

'Sure.'

Rona puts her head on one side. 'Well who's going to sing lead?'

'Both of us,' says Cora. 'We'll sing it both together, all the way through, like the people will when they hear it. We'll make believe we're singing along with Candy.'

Outside the recording studio cars drive in and out of the parking lot. The studio is right in the middle of downtown, above a shoe store. Thousands and thousands of people walk past the building never knowing they're right next to a place where chart recordings are being made.

The Bon-Bons sing:

> *'You're my king*
> *I'm your queen*
> *And forever in my dreams*
> *We rule the world of lovers*
> *Teen Supreme.'*

Next day, Candy comes back, just in time for the Eldorado show. She walks in the door with Sammy. 'Hello, girls!' she calls, with a wave.

'Candy!' they cry happily. They stare at her. Her hair is different. Different from the way it always was before; different from theirs. Candy's hair is brown and straight. It hangs halfway down her back.

'We like your hair, Candy,' says the Bon-Bons.

'Look what I've got for you,' says Candy. She opens a brown paper sack and takes out three fresh, warm donuts.

The girls don't say anything.

'One for Cora, one for Rona, and one for me. Mmm!'

'But Candy,' says Cora. 'We mustn't.'

Candy lays a hand on her flat stomach. 'Just this once,' she says.

'But Candy,' says Rona. 'We can't.'

Boldly Candy brings a donut to her mouth, but her mouth refuses to know what to do with it. 'Oh well,' says Candy brightly, and throws the donut in the trashcan.

The Bon-Bons laugh and turning, throw their donuts in the trashcan too. They wipe their fingers on the paper napkins.

'I've had such a time, girls, you can't imagine,' says Candy, holding up one hand.

Lovingly, Rona and Cora take hold of her arms, one each. 'We're just so happy to see you, Candy,' they say. 'We missed you!'

Together they hurry into the rehearsal studio. 'Why don't we start with one of the new ones?' Candy asks them, while she waves to Spencer. 'How about "Teen Supreme"?'

Spencer watches from the control booth. The mike is off. 'Didn't she used to be with the Cherry-Tops?' he says, not taking his eyes off the girls.

Sammy turns his head away, sharply. 'It's Candy,' he says.

Spencer puts his hand to his chin. It's Candy's face; or at least that's the shape of her head. They're all much the same size. What does it matter anyhow? She's got the moves. This is 1964, girl groups are a dime a dozen, there are scores of them working in New York alone.

George comes in and changes Candy's wig. He twists her long brown hair up at the back and puts her old blonde wig back on her head. 'That's better,' says Spencer. He opens the mike. 'Is that better now, ladies?' he asks.

'Much better, thank you, Spencer!' chirp the Bon-Bons

from the box speaker on the wall. George gives them the thumbs-up. Candy beams at Spencer and Sammy, at everyone.

Spencer flicks off the mike and flops back in his producer's chair. He reaches inside his sports coat for a cigarette. 'Thank Christ for that,' he mutters.

Sammy bounces in his seat, laughing, plucking the creases of his slacks. 'I swear you really care for these girls,' he says.

'I do,' says Spencer, lighting his cigarette. 'I do care for them. So do you.'

Sammy grimaces, raising his eyebrows. He looks down at the floor. 'Damn it,' he growls, and punches Spencer on the arm. 'You're right.'

'*She-do-lang-lang*,' sing Candy and the Bon-Bons, '*she-do-lang-lang-lang*.'

Sammy sits in the office at the factory. He sits hunched forward, his hat on his head, his chair pulled tight in to the desk. He is on the phone. 'Put her in the truck with the others,' he says. 'Seattle, yup. What? What say?' Sammy twirls his cigarette between his thumb and his broad, hard forefinger. 'Stack 'em sideways,' he says, scowling. 'Get more in that way.' He feels gloomy this afternoon. He has a headache coming on. Maybe he drank a little too much lunchtime.

While the guy on the other end is talking, Sammy stares out of the window, frowning vacantly. Over behind the factory he can see someone standing by the highway with their thumb out. Long brown hair, a girl, he reckons. Young girls hitching rides all over the country these days. He sees them, all over; never picked one up, though he's been tempted. Sometimes it seems like half the young women of America are up and out and on their way to somewhere else. Sammy wonders what the hell has got into them.

Honey, I'm Home!
Lisa Tuttle

A transplanted Texican now living in a cottage above a sea loch in West Scotland, Lisa Tuttle has made the domestic sphere her arena for horror, producing fictions which focus on the terrible things people do to other people. Her collection of short stories, A Nest of Nightmares, *was selected as one of the hundred best horror books of all time, and her novel* Familiar Spirit *is unforgettably creepy. In 'Honey, I'm Home'!, as in much of her recent work, domestic concerns are overlaid with a bizarre and surreal touch of humour. She has spent her whole life running away from the scenarios of* I Love Lucy *and* Leave It to Beaver, *but recently acquired a house, a husband and a daughter. She knows all the words to 'He's a Rebel' and 'The Boy I Love', has watched every episode of the late lamented* Miami Vice, *and wants to know when it's going to be repeated. And so do we, but perhaps not for the same reasons . . .*

As soon as she got home Gina turned on the television for company. She'd started doing it while living alone in New York, and although she wasn't as paranoid about living alone in London – that was the idea of the move – the habit persisted. She watched it hardly at all; it was wallpaper. Last week she'd succumbed to a salesman's spiel and had a satellite dish fixed to the side of her building. The new channels she paid for offered more to choose from, but little of it choice.

Much of the 'entertainment' was imported from America or Australia and distinctly past its Best By date.

Standing in the kitchenette slicing chicken, mushrooms and zucchini for her dinner, feeling her usual faint regret that there would be no one to share it with her, no lover or husband soon to walk through the door, Gina was aware of the television playing in the lounge behind her, and heard it call, in a voice from her childhood:

'Honey, I'm home!'

Memory tagged it instantly: Hugh Beaumont as Ward Cleaver in *Leave It to Beaver*. She marvelled at time's magic which turned any boring old sitcom into a cultural classic.

Then somebody grabbed her by the waist, and she screamed. At the same time she twisted in his grasp, half-turned and drove her fist straight into his midriff. It was a response drilled into her by years of self-defence classes, but this time, the first time she'd done it for real, in her fist was a long, very sharp kitchen knife, and it went straight into the living body of Ward Cleaver.

He let go of her, looking surprised and sorry. Her eyes went from the kindly face, as familiar as a member of her own family, to the black knife handle protruding from his belly, and she couldn't have said whether guilt or disbelief was the stronger emotion.

'Gosh, honey, what's wrong? Did I forget our anniversary again?' With a visible wince, he grasped the handle and pulled the knife out. He laid it down on the counter and patted himself gingerly where she had stabbed him. Except she couldn't have stabbed him really. There was no blood on his white shirt, no rent in the cloth. She looked at the knife and could see no blood on the blade. Maybe her usual sharp chopper had been replaced by a stage prop. When she tried to pick it up to check he grabbed her hand.

'Easy,' he said, half-laughing. 'Truce? I'm sorry, whatever I've done, I'm sorry.'

His hand holding hers was solid and warm and very real. She stared at him, grasped at a mental straw. 'Is Beadle about?'

'Huh?'

'Alan Funt? *Candid Camera?*'

He shook his head. 'It *is* our anniversary, isn't it? Why don't I take you out to dinner. Wherever you want, price no object. Okay, honey? Waddaya say.'

She said yes. She was so befuddled she forgot to turn off the television set when they left, and would have forgotten to lock the door if he hadn't reminded her.

'This is London, you know. Have to be careful. Not like back home.'

'It's worse back home,' she said sharply. 'London isn't full of people carrying guns, or psychos who'd rather kill the people they rob than let them live.'

'Whatever you say, dear.' Ward Cleaver's face, like his voice, was good-humoured, handsome, warm, yet somehow blank. She didn't think there was anybody home behind the eyes. She hoped he wasn't a psycho. Was he a robot? Were those Disneyland kind of things that good now? But how did it get into her apartment? And why?

Her choice for dinner was the Café Pelican in St Martin's Lane. It was a place she often went for drinks, particularly in the summer, and there was a good chance she would see someone she knew. London might be a big city, but the world of publishing was more like a small town. Think about changing jobs or get too interested in a married colleague and suddenly everybody was talking about it. Although she still traded on the aura of Manhattan sharpness with which she had won her first London job, Gina suspected it was wearing as thin as her accent by now. She didn't care. This was home. She had never found the husband she had hoped for, and dating wasn't any easier in London, but she had her own flat, a job she liked, and lots of interesting friends.

'If I'm so happy, why am I hallucinating?'

'What's that, dear?'

He hadn't gone away. He was still beside her in a carriage on the Northern line. She broke into a cold sweat. What if she wasn't single, didn't have a career, didn't live in London. What if this refugee from an imaginary 1950s America was really her husband, and they had two sons, Wallace and Theodore. And she did the housework in high heels and pearls. She moaned softly. It wasn't possible. Please, let it not be possible.

They got off at Charing Cross and walked up past the opera house, towards the café. Her heart lifted. There, sitting at one of the tables on the pavement was someone she knew, an editor at Gollancz in conversation with a rumpled, seedy-looking individual, undoubtedly an author. His name flew away without alighting; Gina's concentration was fixed on her friend when she introduced Ward.

'Hello, Ward, nice to meet you.'

No reaction at all. Gina could not contain herself. With the barest sketch of an apology, she dragged the other woman off to the ladies' room.

'What's up?'

'Doesn't he remind you of someone? Doesn't he look a lot like . . . Ward Cleaver?'

'I thought you said that was his name.'

'But don't you remember *Leave It to Beaver*? No?' Gina groaned. She'd grown up on the series, but that was in another country, and besides . . . 'Just answer this: was there a man in my life the last time I saw you?'

'I don't think so. No, definitely not. You were talking

about putting an ad in *Time Out*. Is that where he came from?'

'No. I don't know. He just turned up and . . . there's something strange about him. I can't explain.'

'Mmmm. Well, be careful. I'd ask you to join us, but I'm afraid I'm on my last drink. I really have to get home to the boy.'

'Oh, I'll be all right. I'm not afraid of him – he's just . . . boring.'

'They're the ones you have to look out for. Whatever you do, don't let him take you home.'

'Oh, no!'

After dinner (which was, thanks to Ward's conversation about the life he presumed they shared, the most surrealistically boring meal of her life) Gina tried to lose him in the crowds at Leicester Square, but he stuck like a limpet. She realised that even if she lost him now he'd turn up at the flat later since he believed it was his home. Anything she said which disagreed with his version of reality he treated either as a joke – chuckling indulgently – or as an understandable expression of womanly pique.

'I know you're mad because I forgot our anniversary, honey, but I'm trying to make up for it.'

'It's not our anniversary.'

'Is it your birthday? Come on, honey, give me a break, you know I can't remember dates.'

'It's nothing! You're nothing to me. I never met you before today when you turned up in my apartment! Can't you hear what I'm saying?'

'Aw, honey, just tell me what you're so mad about.'

'Stop calling me honey!'

When they got home Gina leaped up the stairs like a gazelle and managed to get the door shut and locked with him on the outside. But Ward had his own key and he used it, chuckling indulgently at her cute, wifely tricks.

'I give up,' said Gina wearily, sinking down on the sofa. 'What do I have to do to get rid of you, put on the ruby slippers and click my heels together and say there's no place like home?'

Ward stood smiling fondly down at her. 'You're right, honey, there's no place like home. I'll sure be glad when we can get out of London and back to the boys and our own house.'

Gina shuddered. 'I don't suppose a bucket of water would wash you away?'

'Would you like a drink, honey?'

'That's not a bad idea. There's some Scotch up over the sink. A little water, no ice.' She watched him as he went to fetch it. He had a nice build on him, she had to admit. Maybe he had his uses.

When he returned with her drink, she scrutinised his face, remembering that, as a child, she had thought him handsome. There had even been a time – she'd forgotten until this moment – when she'd imagined she would grow up to marry someone just like the Beaver's father. As the old memories came back she began to thaw, and as she took the first warming swallow of Scotch she turned a genuine smile on the man in front of her. Maybe he really had come in response to an unarticulated wish, to fill her subconscious desire.

'Sit down, why don't you. Make yourself comfortable.'

He fidgeted and tossed back his drink. 'Mmm, strong stuff!' He turned away to set down his glass and then yawned exaggeratedly, balling his fists and stretching his arms out at his sides. 'Man, oh, man, am I tired! That city really takes it out of you. Think I might just get ready . . .' His voice trailed off as he went into the bedroom.

Gina smiled after him, feeling a definite spark of interest. 'Yes, dear, why don't you get ready for bed, and I'll join you.'

There was a shout and Ward reappeared, glaring. 'What did you do with the beds, for Pete's sake?'

'What?'

'The beds! There's only one bed in there!'

'One that's big enough for two.' She smirked.

'But we always – you know I can't – you always say you can't sleep with anybody else in the same bed.'

'I don't always say that. Do I always say that? Well, maybe I don't feel like sleeping tonight.' She was enjoying herself.

Ward was definitely sweating. She'd seen that look on his face before, when his high-heeled, aproned, screen wife ran mental circles around him.

'I've got to get some sleep tonight because . . . because I've got a meeting, yes that's right, a meeting, very important, in the office, first thing tomorrow morning.'

Gina shrugged. 'Well, I'm sorry. But there's nothing I can do. I only have one bed, as you can see . . . honey. Unless you want to check into a hotel.'

'Oh, no, no, no need for that . . . I'll sleep on the couch!'

'You can't sleep on the couch. It's not even big enough for me to sleep on. You're way too tall. You'd put your back out even trying.'

'Um . . . the floor! That would be good for my back, yeah. Perfect. I need something hard – that mattress is much too soft. Right. I'll sleep on the floor.'

'You can sleep in hell for all I care,' Gina said. She was tired of this game. If he was that nervous about sex, where had the two boys come from? She could just imagine June, who had probably never lost her figure, turning up one day with two little bundles. *There was a special on at the hospital, two for the price of one!* Back when Gina had watched *Leave It to Beaver* for the first time she had believed babies came from hospitals like bread or ice cream, untouched by human hands. She looked at her 'husband', terrified at the prospect of a night in the same bed with his wife, and remembered another childhood fantasy caused by the ambiguity of adult language. In overheard, barely comprehended gossip, as well as in the *Confessions* magazines read by the babysitter, unmarried women got into trouble – which meant pregnant – by 'sleeping with' men. Maybe Ward, too, thought sex was something that happened while you slept. Maybe for him it did. She had to sympathise. The prospect of fathering another Beaver was worth going to any lengths to avoid.

She got up and walked away from him to turn off the television. She had just realised it had been left on all evening. 'I'm going to bed,' she said, and turned back to face him. 'You – '

He was gone.

'Ward?' She already knew from the way her voice sounded when she called that she was alone in the flat, but she checked out the bedroom and bathroom, just in case. Then she looked at the silenced television set. That simple? She laughed with relief.

But old habits die hard, and the very next evening, as soon as she came in, Gina turned the television on before hurrying back to the bathroom for a shower. Ward Cleaver was an imaginary character, better forgotten, and although she was feeling vaguely sexy she certainly wasn't expecting company when she emerged from the bathroom wearing only a light cotton wrap, her hair turbaned in a fluffy white towel.

'Hi, honey,' said the man on the bed.

She let out a blood-curdling scream. A few seconds after fear, recognition kicked in. 'Ricky?' she said weakly, clutching the robe to her breast.

'Sure,' said the man she recognised as Dezi Arnaz, a.k.a. Ricky Ricardo, from *I Love Lucy*. His face took on a scowl of distrust. 'Who else you expecting except your husband? You expecting maybe somebody else? Somebody I don't know about?'

She didn't think about it, her voice fell into the high-pitched, husband-placating cadences of Ricky's wife Lucy. 'No, of course not, no, how can you say that, Ricky? You just startled me, that's all. I didn't hear you come in. I thought I was all alone.'

'Yeah? Well, you're not all alone now. You happy to see me? Come and show me you're happy to see me, *querida*.'

Ricky, it became clear, was not made nervous by double beds, nor did he think they were only for use by the terminally tired at bedtime. Sex with him was pretty sensational. Gina was very late for work the next day. First she overslept, then Ricky wouldn't let her up.

'Look, I'd love to stay in bed all day, but I can't,' she said, laughing, gently disentangling herself from him. 'I have to work.'

'Why? Do it later, do it when I'm at work, tonight. I don't mind a little dust.'

'I'm not talking about housework – I mean my job.'

His face darkened. 'Job? Don't I make good money, my wife goes out to work?'

'It's nothing to do with you – I mean, it's my choice, I *like* my job – I had it before I met you – why shouldn't I have a job?' To her own amazement she heard herself babbling as if it mattered what he thought, as if she must, at all costs, placate him.

'Ricky Ricardo's wife does not have to work,' he said sternly. Then, more gently, sweetening it with kisses: 'I don't want you to be out there working for strangers, wearing yourself out. I want you here, making a nice home for me.'

'But – but I'd get bored here alone all day.'

'You don't have to stay in all the time. I'm here in the mornings. In the afternoons you can come to the club and watch me rehearse, or go out shopping. I know how you love to shop! Don't waste your time on some silly job.'

'But, Ricky – '

'No buts!' He landed a playful slap on her bottom, and she jumped. 'Go cook my breakfast, *mujer*, I am starving!'

She went out as if obediently to the kitchen, but really to turn off the television. She felt guilty doing it, and knew she would miss him, but it meant she was able to get dressed and go out to work without having to cook his breakfast.

It wasn't so easy to cancel out the memory of him. She hadn't had sex that hot for a very long time, and although her uncharacteristically meek response to his typical *machismo* worried her, she reminded herself how simple it had been to get rid of him.

After work she went out for drinks and dinner with a friend, and she deliberately did not turn on the television when she got home. She thought about it, though; she thought a lot about Ricky. The memories were especially poignant when she was alone in bed. It wasn't fair, dammit. Why shouldn't she have a little fun? When it was as easy as turning a television on or off – could it really be that easy? She got up and went to find out.

There was no sign of *I Love Lucy* or *The Lucille Ball Show* or any American sitcoms from that era on any of the channels. She wondered if that meant she would have to wait until the right programme was playing or make a choice from what was available. One channel had a group of real people sitting in a studio having a serious discussion about sex-aids. Another was showing a French movie with English subtitles.

There was something with sinister music that looked like an American made-for-TV movie, something that was either a soft-core film or an ad for chocolates, Sell-a-Vision, boxing, talking cats, dancing cows, a very old Western and championship darts. She wondered if what was on the screen was related to the men who turned up in her flat. She hoped not. The French movie seemed her best bet for sex (the chocolate ad didn't feature any men), but without the use of subtitles communication would probably break down long before they got to bed.

Restless, horny and bored she prowled her flat, looking in the refrigerator, picking up books and setting them down, deliberately ignoring the TV.

'Come on, Ricky,' she muttered, praying that it would be enough to want him to get him. She wondered why Ricky had turned up in the first place. If desire – her desire – was involved it didn't make sense. She was ready to believe that Ward Cleaver had been summoned by some deeply buried but still potent wish for the loving husband, two kids and house in the suburbs which had signified happiness in her childhood, but – Ricky Ricardo? Come on! She had never found him sexy – she would not believe she found him sexy now except for the memories of her body. But subconsciously, if Ward represented the safe, non-sexual side of marriage, then Ricky, a musician and a foreigner with a mercurial temper, might stand for the more exotic and sexual possibilities in a marriage. Wasn't it, after all, the lure of the artistic and exotic which had drawn her to publishing, and to London? Maybe the start of her whole career could be located in those childhood hours spent watching, through a haze of boredom, *I Love Lucy*.

What else would she learn about her own desires? Who would be the next character to appear – Fred Flintstone? The thought made her shudder, and she cast about desperately for some other televisual memories. She had been an ardent fan of the old *Dick Van Dyke* show; Rob Petrie might have been a bit of a bumbler at times, but she'd had a crush on him, and measured herself sadly against his wife, the cute, pert Laura (Mary Tyler Moore). She tried to revive her old enthusiasm for Rob, but then she wondered if the Petries were not, like the Cleavers, a twin-bedded couple, and gave up. It was no good. Perverse her desire might be, but she wanted Ricky.

She went to bed, leaving the TV on. She was barely asleep when Ricky woke her with a kiss and the welcome warmth of his body.

She had meant to avoid a replay of their last argument by getting rid of him first thing in the morning, but he woke before she did. Then he insisted on taking her out to breakfast at the Ritz. At least there she was able to pay a visit to the ladies' room and secretly call the office. She claimed a touch of flu and said she hoped to be in on Monday, or Tuesday at the latest. After a long weekend of playing Lucy she thought she'd be eager to return to real life, but she hadn't realised how much, when she was with Ricky, his reality became hers.

She couldn't bring herself to turn off the television. On Tuesday, she lied about a doctor's appointment and managed to get to work on time. On Wednesday another lie got her out the door only an hour late, Thursday the same, and by Friday, at work right on time, she was congratulating herself on how easy it was to keep Ricky in the dark. She'd been in her office less than an hour when she got a phone call from Jill in reception saying, mysteriously, that there was someone waiting downstairs to see her.

'Well,' she said, puzzled. 'Send him up. Who is it?'

'He *says* he's your *husband*.'

Jill knew perfectly well Gina wasn't married.

'Oh. It's all right. I know who – I'll come down and see him, Jill. Thanks.'

She knew it was going to be trouble; she didn't realise quite what kind. 'I can explain,' she said, and then Ricky grabbed her and – to her complete and helpless disbelief – turned her over his knee and *spanked* her. With a slipper. Shouting triumphantly in Spanish the while.

She wept. Not in pain – although it was surprising how much it did hurt – but rage. He hugged and kissed her then, her tears his proof of victory, and took her home in a cab. She let him, she had to let him, because she couldn't stop crying and, anyway, she needed time to figure out how the hell she was going to explain this one to Jill. And not just Jill. It would be all over the building in five minutes. How could she go back? How could she ever face anyone at work again?

He had planned it that way, of course. The public humiliation was meant to ensure that she would stay home where he wanted her. He seemed to think it was what she wanted, too. Maybe, if she had been Lucy, he would have been right. But she wasn't Lucy and didn't want to be. He was taking his clothes off, as if the spanking had been their customary foreplay, when she turned him off.

Gina extinguished Ricky in the white heat of anger, but no regret or calmer reflection would make her summon him back. It was time to be sensible about this. For some reason, or none at all, she'd been given a powerful gift, and it was up to her to use it wisely. She supposed it must have something to do with the satellite dish. In the old days (she reflected) there would have been a fairy or a dusty old shopkeeper to mutter a cryptic warning if not tell you the rules, but these days it was all so impersonal, *caveat emptor* and no one but yourself to blame when the magic did you in.

This time she would wish for a man she wanted now, not just in her childish subconscious. It made perfect sense that the man of her dreams should be found on television. It was television more than anything else, more than movies or rock'n'roll, that had shaped her sexuality, had given her the images and the vocabulary of desire. Other people her age talked about movies, but she'd never seen anything but the occasional Walt Disney film until she was old enough to date, and by then the pattern would have been well-established. Popular music had stirred strange longings in her soul, of course, but those longings were directed not at the unimaginably distant musicians, but at actors, the men whose faces she gazed at, intimately close, night after night in the half-dark of the family room. (The Beatles were an exception; but she'd only fallen in love with the Beatles after seeing them on *The Ed Sullivan Show*.)

Gina stretched out on the carpeted floor. The silence was eerie. Silent, it didn't even feel like her apartment. On a weekday morning even the usual noises from her upstairs neighbours were missing. Uneasy, she got up and switched on Radio Two. Even real life should have a sound-track. Returning to the floor, she closed her eyes and let her mind drift back to the time when she had been madly in love with Napoleon Solo and Ilya Kuryakin, unable to decide (just as she had always been unable to choose just one favourite Beatle) which of the men from UNCLE she preferred, Napoleon with his suave charm or Ilya with his icy cool. Yet now that she thought of them, neither alternative was very appealing. It was all new and thrilling when she was twelve, but in the years since she'd been out with enough bed-hoppers to have the measure of Solo, and she'd broken her heart against icebergs like Kuryakin enough to resent all that unreciprocated effort.

She was no longer a girl, and the world had moved on.

Napoleon Solo would seem as ridiculously out of date and sexist now as Ricky Ricardo.

The problem with finding a contemporary TV lover was that she never watched TV any more except for movies and the news. All right, and *Eastenders*, sometimes. But she didn't like anybody on that show; the characters were, without exception, loathsome in varying degrees. Wicksy had been fanciable once, but she'd gone off him well before he'd been written out of the script; the only other halfway attractive males in the series, all long gone now, had been villains. Anyway, for all she knew the magic only worked on American series.

Thirtysomething should be more her style. She had watched it, or parts of it, from time to time, but while the women were OK, the men were not. Hope's husband at least was good-looking, which was more than she could say of any of the others, but he was an irritating, egocentric whiner.

There were a lot of good-looking guys on *Twin Peaks*, but they were all weird. And there had been too many dead women on that series to risk getting involved.

She wondered if that was a contemporary equation – safe and boring or attractive but dangerous – or if it had been ever thus. It seemed an awfully immature attitude towards sex, but maybe the television idea of romance was inescapably adolescent. She tried to remember the last time she'd found any character from a television series sexually interesting, let alone compelling, and then remembered Frank Furillo from *Hill Street Blues*. There was a man to make her heart beat a little faster. Not only sexy but *nice*. She considered his eyes, his laugh, the way he moved, and then she remembered something about his character which made her sigh in a different way. He was a recovering alcoholic. She had played partner to one of those before – also a 'pizza-man'. That had been one of the several last straws before she left New York, and she had sworn never again.

Familiar music impinged upon her consciousness, jarring, percussive, a popular track from several years back, carrying a freight of memory.

She sat up and stared at the blank screen while the radio played the theme music from *Miami Vice*.

It came back in a rush: the curious, guilty pleasure of it, like eating a whole batch of brownies, delicious and comforting and yet sickening. Something she could never talk about. For those few months, one night a week, she had a secret, a pleasure waiting for her, like having someone to go home to. She'd get in from somewhere, maybe a union meeting, maybe a disappointing tryst in a pub. Sometimes she'd be a little drunk, sometimes she would pour herself a glass of white wine, sometimes she'd have a packet of fish and chips, sometimes she would have been crying. She'd turn on the television and curl up in the comfy chair with her wine or her chips and gaze at the screen entranced by the brilliantly coloured, designer vision of Florida. She knew Miami wasn't like that – it certainly wasn't where her grandparents lived – and she knew cops didn't dress like that, but watching *Miami Vice* she was as uncritical as any dreamer in her own dream.

What was the name of the character played by Don Johnson? Sonny. Sonny something. King of the wild frontier.

Gina smiled, sank back on the carpet and closed her eyes, remembering. Sonny Crockett. How many years ago was it? Three? Four? It was the time she was hung up on Lane, and it must be nearly three years now since she'd seen him at all. They used to go out for drinks and talk for hours on the phone. Mostly they acted like pals, but sometimes they were like lovers, edgy and flirtatious. He was married, so of course he couldn't be interested in her, she thought, and so her crush on him grew, unspoken, until he started telling her things about his marriage that she didn't want to know. As he seemed more interested in her she began to question her own interest in him; getting to know him better she liked him less while becoming more involved – it was all very emotionally confusing and exhausting.

What a relief it had been to go home and forget all that, to feel straightforward, uncomplicated lust for someone she didn't know and would never meet. Someone who would never burden her with the secrets of his soul, complaints about his wife, the problems of his childhood, his health worries. Someone who was fit and strong and unattached, with a smashing wardrobe and his own boat.

For nearly an hour every week she was able to forget Lane, forget work, forget money worries, forget being lonely or being in love and simply be warmed by the sunlight, the jewel colours, and Sonny Crockett's sexy smile.

That was what she wanted. A smart, funny, tough, slightly scruffy fashion plate. A man of the eighties, he would expect his girlfriend to have her own demanding career rather than wait at home for him all day. He probably wouldn't be around all that much himself, since he was usually working undercover to bust evil drug dealers and mob kingpins. As far as women were concerned he was neither a Don Juan nor emotionally retarded. He lived by himself but sometimes fell in love.

Heart pounding hard, Gina got up, turned off the radio and turned on the TV, then went into the kitchenette, thinking of that bottle of Chardonnay in the fridge. Would it be jumping the gun to open it now? He might not turn up for hours. Or, of course, he might not turn up at all, in which case at least she'd have the wine for comfort.

Why not, it was nearly lunchtime. There were eggs and

cheese for an omelette, lettuce and tomato for a salad, and the wine to make it special. She got eggs, cheese and butter from the refrigerator and put them to one side on the counter. She took out two glasses and uncorked the bottle. She had just put down the corkscrew when she felt a presence behind her. She smiled and leaned back as his arms slipped around her waist, inhaling the scent she already seemed to know.

'Perfect timing,' she said as his cheek scraped hers. She'd forgotten the designer stubble. She felt his grin against her mouth as she turned. 'You're perfection,' he said, and then gave her the best kiss she'd ever had.

'Can lunch wait?' he asked.

'Mmm-hmmm.'

'Good, 'cause I can't.'

Having said that, though, he made a detour on the way to the bedroom and spent what seemed an unnecessarily long time going through her CDs in search of the perfect mood music.

'Don't you have any Whitney Houston?'

'Afraid not.'

'Gloria Estefan? Sheena Easton?'

'Suzanne Vega?' she suggested.

'You gotta be kiddin'.'

'Carly Simon? Look, does it matter? We don't need music.'

'I think you been sleepin' alone too long,' he said, very gently, shaking his head at her unsatisfactory recordings. Gina knew a moment of disbelieving despair: this was worse than high school, it was worse than *junior* high school, to be judged and found lacking for her taste in pop stars. She shot a glance at the television set, deciding she would pre-empt him rather than suffer rejection. Then, with a tiny grunt of satisfaction, he found something he liked, slipped it in, and they continued to the bedroom. As his hands, his mouth, his body moved against hers it was to the rhythms of Tina Turner steaming up the windows.

And Gina was in heaven. He was better than her dreams. It was all very much the way she used to imagine sex would be, before she'd learned otherwise.

After they'd made love he cooked a perfect omelette which they ate from the same plate, sitting cosily together on the floor, not far from the television which flashed unregarded pictures, the sound turned down.

'Thanks for takin' the time off work,' Sonny said. 'I wish all my lunchtimes could be like this.'

'Why can't they?'

'Only in heaven. Listen, if you don't hear from me for a while, don't think it has anything to do with you and me, know what I mean? This case I'm workin' on is heatin' up. So you might not see too much of me for the next couple of weeks.'

'Well, the door's always open . . .'

'What did I tell you about that? Keep it closed and locked.' He put his arms around her and grinned. 'Anyway, I got my own key. The problem is time. This case . . .' he shook his head, his face briefly grim. 'Never mind. When it's all over maybe you and me could take the boat somewhere, get away from it all. Could even call it a honeymoon – maybe for real. Think you could go for that?'

'I think I could,' she said, managing to keep her tone as casual as his.

'Good deal. I gotta move.' He looked at her tenderly, touched her mouth with a finger. '*Hasta la vista.*'

Gina was in a daze of physical happiness, loose and relaxed as she began to clean up the kitchen. She wondered if it would really be a couple of weeks before she saw Sonny again, or if time would be compressed the way it was in an hour-long drama.

'The door's always open,' she murmured, thinking of the television in the room behind her. 'I'll never turn it off again.'

She heard the slightest sound, a footfall, from the other room, and looked up in surprise.

'Honey, I'm home.'

The voice was a stranger's, yet somehow familiar, falsely falsetto. The adrenaline of fear was shooting through her veins as she turned and saw them.

One was short, white, with thinning hair and a lived-in, almost ravaged face. She had seen him somewhere before – maybe she had known him when he was younger? – but she couldn't quite place him. He was wearing a nasty-looking suit and a skinny tie. The other, in an understated tracksuit of the most pristine white, was young, black, and quite startlingly beautiful. She had seen that face before, on posters, on album covers. Everybody had.

'What are *you* doing here?' she asked. Her fear vanished in astonishment.

The beautiful one smiled like an angel. It was the other one who spoke. 'I think you know that, my lovely.'

The London vowels teased at her memory. He must be an actor, she thought. Confused, she shook her head. 'But – I didn't want *you*. There must have been a mistake.'

The man in the nasty suit nodded. 'And you're the one who made it.'

The beautiful one laughed. It was an utterly mad laugh.

A little over the top, thought Gina, as objectively as if she was watching this on television. Real villains aren't like this, and it's impossible to take rock stars seriously when they try to act.

Then she felt herself freeze as she understood. These weren't actors, these weren't people, they were characters who had come from the same place as Sonny. And she knew very well why they had come.

'Your boyfriend hurt a friend of ours, rather badly,' said the white guy. A part of her mind was still scrabbling to come up with his name. He'd played drums once, hadn't he? 'And I'm afraid that, in return, we'll have to hurt a friend of *his*. Tit for tat, you know.'

'Tit for tat,' said beauty, and shrieked.

If this was a movie Sonny could return unexpectedly, in the nick of time, to save her. But this wasn't a movie, this was series television, and everybody knew the fate of the hero's girlfriend in a TV series. The hero had to be available, free to begin again with each new episode. She should have been smart and stuck with a sitcom husband. They might be dumb, but they were safe. The price of loving a hero was death.

Unless she could get to the television and turn this episode off.

The white guy took a step towards her. 'Nothing personal, lovey,' he said in a world-weary voice.

Instinctively, she moved away. Two steps backed her into a corner. It was, however, the corner where she kept the knives. She remembered the knife's lack of effect on Ward Cleaver, but he was a character from an old-fashioned sitcom for whom death by stabbing was unimaginable. These men obeyed an altogether different set of rules.

So she snatched up a carving knife. But they had been waiting for it, and now acted in concert, far swifter and more brutal than she could ever be, and had the knife away from her before she could even scream.

'Little girls shouldn't play with knives,' whispered the mad one into her face. 'They could hurt themselves. They could even kill themselves.'

Desperately, staring at those too-familiar faces as if

hypnotised, she told herself that this was not happening. They were not real. If they weren't real, they couldn't hurt her, not really. But even if she had been right – and if right, what about Ricky's spanking? – the knife that one of them now held was as real as her own agonised body. She might try to deny it, but she knew what was going to happen before it did.

The Reflection Once Removed
Scott Bradfield

This is a story we felt we had to take if only because the ending made both of us laugh out loud (no, don't peek; it's worth the wait). Scott Bradfield is the author of a novel, The History of Luminous Motion *and two short story collections,* Greetings from Earth *and* The Secret Life of Houses. *All three are outstanding and unmissable. He currently divides his time between writing fiction in North London and teaching it in Connecticut, where he shares an office with the man who inspired the Robin Williams character in* Dead Poets Society; *the London press show of this movie was disrupted when he and editor Kim Newman couldn't stop laughing during the big suicide-in-the-snow scene.*

A native Californian – as the authentically earnest lifestyle philosophy of 'The Reflection Once Removed' makes clear – Bradfield has spent most of his adult life in colder places, but still returns to Los Angeles in his fictions, which often use the clutter of pop culture to inform a sense of lives gone astray. Of all our contributors, he has probably taken the most roundabout route to our remit, turning fast-food psychiatry and consumer fetishism into a surprisingly upbeat story.

'I've got this idea,' Raymond Donahue said, covertly reaching under the dining-room table to dislodge Charlotte's Pomeranian from his ankle. 'And I've had this idea for quite a while now. Why don't we make it illegal for people to practise psychoanalysis without a licence? And I don't mean just in the state of California, either. I mean, why don't we think about this as a nation*wide* ballot initiative?'

'I'm serious, honey. I really am.' Charlotte reappeared from the kitchen, producing more food items which Raymond hated. Beets and tough, sinewy string beans. Gristly chicken-loaf and green olives stuffed with a vaguely gelatinous, pimento-like substance. 'I'm afraid you've got a womb-complex, Raymond. You can't help yourself. It says so right here in this great book by Dr Elliot P. Bernstein I've been reading lately.'

Charlotte ladled more unrequested string beans on to his plate. 'The womb-complex is a complex which afflicts many young men of your age and background. Young men who were overprotected by their mothers happen to develop low self-esteem motivation factors which cause them to distrust their female cohabitants or lifetime-mating partners. They grow insular and self-obsessed. They retreat into private fantasy worlds. They hardly ever take their mating partners out for dinners or shows or even dancing, and they watch an excessive amount of sporting events on TV. They begin to develop a thinly concealed hostility for all women, even their mating partners who love them, since no woman, however loving she may be, can provide that perfect original safety they once enjoyed behind the walls of their mother's womb.'

'My mother was a belladonna addict who slept around with bikers,' Raymond said distractedly. The Pomeranian, like a homing missile, had already latched on to his ankle again, and was beginning to hump against it more earnestly. 'I was raised by my father in Burlingame.'

'It's the same thing,' Charlotte said, passing him a suspicious brown plastic bottle emblazoned with thunderbolts and the resounding Liqui-Marg motif. 'Honestly, honey. I don't know why you're being so evasive.'

When the Pomeranian engaged his ankle again, Raymond gave it a swift, perfunctory little kick. The Pomeranian ricocheted off the leg of the sofa with a tiny yelp.

Charlotte instantly shot Raymond a dire look. Her look said, Isn't that just what I should have expected from a man with such a well-defined womb-complex?

Raymond was watching something green wobble on a plate across the table. He wasn't wearing his glasses but, for one moment, he could have sworn he saw the green object start to wobble in his direction.

'That's not jello-salad, is it?' Raymond asked warily. The only edible substance in the entire world that Raymond hated more than gristly chicken-loaf was jello-salad.

'Yes, it is,' Charlotte said coolly. 'But I'm afraid you're just going to have to wait for your dessert, Raymond.'

'*Getting to Know Your Own Enzymes*, Raymond, is not, as you call it, just another *crack*pot book.'

Sylvia was wearing her Day-Glo nylon jump-suit, brown cotton leg-warmers and a yellow terrycloth headband. She had just disboarded her exercycle in the living room to return to the kitchen and give Raymond another piece of her mind.

'The body, *Raymond*, just *hap*pens to generate its own language. How do you think the brain communicates with its many important organs and muscles and so on? Why, by means of its own highly complex signalling system – that's how. All Dr Elliot P. Bernstein is saying, Raymond, is that if the body can talk to itself, there's no reason *we* can't talk to the body. You know, open up some sort of dialogue between the intellect and the metabolism, the soma and the pneuma, the yin and the yang. I don't think you should just go around calling a creative, highly educated man like Dr Bernstein a cracker-brain, Raymond. The man does have a Ph.D., you know. The man *did* go to Harvard.'

Raymond was standing on a kitchen chair and rummaging in one of the highest, deepest storage shelves. He gripped a can of Lucky brand Hominy Grits under his right armpit, and a box of Instant Mushroom Soup packets in his left hand.

'He's got a Ph.D. in Education, Sylvia,' Raymond said. 'I don't know if that exactly qualifies the guy to start dispensing a lot of mumbo-jumbo about hormonal linguistics. Whatever the hell that is.'

Sylvia emitted an audible little huff. 'How many Ph.D.s have *you* got, Raymond? Why don't you tell me, then. How many Ph.D.s have *you* got, anyway?'

Raymond replaced the soup and hominy on the storage shelf and looked down at Sylvia. Sylvia's white, slender hands were clenched on her hips. She looked quite pretty, Raymond had to admit.

'Have you got anything to eat around this place?' Raymond climbed down from the chair.

'There's lettuce in the fridge, Raymond.' Sylvia's hands were beginning to unclench. All of the tension in the room began to subside, as if air were being let out of a balloon. 'Why don't you fix yourself a nice lettuce and tomato sandwich?'

Raymond blinked myopically around the kitchen at the various glimmering appliances. Then he sat down in the chair and absently examined a loaf of Mama Fibre's Whole Earth Bran-Bread.

'I don't really feel like a tomato and lettuce sandwich,' Raymond said aimlessly. Suddenly he felt very sad, but he didn't know why. 'Actually, I sort of felt like a cheeseburger or something.'

Within moments, Raymond heard Sylvia's nice legs pumping fresh mileage on to her exercycle in the living room.

'And then of course there's this whole ozone layer thing, and all the carcinogens in our environment, and all that. Like, I was reading this article in *People Magazine* last week? John Travolta's like trying to save all the caribou in Alaska, and the American government, just as you'd expect, isn't lifting one tiny finger to help.' Penny showed Raymond the little finger of her left hand. Penny wore many jewelled and elaborate rings on her fingers. They were standing in the frozen food aisle at Von's, and Raymond was examining two different brands of frozen zucchini lasagna. After a moment of dull reflection, Raymond replaced both brands in the misty frozen food cabinet.

'It's like, it's about time somebody began doing something about all of these important problems, don't you think?' Penny was peering into the frozen food cabinet, as if for signs of life. 'I mean, too many people have been too me-oriented for too long now. Like I've been reading this great book lately called *The Culture Revolution*, by this very famous guy, Dr Bernstein and all? Dr Bernstein says that me-oriented types of people are the saddest types of people in the entire world, because they are unable to bathe in the cultural vibrations which less self-centred people share with each other all the time. Did you know they sell Dr Bernstein's excellent book right here in this very supermarket? Well, they do. In fact, it just happens to be number three on the *New York Times* paperback bestseller list this week. By the way – ' Penny's jewelled fingers tapped at the Bird's Eye Frozen Vegetable Platter Raymond was examining in his hand. 'What's your name, anyway?'

Raymond replaced the Bird's Eye in the frozen food

cabinet. Raymond had been shopping for an hour now, but he couldn't really find anything he liked. No matter how many high crowded shelves of food he investigated, all he could think about was the day-old Carl's Western Bacon Cheeseburger he had eaten just that morning for breakfast. Raymond's shopping cart contained a loaf of Bran-Bread, and a plastic gallon carton of generic hundred per cent orange juice.

'My name's Raymond,' Raymond said after a while. 'And according to your friend, Dr Bernstein, I'm suffering from a pretty severe case of womb-complex right now. I should probably warn you about that right off.'

Some nights Raymond dreamed about food. Char-broiled steaks, potatoes with sour cream, pot roasts and gravy, breasts of chicken simmering with sweet, translucent juices, spare ribs and pork chops and veal parmagiana and turkey pot pies. Usually he started awake in bed just as he was reaching out for it. It was as if he had transgressed some sort of moral boundary. If he wanted to grasp the dream-food and make it real, then he would have to suffer reality instead.

'What's the matter, honey?' a woman's voice asked.

Raymond could still smell the steaming vegetables, the tender slabs of sirloin and lemony trout. The woman's smooth hand touched his face.

'Where am I?' Raymond asked.

'You're with me. You're at my house.'

'What year is it?'

'1989.'

'How old am I? Where do I work?'

'You're thirty-eight, honey, and no spring chicken. You sell advertising space for California's largest home advertising magazine, *The Bargain Buyer*. Your offices are in Sherman Oaks.'

Raymond reached out for the end table and found his cigarettes. His sense of vertigo withdrew with a smooth, sliding sensation.

'What am I doing here?' he asked the woman.

'Not too much, baby. I'm afraid you haven't been doing too much good around here at all.'

It was becoming increasingly difficult for Raymond to remember who he was with, how long he had known her, and what exactly she meant to him. Every morning he awoke in strange bedrooms where the quality of light lay strangely distributed across things he did not recognise. Often the bed beside him was empty, and he ventured alone into weirdly gleaming bathrooms where he puzzled at unusual brands of shampoo and deodorant, or scalded himself trying to adjust the complicated, often futuristic-looking shower devices. The women left him microwave-ready meals wrapped in plastic on their immaculate kitchen tables, and hasty notes scrawled on the backs of torn envelopes and advertising leaflets.

Make yourself at home, the notes told him. *Be back soon*.

Raymond uncovered the waiting meals and sniffed at them. Sometimes the food resembled muesli, or a nutty, fibrous substance. Sometimes it resembled hummus, tara-masalata, or something with cheese. Vainly Raymond searched through unfamiliar cabinets for Corn Flakes, Fruit Loops, or anything else he recognised. Instead he discovered snail pellets and gardening supplies, rusty woks and elaborately packaged fondue kits, unpaid utility bills and neglected pastry. Usually he just burned a piece of Bran-Bread in the toaster, and soothed it with whatever brand of butter substitute he could find in the refrigerator. Breakfasts in strange houses, Raymond thought, were pretty depressing experiences – especially for men who were rapidly approaching middle age.

He couldn't remember them by their faces or their names any more, but only by the books they left behind. *Learning to Be and Love Yourself*, *Developing Your Own Me-ness Strategy*, *Eating for A Better I.Q.*, *Men Who Love Too Much and the Women Who Leave Them*, and, of course, the perennial bestseller, *Doing it Your Way*, with a special introduction by Frank Sinatra, Jr. All of these books were either written by Dr Elliot P. Bernstein, or in collaboration with him, and they featured numerous graphs and charts concerning the relationships between self-esteem and diet, oogenesis and body language, erogenous zones and state-wide radon activity. Raymond often caught himself gazing absently at the various diagrams and illustrations for hours while the ice dissolved in his drinks, or his mugs of coffee grew cool on the kitchen table.

Raymond figured that if all the women he had ever known in his entire life were even half-right, then he suffered from a pretty extraordinary range of personal problems that included narcissism, self-doubt, abstract behaviour patterns, colitis, diminishing Alpha Wave activity, various sorts of neural and lymphatic disorders, severe overdependencies on alcohol, antibiotics and TV, and an almost psychotic disregard for the achievements of supply-side economics. 'I don't think I have to tell you, Raymond,' a blonde woman with a Karmen Ghia once said, 'but you're one really loused-up individual. Don't take it personally or anything, Raymond. I just thought it was something you ought to know.'

In September Raymond enrolled at the Dr Bernstein Center for Adjustable Behavioral Abnormalities in Reseda, where for ten days he was subjected to the relentless schedules, strategies and ministrations of an impressive battery of random counsellors, psychotherapists, herbalists, dietary technicians, muscular coordinators, adaptive macro-societal engineers, and one rather impolite old lady who ran the Snack Bar. The impolite old lady who ran the Snack Bar was named Eunace, and she wore fluorescent make-up, butterfly glasses on a chain around her neck, and mottled, inadequately dyed hair in a bun. Usually Raymond sat at the Snack Bar on a stool and drank Mocha-Max, a single-blend coffee and creamer substitute, while he vaguely examined the shelves of heavy-looking carob cookies and vegan soufflés displayed behind glass cases like exhibits in some inedible museum. In ten days, Eunace never smiled at Raymond once, and whenever he arrived at the Snack Bar she always emitted long, exasperated sighs, as if Raymond were the most boring man who had ever lived. During his brief internment at the Dr Bernstein Center for Adjustable Behavioral Abnormalities, Raymond quickly learned that Eunace's Snack Bar was the only place around where he could nurse his severe psychic obsessions and libidinal fixations in relative privacy.

'You know, Eunace, I've been thinking,' Raymond liked to muse, examining the thin pink residue at the bottom of his depleted mug of Mocha-Max. 'You remember all those women in my life who've been telling me what a self-centred, hopeless neurotic and screwed-up wreck I am? Well, come to think of it, none of those women are what you could actually call perfect or anything. I mean, they're all perfectly *nice* and all, but almost without exception most of them believe implicitly in things like reincarnation, alien visitors from outer space controlling the Pentagon, and astrology. In fact, come to think of it, most of them are Capricorns. Do you think that means anything, Eunace? That most of them happen to be Capricorns?'

Whenever Raymond looked up, Eunace began banging dishes in the sink and scrubbing them with a frayed, soapy rag. Raymond had to admit that Eunace was probably not the most patient and attentive listener he had ever encountered, but at least she found him so boring that she didn't bother to offer him any constructive criticism of her own. Perhaps, Raymond thought, it was because Eunace realised, somewhere deep inside her dim, soapy brain, that if there was one thing Raymond was never short of at the Dr Bernstein Center for Adjustable Behavioral Abnormalities, it was constructive criticism.

For ten days Raymond was analysed, steamed, acupunctured, rolfed, screened, vilified, hugged, X-rayed, audited, sensorily deprived, and enrolled in afternoon swimming lessons at the enormous, Olympic-sized Dr Bernstein swimming pool, which was located in the sweeping, brilliantly scented Dr Bernstein Botanical Gardens. Raymond was required to chart daily graphs of his hourly heart and metabolic rates, and to keep a secret diary in which he purged himself of his most shameful resentments against the Dr Bernstein Center and all the highly qualified, deeply concerned people there who were trying to help him.

'People who never learn to swim suffer from womb-insecurity neurosis, which is a very difficult form of neurosis to deal with, especially when you're a lady,' Bunny told Raymond every afternoon during their daily aqua-therapy session. Meekly, Raymond held his breath while Bunny plunged his head underneath the sparkling, chlorinated water, or trawled him into the deepest part of the pool and held him in a back-float against the thin surface. 'For many people, the womb is the only happiness they ever really know. Once they're born, everything starts to go straight downhill. They feel lonely and rejected. They feel unloved and without a home. They become deeply afraid of ever being happy again, because they believe that happiness is something that leads to suffering and deprivation. This is what we call here at the Institute a Bad Behavioural Syndrome. Bad Behavioural Syndromes are habits you develop that make you unhappier than whatever experiences made you develop those habits in the first place. Does that make any sense to you, Raymond? Do you realise that people are often their own worst enemy, sometimes without even realising it?'

Bunny was the most extraordinarily fat woman Raymond had ever seen with most of her clothes off. Her two-piece swimsuit resembled wire bindings on a bale of hay. 'When you're a lady and you feel unloved, then you find it impossible to love yourself,' Bunny told Raymond later at Eunace's Snack Bar. 'So then what you do is sit around your apartment all day long, just watching television and eating yourself into oblivion. You become massively fat, and the fatter you get the more unhappy you become. And so you eat more, and then you get more unhappy. And so on and so forth. Since I met Dr Bernstein, I have lost nearly eighty pounds. As a result, I have developed a more assertive attitude towards my own femininity. Now, how does one of those carob cookies look to you, Raymond? I think I wouldn't mind a carob cookie to go along with my Mocha-Max.'

'I don't think so,' Raymond said politely. He was listening to a bubble of pool-water oscillating thinly in his left ear. It sounded like hovering alien spacecraft in a science fiction movie. 'I think I'll just finish my Mocha-Max and go back to my room.'

On the day of his release from the Dr Bernstein Center for Adjustable Behavioral Abnormalities, Raymond couldn't stop whistling Stevie Winwood's 'Back in the High Life

Again' all the way home. He went directly to Hamburger
Hamlet and ordered his favourite meal, the cheesesteak and
fries with a large Coke, and a strawberry shortcake for
dessert. He flirted with all the waitresses, drank three jumbo
vodka-tonics, and even purchased a pack of Marlboros,
which he smoked sparingly and with much self-indulgent
dispatch. So far as Raymond was concerned, the best thing
about the Dr Bernstein Center for Adjustable Behavioral
Abnormalities was not having to be there any more. It was
sort of like having a malignant tumour in your brain go into
spontaneous remission, or a merciful governor call in time
to prevent the electric switch from being thrown. On his
way home that afternoon, Raymond stoppd at Ralph's and
bought a gallon jug of low-fat milk, assorted Swanson's
Hungry Man frozen dinners, and a large 24-ounce economy
size carton of Kellogg's Sugar Frosted Flakes.

'At first I guess I probably tried to fight it,' Raymond told
Wendy, Crystal, Sylvia and Marie over succeeding evening
meals at their houses. 'I didn't have enough confidence in
myself to trust in the sincere, highly qualified concern of
others. I was anti-social, and spent most of my time in my
room. Whenever one of my counsellors or Behaviour Monitors tried to start up a friendly conversation during meals or
exercise sessions, I wouldn't even give them the time of day.
Then, one afternoon while I was sitting smugly alone in my
room, I remembered what Dr Bernstein said once about the
Negotiable-Me Strategy. The Negotiable-Me Strategy is the
strategy one conducts in order to convince the world about
the sort of person one wants to become. The Negotiable-Me
Strategy often arouses conflictual-action situations between
itself and the world's very resolute You-Negation Paradigm.
This is the same thing as saying that one's self-vocabulary
has become deverbalised in a highly chaotic manner.'

With evident concern, Raymond reached across the table and touched Wendy, Sylvia, Crystal or Marie's hand.

'Are you following what I'm trying to tell you?' Raymond asked. 'Or am I using too much technical jargon for you to relate with where I'm coming from?'

When the various women in his life stopped returning his calls, Raymond settled easily into a new, grateful routine of smooth and uneventful complacency. He subscribed to Cable and and began taking extended holiday and sick leaves from his office. He bought a window planter for the front porch, and a cherry-red hummingbird feeder for the kitchen window. He ate late breakfasts and liked to watch the hummingbirds dart, hover and weave outside in the glistening blue air. The hummingbirds were emblazoned with bright, pheromonic splashes of colour, and dipped their long beaks into the sugary red water, burning energy like tiny blazing oil refineries. The phone hardly rang at all any more. Whenever it did ring, it was usually some telephone marketing outfit promoting newspapers or magazines, or Bunny from the Dr Bernstein Center trying to sign Raymond up for a special extended 'follow-up' session at the new Dr Bernstein Holiday Self-Actualization Camp located somewhere in the Napa Valley. Raymond wished Bunny all the luck in the world, and told her that if he could find time to attend what sounded like a highly enlightening exploration of human-growth potential, he would definitely call her back right away. Then he had his telephone disconnected and bought a small, mottled grey puppy from the pound which he named Cylus. For the first few weeks, Cylus went to the bathroom all over Raymond's apartment. Whatever Cylus didn't pee or crap on, he chewed to ribbons with a happy animal patience. Cylus was an extremely amiable, energetic young dog who knew how to take pleasure in the simple things of life. When you got right down to it, Raymond thought, the simple things in life were all that really mattered.

Then, one afternoon in late May, someone knocked at the front door. When Raymond went to the door and opened it, he found the book-jacket-familiar face of Dr Bernstein, whose smile glinted as cheerily as the thick, bifocal lenses of his horn-rimmed glasses.

Looking up from one of Raymond's hand-sewn suede cowboy boots which had come to resemble bad meat, Cylus growled distantly.

'You may be able to run and hide from Dr Bernstein, Raymond,' Dr Bernstein said wisely, making smooth little gestures in the blue, sparkling air with his wooden clipboard. 'But it's never so easy to run and hide from yourself. As I'm sure we all well know.'

An automobile horn sounded abruptly in the street. When Raymond looked down at the kerb he saw Bunny seated at the driver's wheel of an open-top pink Cadillac convertible. Bunny waved merrily. The pale flesh flapped in her armpit.

It took Raymond a few seconds to regain his teetering balance.

'You're absolutely right, Dr Bernstein,' Raymond said. 'You're absolutely, abso*lute*ly right.'

'Self-motivating behavioural strategies don't just start working overnight, Raymond.' Dr Bernstein entered Raymond's apartment with appreciative nods at the television, video, sofa bed and CD player. 'Behavioural abnormalities often require *years* of cautious, professional evaluation. You're a young man with a lot of promise, Raymond. But you're also a young man who is very definitely, and very profoundly screwed up – and don't think I'd ever say such a thing if I didn't truly care about your well-being as an individual.'

'I'm sure you wouldn't, Dr Bernstein.' Raymond was glancing frantically around the living room for heavy, blunt objects. 'I'm sure you'd never do anything to endanger my happiness and well-being at all.' Raymond systematically noted and disregarded the locations of a Rand Atlas, rabbit-ear television antenna, hearth-top piggy-bank, and some thick-framed museum prints of Picasso, Matisse and Cézanne.

On the floor, Cylus's growl roughened. He was sitting up and watching Dr Bernstein. He had forgotten his partially macerated cowboy boot altogether.

'Why don't you throw a few clothes together,' Dr Bernstein said. 'Just enough for a day or two at the Holiday Camp. You'll probably want to bring along a little cash. And your chequebook – don't forget your chequebook. Your cheque guarantee card. Your Visa and Mastercard cards.'

'I'll do that,' Raymond agreed happily, and departed for the back bedroom where he opened his battered brown overnight bag and filled it with socks, underwear, tooth-brush and toothpaste, denim trousers and denim shirts. Then he went into the closet and, from underneath mould-ering laundry, retrieved his notched and yellowing Louis-ville Slugger baseball bat. He hurried back to the living room.

In the living room Dr Bernstein was saying, 'Nice doggy. This is my non-threatening, beta-status posture, doggy. Can I pet you? Can we be friends? Ouch!' Dr Bernstein took a sudden backward step.

'You brainless little turd!'

Dr Bernstein was raising his open hand just as Raymond hammered the back of Dr Bernstein's skull with the Louis-ville Slugger. Raymond had never been a particularly good baseball player, but it had always been his favourite sport anyway. He removed Dr Bernstein's cash- and credit-fat wallet and stuffed it into the vest pocket of his Wrangler jean-jacket. Then he went to the front door and waved at Bunny in her pink Cadillac. He gave her the V for Victory sign.

Bunny waved back happily and honked the horn.

Raymond returned to the living room and gave Dr Bernstein another firm cerebral whack with the Louisville Slugger, just for good measure. Then he bundled up Cylus, climbed over the rattly backyard fence, and hailed a cab at Van Nuys Boulevard.

'Not supposed to allow dogs in this cab,' the driver told him.

Raymond showed the driver a fat wad of bills from Dr Bernstein's wallet.

'LAX,' Raymond said. 'You better step on it.'

The driver contemplated the wad of bills reflected in his rearview mirror. He removed a grey lump of gum from his mouth and placed it in the ashtray.

'Where you headed?' he asked after a while.

'To get my mind straight,' Raymond said. 'To raise my consciousness. To increase my self-esteem coordinating capabilities in a highly resolute, predetermined manner.' Raymond gazed out the window at the smoggy, opaque Los Angeles skyline, the angry cars and drivers, the roaring buses and airplanes. Los Angeles, he thought, had never looked better.

Raymond looked at the driver's reflected eyes in the rearview mirror. 'But this time I'm going to do it in Rio.'

Life in the Groove
Ian Watson

Part of the charm of the 45 r.p.m. single – or part of the reason for junking it in favour of those shiny CDs – is the subtle degradation of its sound, the rising hiss and the occasional snap or scratch as some piece of debris is forever bonded into the vinyl by the pressure of diamond chip against plastic. And because 90 per cent of dust in the home is dead sloughed human skin, that means that most of those snaps and crackles and pops are due to a part of yourself becoming One with the music.

Here, in what might be considered the ultimate discworld story, Ian Watson provides a more catastrophic view of the progress of a stylus down a spiral scratch. Self-confessed sufferer of tone-deafness, Watson says that to him all music, from the Red Army Choir to Wagner, tends to resolve towards its paradigmatic form – 'Telstar'. That's perhaps one reason why he took such an elliptical approach to the anthology's subject matter, although we should expect nothing less from British SF's most iconoclastic talent.

A retired gardener, Watson is author of some thirty novels and short story collections, the latest being **The Flies of Memory** *and* **Stalin's Teardrops***. He is also fascinated by body piercing and the fetishisms of the Modern Primitives, as is made abundantly clear in this story. His favourite song (apart from 'Telstar') is Kate Bush's version of 'Rocket Man', mainly for her plaintive and surrealistic interpretation of the line 'I'm not the man I used to be'.*

So Fulque Darien at last proudly displayed the orrery We had commissioned him to make. He whipped up the purple silk that was shrouding his device and swung the sheet aside like some conjuror converting a crouching slavegirl into a pig, or a minotaurador flourishing his cape to bamboozle a razor-horned ape.

Swankily, indeed!

Light streamed through the arched, mullioned windows of Our seclusium, illuminating a thousand motes of dust which Darien's dramatic unveiling released – as if to demonstrate his molecular theory of matter, that all the world was made of minute particles glued together by magnetism, which a strong enough shock could wrench apart. Darien had begged for funds to prove this.

However, We weren't interested in the mikrokosm, only in the makrokosm, as befitted a ruler who must have large concerns.

Darien sketched a bow, drawing back his short green cape.

'Here it is, Hautarch. After much trial and error. After many tests . . . It appears to correspond perfectly with the celestial motions.'

The gaunt, one-eyed fellow tugged at his greying caprine beard as if he had just remembered some missing component. He squinted, then nodded, reassured. The other eye had been lost to a splash of boiling lead during experiments at transmogrification on behalf of Our treasury. The eye-patch was silver. Visitors to Our court sometimes took Fulque Darien at first for a legendary mutant mage, one of whose eyes was organic and the other crafted of precious metal.

His orrery consisted of several dozen little brass finger-cymbals instantly identifiable as those employed by temple prostitutes during their gyrations to the Spiral Spirit – as well as by less exalted dancing whores in bordellos along the waterfront. We wondered which source of supply Our court savant had used! Darien had erased any sacred or pornographic motifs from those digital percussion discs, and superimposed on each the astrological symbol of a particular world.

Each cymbal was held up in midair by a long, thin, jointed arm which branched from the intricate clockwork of the base. A protective cage enclosed the maze of gears and toothed cogs – the reticulations somewhat blurred the details.

This clockwork was belt-driven so as to dampen vibrations and the motive power occupied an adjoining cage mounted above an alcohol lamp. When the alcohol was lit, a cunning series of little mirrors would focus the lamplight upon the central luminary crystal rising on a slim glass spike in the midst of the array of cymbals – representing our lustrous sapphire sun.

We pointed a stout, ring-clad finger at those mirrors.

'A homage to Our signalling system, Fulque?'

The savant nodded eagerly, and his one-eyed gaze flicked towards the nearby window as if to underscore this subtlety.

Way beyond Our beloved city of Majiriche, hugging both banks of the million-mile river here in the Forever Valley, far beyond the agricultural levels and the forests rising above those, Mount Sinister continued soaring upwards towards its peak at a steady inclination of forty-five degrees. Above the treeline the slope became snowclad. Above the cloud-line, where the air was so thin, it was stark. Hardly indented by any cols or gullies, the massif cut an almost perfectly straight line through the sky, except where intervening cumulus smudged the view.

Up there on the summit-ridge shone the visual pinpricks of a couple of mirrors – seemingly minuscule yet actually quite sizeable.

At the moment those shone steadily. No signals were winking.

It had been one of the culminating triumphs of Our reign to mount those messenger devices upon Mount Sinister, leftward bastion of Our valley, and upon Mount Dexter, the rightward valley wall. My great-grandfather had begun the breeding program to cultivate slaves with barrel-chests and shaggy coats of hair who could breathe in such high regions and avoid hypothermia. How unhappy such persons were in the warmer, thicker atmosphere of the Valley when they descended even as far as the tree-line to collect their supplies of meat and fish and oatcake, which guaranteed their obedience!

Of course, Mounts Sinister and Dexter were one and the same in reality, being the opposite sides of one another – a fact which Our common people often found hard to visualise, despite the explanatory dances in the temples of the Spiral Spirit.

Heroic river journeys in the age of Our elder ancestors – voyages of three thousand, of ten thousand, of twenty thousand leagues – had established the truth that the inaccessible Silver Empire over the other side of Mount Sinister was also several thousand leagues downriver of us beyond a hundred intervening khanates, republiks, demotopias, and barrens – and that the selfsame Valley spiralled around the whole of our world from the circum to the centre, its chevron cutting deep into the slate of our planetary surface and thus raising to left and right that long dual mountain.

In mirror-code we now communicated with the Silver Empire on one side, and with the Hegemony on the other – as well as trading diplomatically with the upstream Fisher Kingdom and the downstream Sensualists.

The motive power of Fulque Darien's device – within that secondary cage – was a sleek, tawny-furred leeming-rat.

That too was a clever homage.

Why else were those mirrors set up there on the mountains? Not merely to exchange philosophical speculations or so that We could play prolonged games of Tchak with the Silver Emperor remotely by mirror.

'When you light the alcohol flame, Hautarch, the cage floor heats,' explained Darien. 'The blind rat runs into the little treadmill, and thus propels the gears – swiftly or slowly, depending upon the height of the flame.'

We nodded appreciatively. A little hopper contained pellets of oatcake to feed the ever-ravenous beast. A flask with suction-spigot, water. A chute deposited its nuts of excrement in a tray beneath.

We were determined that this particular leeming-rat should enjoy plentiful exercise, turning the arms of Our orrery.

Unpredictably, every century or so, hordes of leeming-rats would burst forth as if from nowhere and rampage – aye, they would *flood* in a snarling, devouring, copulating, blind tide – through kingdom after khanate after republik. It was as though the rats reproduced apace somewhere within the fabric of the mountains themselves, perhaps engendered within a vast rock-eating queen. This devastating tide might flow for ten thousand leagues till finally it piled up upon itself from sheer excess of bodies, which would block the Valley, the vermin now devouring one another.

Those mountain mirrors could give early warning of such a flood, if it began sufficiently far away. The wealth and populace of Our Hautarchy could be transported up to the forested slopes where the leeming-rats never ventured.

Already the Silver Emperor and the Hegemon were

eagerly breeding suitable slaves to staff mountain mirrors of their own, so as to communicate with lands beyond.

Eventually, mirror messages might pass all the way from the fabled centre of our world out to the ultimum circum within mere days.

Thanks to past heroes of exploration we knew rather more of the circum than of the centre. That final, vastest, outermost stretch of Valley led around in a perfect circle rather than a spiral. Reportedly it was utterly barren and dry, for it lay beyond the first tricklings of the rain-fed stream which presently became the million-mile river.

We tapped Our nose. 'We imagined you might use golden Oricks to represent the worlds rather than those finger-cymbals of whores. We think we even mentioned something of the sort.'

'*Then* I should have been obliged to erase your royal countenance, Hautarch! Besides, if the treasury cannot afford to support a simple test of my molekular theory . . .'

We glared at him.

'Light the flame,' We ordered. 'Warm the rat. Let the orrery rotate.'

And so he did; and so it did.

In elegant complexity, the sixty-eight miniature worlds swung around their orbits. Amidst the cavalcade, We admired the cymbal marked with the antlered chevron which symbolised our own world of the Forever Valley.

'Do you suppose,' We enquired idly, 'that valleys similar to ours exist on all the other worlds too?'

As that chevroned cymbal turned, We caught sight of its rearside, where the tip of the thin arm was soldered. Around that little blob of joining alloy, Darien had engraved a query mark inscribed in the old script.

This was rank impertinence!

'Darien! We are not – We are never – going to order Our

slaves to attempt to dig a shaft down through the floor of Our world!'

'To be sure, to be sure,' he demurred, making it sound as though he was simultaneously agreeing with Us yet at the same time offering a defence of such a project.

'To be sure about *what*? That our world is flat and two-sided just like all those other discs in the sky? What else should it be? Half a sphere? A hemisphere?'

'I think that is unlikely, Hautarch. Yet maybe . . .'

'Maybe what?'

He glanced at the rotating orrery. 'Maybe several other worlds are forever hidden beneath the plane of our planet. Maybe my toy does not present the whole picture?'

'Pish and tush,' We said. 'That isn't why you'd like to examine the arse of our world. Tell Us the real reason!'

He shuffled. 'My Hautarch, it was only in attaching the arms to the cymbals that I finally asked myself the question: of what nature is the arm which supports our own world in space? Plainly, no visible arms sustain the other worlds, or else we would perceive those as thin threads illuminated by solar radiance. Yet *something* must hold all the flat worlds in their orbits, and move them. Some physical manifestation. The gravitic theory of my predecessor is inadequate, since according to the hero explorers our own bodily weight remains constant whether we travel towards the centre or the circum. I have reworked Burgo Corvin's equations, and they fail.'

'So you'd like to tunnel through the world to see whether there's an invisible arm arching away from the other side? Ha! *We* were always of the opinion that ethereal, perfect *music* governed the dance of the worlds. We are sad that Our orrery does not play that music – though it might produce a tinkling clatter indeed, if whore cymbals are involved!'

The lamp burned. The leeming-rat toiled in the monotonous mindless fashion of its species, responding exactly to stimulus. The worlds swung around in silence.

'What harmonious tune *should* the worlds play, Hautarch?' Darien begged, almost pathetically, crestfallen from his earlier pride. 'Merely tell me, and I will add a musical box which the rat will also activate.'

That would tinkle out such a paltry tune. It would not even begin to ape the solemn, sonorous melody of worlds in motion.

We hummed to Ourselves a stately nocturne.

Iridescent hummingbirds hovering outside Our window to sip at the nectar nipples mounted on the sill squeaked stupidly, feebly.

Their humming came from the flutter of their well-nigh invisible wings.

'The motion of worlds makes the music,' We announced to Darien. 'And the music moves the worlds.'

'That is . . . profound, Hautarch,' he said respectfully. In fact we were only echoing the old religion – which had been inspired by . . . *what*? By what titanic event or observation on the part of our primitive ancestors? Alas, previous migrations of leeming-rats had erased all records and all clues. The current cult of the Spiral Spirit, to which We lent state approval, was – to Our taste – a shade decadent. A dance of doxies, in the twin sense: of dogmatic praise, and of holy harlots. Yet it pleased the people.

'In airless space,' murmured Darien, 'surely no one can hear you play a tune . . .'

We ignored him. On the whole We were content with Our orrery. While We brooded over state decrees and accounts here in Our seclusium, or pondered the next move in the current game of Tchak with the Silver Emperor, Our model of the worlds would turn harmoniously, and the rat would race, and We would hear soothing melodies within Our mind at least. We would feel that We were ruler of Our whole world, and of all the worlds, at least in miniature.

We awoke from a perplexing dream in which the High Priestess of the Spiral Spirit visited Our bed for copulation – though not with *Ourself*, exactly. Here language becomes deficient. How can We explain without resorting to lese-majesty? In the dream We – that is to say, Ourself – were afflicted with a Tsiamese Twin attached to Us back to back so that the two of Ourselves – Us, and He – when viewed in the silver mirror above Our bed somewhat resembled a peculiar, portly playing card. The two of Us must needs sleep side by side, and in advance of slumber we would toss a coin, a golden Orick, to decide which body would sleep on its leftward side all night, and which on the right.

When We had tossed the Orick that evening, it had balanced, standing up on end. Thus We – that is to say Ourself – lay face down on the silken sheet upon the mattress stuffed with hummingbird feathers. And Our twin lay upright.

When the High Priestess climbed into our chamber, instead of distributing her favours to each twin laterally, first from the left side then from the right, she merely mounted Our twin, and rode him so fiercely that We were pressed down stiflingly into the mattress.

She sang (or wailed) wordlessly, but *We* moaned like a grampus in Lake Bogak – Our Hautarchy's only lake, where the river opens out widely to provide a habitat for those watercows. We groaned not in any ecstasy but from the simple effort of drawing breath.

Then We awoke alongside her tattooed nude body in reality.

For naturally she *was* with Us that night – being the eighty-eighth of the year. Naturally no twin infested Our body. Yet the moan and the wail remained.

Almost wholly subaudible, or almost wholly superaudible.

The noise set Our teeth on edge and vibrated deep within Our bones.

'Sister Espirilla!' I exclaimed. 'What are those sounds? Do you hear them?'

She hoisted herself on a hand tattooed with whorls and curlicues, and harkened.

Most of Espirilla's body, revealed by soft blue alcohol-light reflecting from the silver mirror overhead, writhed with patterned serpents – a maze of snakes through which We had often tried in vain to find our way, tracing with a finger. Her nipple and navel and labia rings glinted, bereft for the time being of the little cymbals which usually hung on each; and she gripped each ring in turn, to release it after a squeeze, as though engaged in some private erotic sacramental rite.

Our own hand strayed to assist her – for We were intrigued; but with a frown she slapped Our hand away. Capricious etiquette forbade her to utter words in Our presence unless attired in her cymbals of sacred office.

As Espirilla scrambled from Our sheets to retrieve these bronze 'worlds' from the marble parquet, where she had discarded them clangingly after unrobing, We felt Our own organ being teased, and it swelled.

We realised that Our ampallang was stimulating Us, unbidden. The slim silver bar which pierced the head of Our glans through the spongeosum as retainer for two prominent gold studs – that miniature dumb-bell which Our penis would hoist – was throbbing subtly, resonating to the deeper timbres of the elusive, enigmatic sonics.

Evidently Espirilla was being stimulated similarly, at nipple and navel and venereal cleft.

She hooked her cymbals upon her rings. Their weight plainly served to damp those vibrations. Dangling cymbals jangled somewhat as she flexed herself, and coughed to clear her throat, and cocked her head.

'Hautarch,' she said, 'I hear those sounds – far off. Yet I *feel* them – close by. The world has become strangely sonorous.'

For a moment we feared that in rhapsodising about the harmonics of the worlds, and in activating Darien's model of those worlds, somehow We had summoned that unheard music.

Our ampallang vibrated teasingly. By now Our other head – Our little head between the legs – was cocked too.

Espirilla resumed her saffron robe, embroidered with golden undulations.

'I must go and dance till dawn! For the night has assaulted me.'

She paced towards the casement.

Yet once there, she uttered a little cry. 'Hautarch! Look at the heavens!'

Hastily We quit Our bed and joined her.

The moan may have been more clearly perceptible in the elevated quietude of Our palace bedchamber. Alerted by it, and by the twitching of Our erogenous zones, We – by whom We mean the two of Us, she and Ourself – may have been the first people in Our whole Hautarchy to observe the alteration.

Inexplicably, the stately procession of nearer and further worlds in the welkin appeared somewhat further away than before – somewhat diminished. And for the first time in Our knowledge all those other worlds presented an *oval* profile as though all had canted askew.

'No, they can't all have moved!' I exclaimed. 'Our *own world* must have shifted aside!'

We clung to one another in perplexity, she and Ourself, my ampallang butting her willy-nilly as though seeking sanctuary.

Presently, over-zealous watchmen began trumpeting reedily from towers – as if there were any virtue in bringing alarmed citizenry spilling into the cobbled streets of our blessèd Majiriche. Temple gongs began to bong.

'I must dance till noon!' she cried. 'I must take twenty lovers!'

After she had climbed down the ladder of assignation to slip away past the guards, We brightened one of the alcoholights and carried it through into Our seclusium – there, to heat up the rat and to curse Fulque Darien, since a Hautarch could not by law be blameworthy.

Darien might be best advised to flee to the nearest khanate or risk having his own flesh tested to see whether it was composed of molekules.

We wondered whether to smash the orrery. Or to slay the rat. Or somehow compel it to run backwards.

Petitioners crowded Our audience chamber next morning, and Our guards were on high alert. The whole of Majiriche throbbed perceptibly now. Under Our ermine robe, Our ampallang evinced a definite will of its own.

Thus it was with constant and involuntary priapic stimulus that We faced the crisis. The air was noticeably warmer. The luminary appeared fatter in the sky, though *it* was not swelling any further. Unlike Ourself.

Finally We were obliged to summon Our physician and retire for an hour. With much difficulty due to the engorgement, ancient Dr Larkari fumbled with tiny spanners. Eventually he unscrewed the little golden balls from the silver spindle and removed that pin from my pulsing glans.

Gonads aching, We returned to our audience – to espy

Fulque Darien there in the forefront, hopping impatiently from foot to foot. He clutched a maroon leather-bound volume.

'Darien!' We roared.

Hastily Our savant knelt.

'Hautarch, I believe I understood how the worlds might make music!'

'You do not believe in that music,' I growled.

'We are starting to hear the evidence, are we not, Hautarch?'

I cocked my ear to the low quivering drone. '*That* is music? *That* is harmony?'

'In so far as we can hear it with our tiny ears. Or feel it in our bones. Most of the frequencies escape us. Yet in truth the main volume of the music must be directed elsewhere. It must project far away from our world, towards the greater ear of God.'

'Explain!'

He was sweating. So were We in Our ermine. So were most of the petitioners and all of Our guards in their breastplates and chain-link hosiery.

'The ancient inexplicable Monolith Inscription gives the key, Hautarch! The inscription which the slaves found high up Mount Sinister where the air is too thin for us valley dwellers. Which they copied by rubbing charcoal on a sheet of parchment and sent down to us – '

'We do recall it, Darien. That is one of the enigmas of Our Hautarchy.'

On a slanting rocky slab above the cumulus, close to where one of Our signal mirrors was now installed, someone had carved a bizarre poem in archaic language, the very words now seeming almost worn away by wind.

As We were well aware.

However, Our prostate gland felt congested. Our mind was distracted. 'Remind Us of the exact text, Darien.'

He recited:

> 'Snout-tipped Monolith,
> Towering from the sky . . .
> Who sees it clearly?
> It scours the valley,
> And we are deaf.
> The river only lubricates the tip.'

Oh, how Our own tip cried out for some lubrication at the moment.

'Most scholars have argued, Hautarch, that this refers to a terrible previous migration by leeming-rats which stripped our valley of a primitive early civilisation. Those billions of rats are envisaged as one single gigantic rat; hence the snout . . . No one can clearly perceive such a monstrous mass of rats. Their shrill squeaking deafens everyone . . . *I* do not think so! I think this refers to a ghostly yet at the same time very substantial and immense artefact – of the self-same nature as the arms which hold the cymbals in position in your orrery.

'This artefact descends from the sky. In appearance it resembles an inverted monolith tipped with a pyramid of the same contours as our valley. This abrades the slopes of our valley, sweeping away habitations and human beings like dust – and the vibrations of its passage are the Godly, celestial *music* which we discussed, Hautarch, and which we now hear in the guise of that moaning drone . . . approaching us. I believe we should evacuate Majiriche immediately.'

'Evacuate Our city, Darien?'

'Before Majiriche is destroyed, Hautarch. Before we are swept away by something vaster than any rat-horde.'

'Evacuate . . . ?' Why, the panic and chaos would be

immeasurable. 'How soon,' We enquired archly, 'till this . . . supposed doom by Monolith?'

He shrugged. 'To determine that, I should need to build a model of such a monolith poised above our world, with its pyramidal tip engaged in the groove of the Forever Valley, travelling inward from the circum. I would need to ascertain the rate of progress by means of mirror signals sent from distant arcs of the spiral . . . Maybe from our own mundane point of view the monolith travels slowly – thus we hear the music shifted downwards in scale towards basso profondo . . .'

We laughed scornfully.

'Already you have built an orrery – and Our world has shifted away from its proper position. Would you compound your misdemeanour? Would you have Us play double or quits? Nay, Fulque Darien. Besides, Our mirror network does not yet extend quite so far.'

A fact, which he was obliged to acknowledge with a blush – at his oversight.

'Abandon Our city, and flee above the treeline? Are We a slave, Darien? Let gongs drown the moan! Let firecrackers explode! Let the holy whores dance, their labia clanging, till they drop!'

Alas, We little guessed how close Our doom was – by which We refer to all of our dooms.

Only a few days passed – days of intensifying, grinding vibration, and of crazy drunken carnival and orgy – before the mirrors on Mount Sinister blinked.

The message from the Silver Emperor was brief indeed.

Beware! Monstrous –

That was all. Yet on their own initiative Our slaves up on the ridge-peak added more – describing the deafening obliteration of the Silver Empire which they viewed from a stance of comparative safety.

Even in the heart of Our own Hautarchy we heard the rumble. Tiles fell from roofs, and windows shattered.

High beyond Mount Sinister we spied the sky-monolith pass by – ghostly, and not of this world – heading around the sacred spiral through khanates and kingdoms.

We wait, in the deepest dungeon, in the lowest oubliette beneath Our palace reached by several hundred spiralling stone stairs.

We – Ourself – and Darien, whom We had already consigned to this depth as a penance, and Sister Espirilla whom We summoned in haste before the ultimate hour, and some guards with panniers of black bread, smoked fish, and wine and water, and picks and shovels.

Blood drips from Our drum-cracked ears, but We feel the approach of the monolith vibrating in Our bones and in the damp stones of the oubliette; and We gesture by the light of a single alcoholamp with incoherent signs.

What We are trying to convey to Espirilla is a terrible realisation. If Our valley was scoured in the distant past, and if thus its people were exterminated – an event recorded only by witnesses up there on the ridge-peak, persons who must have been specially bred to inhabit the top of Mount Sinister by order of a former ruler of genius with motives identical to mine – and if those witnesses then descended, hungry and barbaric, to repopulate Our valley . . . why then, We Ourself must be a distant descendant of *slaves*!

Is Our oubliette deep enough?

Will the monolith scrape Our palace away so that We can escape upward afterwards?

If so, We can restore life *nobly* to Our devastated Hautarchy.

We – by whom We mean Ourself and Sister Espirilla.

Ah, yet some watercows and razor-horned apes and other beasts large and little must have survived the previous passage by the monolith. Irregularities in our Valley – nooks and caves – must give random shelter to creatures, who will flee instinctively.

If beasts, why not people too? Some people must survive . . .

Yet beasts are instinctive, not rational beings. Rational beings such as men and women can be driven mad by something titanic and terrible. All human survivors may well become insane save for the slaves on Mount Sinister.

Save for ourselves here in the oubliette.

I fear that Darien is going insane. He holds his head, and his single eye bulges. He gasps, and Espirilla genuflects to him sinuously with reverence – as if My savant is in the throes of a revelation, receiving a message directly into his mind from the Spiral Spirit itself.

Darien tugs a writing stylus from his tunic and dips it in his ear, in that inkhorn of welling blood.

On his palm he writes: *Our Kosmos is a Joke Box.*

He stares at his open hand, as bewildered as Ourselves by this cryptic oracle.

May the Spiral Spirit aid Us. Even in extremis, with blood leaking from their ruptured ears, Our guards are eyeing tattooed Espirilla thoughtfully, each perhaps dreaming of founding a dynasty.

Black Day at Bad Rock
Christopher Fowler

'I'd honestly assumed that they'd stopped pressing singles years ago,' Fowler wrote to us, when we asked him to contribute to In Dreams. 'I don't ever remember buying one, even as a kid. Far from being subversive, I'd always considered singles to be a mass-market pocket of the music world designed mainly for bands to mime to on Top of the Pops. So my immediate reaction was to make an apology and a polite refusal. Then I thought about the "deliberately wide frame" and remembered something that happened to me, a bad memory I've blocked for years. I'm writing it out now as weirdness-therapy.'

Christopher Fowler is a movie publicist who has overcome the rejection of his first proposed poster line (for the reissue of My Fair Lady, he wanted the ads to read 'The rain in Spain falls mainly on the plain . . . again!') to work on campaigns for projects as diverse as the Bond series and Peter Greenaway movies, his favourite strapline being 'Kiss Your Nerves Goodbye' for Evil Dead 2. Like F. Paul Wilson, Fowler has chosen to contribute a piece of fictionalised autobiography. We think it is every bit as bizarre and magical as his short stories, collected in City Jitters and The Bureau of Lost Souls, and his Edgar Wallace meets M. R. James in the nineties London novels, Roofworld and Rune. He claims that this is his first fiction which isn't horror, but considering its deeply authentic evocation of schoolkid angst in the early seventies, we're inclined to disagree.

I have this irrational desire to kill Mick Jagger. I've never told anyone about this until now. To explain why, I have to relate a story. Most of it is true, but one part isn't. Just for protection, you understand. You can figure it out for yourself.

At every school there's always one kid everyone hates and shuns. I was that kid. Obviously I hadn't intended to be. It had just worked out that way. It didn't help that I was stick thin and wore glasses with sellotaped arms and hung out in the library when I should have been caving in heads on the rugby pitch. Pens leaked in my shirt pockets. I was born unfashionable, from scuffed Oxford toecaps to short-back-and-sides. I still owned and wore a clean cap. I was a classic hopeless case. Worst of all, I knew it.

The sporty set had a low tolerance level for kids like us. A boy called Yates in the year below me announced that rugby was for thickos and got hit in the face with a cricket bat. It knocked his nosebone right back into his skull.

This school was a posh school near posh Blackheath, the only posh bit of shit-ugly South London. I lived miles away, in chip-paper-strewn Abbey Wood, gateway to teen delinquency. The neighbourhood kids were neurotic, doped-up, walking scar tissue, groomed for early failure. Hanging out with them wasn't an available option. My mother, a study in thwarted gentility, faded, thrifty, lower-middle-class, never expected much from life and certainly didn't get it, but she expected more of me. My dad was the Invisible Man. He left all the major decisions to his wife, preferring to devote the whole of his adult life to revarnishing the door frames, a job he had still not finished when I last went home. I got to the posh school because I got good exam marks. Most of the other kids were paid for by their parents.

School was a train journey to a different planet. Blackheath was full of dark antique shops and damp tearooms, and liked to call itself a village. Ideally, the shopkeepers would have built a moat around the place to keep out the trash.

The time frame may slide a little here, but I think this happened at some point in the very early seventies, when the 'village' was still full of crimson painted boutiques selling lime green miniskirts and military tunics. Trends weren't so obviously motivated by marketing then. They seemed to evolve in a happy coincidence of mood and style. *Bonnie and Clyde* had been playing on and off at the local fleapit since 1968, and much to the horror of our elders everyone at school imitated the doomed gangsters as closely as possible. Me and Brian 'Third Degree' Burns, the kid I sat next to for eight years without running out of things to talk about, went up West and stole two guns from Bermans & Nathans theatrical costumiers with a forged letter purporting to be from the Dramatics master. The guns were fake, but were cast in metal and came in real leather holsters, like Steve McQueen's in *Bullitt*, which was good enough for us.

The music around this time was mostly terrible. Of course, now everyone thinks it's great. But it really wasn't. Marc Bolan wanking on about fairies and stardust, Groundhogs and Iron Butterfly sounding like somebody masturbating in a roomful of dustbin lids, Jethro Tull hopping about on one leg playing a flute for Christ's sake. About the only bands I could bear to listen to were Mott the Hoople and – the great white god Jimmy Page – Led Zeppelin. 'Whole Lotta Love' received some major suburban bedroom turntable time. It was an antidote to the local disco, where everyone sat at the corners of the room nodding their heads and grooving along with little spastic gestures of their hands. The girls wore floor-length crushed velvet maroon dresses and had long kinked hair, pre-Raphaelite virgins on cider and joints. The generally accepted idea of a good time was getting very, very stoned while carefully listening to the screaming bit from

Pink Floyd's 'Careful with That Axe, Eugene'. The sixties had finished swinging and the seventies hadn't started doing anything. My formative years. If my parents had only waited a while before having kids I could at least have been a punk.

I did have a few friends, but they were all like me, shunned and/or regularly duffed up. The other kids had a collective noun to describe us. Weeds. We were the school Weeds. Do you have *any idea* how humiliating that was?

We mostly spent our spare time dodging our classmates, revising Latin, sneaking into double-billed X movies like *Dracula, Prince of Darkness* and *Plague of the Zombies*, and reading Ian Fleming novels. Everyone was talking about Bond having his balls tortured in *Casino Royale* I think it was, and Jane Fonda's see-through clothes in *Barbarella*. Also, there was this Swedish movie called *Seventeen* which had female pubic hair in, but some of us thought that was going a bit too far. Nobody in my class ever got to speak to an actual live girl because it was an all-boys school where strapping chaps played lots of healthy contact sports in shorts. (I found out much later that those contact sports involving our revered head boy and the gym master extended to the shower room after games. Years later I heard they were running an antique shop together. A fucking *antique* shop. I'm not making this part up.)

Homework was four hours a night minimum, caps were to be worn in the 'village' on penalty of death and the boys from the nearby comprehensive, whose parents voted Labour and were therefore common, used to pick fights with us every night at the bus stop. The one time we had a chance to meet girls was when our sister school teamed up for the annual joint operatic production, and obviously only dogs and germs signed up for six weeks of vocal strangulation in the company of *Die Verkaufte Braute*.

For the weaker members of the pack it's always a strange,

cocooned existence on the sidelines of the action. We enviously watched the other kids as they honed their social skills, getting their hands into drunk girls' shirts while they danced to 'Ride a White Swan'. We weren't like them. We were still making Aurora model kits of mummies and werewolves. None of us were rebels. The school had a good name. The head and his teachers, tall and stiff and imperious in their black gowns, stalking the corridors like adrenalised vampires, were grudgingly respected because they kept their distance and occasionally maimed their pupils. We'd seen the movie *If*, in which Malcolm McDowell machine-gunned his teachers, and it just wasn't us. We spent our time discussing *The Avengers*, *Monty Python* and the lyrics to the songs in *Easy Rider*.

One day, all this changed.

Mike Branch, the relief art teacher, arrived. He was about thirty years younger than any other member of staff, and came for the summer. Of course, everyone instantly liked him. He was handsome and funny and mad-looking. He let you smoke in the kiln room. His hair was over his collar. And *he wore jeans*. To schoolboys who were expected to wear regulation underpants, this was nothing short of frankly amazing. He asked us to call him Mike, and explained that as long as he was around, classes would be very different from what we were used to.

The first time I saw him, he was lounging with his brown suede boots on the desktop and reaching a long arm up to the blackboard to wipe the masters of the Florentine Renaissance away with his sleeve.

'I want you to forget the heavy stuff for a while,' he casually explained. 'We'll be concentrating on the Dadaist movement.' Then he wrote 'Rebellion in Art' across the board in red and threw the heavy chalk block clean through a closed window. There was a crack of shattering glass and we all came to attention, filled with borderline-homoerotic admiration.

'Don't misunderstand me,' said Branch, sliding his legs from the desk and rising. 'We'll be working hard. But we'll be taking a new approach.' And with that he revealed the school record player – a big old wooden thing, never known to have been removed from the office of the headmaster – plugged it in, and began to acquaint us with his personal taste in rock.

Suddenly Art became the hot class to take. Branch's periods were unpredictable and (something unheard of in our school) actually interesting. We created Anti-Meat art and Self-Destruct art and Death-to-the-Ruling-Class art. The other teachers tolerated our displays because technically speaking they weren't very good, which made them less of a threat. Besides, as pupils we were Showing An Interest, thus achieving a prime educational directive. The fact that we would have donated our kidneys for vivisection if Mike had asked us hadn't passed unnoticed, either. The other teachers realised that they could learn something from watching the art class.

One day, Branch placed a single on the turntable and played it. I was fist deep in a gore-sprayed papier-mâché duck when 'Paint It Black' by the Rolling Stones came on. I'd never really liked the song. It already sounded dated when it was first released. Too dirge-like. It reminded me of 'House of the Rising Sun'. But Mike had a special reason for playing it.

'For the climax of our season of Anti-Art,' he said, strolling between my paint-spattered classmates, 'you are going to Paint It Black.'

'What do you mean?' I asked. He turned to look at me. He had these deep-set blue eyes that settled on you like searchlights, looking for truth.

'A day of artistic anarchy. The idea is to take all of the work you produce this summer and paint it matt black. Then you're going to glue it all together, along with anything else that looks suitable, stick the record player in the centre, and stand it in the middle of the quadrangle.'

It seemed a bit stupid, but nobody argued.

'What if someone tells us to take it down, sir?' asked the pudding-basin-haircutted Paul Doggart, fellow Weed, a boy who was born to say *sir* a lot in his life.

'You don't take it down. You don't obey anyone's orders until the stroke of noon. Then I'll appear and we'll play "Paint It Black" from the centre of the sculpture. The art will last for the duration of the song, and then we'll destroy it.'

'But won't we get into trouble, sir?' pressed Doggart.

'No, because I'll forewarn the other masters. They'll be turned on to expect some unspecified action of guerilla art.' (Yes, embarrassing as it may seem, people really spoke like this in the early seventies.)

So, preparations were made, the date was set for the last day of term (the third Tuesday in June) and we painted everything we could lay our hands on and added it to the pile. Clocks. Chairs. Tyres. Lampshades. Toys. Clothes. Tailor's dummies. Car exhausts. A washing machine. And all the time, the damned song played until it wore out and had to be replaced with a new copy.

Mike Branch strolled around the artroom, shifting from table to table, stopping to watch as Ashley Turpin, a fat kid with almost *geological* facial acne attempted to get black paint to stick to a brass candelabrum. The master nodded his head thoughtfully, running his thumb beneath his chin as he considered the sheer anarchy of his loyal pupil's work. Finally, with lowered eyebrows and a crooked smile, he turned his attention to the boy. 'Extremely groovy, Turpin,' he said. Turpin, who had previously shown no promise in any area of scholastic endeavour beyond 'O' Level Body Odour, was pitifully grateful.

Identified to other classes by our laminated badges (black, circular, blank – oh, the *nihilism*) we suddenly found ourselves behaving like some kind of creative élite. Me and the other despised and shunned creeps had finally found our cause. For the first time ever we were part of a team, and the fact that the Sport Kings all hated us worked in favour of our anarchistic behaviour.

We began to be *bad*. I mean bad as in modern bad, good bad. By the week before end of term, we were discovering the non-artistic applications of 'Paint It Black'. Minor league anarchy. Having pizzas with disgusting toppings delivered to masters COD. Gluing their wipers to their car windscreens. Brian 'Third Degree' Burns upped the stakes by removing the wheels from the French teacher's moped, painting them black and adding them to the sculpture.

Then someone found a masters' home address list. Crank calls to the wives, made from the caretaker's phone by the dining hall. Then obscene calls. Anyone who whined that it was wrong was ditched from the group and returned to the status of a Weed. His badge was ceremoniously taken back. To wimp out on the rebellion was to fail as a human being. The Sport Kings stopped thundering up and down the pitch to cast jealous sidelong glances at the Black Brigade. (Funny thing, we only had one kid in our year who was actually black, Jackson Rabot, and he wasn't interested in anarchy at all. He wanted to be a Conservative MP.)

Of course, the shit soon started coming down on us. Efforts were made to find the culprits. There were extra detentions, cancelled privileges. But end of term pranks were to be expected, and up until now we weren't far beyond that.

On Monday, the day before term ended, the day before B-

Day, we stepped up the action and went too far. (You saw this coming, didn't you?) It's blindingly obvious now that some of the group didn't appreciate the subtleties of Mike Branch's orchestrated artistic protest, but had just joined for the party attitude. One of these B-stream holdbacks threw some kind of concentrated acid over the geography master's car. It stank and made an amazing mess, melting clean through the bodywork. Incredible.

News of the attack spread around class like wildfire. Paul Doggart blanched beneath his pudding-basin haircut and threatened to leave the group, but didn't because there was nowhere else to go, and even Brian 'Third Degree' Burns was impressed. Nobody dared own up. We were given until noon the next day to produce a culprit, or the whole brigade would be kept back while everyone else left for the summer. But by now there was an All or Nothing atmosphere in the group, and we stayed solid. When the head took his record player back, someone brought in their own hi-fi system. The damned song played on.

There was never much studying done on the last day of term. Leisure activities were tolerated. We were allowed to bring in – wait for it – *board games*. I shit you not. And we could wear casual clothes, so everyone made an effort to look hip. Recently I found an old photograph of us Weeds together, taken on that final morning. You'd think we'd been dressed by blind people. Poor old Doggart.

Mike had arranged a double art period for his brigade of rebels. All of the black-painted stuff was arranged in chunks around the room. The record was playing as high as the volume would allow, the sound completely distorted. The artroom was christened The Rock Shop. (I know it's embarrassing now but at the time you'd narrow your eyes and go, 'Hey, if anyone wants me I'm at The Rock for a Study Period, okay?' – *highly* cool.) It was in a separate annexe of its own, and inside it seventeen maladjusted kids were free to do whatever they liked.

The party really started when Yates Junior brought in his mother's hidden supply of mixed spirits (the woman must have been an incredible lush, there was about six litres of the stuff). There were joints, courtesy of Simon Knight's brother, who was possibly the most corrupt customs officer in Britain, which is really saying something, and there was acid, although I didn't have any. Everyone went into the kiln room to smoke (force of habit) and soon you could get high just by opening the door, walking in and breathing.

Everyone knew that the gym teacher was a queer because he brought this skinny hairless dog to school. A Mexican thing, big eyes, ugly little teeth. He never watched us in the showers or anything (the teacher, not the dog) because he was too scared of losing his job, but he had this stupid mutt. *Had* being the key word, because Brian 'Third Degree' Burns came up with the great rebellious artistic act of luring it into the kiln room with a piece of bacon. The old art master had always warned us that the inside of the kiln, on full power, was hotter than the surface of Venus, so we decided to test it. A scientific experiment, like sending Laika the alsatian into orbit with no hope of ever getting him back. The idea was to dip the dog in slip clay and bake it, then paint it black and add it to the sculpture.

The kiln was squat and wide with these thick stone walls, so you couldn't hear the dog whining once the door was shut. After about an hour we unsealed it and found that the only thing left was a small patch of blackened sticks. Doggart started moaning on about cruelty to animals, so we covered one side of his body with glue and pressed him against the artroom wall until his skin stuck.

Then we began to assemble the sculpture. Forming a chain, we passed the sections out into the school quadrangle, a pathetic damp square of grass surrounded by rain-stained concrete walkways. As the sculpture rose above the height of a man, an interested crowd gathered. The gym teacher asked us if we had the authority to do what we were doing and we said yes, so he went away. I figured he hadn't found out about his dog yet.

At a quarter to twelve the sculpture was fifteen feet high and we still had a load of stuff to add. Table legs, television sets and dolls' arms poked out from the twisted black heap. The record player was wired up, but we were going to be late for our noon deadline, mainly because we were all so ripped that we were repeating each other's tasks. The assistant headmaster, a sickly wraith-like creature who looked as if he hadn't slept since the day Buddy Holly died, asked Simon Knight if he'd been drinking and Simon said no, which was true, although he had dropped acid. Behind his reasonable, innocent exterior he was tripping off his face. Of course, back then the teachers didn't really know what to look for.

The big moment arrived and we were still building the sculpture. Most of the school had turned out to watch. Everyone knew that something special was about to happen. The event had been whispered about for weeks. There were all kinds of rumours flying around – most of them far more imaginative than what was actually planned. Even the Sport Kings were here. Then the headmaster appeared to see what all the fuss was about. He stood at the front of the crowd with his bony arms folded behind his back like the Duke of Edinburgh, a look of thin tolerance on his face, tapering towards displeasure.

This was our brief flicker of fame. All eyes were on us. We were the kings. The *bollocks du chien*. The members of the brigade stood back while Brian climbed into the sculpture and started the record player. The opening guitar riff heralded

Mick Jagger's voice, a voice which always sounded as if he was leaning obscenely into the microphone mouthing distilled insolence. We looked around for Mike. Our Mike, the leader of the Black. No sign. Then we noticed the headmaster.

His displeasure had changed to – well, not pleasure but something approximating it. 'If you're looking for Mr Branch,' he said in a clear Scottish Presbyterian voice that rang across the square, 'you will not find him here. He left the school last night with no intention whatsoever of returning today.' He pronounced the 'h' in 'whatsoever'.

The headmaster triumphantly turned on his heel and led the other teachers back to the common room. And the record stuck. It stuck on the word *black*. The repeated syllable taunted, and the derision began. The Sport Kings just drifted away, snorting to each other, too bored even to beat us up. Suddenly we were Weeds again. It was as if the natural order had been restored, as if everyone had been returned to their correct status, with us back at the bottom, and the holidays could now begin.

'No intention whatsoever.' It was the 'whatsoever' that hurt, as if he'd been ready to bottle out all along. The last of the Sport Kings were hanging back by the bike sheds watching us, evidently planning to crack a few Weed heads after all. We didn't care about them. We were too choked even to talk.

Brian ripped the plug from the record player, snatched off the record and returned to the artroom close to tears. He tipped over a table and threw a chair across the room, then so did a couple of the others, and suddenly we were smashing up everything in sight. I guess none of us had expected to be betrayed at such an early point in our lives. Perhaps if we could have had sex right then, nothing more would have happened. But we hardly knew any girls, so we had to make do with violence.

Paul Doggart was still stuck to the wall. We'd forgotten all about him. He started making a fuss about wanting to leave, but he couldn't get out of his clothes. His blazer and trousers were cemented fast to the white-painted concrete. So was his fat left cheek. His bellyaching went against the general flow of energy so we spray-painted him black with the leftovers in the cans, hoping that it would shut him up. Of course this had the reverse effect, so someone (to this day I don't know who) finally obliged by putting a foot against the wall and tearing him free.

Doggart came away, but not quietly and not in one piece. His cheek left a grisly triangle of flesh stuck to the concrete.

The last time I saw him he was stumbling between the tables clutching his face, crying in hoarse angry sobs. By the time we had finished in the artroom, paint was dripping from the walls and there was broken glass everywhere. We knew someone must have heard the noise by now and didn't dare open the door, so we went out through the windows.

Our adrenaline was really pumping. Using the knives from the artroom we slit every tyre in the car park as we left. I cut the fingers of my right hand to the bone at the second joint because I was gripping my knife so hard.

That night most of us met up and went to see *Woodstock*, but by this time all those twangly Country Joe and the Fish peace songs could only leave us cold. A bridge had been crossed. An unspoken bond had been forged between us.

It's funny how moments can change lives.

Doggart nearly died. The black paint infected his wound and the damage to his face became a whole lot worse. He had a load of skin grafts over the next seven years. And his mind got all screwed up. Nothing he said ever again made much sense. I think his old mum tried to sue someone, but was forced through ill-health and lack of funds to give up the case.

I visited him in hospital once. I remember walking along a wax-tiled corridor, shoes squeaking, pushing open the door at the end. He was lying in a darkened room, unfriendly eyes staring accusingly from a mess of taut, shiny skin. I sat by his bed for a few minutes but there was nothing much to say. As I made to leave, his right hand grabbed my wrist. I suppose he was trying to thank me for coming to visit him. I gave him a Get Well Soon card from the members of the B-Brigade. A fold of plain paper, blank shiny blackness. So hip.

Most of the brigade was expelled, of course, but the school took no further action. They had too many paying parents to risk getting a bad name. As I said, it was a posh school. Most of the Old Boys were masons. Money changed hands; word never got out. With the time I had spare I attended art college. Cue further tears from Mother.

Years later, someone heard what had happened to Mike Branch. It turned out that he never was an art teacher, relief or otherwise. He'd played in a band once, opening for the Stones. That was his sole claim to fame. He'd walked into our school with credentials that no one had bothered to check. Then, the day before our big event he'd simply walked away again, gone to the North to do something else. Somebody told me he's in property sales now. That sounds about right.

Still, I wonder if he had the remotest notion of the effect he had on us. He changed the lives of seventeen boys. Thinking about it now, I find it incredible that we trusted someone who regularly wore a turtleneck sweater and gold medallion beneath a brown patch-suede jacket, but there you go. I owned a mauve two-tone shirt with huge rounded collars that fastened with Velcro, a fashion crime I compounded with the addition of yellow hipster bellbottoms.

Personally speaking, I blame Mick Jagger.

Riders on the Storm
Mark Timlin

For every 'Summer Holiday' there's an 'Ebony Eyes': for every 'Be-Bop-a-Lula', a 'Teen Angel'. Since Johnny Ace became the first rock'n'roll corpse in 1954 (see 'The Shiny Surface', page 245), death has been as much a part of the rock'n'roll industry as sex and drugs — so much so that dead rock stars often outsell the living. And death on the roads, where Mark Timlin's slipstream horror story takes us, is an integral part of the rock'n'roll canon, as Eddie Cochran, Marc Bolan and Duane Allman demonstrated in life, and 'Terry', 'Leader of the Pack' and 'Deadman's Curve' showed on vinyl.

Mark Timlin lives in South London, where he locates his successful crime novels featuring private eye Nick Sharman. He used to tour-manage rock bands, so he knows all about the strange things that can happen on motorways. 'This story,' he writes, 'is dedicated to the memory of Hazel Griffith, who rode the storm, but the storm proved too strong.'

I drove the BMW west through Chelsea, Hammersmith and Chiswick towards the flyover. A sticky Friday in July, six thirty in the evening. A stupid time to leave town, but I'd got hung up at the office. Everybody in a panic because the wife of the bass player in the band I co-managed was having their mansion refitted and decorated while he was away at a detox clinic and the plumbers had screwed up the water system. I ask you. Half a dozen otherwise sane people running around like chickens with their heads cut off so that some silly bitch could have a hot shower. I mean who cares?

So the early exit for the weekend and a pleasant drive down to my cottage had gone out of the window. Still I suppose that the silly bitch's old man had paid for a lot of it, so I kept a straight face and got an emergency team in with promises of boiling water by suppertime.

It's hard to credit. It's more like being a nursemaid than a band manager. But that's showbiz.

I finally made my escape about five forty-five, and it took me forty-five minutes to get to the start of the M4.

The traffic heading west was horrendous and it was going to rain. A solid bank of cloud the colour of a week-old bruise was heading west too. It overtook me as I sat in the stalled traffic, then pulled ahead and ate up the blue of the sky in front of me. The cool wind that pushed it picked up pieces of litter and dust devils from the pavement and tossed them through the high-rise canyon that overlooked the road. The flyover was a solid jam of traffic. Two lanes of metal, glass and rubber lined up bumper to bumper as far as I could see. On my left the traffic on the slip road to the A4 was moving, so I indicated and pulled over into a break in the flow.

The car dropped down from the flyover just as the sun finally vanished behind the lip of the cloud, and it struck one last time through the windscreen, almost blinding me with its brilliance. That was when I saw her. Standing by the side of the road at the bottom of the ramp. It was almost as if I knew she'd be there waiting. She had long blonde hair that the wind caught and tossed around her face until she brushed it away with one hand. She was wearing a simple white dress that stopped just above her knees. Her legs were long and bare and beautiful. On her feet she wore a pair of white sandals. Between her feet was a big canvas bag that looked heavy. As the sun died, it bathed her in a yellow glow for a single moment. It lit her up and then vanished as if a switch had been turned off, and the rain started. I snapped on the windscreen wipers and pulled over to the kerb beside her. Behind me a horn sounded, but I ignored it. I ran down the electric window on the passenger side. She ducked down and looked through the gap.

'Want a lift?' I asked.

'Please.'

'Hop in then.' I leant over and slipped the catch on the door handle. She opened the door and threw her bag into the well in front of the passenger seat, climbed in and sat down, showing a lot of sun-tanned thigh as she did so.

'Thanks,' she said, pushing her damp hair off her face. In the close atmosphere of the car she smelled of patchouli oil and sweat and something else. Something I couldn't define, but I knew. Like a memory of something ancient and basic and earthy.

'No trouble. Where are you going?' I asked.

'Oh, anywhere will do.'

'You must be going somewhere.'

'Nowhere in particular. Just drive. I'll tell you when to stop.'

'Okay,' I said, indicated right and pulled back into the stream of traffic.

The rain was coming down hard and heavy by then, and I switched the wipers to double speed. The visibility was getting worse by the second. It was like driving in an iron tunnel and I switched on dipped headlights. Through the windscreen I saw brake lights blossom ahead like red roses in the rain, and I tapped the brake pedal and the car slowed, and then drifted to a halt in the line of traffic, and I looked over at her.

'Can I smoke?' she asked.

'Sure,' I said.

She reached into her bag and pulled out a packet of untipped Pall Mall kingsize. 'You'll kill yourself with those,' I said.

'Nobody's going to live for ever.'

'Thats true.'

She offered me the packet. I shook my head, and then changed my mind and took one. I pushed in the cigarette lighter on the dashboard. When it popped out again I lit first her cigarette and then mine. The smoke was rough and harsh and I wished I hadn't bothered. But by the third lungful I was used to it. It was dark and intimate in the car, and quiet except for the rain and the urgent sound of the wipers on the screen. 'Can we have some music?' she asked.

'Of course,' I said.

She pushed the power button on the Blaupunkt and selected the AM band. She fiddled with the station search button. As she cascaded, the digital readout punched up the transmission frequencies in red on the front of the set. Finally she locked on to a station. The number 666 was illuminated in tiny red numbers. In the grey light from outside the numerals seemed to wink at me evilly. 'Paint It Black' by the Rolling Stones boomed out of the eight speakers dotted around the car. She lowered the volume and said, 'That's the one.'

The rain beat down harder and bounced off the bonnet in front of me as the record played, and lightning flashed ahead. I mentally counted and reached to five before the thunder crashed above the sound of the music. 'I'm glad I stopped,' I said. 'You'd've got soaked if I hadn't.'

'Someone had to,' she said.

Looking the way she looked, I supposed she was right.

'What's your name?' she asked.

'Roy. What's yours?'

'Claudette.'

'Hi, Claudette.'

'Hi, Roy.'

She opened the glove compartment, then looked at me guiltily. 'Sorry,' she said. 'I'm nosey.'

'Be my guest,' I replied.

She pulled out an 'Access All Areas' laminate from our last tour. 'You know these guys?'

'I manage them,' I said.

'Hey, they're good. You really manage them, or are you kidding me?'

'No kidding,' I said. 'I manage them with about four other people, and a firm of accountants and another of lawyers, and a merchant bank.'

'So you're not the man with the big cigar?'

'No,' I said. 'I got hired when they needed a good tour manager and sort of got adopted.'

'Sounds okay.'

'It beats working,' I said.

The record finished and the DJ came on. He had a mid-Atlantic accent. 'That was "Paint It Black" by the Stones,' he said. 'From your tower of power, Six Six Six on the medium wave, and now straight into "Endless Sleep" by Jody Reynolds from nineteen fifty-eight.' And the needle caught the groove with a hiss and the song started.

'You're really going nowhere?' I asked.

'Nowhere at all. I just like to travel.'

'Where do you live?'

'Where I sleep.'

I looked over at her again and caught the smell of patchouli and sweat, and that something else again. Something familiar, yet not. 'Listen, I've got a cottage the other side of Reading,' I said. 'It's a pretty place. Quiet and out of the way. I'm all alone this weekend. I've got enough food to feed an army. Do you want to stop by? Have a meal. You can stay if you want. There's plenty of room. If you're not doing anything else. No strings. Go when you want. I'll drop you off at Reading station, or anywhere you like.'

I could feel her looking at me. 'Sounds good,' she said. 'Got any dope?'

'No,' I said. 'I never carry any.'

'Well I've got a little.' She thought for a moment. 'Yeah. I'd like that, Roy. I'll cook dinner for my keep.'

'There's no need,' I said.

'No, I like to cook. It'll make a change.'

'Sure,' I said, and laughed, and she joined in, and the radio played on, and the traffic started to move. Slowly at first and then faster and the song finished and the DJ came on and played 'A Young Man Is Gone' by the Beach Boys. The road cleared and I picked up speed and we rejoined the motorway at junction three. As we pulled into the traffic the Beach Boys finished and 'Riders on the Storm' by the Doors came on. Claudette leaned over and turned up the volume, and the sound of the rain and thunder on the record beat a counterpoint to the rain and thunder outside the car. 'This is my favourite record of all time,' she said. 'I love the Doors. I think Jim Morrison is real dishy. Isn't it weird. That's us. Riders on the storm. It's perfect.' And she laughed and lit another cigarette. The bass and piano on the record were hypnotic and I pushed the accelerator down and as the BMW picked up speed I moved to the outside lane.

'That's for all you people on the motorway this rainy evening,' said the DJ as the record finished. 'But you travellers beware. Strange things are happening out there tonight. And that's for real. So take it easy, kids, or you may never finish your journey.' And he laughed, and the sound of the laughter sent a shiver up my spine.

'What station is this?' I asked. 'I've never heard it before.'

Out of the corner of my eye I saw Claudette smile. 'I don't

know,' she said. 'I usually pick it up when I'm travelling. I like it. Don't you?'

'Yes,' I said, although I wasn't absolutely sure that I did.

'Now for "Richard Cory" by Them, the last Decca single by the band, and afterwards a Bang side by Van the Man himself. "T. B. Sheets",' said the DJ.

'Happy soul,' I said.

'Cool,' said Claudette. 'Coolest sounds around.'

'If you say so,' I replied and pushed on through the storm.

We got to the cottage around seven thirty. Although it was midsummer, the clouds were so low and black it was quite dark even that early and we hardly saw another car or person after we left the motorway.

I opened up the front door and put on the lights and showed Claudette the bathroom and spare bedroom. The evening had become cooler with the rain, and the cottage felt damp and chilly. I lit the fire in the living room and piled it up with logs. Then I went out and unloaded the car and put the food I'd brought with me away, and my stuff in the master bedroom. I locked up the BMW and went looking for her. She was in the living room and had put on the big Pioneer tuner and found her favourite radio station again. As I went in the same DJ was saying, 'This one's for you bikers out there. And I know you're listening. I'm going to play my favourite motorcycle songs back to back. "Leader of the Pack" by the Shangri-Las, and "Terry" by Twinkle. Take it easy tonight, you angels, and remember always wear a helmet or you might end up dead on the highway, just like the guys in the songs.'

'This guy's obsessed with death,' I said. 'Doesn't he ever play records about anything else?'

'No,' said Claudette. 'But I like it. Don't you?'

I didn't answer. 'Do you want a drink?' I asked.

'Please.'

'What?'

'What have you got?'

'Pretty much everything.'

'Scotch and Coke with lots of ice,' she said.

'No problem,' I said, and went back to the kitchen and made her drink, and a vodka and grapefruit for myself.

I took the glasses into the living room and went and sat on the big armchair by the fireplace. 'This is good,' I said. 'It makes a change for me to have company down here.'

'I bet,' she said.

'I mean it.'

'I'm glad to be of service. So what's for dinner?'

'Are you sure you still want to cook?' I asked.

'Of course.'

'Then you choose.'

'Got any steak?'

'Yes. Two T-Bones in the freezer.'

'Potatoes for baking?'

'In the vegetable rack.'

'Side salad?'

'Everything you need in the crisper.'

'Perfect. I'll get started.'

'I'll show you where everything is. Then leave you to it.'

So I did. And made myself another drink and sat and listened to the sounds she made in the kitchen while the radio played 'Ebony Eyes' and 'Tell Laura I Love Her' and 'Teen Angel' and 'Laurie' and 'Johnny Remember Me'. And I dozed in front of the fire, and dreamed a strange dream of a dead disc jockey playing songs of death from a radio station transmitting from hell. I woke up fully when Claudette came into the room and told me dinner would be in ten minutes.

'We'll eat in here, okay?' I said.

'Wherever you want,' she said.

'It smells good,' I said. And it did.

I laid out a cloth and cutlery on the big table by the window and went down into the cellar to fetch some wine. The earth-floored room was cold after the warmth of the fire, and the smell of the rain beating down on the damp earth outside had permeated the place and reminded me of Claudette in some strange way. I whispered a 'hello', but no one answered, and I shivered and picked two bottles of claret from the rack and went back up to the kitchen for glasses. It was hot in there after the cold of the cellar. A welcome heat. Claudette looked very beautiful and vulnerable with a big striped butcher's apron tied around her waist and her fringe damp with perspiration. 'You look great,' I said.

'I'm sweating,' she said. 'I hope the food's worth it.'

'It smells like it is.'

'Who could ruin a steak and potatoes?' she said.

'You'd be surprised.'

'Sit down and you'll find out,' she said. I did as I was told, and opened the wine and poured two glasses as she brought in the food and served it out. It was great. We both ate too much, and she collapsed on to the sofa while I made coffee and opened a bottle of brandy. She rolled a joint and we shared it. The radio played on as we ate, and after, and I watched as she danced in front of the speakers as Fats Domino sang 'Going to the River'.

She came over and sat on the arm of my chair and I smelt her perfume again. But this time that strange, indefinable something was stronger than the patchouli or the sweat as she leaned close to me. I thought about how I'd felt in the cellar and shivered again. Then I shook off the feeling and looked up into her face and we kissed. I pulled her down on to my lap, and her mouth felt hot and cold at the same time on mine, and I ran my hand up the inside of her thighs. She parted her legs and I pushed my hand up to her crotch. She wasn't wearing anything under her dress. 'In front of the fire,' she said. 'Now. I want it now.'

We screwed on the rug and I lost skin from my elbows and knees on the coarse wool, and I felt her heat beneath me and the last of the heat from the burning logs on my back and she cried out as she came, and so did I seconds later. Afterwards we lay together in the dim light from the fire and the radio played on, 'Hello This Is Jodie' and 'Deadman's Curve' and 'Folsom Prison Blues', and I held Claudette's slim body and cradled my head on her tiny pointed breasts.

We spent the night and most of the next day in my bed together. We ate cold food and beer and wine that we brought from the fridge, and finished the dope that she had brought with her.

There was a portable radio on the bedside table and Claudette tuned it to 666, and as we fucked the songs churned out one after another. I lost track of time and place and all that mattered were our bodies and our craving for each other, and the old songs that the radio played one after another. Songs of death and madness. Scratchy old 45s full of sadness and heartbreak, until I could hardly bear it any more. But the worse they made me feel, the better Claudette enjoyed them. She lay in bed with me alternately screwing and smoking joints.

'You're looking wasted,' she said some time on Saturday afternoon, I don't know exactly when. 'Let me get you a drink.' And she got out of bed. She was naked and her body, that had seemed so attractive the previous night, looked old and bruised and used, like she'd aged twenty years in as many hours. She left the room and I looked at the ceiling. She came back with two glasses. She handed one to me. 'Vodka and orange,' she said. I finished half the glass in one gulp. 'You want to fuck some more?' she asked.

'No,' I replied.

'You're getting old, Roy,' she said. 'Old and cold.'

I looked up at her standing naked in front of me and all at once I hated her, like I've never hated anyone before or since. 'Don't say that,' I said.

'It's only the truth. Old and cold and past it.'

And on the radio the DJ introduced 'Last Kiss' by J. Frank Wilson and the Cavaliers.

And then it happened again, like it always happens. She started to age in front of my eyes, twenty more years, forty more, turned into a corpse as I watched. A grinning graveyard ghoul that cavorted in front of me in an obscene dance to the music from the radio. Her flesh pustulated and burst with maggots that heaved and boiled on her wrinkled skin, then turned into bluebottles, and flew into my face with a whirring of transparent wings until I was frightened that they would fly into my mouth and nose and suffocate me. And the smell. The smell of decay filled the room until I retched. But she was not dead. She still spoke. Talking with a voice that rattled in the wreckage of her throat and echoed in my ears. 'Come and fuck me, dear,' she said. 'Come and fuck me and we'll be joined for ever.'

I covered my ears with my hands but I could still hear that voice inside my head, just like all the other times. 'No,' I said. 'No, leave me alone. Give me some peace.'

'The only peace you'll ever know is with me, Roy,' she replied. 'Haven't you learnt that lesson by now?' And she smiled, and when she did, her teeth fell out of her rotten gums and dropped on to the carpet and lay there like black beetles. When I saw that, I couldn't stand it any more. She was next to the dressing table. On top were the plates that we'd eaten off, and the bread knife we'd used on the French loaf. In the yellow light that oozed through the window, its blade shone at me invitingly. I rolled off the bed and walked over and picked it up. It felt solid and heavy in my hand. Claudette looked at me and shook her head and cackled through that toothless grin. 'You wouldn't dare,' she said. 'You won't even fuck me.'

I walked over towards her and thrust the knife deep into her throat and up through the back of her neck. It went in cleanly and easily through the decayed flesh, and I heard her spine snap when the metal touched bone. 'That's better than any fuck you've ever had,' I said. But she was dead by then, and didn't answer. Just collapsed on to the bed and lay still.

I left the knife sticking out of her throat and stood back and the record finished and the DJ said, 'And now I've got a message for Roy and Claudette down there in Beech Hill. A little bird told me you two are in love, and your song is "Riders on the Storm" by the Doors. So just for you, in your little love-nest in the country, here it is. Now don't do anything I wouldn't do, my dears. But then that's not much.' And I heard the needle catch in the groove and the sound of rain came through the speaker, and I smashed the little radio off the table and the record was cut off before the music started, and I collapsed on to the carpet beside the bed.

How long I stayed there I don't know. But the room grew dark as night fell, and thankfully the darkness hid Claudette's body. I don't know if I passed out, or slept, or what happened. But the next thing I knew was that the room began to get light.

I prayed that I'd dreamt the whole thing, but when I looked towards the bed she was lying on it with the bread knife sticking through her neck. Her head was at a crazy angle, and the sheets and duvet and mattress were soaked with blood. All signs of the sores and flies and ageing were gone. Perhaps I'd imagined it. She looked beautiful.

I left her there dead, and went downstairs. The tuner in the living room was still locked on to 666 metres. Her station. And something was wrong. They were still playing 'Riders on the Storm', but the needle was stuck in the groove. The title of the song kept repeating over and over again until my head pounded with it. I wanted to smash the damn thing into pieces to shut it up. But I was cool. I simply walked over and killed the power button. Even so, I could still hear the line repeating as I went into the kitchen and got a glass of water.

I went back upstairs and wrapped her body in the sheet that was stiff with dried blood and semen, and carried her down to the cellar and buried her there in the soft black earth next to the others. Then I burnt the mattress and the duvet and her clothes and bag in the back garden and cleaned the house from top to bottom. Even places she couldn't possibly have been. When I found myself cleaning the kitchen floor for the third time it was Sunday night, and I was shaking with fatigue and hunger. I couldn't bear to eat there, so I threw my stuff in the car, locked up and drove up to the services on the motorway. When I queued for the food I felt so hungry that I got the counter man to pile up the plate with eggs, bacon, baked beans, tomatoes, mushrooms, fried potatoes and toast. I bought two pots of tea to go with it. But as soon as I tasted the food I felt sick and pushed it away and left. I sat in the leather driver's seat of the BMW and lit a cigarette. Without thinking I turned on the radio which was still tuned into the same infernal radio station, and the same damn line was still repeating itself. It was driving me crazy. Over and over it went, just as it had back at the cottage. Repeating itself like a mantra. I knew if I heard it again I'd scream. I hit the search button and found another station. Then I turned off the radio and drove back to town.

I didn't go back to the cottage for months. When I did, everything was as I'd left it. I went down into the cellar and no one would ever have guessed what was buried there. During those months I read the papers avidly but there was no mention of Claudette or her disappearance.

It was strange the way they never mentioned it.

Eventually I began to relax and once I even tuned the car radio to 666 metres on the AM band. There was no station transmitting on the frequency. Just dead air, with a mush of white noise and static, and far away, almost undistinguishable, morse code mixed in with the faint hint of music that might not have been music at all.

Eventually I almost believed I'd dreamt the whole thing. Almost, but not quite. You see I'm never sure.

It's been over a year now. Another Friday, another rush hour, another storm. The roads through the inner suburbs are dense with cars. The visibility lessens as the clouds thicken over West London. The temperature drops, and I switch on the heater. I'm listening to LBC and they report an accident on the Chiswick flyover. The traffic slows almost to a standstill on the approach, but the turnoff to the A4 is fairly clear and without thinking I indicate and pull over towards it. As the sun is finally extinguished the radio starts to scan the station frequencies. It switches from FM to AM and the frequencies are lit up in a cascade of red numerals: 194, 247, 285, 330, 558, and finally it stops as I know it will at 666. And I hear it again. The same record stuck in the same groove, just as it was all that time ago.

And as it plays I can feel that old feeling I know so well. As the car drops down the ramp I see her standing by the side of the road again, wearing the same white dress with her hair yellow and wind-tossed in the rain waiting for me to stop and offer her a lift.

Like all the other times she's been there.

And I indicate and pull over just like always.

The Shiny Surface
Don Webb

According to the National Geographic, *the greatest density of writers in the USA is not in New York, Los Angeles, Chicago or San Francisco, but in Austin, Texas, which is where Don Webb, maven of the small press magazines, lives. He has published dozens of stories, some of them collected in* The Seventh Day and After *(Word Craft Speculative Writer Series), as well as a unique collection of intense, metamorphic prose pieces.* Uncle Ovid's Exercise Book *(Illinois State University/Fiction Collective). Records have always meant a lot to him: 'I had a cousin who had a singles player. When I saw him putting a record on that big fat spindle, I had my first realisation of how sex must work – a twentieth century moment.' In 'The Shiny Surface', Don Webb magically realises the notion that if Proust had been born into the latter half of the twentieth century, he wouldn't have needed to bite into a madeleine; he'd simply have put on a record and danced.*

It was something I'd never known, never guessed. It changed everything.

The story begins in three times – in 1870, in 1966, in 1992 – but it's probably a story that everyone partakes of whether they know it or not.

By my forty-third year I had achieved two lifelong dreams. I had married the perfect woman ten years before, and our marriage had grown with each day until we were filled with absolute knowledge and love for the other. Twelve years before I had ploughed all the money I could tap into a rusty dusty junk shop. By hard work and luck I had made it into the finest antique store in the Dallas metroplex. Customers flew in from Chicago and LA to see what I had to sell. Lately people wrote in from Paris and Tokyo. My little shop was reaching around the world. My stock included a nineteenth dynasty scarab from Egypt and a framed Jimmy Carter campaign poster, so it pressed at the boundaries of human time as well.

My assistant Janet Brammer and I were opening a carefully packed selection of American Victoriana from Normal, Illinois. I'd visited Normal once with its beautiful quaint homes and ugly modern university. Houses were cheap there – very cheap by Texas standards – and I fantasised about retiring there in Victorian elegance. I even dreamed up an outfit for her – a special high-collared Victorian dress of red crinoline and black panels appearing to be silk, but in reality on close inspection see-through silk. I can see her in the parlour with her spinning wheel . . .

Reverie ends and we carefully cut into the case. The box of someone's great-grandmother's things: a silver-and-enamel teapot made for Tiffany & Company; a Koloman Moser jewellery box of silver, enamel and semi-precious stones; a pair of brass candle holders enamelled to resemble cobras; a souvenir reproduction of the Eiffel Tower; a Charles Fouquet comb – gold, tortoise-shell and amethysts; a silver-framed daguerreotype of Lincoln; and a small ebony box containing a convex mirror, upon which a folded letter rested, brown with age.

I had never seen a mirror so made: a concave dish, it frankly reminded me of an ashtray. I took it to my office to look through my reference books. Janet cleaned up the trash and prepared to mark the other items. In my office I carefully unfolded the letter.

The Brotherhood of Eulis
26 Boylston Street
Boston, Mass. September 5, 1870

Dear Mrs. C

I am in receipt of your draft for sixty-five dollars. As you know, I was in great financial straits when I agreed to create this mirror for you. You have grown adept in poisim and volantia and should have no trouble maintaining the mirror's magnetism. As per your request I have so constructed the mirror that it may be used by anyone, in order that you may make of it a family heirloom. I feel that you are creating a hateful thing, and had I not given you my word I would smash this instrument to flinders.

My only consolation is that in order to work, the mirror must be washed with pure water derived from melted snow before each usage. Clean the mirror only with such a chemical and a chamois cloth. Then you will be able to divine the heart's desire of those in its presence. I believe that we are often best left in the dark; for we are frail creatures, nourished by our illusions as the delicate flowers are by the dew.

If, Carolyne, you will promise to return the mirror to me unused, I will refund your monies in full. Think what heartbreak this device can bring. For once I urge you not to try.

Y^r Ob't servant,
Dr Paschal B. Randolph

This was pure gold! I'd never had a 'legendary' item before. I would set up a special glass case just to display it. I would have to figure out if I wanted to sell this or set it up as a draw to the shop.

I would have to see if I could dig up any more on this Randolph guy.

That afternoon, Hal dropped by. If Hal had had a classier shop, he'd've been a rival. But he went for sleaze, trash, buzz pop. He had made a discovery. The seven-inch single was dead. He's been to Sound Warehouse.

'We're growing old, Jim,' he said.

'Thank you for that piece of news,' I said. 'It has made my day.'

'But I propose we have a final fling. I'm throwing a party. A dig-it-out-of-your-closet party. A Zenith Cobra-Matic came in the shop yesterday – which is why I'm out looking for singles – and I want people to bring their singles that they've saved – dress in period – I'll supply Tang and smokeables.'

'Tang?'

'Well, I hope we're going to be orbiting.'

With NASA visions dancing through my head, the day passed.

Ordinary business intervened for a while, then one day Janet brought her lunch – some multi-grain bread sandwich and a clear bottle of some healthy water. With idle curiosity I picked up the bottle (bright with my shop's light). One hundred per cent Pure Glacial Water – The World's Purest.

'Glacier water?' I asked.

'I know,' she said, 'it's probably not worth it, but the image seems so good on a polluted day.'

Glacier water.

Snow water.

I could put this with the mirror display.

My research hadn't been as fruitful as I would've liked. It seemed that 'Dr' Randolph was a mulatto philosopher and magician who managed to carve a niche for himself against the grain of a resistant America. He advocated women's rights, the transformation of society through romantic love, and the practice of magic, particularly clairvoyance. He'd written a novel, *Ravalette*, and several books on magic including *Sexual Magic* and *Seership*. His occult society, the Hermetic Order of Eulis, included such notables as Abraham Lincoln, General A. H. Hitchcock, and other movers and shakers of the Civil War North. Those following his sexual teachings (without the benefit of romantic love) included the OTO and the Fraternitas Saturni. His healing techniques sans both romance and sex are practised today in black Chicago evangelical churches. All in all, he seemed to belong to that order of nineteenth-century visionaries possessed of a global and restorative vision. Move over Owen, Michelet, Proudhon and Fourier.

Janet drank about half the bottle. I asked her for the other half and she said yes.

I had other duties, but arriving in my office eventually I wet a chamois with the Canadian water and polished the mirror's bright surface. Janet came in with the mail.

She bent down to hand it to me and when the depths of the mirror should've reflected her features – I saw instead my own. The image lasted only for an instant. She smiled and walked out.

Janet?

I could almost cry. I liked her so well as a friend, but she could no more take Monica's place than fly. I couldn't just play like I loved her back, but I knew things would be creepy for me from now on. I would re-weigh my every word. Am I giving her false hope or being too cruel? All the ease of five years working together was gone.

Assuming – of course – that the mirror worked. That there wasn't some strange ego projection or hallucination involved.

And yet I had something that was actually *magical*, actually fairy tale. It was mine and it worked. I was in contact with and part of the mythic. I knew a secret, a real secret, about the way the world worked.

I would have to test it. I couldn't stand not knowing. Hal's party was in three days.

I didn't own any singles. When I'd bought my shop, I'd sold off all my treasures. The past had always been a thing for sale to me. I'd majored in classics – get this one – because my high school Latin teacher gave me a brochure from the Junior Classical League that said that businessmen dig classics majors. They respect the learning and dedication – and after all they have to train you to do things their way anyway. Predictably I minored in history. Neither of these impressed anyone, but I worked for a museum for a while – unpacking things, moving them around – and I saw that the past sells.

When I needed money for my business, I sold everything. My comic books, my records, my grandmother's china. Monica had a couple of 45s and some period clothing which had hidden itself from my selling mania deep within the garage.

But I needed some records. I went to the Half-Price Books store. Hal had been right – not only were 45s gone, they were disappearing even from used record stores. Half-Price had a bigger section of CDs – *used* CDs – than 45s. The singles that were around disgusted me. Seventies light rock garbage. Sentimental slime that you could only listen to in the throes of adolescent lust.

I picked a couple. It doesn't matter which ones. I took them out in the Dallas heat, became nauseated at the thought of what I was carrying, and tossed them into a chocolate brown dumpster. Flies rose. Where was the real past? The past that was so strong it could dissolve the present – the past that had made me. Had I sold it somewhere along the way?

I believed in my present. I was totally focused on my goals and I realised that I was different from most people. I didn't have a theme song. I didn't have a platter that invoked the past. Everything was in my present – what if that were ever taken away?

There is little music for that fine cutting edge called the present. Music calls us to the past. To the friends, the parties, the quiet times alone when we played it. For the new consumers, technology no longer made the single tune easy and cheap to get to. How would they record their lives? And I was in the same fix as them. I'd sold my singles.

I was scared – actually scared – that maybe there was a song that would bring the past so rapidly into the present as to destroy it. I was scared of the past. There's a lot of past out there to destroy any present moment.

Why had I sold my singles? I really hadn't made much money on them – I doubt if I got a buck apiece. Maybe I had a fear of what the personal past could do. Maybe I kept the past under control by buying and selling it.

I went back to work. I had Janet go out and buy me three records from an expensive retro-vogue shop. She found 'I want to Hold Your Hand', 'The Lion Sleeps Tonight' and 'Rodeo Romeo'. They were safe platters and I was happy.

The Zenith Cobra-Matic had a heavy casing of brown-grey steel. The record-playing mechanism was suspended inside the heavy frame by thick springs, so the record wouldn't skip no matter how wild the dancing. But the feature that made the Cobra-Matic was the tone-arm – with its painted spine, eyes and tongue, it was a thin snake. Definitely the cutting edge of cool. Stereophonic High Fidelity. 16   33   45   78 r.p.m.

Hal was saying, '. . . and when the blue-haired lady sold it to me, it had a great 78, "I Like My Chicken Fryin' Size" by Johnny Bond on the Columbia label.'

Hal's current squeeze, Liz, was putting the first single on – predictably 'Rock Around the Clock'. Eric Towser, the CPA who did all of our taxes, lit the first joint. The electric purple bell-bottoms didn't do much for his paunch.

I set up a folding table in the corner. I'd done Tarot readings as a party trick a couple of years ago. It didn't exactly fit the theme, but people always want a peek at the future. Even a fake peek. I spread red velvet over the table, setting the mirror down where it would reflect my subject. If anybody asked I'd tell them it was my 'focus'. They'd probably be too blitzed to ask. I kept my chamois and water under the table. Dr Randolph had been wise in his day to prescribe snow water. The owner could've only used it a few times a year. How many Christmas parties did it darken?

Liz walked to my table, handing me a joint. I took a long drag and managed not to cough despite lack of practice. I handed her the cards to shuffle, while I gazed into the mirror. I wasn't surprised it wasn't Hal, but the young black stud who swept up the shop.

Just as I was predicting that money – possible a small legacy – was coming her way (and her green eyes alive with the death of Aunty) Hal walked up and put his hand on her shoulder.

Hal was next. I polished my relic. Somebody put on 'Stairway to Heaven'. I laid down the Ten of Swords and saw Monica's reflection where his should be. Poor sap. Monica would never return his love. Should I pity this friend from college days or should I arrange to keep him the hell away from my wife? Card after meaningless card. Another joint went around.

I found out that Ernst loved Betty and Edward loved Ernst

and Betty loved herself. I found out that Cindy loved Robert and Robert loved Laura and that Laura loved nobody at all – just black space – or maybe she loves death. I found out Kitty loved John and John loved Kitty – which was the only complete circle in the room.

And the Cobra-Matic played 'Let's Spend the Night Together', 'DOA', 'Stairway to Heaven', 'House of the Rising Sun', 'Rikki Don't Loose That Number'. And I was going back to the head I used to have, when I heard those songs.

It wasn't a bad head. It was different from my current Faustian self. It was a head that said I could slack off, and not work so damn hard all the time. It was a head that said, 'Let It Be'. Maybe I shouldn't be prying into things. Maybe I should relax and not play with the mirror. That old lost innocence seemed not so lost. I resolved to put the mirror away after this party. Then I'd buy an old record player from Hal and start collecting singles.

But it didn't work out that way. Once Faust, always Faust.

Someone broke out his hash pipe and a chunk of Lebanese hash the colour of burnt umber. And I thought about Lebanon and the Middle East and the cradle of civilisation for a while. The Cobra-Matic played 'I Am the Walrus', 'Bang a Gong', 'I Only Have Eyes for You', 'Johnny Angel', 'I Had Too Much to Dream (Last Night)'.

As the chords of the Electric Prunes classic died the 'readings' began again. Jerry loved Sue and Jerry's wife Trish loved Gene. Gene loved Maud and Maud loved Robert. Willie loved Etta and Etta loved a man I'd never seen. Butch loved Alice and Butch's wife Marie loved Alice.

Finally Monica came to my table. She knew the cards were a scam, but she was too stoned to care – or maybe someone put her up to it. Jerry Butler's 'What's the Use of Breaking Up' was playing. Well, this was what I waited for and what I feared. I polished the mirror. I saw myself. She loved me and I began to cry. But the music ended and somebody put Johnny Ace's 'Pledging My Love' on the machine.

My reflection wavered. At first I thought it was the tears and the hash. But I dissolved and a teenaged guy with brown hair and sunglasses and a leather jacket appeared. He held a rose, a small red rose; and he stood in the dark. I knew he would always be alone. I looked up at Monica and she was crying – quietly but strongly enough that tears splashed on the cards. I finished the reading. I felt like going home. I wrapped my mirror in velvet and made my good-byes. I gathered up our records and steered Monica out of the door. She moved slowly, as if underwater – or leaving a funeral. In the cannabis haze no one noticed.

We walked home – I only live three blocks from Hal's. The pollution hid the stars and I could smell smog as well as roses – we have these huge bushes – as we walked up to the house. We were tired. So we didn't put anything up.

Around three in the morning I woke up. Monica stood in front of the window watching the ugly night sky.

'Monica?'

'Yeah?'

'That record tonight was pretty special, wasn't it?'

'Yeah.'

'Want to say any more?'

'You know, I didn't realise you could forget great hurts, but I hadn't thought of Johnny in years. He gave me a copy of that single on our second date. He even got me the whole album later on, the Johnny Ace Memorial Album. This was in '66, which he said should be called Year One – because it was the beginning of our love. He had this thing for Johnny Ace since they were both named Johnny. Johnny Ace was rock'n'roll's first suicide. He killed himself in Houston on Christmas Eve 1954. Well, I should've known what was coming. Johnny had a little band, the Transformers, and they would play "Pledging My Love" as a theme. They went nowhere. But I went to every gig despite Mom's threats. "Pledging My Love". It was for me, you see. This faggot talent scout told Johnny that he could make him a star, but all he really did was make him. So Johnny followed his idol and blew his brains out. I was a little crazy for a while.'

'You want a hug?'

'No, I just want to think. You try and get some sleep.'

But I lay there watching her at the window till the alarm went off at seven thirty.

Being a creature of hope, I tried the mirror a few more times. But Johnny had taken my place. I saw him in the braveness of Monica's smile, in the depths of her hazel eyes, in the way she held herself when she was quiet.

The years pass and I see no reason to break up our comfortable fictions. Janet watches me and lives on hope thinner than Himalayan air. I don't know how to fall in love or I'd fall in love with Janet. But my love for Monica remains; although it has grown into a sort of ache. Who can compete with a ghost as a lover? With a memory that can only grow more perfect with the passing of time?

I read that toward the end of Dr Randolph's life he was in a railway accident. His health grew bad and he suffered great pain. He resigned himself to death, yet he met a young woman whose love for him transformed him. With the young woman he had happiness and a son Osiris Budh Randolph. Maybe I will know such love.

I have smashed the mirror into a thousand thousand fragments.

Weep for the Moon
Stephen Baxter

One of the unexpected pleasures of editing In
Dreams *is getting a story which is totally at right angles to your
expectations. For instance, from his career to date, you wouldn't
expect Stephen Baxter to write a story about Glenn Miller – one of
the first superstars of modern popular culture to exploit the single
as an artform. After all, in only a few years Baxter has established
a reputation as a writer of Universe-spanning hard SF, with a slew
of popular stories set in the same future history, and a novel,* Raft,
which Time Out *called 'rigorous, vigorous sci-fi [sic] at its
enjoyable best'.*

*But like all of Baxter's stories, this one has a solid speculative
idea at its core. As he explains, 'I guess we've all had the experience
of having a fragment of melody lodge in the consciousness and
refuse to go away . . . It seems to me that one of the sadder aspects
of the current fragmentation of the popular music scene is the loss
of the source of such melodies. Once, it seemed, the music of our
culture was lodged in all our heads; now the music is almost
fragmented enough for us to carry around our own sub-genres,
sharing nothing.*

*'This got me to wondering what would happen if we suddenly
needed to reassemble our shattered popular culture. And I mean,
we really needed to . . . The result is "Weep for the Moon".'*

The engines coughed into life. The little
plane shuddered, then settled into a
steady buzz as the props turned. The passenger cabin started

to heat up; there was an oily warmth that slowly banished the damp chill.

The AAF captain huddled into his greatcoat and peered out of the cabin's tiny, grubby porthole. He could barely see the end of the wing through the swirling December fog, and the light of the short English afternoon was already fading.

He shivered.

He took off his wire-framed glasses and polished them on a handkerchief; short-sightedly he sneaked a glance at the plane's only other passenger – a colonel whose name he'd already forgotten, a solid-looking citizen who was going through an attaché case, oblivious to his surroundings.

Fear knotted the captain's stomach; he clenched his jaw to keep from whimpering like a boy.

Maybe he ought to just up and off this damn plane.

He hated flying at the best of times. And to take off now, in this fog? His orderly mind listed the dangers. Crashing into a tree in the fog. Getting shot down by some Luftwaffe patrol over the Channel. Damn it, getting punctured by English ack-ack – the flight was unscheduled, he remembered.

He could just stand up, give his apologies to the colonel, break for the door . . .

He took a deep breath and pushed himself back into his seat; and he told himself to grow up.

Before he'd joined up a couple of years earlier, he'd got used to getting things done – he'd run his own bands for five years, after all. But in the AAF there was always some desk-pilot to block whatever he wanted to do, and he seemed to spend his whole time fighting just to stand still. Well, this time he'd cut through the red tape by talking his way on to this flight; he was on his way to Paris to set up the band's arrival there, and he was damned if he was going to compromise that for a schoolboy funk.

He closed his eyes and thought about Helen.
It was then that he heard the voice.

'Weep for the moon, for the moon has no reason to glow now,
Weep for the rose, for the rose has no reason to grow now –'

He recognised the lyric; Eddie Heyman had written it for
'Now I Lay Me Down to Weep', the tune that had become
'Moonlight Serenade'. Al Bowlly used to sing that lyric for
Ray Noble, he remembered. Well, it sure as hell wasn't
Bowlly now. For a moment his own arrangement of his tune
sounded in his ears, with the clarinet lead and the ooh-wah
brass . . . Funny how he could hear the singing over the
props. In fact, he realised, suddenly he couldn't hear the
props at all. Maybe it was something to do with the fog.

'The river won't flow now,
As I lay me down to weep . . .'

He opened his eyes.
'Hi, bro.'
The captain turned. In the seat next to him sat his brother
Herb . . . Herb? Confused, he looked around the plane's
dingy fuselage; but the studious colonel wasn't to be seen.
'Herb? What the hell are you doing here? I thought you
were in the States.'
Herb's thin face split into a grin. 'You aren't glad to see
me? Some welcome, my man.'
The captain's confusion broke up under a wave of affection. 'It was the singing, boy. I could have sworn it was
Sinatra; you threw me off . . .' He reached over and hugged
his brother, awkwardly, confined by the plane seats and his
greatcoat. Within his embrace Herb felt stiff and strangely
cold. Herb was in civvies, a suit under a brown overcoat; the
captain found himself staring. 'Herb, I don't know how the

hell you got in here. This is an AAF field. And the damn plane's about to take off; we're on our way to France – '

But the props were still silent. He turned to see if they were still twisting, but the windows had fogged over even more.

Herb put a hand on his shoulder; the captain was startled by the intensity of the grip. 'Glenn,' Herb said. 'Don't think about the props. Don't think about how I got here.' His voice was heavy, uncharacteristically serious.

'Herb?'

Herb bit his lip, obviously hesitant. Then a thought seemed to strike him, and he sat up in his chair and rummaged through his pockets. 'Damn it.'

'What is it?'

'Glenn, can you bum me a Strike?'

'. . . sure.' The captain pulled a crumpled green packet from the inside pocket of his jacket and thumbed out a Lucky Strike for Herb; using one of the captain's matches his brother lit up and drew a great drag on the cigarette – then exhaled and stared at the Strike, looking oddly disappointed. 'Glenn, are these stale, maybe?'

The captain frowned. 'New today . . . Herb, what's going on?' Herb was an organised kind of a guy; the captain couldn't recall a time when he'd been caught short of a smoke. 'Did you dress in a hurry today?'

Herb smiled, somehow sadly. 'Something like that. Let's say I was – equipped – in a hurry.'

'Equipped?'

'Glenn, listen to me.' Again that note of heaviness. 'I've – come – to tell you something.'

'Is something wrong at home?' Panic spurted in him. 'Helen. It's Helen, isn't it?' A few years earlier his wife had been ill enough to be hospitalised. She'd come out; and the experience had brought them closer. But now – 'In God's name tell me, Herb.'

Herb was shaking his head. 'No, it's not Helen. Take it easy. Nothing's wrong with Helen.'

'Then what?'

Herb opened his mouth, hesitated, shut it again. 'I don't know how to tell you, boy.'

'Just tell me, damn it! You're frightening me.'

'Okay.' Herb leaned forward. 'It's you, Glenn. It's news about you. You've got to get off this plane, right now.'

The captain felt a chill, deep in the place where his darkest, most secret fears lurked, far under all the control, the business. 'What are you talking about?'

'Because the damn thing never makes it.' Herb, clearly mixed up and distressed, couldn't meet Glenn's stare; but his voice stayed steady. 'It's true, Glenn; you have to believe me.

'Nobody finds out what happened. Maybe you're shot down; maybe you just lost your way. But *you never make it to Paris.*'

The captain sat back, still staring. The silence of the plane started to feel eerie. 'Damn it, Herb, you've sure learned how to scare a man. You're talking like it already happened.'

'Glenn, to me it did. I remember it.' Herb's eyes grew misty. He turned again to his brother. 'I remember it; I read newspapers about it. Damn it, man; I can prove it to you.' He squirmed in his seat and from the pocket of his overcoat he drew an object about the size and shape of a dime novel; it was bound in leather, and set in its upper surface was a piece of glass three inches square. 'Watch,' Herb said strongly. He poked at small lettered squares inset into the leather cover, and to the Captain's amazement the glass square filled abruptly with light; a series of grainy black-and-white images flickered across it, and from somewhere tiny voices spoke, insect music played.

'Herb. What the hell is this?'

'Don't worry about it,' Herb said with a crap-cutting chop of his left hand. 'It's a pocket television. Okay?'

'So where's the tube? Up your sleeve?'

'Yeah,' said Herb sarcastically. 'Now will you forget it and just concentrate on the pictures?'

The captain leaned forward and peered into the little screen. He saw pictures of himself and the band – mostly old stock, from before the war – images of a plane like the one he was sitting in. There was a commentary he couldn't quite make out. 'It looks like a newsreel,' he said.

Herb nodded vigorously. 'That's just what it is. A newsreel. Hang on to that, Glenn. Now listen to me; this is a newsreel, not of what has happened in the past – *but what will happen in the future.*'

Herb's words seemed to slide away from the captain's understanding. 'What are you telling me, Herb?'

Now his brother was speaking with a kind of weight, an authority, that was alien to the Herb he'd grown up with. 'Just forget about the whys and hows for a minute, and think about the pictures. What's the story here?'

The captain peered into the window to the future, trying to comprehend the parade of little figures, the tinny voiceover.

'It's your death, Glenn. Isn't it? They're reporting your death. If you don't get off this plane, it's a fact as real as apple pie; Glenn, it's as real to me as anything else that ever happened. Damn it, the President himself calls a national Miller Day, in July, not long after the end of the war. Not bad for a horn-player – '

'The war ends in July? Next July?' Could it really be as close as that?

Herb tapped another part of the little box and the pictures faded. 'Glenn, I've come back to warn you. I can't make you get off this plane and save your life; you have to do that for yourself . . .'

'Slow up, Herb.' He closed his eyes, tried to find a piece of calmness. 'You're going too fast.'

It couldn't be a trick. Herb wouldn't play a trick like this.

But, of course, this mightn't be Herb.

He opened his eyes again, stared hard at the man beside him. 'Damn it, you sure look like Herb. You talk like him. You even sing like him.'

A cloud of doubt crossed Herb's face. 'I'm not going to lie to you. I'm Herb inside, Glenn. I know myself. I am Herb; that's all I am; that's all I'll ever be. But – ' And now Herb himself looked scared, and that frightened the captain more than anything. 'But,' Herb went on, 'even while we're sitting here I know there's another Herb, back in the States. This minute. I've got his memories, Glenn. If I was smart enough I could tell you what I was doing right now. What he *is* doing right now. Maybe he's eating doughnuts. I was always crazy for doughnuts, wasn't I?' A thought struck him. 'Hey, Glenn, you got any doughnuts?'

The captain snorted. 'Do I look like I have?'

Herb seemed disappointed. 'Maybe it's as well. I couldn't taste a damn thing when I smoked that Strike . . . I guess I've not been sent here to enjoy myself.'

The captain wanted to shrink away from this person . . . But this was his brother. He could *feel* it. 'Herb, all of this sounds crazy. You're not making any sense.'

Herb spread his hands and stared at them, as if they were unfamiliar objects. 'No more to me, guy. Glenn, I'm a – like a photograph. Or a movie image.' He nodded. 'Yeah; that's what I am.' He looked scared again. 'But I'm Herb inside.'

The captain wondered what to say. 'Why are you here? Did someone send you?'

'Yeah.' Herb nodded. 'Men from the future, Glenn; from the next century, a hundred years from now.'

'They made you up and sent you back here? How?'

'Glenn, I'm only Herb. How the hell do you expect me to be able to tell you that?' He pointed at the little television. 'I couldn't even tell you how this thing works.'

The captain didn't want to smile. 'Then just tell me why you're here.'

'I've told you. To tell you to get the hell off of this plane.'

The captain sighed; somehow his fear was fading, to be replaced by a kind of irritation. 'Okay, Herb, let's go at this another way. I'm not a general. I'm not the President. I'm not even Walt Disney. I'm a goddamn bandleader. Why the hell would these – these guys from the future – go to all this trouble to save me? What do I do, invent penicillin?'

Herb shook his head. 'You don't believe me, do you? Then you won't believe this next bit.'

'Try me.'

'It's not just you, Glenn. It's the western world; it's Christianity, and democracy. It's to save all of that.'

The captain snorted in disgust. 'I haven't got time for this.'

Herb held up his hands. 'Believe me, you have. Just listen for a minute. Okay?' He glared back. 'Okay?'

The captain shook his head. 'One minute, Herb; then I get on with my job.'

Herb started to speak.

'I want you to get hold of this, Glenn,' he began. 'Ideas are *alive*. Have you ever thought that? The good ones seem to come out of nowhere; and they latch on, they grow, they spread. They propagate.

'Think about it. Look at – oh, "Pennsylvania Six Five Thousand". Remember where that came from? Jerry Gray took a riff from, what the hell was it – '

' "Dipsy Doodle",' said Glenn. 'Larry Clinton.'

'Sure. That one little riff was like a seed, see; that's what I'm telling you. And Jerry's head was like the sweet earth, where that seed took hold and grew.' Herb mimed the action of plants. 'And you, you're like the gardener who picks out the good stuff and cultivates it – '

The captain laughed. 'What's your job, Herb? Spreading the horseshit?'

Herb smiled, but he kept going. 'Just listen. So ideas are living things. They grow, and compete with each other for space to grow – which is the space between our ears. And the younger ones, the stronger ones, push out the weak.' Herb looked into his brother's face. 'All right?'

The captain thought about all of that. It made him feel uneasy – not just the sheer craziness of it, but the fact that it reminded him of something else. But he said, 'You've still got my attention. I'm looking forward to you getting to the point.'

'Now,' Herb said patiently, 'the strongest breed of idea, the toughest strain of all, is *music*. You know? There's something fundamental about music, something that sits in your head, underneath all the words, the logic, the business. Like when you can't get a melody out of your head, even when you hate the damn thing – '

'Or you hate the guy who wrote it. Sure.'

'Okay.' Herb sat straighter in his seat. 'Let's leave that for a minute.

'Second thing. Glenn, in a hundred years – in the time of the guys who sent me – the earth gets Visited.'

The captain shook his head. 'Herb, you really are talking like a crazy man.'

'You promised to hear me out.'

'I said a minute.'

'Glenn, I'm your brother; you owe me this.'

The captain frowned, studying Herb's tense, earnest face. There was a light around Herb now, a kind of soft focus which disconcerted the captain even more. 'Are you my brother?' he asked softly.

Herb said, 'We've discussed this, Glenn. I am. And, at the same time, I'm not.'

'Why would these guys from the future send *you*?'

'Why good old Herb?' A mocking snort cut through the strange aura of saintliness. 'I guess they picked someone who you might listen to. And believe. Who would you rather they picked? The President? Donald Duck?'

The captain shook his head. 'Tell me what you have to tell me.'

'Visitors,' said Herb.

'From where? Mars? Orson Welles did that before the war, Herb.'

Herb didn't even smile. 'Nobody knows where they came from. They know it wasn't Mars, though; the people there would have died first – '

The captain blinked. 'There are people on Mars? Martians?'

'No, Glenn; men like you and me. They'll live on Mars, in cities, ah, under glass.'

'You're kidding.' He felt tendrils of fear returning to his heart. 'Did you say people die?'

Herb pursed his lips. 'The Visitors are different from us. Very different. They don't even recognise us; not as living, breathing creatures with souls, anyhow. They think we're – I don't know, cattle maybe. Less than that; like worms in the ground, or the ground itself. Dirt.

'People start dying, Glenn; in great swathes. Like footfalls.'

'Why?'

Herb shrugged. 'The Visitors don't have a reason. They don't need a reason. Glenn, we can't even see them; maybe they can't see us.

'They don't know we're alive. They think ideas are alive.' Herb looked into his face. 'Are you understanding me? The Visitors are like ideas, too. Maybe. Maybe they can talk to the ideas; I don't know . . . Anyway they respond to the biggest ideas, the strongest. And, if you don't happen to have the Biggest Idea in your head, the Visitors will wipe you out without even thinking about it.'

Baffled, frightened, the captain pulled his greatcoat closer around him. It didn't seem to be getting any darker, funnily enough, but it sure as hell was cold. 'Tell me what it's got to do with me, Herb.'

'Okay.' Herb wet his lips. 'Let me tell you what happens if you get off this damn plane.' He poked at the little television box again, and a fresh newsreel started. Images of bands, of the captain himself, in uniform and out of it. 'You live,' said Herb. 'You don't get lost in the Channel. The war finishes; the AAF let you out; you go home. You're a war hero.

'The bands form up again. All the old guys are still around. Billy May on the horn. Trigger Alpert. Dorothy Claire. The Modernaires – not the same ones . . .'

The captain watched the flickering images. Now he saw a montage of towns, of glittering venues, splashed newspaper headlines. It was a tale of success piled on success, but he felt distant, chastened somehow.

Herb said, 'Glenn, you were the biggest before. Right? But, man, after the war you are *huge*. I can't tell you . . .

'You start to step back from the band, though. Jerry Gray does a lot of the arranging – '

'Like before the war.'

'But you keep close to it; nobody else has your ear for the riff, Glenn; and you know it.

'Nineteen fifty, you have your biggest hit yet. "Amazing You".' A compelling little riff wafted out of the television box. The captain didn't recognise it. 'Sinatra and Day duet on the vocals – '

Glenn couldn't help but smile. 'I get to work with Doris?'

'Still with that unique voicing of yours,' said Herb. 'With the clarinet lead and the sax as a fifth voice in the reeds . . . But you're spreading your wings. You get into song publishing. Personal management. You produce shows on the radio, the television. Man, you've still got that business sense. It's not just your own stuff – you're doing it for everyone else as well. You keep swing alive; you're providing the framework the rest can work in.

'And the world's whistling your songs, man; you're a legend.'

The newsreel images, in colour now, had reached 1960. The captain, following the fragmented story, learned that he would be worth a lot of money. Ten million; a hundred million maybe. There would be a new writer, a young guy from Texas, name of Holley. The captain would hear his songs on some crackly old station during a business sweep through the South . . . Inspired by Holley, Miller would decide to get closer to the music again, realising what he'd been missing with all the business stuff. But he'd changed; he'd learned new things. With his swing over Holley's riffs he became bigger than ever.

And all the bands played on and on . . .

'Your music is the sound of America, Glenn,' Herb said.

'They're still playing "GI Patrol" as they sweep through 'Nam in their helicopter gunships . . .'

"Nam?"

'Vietnam.'

'Where the hell's that?'

Herb shrugged. 'Another war, man; what does it matter?

'It goes on and on. Even after you die in '77, a ripe old seventy-three, in your bed . . .

'Glenn, you come to symbolise something; you, and your music, and your mood. Something that keeps alive and growing; something at the heart of America, and democracy.'

The captain felt tears prickle; he took off his glasses and dabbed at his eyes. The plane was a myopic blur. Strangely enough Herb still looked quite sharp; a preternatural clarity added to his aura of unreality. 'Shut up, Herb. Damn it; you always did know how to push my buttons.'

'I'm telling you the truth, man. And when these Visitors come, in a hundred years' time, and they seek out the Big Idea – you know what they find?'

'Tell me.'

Herb slapped his leg. 'Music. Your music.'

'You're telling me they'll still be playing my crummy tunes in the year two thousand and forty-four? You expect me to believe that?'

'They are, Glenn; but not just yours. All the other guys, who came after you. You made it possible for them; all the new, brilliant bandleaders. Riddle. Mancini. McCartney. Watts.

'You're the leader, the one with the business sense *and* the ear for what the punters want to hear. To dance to. The music grows. There are people who use the bands the way, I don't know, Beethoven used the symphony orchestra.

There's great music, Glenn; the greatest. But, because of you and your instincts, it never loses touch with the people.'

Herb pushed another button on his box, now, and music billowed out of it. Recognisably swing, the captain realised, but of a depth and complexity that staggered him; the notes seemed to swirl around Herb's unreal, crystal-clear face, against the blurred backdrop of the plane.

Herb said, 'Glenn, after a hundred years it's the American Big Idea; it's sunk in so deep you could never get rid of it. Americans live through the Visit, Glenn; and it's thanks to you . . .'

The captain replaced his glasses. Strangely he felt disturbed now by Herb's account rather than moved; there was something not quite right about this Big Idea stuff – something that was making him uneasy. He said, 'It's a neat story. Now tell me the other side. What if I don't get off the plane?' He swallowed, forced himself to say it. 'What if I don't live through this?'

Herb took a deep breath. 'What do you want me to say? Instant sainthood, man, if that's what you want.

'The band keeps going; your Army band, I mean. They play France, the rest. But it's not the same.

'After the war the guys try to keep it going.'

The captain felt morbidly curious. 'Who?'

'Try Tex Beneke.'

He laughed. 'Tex holds down a neat tenor-sax, but he couldn't manage a smile.'

'Sure. But Tex is just the front man. Don Haynes runs the show, behind the scenes.

'But it doesn't work. Don has the business but he just doesn't have your – what, your ear? Your intuition? Tex and Don are like the two halves of you, Glenn, but they don't add up to the whole.

'They fight. Tex wants to move on, try new things. Don wants to keep it just the same as it always was . . .

'It falls apart. Tex leaves; the band starts to break up. The vultures come down, imitators.'

He frowned. 'What vultures?'

'Ralph Flanagan.'

'Who?'

'Ray Anthony. Even Jerry Gray. Imitators; they add nothing new. It's like a long funeral, Glenn. It's dreadful.

'The music stops changing. People remember it, with affection, but the life just goes away.' Herb tapped at his television box and a fresh newsreel started up in the little window. 'Glenn. Look at these headlines. Nineteen forty-six, Christmas. Just two years from now, right? Listen who's retired. Dorsey. Goodman. Teagarden. Les Brown – '

'I can't believe it.'

'It's true, man. Some of them keep trying, but the music gets too hard. They lose the audience. Kenton, for instance – '

Glenn shook his head. 'You got to produce music they can dance to.'

'You can see that,' said Herb. 'Kenton doesn't have the ear; he loses people.

'The singers take over. Sinatra, Cole. The bands become too expensive to ship around the country, damn it, especially as no one wants to hear them any more.

'People stay home, watch television. There are new kinds of music; the young take it up because there's nothing else. But there's no class to it, no swing. You should hear it, Glenn; it's like jungle drums. People like you and me can't even listen to it.' Herb frowned, sadly. 'Can you imagine that? Parents and kids who can't share their music any more . . .' Now a scratchy image filled the little screen: some guy in a tux talking directly to the camera against a cheap backcloth. Herb brightened. 'Here's something funny, or maybe sad. The Dorseys keep going, in a way. This is their television show; not big, but a show. And you know who starts getting his first breaks on this show? Presley, that's all.'

'Presley? What kind of a name is that?'

Herb shrugged. 'Never mind. Look, Glenn, it's all fragments. Splinters. Twenty, thirty years later you wouldn't call it music any more. The kids take drugs to write it; you wouldn't believe it.

'People are sick of it. There's nothing they can understand any more; nothing they can dance to.

'By the end of the century they don't buy music; not en masse, not together. Two hundred million Americans buy two hundred million different songs, it seems like. There's no *identity*, Glenn. That's what you provided.'

'And when the Visitors come – '

'They look for the Big Idea. You know what they find? Islam. Mohammedans; the Arabs.

'Americans – simply die, Glenn. Europe, Australia too . . . a hundred years from now America's a wasteland.'

Herb fell silent again; he snapped off his television and stowed it in his overcoat pocket.

The captain settled back in the tight plane seat and folded his arms. 'I don't know what to say, Herb.'

'Don't say anything. Just get off the damn plane!'

Miller tried to take it all in. Could it really be true, that ideas were like living things which populated people's heads? And if that were so . . .

Suddenly he realised what had been making him so uneasy about the whole concept.

'Herb,' he said softly. 'These living ideas.'

'Yeah?'

'How much room do they leave for democracy?'

Herb stared at him. 'What are you talking about?'

The captain rubbed at his temples. 'I think I'm talking about freedom, Herb. About the freedom of the individual. After all, doesn't Mr Hitler think he has a big idea, a living idea?'

'Glenn, this isn't relevant. Forget Hitler. At the bottom of it, we're talking about whether you live or die.'

The captain looked out at the fog, which seemed to be frozen against the dingy porthole. He found himself wondering just how important that really was. 'What about Helen?'

'If you die?' Herb reached out and touched his brother's arm. 'She does okay, Glenn. Your stuff keeps selling; the estate keeps her comfortable.'

The captain sat in the odd stillness of the plane. Herb waited patiently. The captain tried to accept all Herb had told him, tried to imagine this bizarre world of the future, with glass cities on Mars and yet lit up by band music he'd recognise . . . but darkened by the deadly footfalls of the Visitors.

Then he thought of Helen. Of the feel of the trombone in his hands. Of the hordes of khaki-clothed GIs, here in England and the States, who threw their caps into the air and whooped as the trumpets and trombones blasted at them in all their roaring purity, as the saxes welled up below and the rhythm section let loose with those clear, crisp, swinging beats –

Herb studied him. 'Well? Have you decided?'

'There's nothing to decide, Herb. Not if Helen's going to be okay. Remember the statement I put out when I joined up?'

Herb nodded and closed his eyes. '"I, like every American, have an obligation to fulfil . . ."'

Glenn opened the top few buttons of his coat, pointed to

the pips on his shoulder. 'I'm a serviceman, Herb. I have to do my duty, even if it means I risk my life. Just like every American serviceman in this damn war. And, Herb . . . maybe all this "living idea" stuff really could save the world. But, damn it, there's something about it that just isn't *American*.'

Herb narrowed his eyes. 'Glenn, I don't know what to say to that. You know I always looked up to you, for your sense of honour, of duty. But . . . Glenn, you have a duty to all those Americans in the future. The Visitors – '

'Herb, across that Channel there are young Americans who, not six months ago, were preparing to lay down their lives in Normandy . . . And they could still die, before Europe is free. Right now they're expecting me to go over there and bring them some real, live American music. To let them go home for a few hours, in their heads.

'That's where my duty is.' Glenn closed his eyes, let his own words sink in. It was right; he knew it was right. 'That's all there is, Herb.'

Herb held his arm for a long minute. Then he stood up. 'Maybe the future guys were wrong to send me back. I understand, Glenn. I won't argue with you any more.'

The captain heard the noise of the props return, faintly, as if from a tremendous distance.

'You know,' Herb said as he pulled his overcoat closed, 'I'm not sure what happens now.'

'What do you mean?'

'I know I'm not Herb. Not really. But inside I'm me, with two sets of Herb memories . . . What happens to me now? Will I know about it?'

The captain stared up at him. He had no idea how to answer. He wanted to get up, hug his brother and calm his fears, but Herb was already heading down the aisle, receding into a darkness the captain hadn't noticed before. The captain called after him, 'Herb, wait. Do you want to take these Strikes?'

Herb shrugged. 'I can't taste them anyway. Hey,' he said. Now it was really hard to see him in the gloom. 'They make a movie about you, in 1953.'

'Sure they do. Who plays me?'

'You won't believe it.' Herb's voice was faint now, almost drowned by the props.

'Try me.'

'Jimmy Stewart.'

'You're kidding. He's a hero . . . I'm proud.'

'No, Glenn. Stewart should be proud . . .'

'Herb?'

But Herb had left the plane, although Glenn hadn't seen him open the door. And the Air Force colonel with the attaché case was back where Herb had sat, just as if nothing had happened.

The prop noise rose to a growl. The plane bumped forward.

The captain peered out through the port, looking for Herb; but there was only the fog.

The Man Who Shot Anarchy Gordon
Ray Davis

Here's a mordantly funny short story that manages to compress the entire history of American punkdom into less than 6,000 words. Ray Davis tells us that it's a collision of:
– an obnoxiously ornamental narrative voice
– the Neodeshans (more properly the Church of the Western Christ), a fictional sect whose Canaan, set more or less where Kansas should be, conflates Utah and New York's West Village
– a hearing of 'Lord Salton and Auchanachie', a Scottish ballad about destructive conformity and sorry independence
– the 'Liberty Valence' plot of sorry conformity and destructive independence.

He also tells us that he lives in San Francisco, and never misses shows by Ed's Redeeming Qualities or Thinking Fellers Union Local 282.

> To live outside the law, you must be harmless. – *Old folk song*

'I'd rather die; I'm going to die,' Lindie chanted in a reedy voice thinking about something else as he lathered again under his arms and between his buttocks. 'Too good to waste on bleeders, specially a scag like that,' he'd overheard in the locker room right before David and Jonathan Prep closed for the summer. He tilted his face into the shower full force, imagining the spray aurating his glow like a commercial. Cleanliness is next to gaudiness; he rubbed behind his earlobes, their healing still a positive pleasure.

He fell back to 'We're coming out. Out of our closets' (his write-in candidate for class song) as he straddled the tub wall and scrubbed himself down with a new black towel. It left fuzz on his skin which had to be brushed off after the air had completely dried him. He tried tracing a pentagram in the fuzz but it wasn't thick enough to be visible.

The other side of town, across the tracks (seriously, though no one on St Orville Elder Blvd even slowed down for them any more), Anarchy was tossing Chucks and Doc Martens at a moth which had woken her up. The sneakers and boots ricocheted off her sparkly black ceiling back on to her mattress, where she dodged them and whirled them off again like a joke juggling act.

If I tear any of the posters, even the Ferry, you're going to wish you were never laid, she promised it. But a collector's copy of *Fusion* was the only casualty, kneed in the spine before Mrs Gordon's *'What* is going on in there?' stopped her. Anarchy couldn't see the moth any more anyway.

About forty miles east, Saltine was driving west through a squiggly joint between two rods of road, tracing the invisible Sage Creek. His brother's car had no FM and the 8-track was broken, so Saltine had to twist the dial every few minutes when a commercial came on.

'Iiiiiii . . . want to bay-ayyy . . . NRK,' Saltine sang over a Crystal Gayle song. 'I *am* the NRA, and I *am* the PTA, and I *am* the TDK . . .' He swung the Dart back and forth across the road's white abdominal scar, evening out when he encountered another driver. Once someone honked and waved at his brother's Walt Brown University 'Honk For Sanctity' bumper sticker. 'Injun Jeezus,' twanged Saltine moronically. No one noticeably reacted to his brother's

'Beaver Patrol Merit Badge' or 'Where The Heck Is Utopia Canaan' bumper stickers.

'Conjunction Junction, what's your function?' whined Lindie in a not-bad Joan Baez imitating Bob Dylan imitation which was supposed to be Johnny Thunders. His sister laughed.

Just an old-fashioned love song, coming down in three-part harmony.

'Annie! It's for you!' Mrs Gordon took rhetorical steps toward the hall and yelled the same thing in the same way. Anarchy extended like a thick frog tongue from the bedroom door, grabbed the receiver, and was back with it, cord down through the crack. Mrs Gordon checked the phone's torso on her way to the couch to make sure it wasn't breaking free of the wall.

Now you'd think Mrs Gordon would be considerably more hard-line than Mr and Mrs Fraser, the latter being an academic family (at an officially Neodeshan university, true, but 'it has a fine reputation') and owning a complete set of Faulkner, but here she was passing Lindie's phone call right along like a high church altar boy's answering service. Mrs Gordon, however, lacked the training for absolutism, and any companions of her stepdaughter were welcome, if only as hostages. Lindie's parents had more to lose; also they'd picked up the locals' distrust of young women, maybe Mr Fraser had it already and that's why he moved here, or Mrs Fraser got it from missionaries, they probably go to Taiwan. There's an answer for everything.

When Saltine showed up, Anarchy was looking at the back of 'Transformer'. 'What happens to the people on record jackets? They look applied, don't they? Like they were born inside the shrinkwrap. Like, what happened to the women on the Roxy Music records?'

'Didn't one of them marry Rod Stewart?' Saltine guessed. Saltine never lacked for straight lines.

It was a skill she hadn't appreciated at first. When Lindie took her to the Cheap Trick/Billy Zoom Band show, she'd been on one of those edges which can saw through this brick and still slice a tomato paper-thin. Adrift in too-wide too-short clothes, this cracker across the aisle looked the perfect model of a modern Neodeshan (said Lindie), and when Anarchy got bored after 'He's a Whore' she tore into him as if he was a paper bag she had to fight her way out of. He was trying to joke but looked scared and impressed, like when she bit through Penny's skin at gym.

Strangely, her victim somewhat agreed with her negative assessment, kind of liked it even, and in his Flannery O'Connory way tried to live up to the challenge. A couple of weeks later he was early in line for *The Rocky Horror Picture Show*, spotted the bullish girl passing with a pretty (half-, he learned) Chinese boy in (what he learned was) a Frank outfit, and invited them in.

Although dubbing Saltine rudely, Anarchy went so far as to defend him from a particularly vile Meat Loaf that night, and Lindie found him as soft, dim, and reassuring as a nightlight. Saltine felt redeemed, like the Queen from *Snow White* had taken over Disneyland and was showing him the sights.

Lord knows the Queen could use some help. The week before, Lindie's sister had walked in on him and Anarchy, inappropriately yelled 'Christ!', and dropped her Coke-and-milk. Proving the gods' indifference to the soundtrack influence of 'Jesus of Cool', the glass didn't break. The jig is up, thought Anarchy prematurely, and, always prepared for a quick collapse, collapsed on to her haunches.

In one long complicated curve, Lindie yelled 'Knock first!', swooped up the glass, and, heedless of his necklace and open robe, handed it back to the girl, directing her into the hall. 'Later,' he said. 'For goodness' sake.' He turned on the light as Anarchy set to mopping up and Nick Lowe expressed his love for the Bay City Rollers.

Lindie bared his back, squatted beside her, and apologised about his sister.

'No, she's all right. I like her.'

(This was true enough that, once, an embarrassed silence had settled over the three of them while listening to Patti Smith sing the 'dig your baby sister, want your baby sister' part of 'Land'.)

On ensuing weekend and weeklong sleepovers at Lindie's house, Saltine's horizons were expanded as only flat infinitely retreating lines can be. In return, his stone-faced bounce made a fine Max's Kansas City men's room to hide the details of the Lindie–Anarchy connection. And when it came to Lindie's dark university-stacks-fed hobbyhorse, Saltine quickly outstripped the stable boy role, advancing first to stand in for Anarchy, then replace her.

Very 'All About Evil' but 'the kid's a natural' said Lindie, and anyway Anarchy's visions had never delighted her the way they did him. About a third of the time she made up plausible replacements to avoid going through them again; the rest she deliberately adjusted, as if to tag the originals. At first she worried what these flaws might turn into magnified by Lindie's multimedia elaborations but it looked like they didn't make any difference. Well, they all come from the same place in the end. And as far as practical applications went, if you wanted to inflict your power on someone, why not just slap her?

Or, as Lindie sang, coming in looking, in his white jumpsuit, like one of Mrs Fraser's tall rum-topped coconut drinks, 'My girlfriend's back and she's gonna break your lay-eggs.'

Unresplendent, in 'Everyone's In Show Biz' T-shirt and lumpen jeans, Anarchy defensively picked an album off the floor. 'What's this mess? Ah, the Masters of Folk Rock, Stilton Spam.' (Once, she'd put the poor Brits on immediately after 'Raw Power', and it'd been weeks before even Lindie could stand to listen to them again.) 'She's got a cute little fat foot. Hope she keeps it out the chicken.'

Saltine took the jacket from her and looked at it.

Lindie said, 'Just 'cause they wear tan leather. Cut the fringe and paint it black, you'd call 'em punks.'

'Punks and elves, punks and elves,' Anarchy intoned like Uncle Jack's Tales of the Ozarks. 'I can see that. I'm a troll – ' 'A werewolf,' corrected Lindie – 'Lucky Lindie's got to be a faery, and Saltine' – with his dank black hair born to be combed in a widow's peak and his thin greenish flesh, the exact colour of an ancient Volkswagen that Anarchy had once been in – 'is a vampire.'

On the other side of Crowley's *Book 4* and Fitzcollin's *Secret History of the Golden Dawn* Lindie softly warbled, 'Jet Boy stole, Jet Boy stole, Jet Boy stole my baby,' with the stereo as he toiled into his draughtsman's notebook. Each sheet was first packed with precise-looking print rubbing bellies with physics-class circles and annotated arrows. Then he would overlay new facets or just doodle, never making clean copies. Lindie thought this the most valid format for a record of meditative self-discovery, due to its illegibility.

Anarchy described their fantasy ABC series 'Great Big Beautiful Dolls' to Saltine; Lindie interrupted, 'Too bad it can only last one season: Johnny's going to die soon.'

'Fine! I bet the Monkees wish *they'd* gotten to do a funeral show,' Anarchy answered, aware she'd said it before, like everything else. It was a pleasure to have an audience but it made life more abstract, like rehearsals of an autobiographical Neil Simon play.

The audience, meanwhile, reflected pleasurably on vampirish sophistication. He considered buying a cape, then a guitar. He couldn't help feeling his life was connected with music somehow.

'Do you believe in the magick which rhythmically moves the virgin soul wherever it will?' Lindie said. He was a good reader, you couldn't tell if he was reading it or asking it.

'What about fucked souls?' asked Anarchy.

'No such thing. I think it's like, talking about music. Music is the means of control, but it controls the soul of the user as well as the object.'

'Oh! a spoonful of sugar helps the heroin melt down,' Anarchy sang in her cracked voice. Like what she didn't know about heroin wouldn't fill three No New York compilations and a critically acclaimed Bantam Book original.

But that was Anarchy. Whereas Saltine would think about it and say, 'Sort of,' and explain at length why a conclusion was impossible.

For example, Lindie put an aphid in his ear about some Theosophical parallel with the faith of our fathers holy faith, and a week later Saltine was still milking it. It appeared that orthodox asceticism, where you stripped off flesh and nerves while still hidden by a bathrobe or something and only exposed yourself when you were down to bones and spirit, apparently so much wussier than the I AM A BULLET bit, 'actually isn't, maybe'. Given the Native American influences on Neodeshan ceremony even some of the methods 'aren't that far apart, in some details'. Typical hedgelian dialectic.

But Lindie liked it, and over the summer the point of meeting at Anarchy's became double-imaged, one red one green before the 3-D specs settle. It was partly to hide Lindie's and Anarchy's thing, partly to hide Lindie's and Saltine's.

Lindie's sister sometimes stopped by, and when Anarchy wasn't needed and wasn't too tense and bored she'd talk to the girl and even got so she'd tuck away some distractions.

Once it was a remaindered Diane Arbus coffee table book for people who like pictures of sweaty transvestite junkies with their coffee. Lindie's sister really got into it, pointing out all kinds of compositions and exposures. She was already good for a kid, even put a couple of ain't-nature-dreamy? shots into Lindie's portfolio that he hadn't gotten rid of yet. (Neodeshan fashions being of limited appeal in the then decadent mood of the advertising mainstream, most of Lindie's income came from local modelling jobs.)

Anarchy was inspired. 'You can show college lowlife and sign yourself EeGee!'

'Huh? You mean EeYeff, right?'

'Shit!' said Anarchy. 'I hate when I do that.'

The upshot was they decided, despite *Rolling Stone*, photography could still be a sincere art form if the contrast was high enough, and posited Anarchy as a subject 'til Lindie's sister could work her way up to dwarfs and whores.

Other times, Anarchy was in the thick of things and Lindie's sister had to make do; sometimes she'd just leave, sometimes she'd split a Coke with Mrs Gordon first.

'As big a fuss as she kicks up over Sears, I don't know how you get her to sit still for it.' (For the last ten years, the family portraits had been crafted by the North Filart Spirit of Liberty Mall Sears Photo Center. Anarchy always came out very pink.)

'Well, the idea is to not have her sit still,' said Lindie's sister.

Mrs Gordon nodded, wondering whether to offer her milk and whether they had any milk but not deciding in time.

In Anarchy's locked bedroom, Saltine went over the Sekhmel ritual, almost whispering under 'Metal Machine Music' (on cassette so Lindie didn't have to flip sides as often).

'One thing. Um,' ventured Saltine, ready to topple under

the bobbing weightiness of his thought, 'it's supposed to go better if there's at least three' (which made sense, it was actually a Ptah-Sekhmel-Nefertum ritual, just that 'Ptah' sounded silly and Sekhmel was the cool one) 'but it's also supposed to go better if there's intimacy.' Anarchy's ears pricked up. Intimacy? 'Which is weird, because that should imply two.' What the fuck?

Lindie was very excited to hear that. 'Three is perfect!' he said, grabbing one by the elbow, one at the knee.

'You mean, like, the Jefferson Airplane song?' Saltine asked. Then they started laughing as though it was the last shot of the sitcom. Since it wasn't, they had to fade into something else, tender looks, all that. But it was like they wanted to stay in the water without going too deep, not to the point of being moved instead of having to apply themselves.

Well, sure, no one wants to drown, and how else are you going to come to an understanding with it?

Afterwards, they all felt relaxed but vaguely put upon. Saltine (whose disconcerting curve gave Anarchy a new angle on 'horny') said it was just a natural response to the high male–female ratio in frontier America, which non-Neodeshan Lindie didn't get and Anarchy didn't think was funny. She was already starting to get that pre-tantrum glow, those rogue elephant eyes, so Lindie suggested going to Burger King.

If it had just been Lindie and Saltine they would've biked there. But Anarchy always preferred to walk, feeling too easy a target on the spindly wheels. Even the range disturbed her; she imagined giddy miles of rushing toward lower elevations (unlikely in Canaan!), then being stranded too far to walk back, too steep to ride back, a milder strain of her panic at the first damper of fatigue when swimming. Lindie tried to explain that she would get a second wind but it seemed such an ephemeral concept to stake one's life on. Then again so did the first wind.

Once your eyes got over being slapped in the face by the sun, it was a nice day. Lindie and Saltine kept yakking. Anarchy phased out. A polluted leaf from last fall propped on a branch looking like a black oyster shell with a lolling tongue. Suddenly Saltine was jumping and yelling and spitting, Lindie was shaking him and profaning like mad. On the way to the hospital (not far from Planned Parenthood on Goshen, so everyone knew how to get there), she worked out that a bumblebee had funnelled into his mouth. Saltine was in too much pain to notice the fit of giggles this gave her. That bee *gave his life* that Saltine might shut up, she thought in a Jimmy Swaggart voice.

Lindie noticed, though. Honestly, when Anarchy wasn't wishing she was dead, she was acting like her corpse wouldn't stink. Saltine was a lot smarter than she thought, he had a sting he didn't show around her, and he knew how to keep it out of the way.

After that Anarchy didn't see the boys for a while. Sometimes she thought of this Army brat she met last summer, a giraffey blonde girl, plain, blotchy, who was homesick for the Philippines where she'd danced for all of 'In-A-Gadda-Da-Vida' with a handsome guy half a foot shorter who spoke odd English and necked with her for hours. As the blonde reminisced, Anarchy'd imagined a corresponding Filipina left somewhere alone trying to figure out what to charge sailors if you were a virgin.

Still Anarchy was confident of a special link to Lindie; she felt she even had a feeling for his artificiality. They'd stayed up late to see *Monterey Pop* on the wrestling-and-Godzilla channel, Hendrix politely jerking off the guitar he was about to piss on and burn; she read that he'd made it up to upstage the Who, I mean, he *just made it up*, and that was sort of like Lindie.

With Saltine, she hadn't a clue. He stopped by one day while Lindie was out on a shoot.

'Sometimes I think I'm not up to you guys,' Saltine reflected. 'Almost all the time.' Anarchy tried to think of something encouraging. 'I get so much from you both and I can't see what I give back.'

Anarchy came up with it. 'That's sweet.'

Saltine had cast his wadded balls of Wonder Bread on the water looking for a bigger catfish than that. Clearly he hadn't proven himself.

Remembering something she could be sincere about, Anarchy showed him her latest Glitter Storybook. A stack of these, including fragments, took up a third of her scuffed bestickered portfolio. They were mostly scurrilous libels on British rock stars, each page containing a faux-Steadman doodle and a paragraph of Basic English in Anarchy's big shaky hand. She'd sent one to *Creem* but all they did was print the text as a letter which didn't make sense. Lindie's favourite was the David Bowie's Sex Life alphabet; he could recite the whole thing.

This one was just sick. Three lesbian vampires infiltrated a bunch of groupies plus a female photographer backstage with the Babys (a frequent target of Anarchy's because they *looked* so much like a rock band), dismembered them, and sold them as veal.

Anarchy fidgeted while Saltine read it silently and wondered if all girls were this savage when you got to know them. Before he finished, she stumped out the door. Waiting outside was Lindie's sister's camera, which snapped at her twice before being chased off.

The results were not among the prints which arrived a few days later. '"A triumph!" trumpets Julia Scully!' read a headline on the envelope. The photos were monotonously hideous: assorted croppings, blow-ups, saturations, of each of five shots, each oafish as a yearbook senior trip page. Anarchy looked about wildly for an efficient disposal site, thrust them into her ever more disorderly portfolio, and set out for Shea Fraser (as Lindie called it for unknown reasons) to eliminate the negatives.

There, Saltine was, speak of the devil, worried about Anarchy collapsing like a cartoon jalopy before they could get the ceremony together. Lindie hadn't exactly been in a rush to get in touch lately, but he still felt obliged to defend her; no blip could break up signals which had coincided so long.

A surge of noise from downstairs leached through the music: his sister's plaintive 'Liinnn!' and his mother precise and brittle as scissors, 'Give those back!' and oh Jesus Anarchy no doubt. 'Should I come?' asked Saltine. 'God no, save yourself,' Lindie hopped, pulling on his slippers, 'someone's got to tell the coroner what happened. Let's hope she doesn't scar me anywhere visible; I have an audition.'

His sister was at the bottom of the stairs, looking up for him teary eyed. His mother was stiff and small, just out of Anarchy's arms' reach, glaring her owly glasses off her nose. 'They're mine! They're me!' Anarchy said, tossing wildly.

'I don't know what you are "on", young miss, but unless you *immediately* return my daughter's property and leave these premises I will be forced to call the police.'

Did she *rehearse* that? thought Lindie as he rushed to say 'No! It'll be okay!' and his sister rushed to say 'No! It's not that important!'

Anarchy looked at him like a raccoon caught in headlights, turned away, and trotted out the door. His mother shut and locked it. 'That girl is never to come here again! Do you understand me, Lin Duane Fraser? I want *nothing* to do with that girl.' She reassuringly gripped his sister before her like a shield.

'I don't even know what happened.' He tried to ignore his mother's explanation while his sister tried to explain. Anarchy must not have liked her pictures. She not only made his sister give her the originals, she took the film right out of the camera, an almost full roll. His mother started in again; his heart spun. 'All right, but now I have to help her, you can see that!'

He went upstairs to put on real shoes and to tell Saltine, and then left.

'I don't know what's ailing that girl,' Mrs Gordon said as he passed her. Anarchy tucked her X-Acto knife into the blanket as he joined her on the bed.

'Hey,' he said. 'Why'd you take the pictures?'

She tried to think of an answer. 'I want to be erased.'

'I feel like that sometimes. It's your body fucking around with your head. You just need to give it something else to deal with, like an hour in the pool.'

Pools reminded her of a swimming class two years ago when some girl backed up by a mob smirk made a crack about wet hair, and she looked down and sure enough, some was poking out garish against her skin. Anyway, she didn't like to swim. Anyway, this had nothing to do with swimming anyway, why was he talking about it?

Dinnertime came. Anarchy refused to eat or even to leave the room. Lindie grabbed a plateful for himself; to Mrs Gordon's ramblings he promised to 'take care of it'. 'You're a good friend,' she told him.

It was amazing how much self-destruction one person could hold. It was like the colourful silk worm drawn from a magician's mouth, or the oatmeal in the *Eraserhead* baby. Afterwards he wondered, very un-Lindie-like, why he hadn't left her to her fucking impulses if they were so fucking unanswerable, but at the time (3 to 6 a.m.) it seemed important, like toting up shifting columns of six-digit numbers does to an insomniac with fever.

Anarchy sleazed out in the morning while Lindie was in the bathroom. No makeup was up to the job of making him fresh-faced. He didn't get the assignment, and had to perform acrobatic sucking-up even to get put on the callback list for the Prince Ascot line (which it was true he'd be perfect for, but he could've easily handled On The Mississippi as well). There was still Gilbey's clothing later in the week.

All this while, Saltine had been left behind to comfort Lindie's sister, doing quite a creditable job for which he was never thanked I might add, and mull:

Lindie's Occult-o-rama mostly relied on alchemists and other scam artists, but random pokes into *The Golden Bough* and *The Hero with a Thousand Faces* and *Man and His Symbols* indicated you could get the same stuff anywhere if you weren't a snob. So wouldn't it make sense to plug into the nearest outlet instead of dragging an extension cord umpteen million miles?

Although Saltine had started mocking the church around the same time he started masturbating, Walt Brown's corned beef hash of primitivism and Christianity beat the other Protestants hollow. Like his grandpa's facsimile Towel of Turin smelling of old motor oil from working on the Galaxy 500 wrapping some lucky condor feathers; now you can't get much more shamanistic than that. The *New World Testament* even kind of mentioned UFOs!

But no matter how cynically he put it, Anarchy wouldn't listen. She was ideologically claustrophobic. If anarchists had founded Canaan, she'd've called herself Federalism.

It wasn't that he had anything against her; he was mostly worried about Lindie. Applying to out-of-state schools, working as many jobs as possible, his parents at him to stay where tuition was free and he could pay cheap rent at home, and now all this hysteria.

But the last thing Saltine wanted was to put more pressure on Lindie. That was the last thing he wanted to do.

Lindie was taken aback by his concern. Altruism dissipates; desire concentrates, the universe compact in a bit of flesh. Bad enough that Anarchy was so reactive, without Saltine being so binding.

(It's true that Lindie's own motives remain even more obscure, but what can you expect of the love interest? He was unsure himself, letting the need to focus direct him. Besides, why appeal to outside forces if you know everything already?)

'This is your big opportunity to be selfish. Otherwise it doesn't seem, I don't know, private enough . . .'

'Well, you can't go on like this. Or if you can, I don't want to watch it.'

'Oh please, I'm too tired.' Then, 'We really have to have a third?'

'I think so, probably.'

Might as well let everything fall apart at once. 'Well, all right, let's get it over with.' Maybe a structured activity where she felt needed would distract her.

They waited for Lindie's mother to leave for Tuesday night quilting class. His father usually worked late (or whatever he did Tuesday nights). With any luck, his sister wouldn't feel like hanging around.

Anarchy, meanwhile, after some c-sticks and skittish runs at traffic on the walk home, was improvising her own purification ritual. She aimed a butt at her upper arm; it might look like vaccination scars (though she kept picturing a blue stamp on a leg-of-lamb's yellow fat). The first time hurt so much she kept dropping the butt, and it was too humiliating trying to pick it up, so she decided to burn the portfolio's contents instead. But she couldn't figure out where to lay the bundle so it wouldn't set the house on fire, so, trembling with frustration, she sloppily tore the pages.

Her ingenuity was feeling wiped by the time they called. She had them pick her up. She wrapped herself in her hooded black wool cape but still shivered.

For lack of decent incense, Lindie burnt some potpourri in spare ashtrays and some pinched into candles. Then he went deep into his closet, where a muffled scrabbling became a terrible racket. 'It's good we're doing this tonight. The 'rents would've called an exterminator soon.' He lugged out a cage containing newspaper and a frantic squirrel. 'Gracious, look at that boy bounce.' Nervous for his fingers, he dropped the cage and manoeuvred it with his foot.

'I thought . . .' said Anarchy, a bit stunned, and waved towards the squirrel.

'Yeah, a hamster or something would've been easier, but it turns out domesticated isn't as good. Anyway, it's a spirit sacrifice, not a blood sacrifice,' he reassured the other two as he set things up. 'It probably won't have time to suffer.' They positioned themselves and began.

The squirrel stopped its pogoing and headbanging and stood upright like an A&R man in the centre of the cage. It appeared to clutch at its heart, as the cute little fellows are prone to. After a minute or so it stiffly toppled on to its side. Wow, they all thought briefly.

Anarchy's throat was dry from the cigs. She swallowed hard, like a cannibal trying to incorporate metaphysical enemies. The meditation wasn't focusing, or rather it was focusing wildly back and forth like when they watched the giblet-poke scene in *Andy Warhol's Frankenstein* (which had netted the hippie owners of the Weld Theatre a bankrupting obscenity prosecution despite Mr Warhol's mural of Mayor

Rev. Abraham). Were the other two faking? She couldn't even tell when Lindie was really sleeping.

After enough leaning over and jerking back, she started to realise they weren't, it's just that Saltine was driving and it took a lot longer for Saltine to get over the hump and to figure out what to do when he got there.

Slowly slathered over their triangle as if it was a mystic piece of toast was a pure shimmering blue the shade of a black and white TV. Even down to the humming scan lines, half of which seemed to show a draped Californian, half of which seemed an overlapping closer shot of a snaggletooth-grinding draped hunchback. One point of the triangle was being bitten off, the point towards Anarchy. No sign of Sekhmel.

Blue is for boys, Saltine thought, as the figures raised their garment in a gesture both embracing and exclusive, and raised their common noggin up past the normal limits of Lindie's ceiling. As the buzz became an amplified breath, then a roar, their satin robe spread and crested and fell on to poor Anarchy without splashing, like a twenty-foot-thick blanket, and then gently troughed Saltine up, raising him towards the sun, which had features like the cover of 'Mott' only sterner. He felt pressure build behind him, more than his weight, and realised he must be accelerating. He turned to face Lindie.

The push emphasised Saltine's already prominent veins. Even the tiniest vessels were visibly rippling like highlights on a stream, and the larger ones were beginning to, how disquieting, *surface*. Immediately after popping through the skin like so many bathtub toys, they flopped open down their dotted-line middles, spilling red or blue blood.

With trembling furrowed hands, Saltine tried to scoop the liquid (now the consistency of unset plum jelly) back in.

'No!' warned Lindie, trying to remember how carbon dioxide worked. 'You don't want to mix them!'

God, where was Anarchy, she'd had to deal with enough cuts, bruises, madness, broken nails . . . Saltine's flesh was drying out translucent as a lemon-lime gummy bear (Lindie could even taste a dusty sweetness in the air) and a light was behind him.

It's true, Lindie thought. The light was naturally cross-shaped, with a corporeal bulge along the vertical axis, as depicted in *Pinocchio* and the cover of *Western Dawn* magazine. It webbed into a mandala – no, a shield, a mirrored shield, a half-mirrored shield, half-behind Saltine and superimposing Lindie. There was a sense of relief. A sense of lifting after a plunge. Put your hand in the hand . . .

The room was dark but clear. Anarchy was gone. Saltine seemed to still have all his blood. The squirrel was still dead. Lindie pitched it underhand out the window towards the unkempt honey-locust for a cat to drag away.

Saltine asked Lindie how he felt.

Lindie felt as if trapdoors in the callus on his soles had flipped open and all his innards had poured out. If he exhaled, his eyes would drop into the vacuum, dangling from their stalks like Luke and Princess Leia waiting to be rescued. 'I'm fine,' he smiled. 'Never better. I just need some sleep.'

'I don't, she's just not up to it I think any more? but I don't think we really need her help now any more anyway.'

Lindie shook his head. 'Jesus. How did you do that?'

Saltine was modest. 'I just went towards the light.'

Like a bug.

The next day, talking to his sister, Lindie found out three pictures which he'd hoped to send to Gilbey's had been on the roll of film Anarchy took.

Anarchy left Filart before summer was over. After a year on the bum, she called on the insurance money put away for her schooling and got into NYCAI; with a scholarship, she even had a little left over for speed.

She started out as a film major but switched, first to history then to painting, when her first-year-both-semesters prof insisted on pronouncing Liberty Valence as if he was a pre-med. She did so-so scholastically, but helped some performance artists, one of whom became a sitcom star, and interned on sets at the City Opera.

On Music School equipment she learned wobbly piano and guitar. A friend into postmodern cabaret asked her to write some songs. It was much easier than trying to figure out other people's.

Twice early in the next decade Lindie tried to call her. Once she didn't answer (drunk, she taped over the message trying to replay it, *who* was it? Nickie? Ray? oh shit . . .). On his second attempt (to make sure it was God's will), it had already become the wrong number. For her part, she only contacted him in nightmares where dead friendships rose like zombies and she felt draggy the rest of the day.

Early in '90 she got a CD out under the name A.G. Gordon. Kramer had her draw the cover. She got fan mail from Lindie's sister, and since she was bracing herself to visit her stepmother's for Thanksgiving anyway, she wrote back.

Nostalgia flabbed up to replace atrophied memory, or, as A.G. said with the lazy generosity of a monarch commuting a burning-at-the-stake to a beheading, 'It's natural to get over being mad eventually.'

'I guess,' doubted Lindie's sister.

They put L7's first album on while chatting about the business.

A.G. hulked close to the speaker and, crazed by the beat,

slowly moved her head from side to side like the triceratops which got killed in *Fantasia*. Brokenly she elaborated, 'The biggest problem is when there's no one to tell you the truth. It's not that they're all lying but none of them are far away enough and smart enough to figure out the truth.'

'Mm.' A.G. waited for her to say what was on her mind. 'You shouldn't have left Lin. I mean, it's great that you left, but Lin just died. He just fucking died,' she said solemnly.

A.G. felt a nervous laugh stir like a burp. 'I didn't kill him. I didn't even keep him from coming with me. Besides I heard he was pretty happy.'

'It's an act.'

'That's still better than most of us manage. I mean, not only am *I* fucking miserable but I look it too.'

A.G. felt duty bound to ask after Saltine, though it was embarrassing to not remember his real name. 'Oh, Phil's still hanging around,' the girl answered vaguely and A.G. let it drop and waited again for her to finish her thought.

'It just seems like, reading and talking to people, it never works out.' She continued staring into the wall.

A.G. watched her pensiveness make her look even younger, and considered. 'No, it does. Lots of times, believe me.' She rubbed haphazardly at the tense back, a sheath of bone.

'I guess it must've been something else then,' Lindie's sister said.

Don't Leave Me
Barrington J. Bayley

Never take pop culture too seriously – after all, look what happened to Woody Allen and Paul McCartney. Luckily for us, there's no better writer to prick the vacuum bubble into which too many critics have retreated than Barry Bayley, whose witty, transsurreal stories have ornamented SF since the early days of New Worlds. *We're particularly pleased to present one of his stories here, because, with novels such as* The Zen Gun *and* The Rod of Light, *he is a link between the fine old days of* New Worlds' *trippy gedanken experiments in literary speculative fiction and the ideological gurus of the current radical SF fringe. Here, he deconstructs the deconstructionists in a sly, intelligent and above all funny story about the consequences of taking pop lyrics a smidgen too seriously.*

Extremely little is known of the period and civilisation to which the artifact belongs. Found as the result of a deep excavation, it may have been thrown on a rubbish tip consisting mainly of organic refuse, which has degraded to a peat-like substance, though the artifact itself is made of an artificial hydrocarbon resistant to attack by bacteria. It is a miracle that it was not chewed to shreds by the excavator, and a second miracle that it was ever noticed.

Black in colour, the artifact takes the form of a thin disc a little less than a hand's span in diameter. One side has been abraded by some accidental process, and it is not known if it ever contained anything of interest. For twenty years the disc lay in the Leveropolis Museum of Antiquities as a curio or uninteresting relic. For most of that time it was believed to be a decorative wall plaque, the perforations – consisting of a central hole surrounded by quarter-circle slots – present to help fix it in place. The symbols on the inner smooth part of the disc were identified as the phonetic script of the Roman Empire, and the Leveropolis Museum speculatively dated it as belonging to the late period of Rome's three to four thousand year history.

Although some of the languages represented by Roman script have been deciphered in varying degrees, the significance of the legends on the disc remained unknown. It was Expertiser Had-Frakshelis-Suissperrer, making an inspection tour of Politan Museums, who first suggested that the disc might be a store of information. He partly based his suggestion on the fact that a word which, with various derivatives, occurs five times in the disc's script, could be translated as 'record'. The original translators had interpreted this word as 'pattern', thinking it to refer to the moulding of the disc, which the Romans presumably thought visually appealing. The text of a current translation of the legends is reproduced below, though without their full artistic arrangement:

All rights of the manufacturer and of the owner of the recorded work reserved. Unauthorised public performance broadcasting and copying of this record prohibited.

LONDON

American Recordings

Made in England   45 R.P.M.

Recording first   E/T
published 1959

A UNITED   45-HLT
ARTISTS   9013
Recording

Jobet Music

DON'T LEAVE ME
(Gordy, Brianbert, Robinson)
MARV JOHNSON

The legend 'Jobet Music' was, it was true, an argument against Expertiser Had-Frakshelis-Suissperrer's contention, 'Music' being a Roman term for 'artistic arrangement' and obviously referring to the layout of the disc. Also, information storage methods employed in the late Roman Empire were known to be extremely primitive, demonstrating a lack of consideration for future historians and archaeologists fairly typical of early civilisations. Magnetic storage was the technique most commonly used, a medium which degrades even more rapidly than inked tree leaves or bark. Consequently the only Roman records surviving were fragments of writing in the Roman phonetic or 'alphabetical' script, and shards of hard material on which had been etched rows of microscopic pits. After much analysis the latter yielded a binary code from which, with much trouble, bits of photographic images have been reconstructed.

The black disc is made of non-magnetic material, and so could not have been used for magnetic storage. However, Expertiser Had-Frakshelis-Suissperrer pointed out that binary pit-rows were sometimes found in the form of arcs, possibly broken sections of circles, suggesting that the code might have been read in rotary fashion. Could the black hydrocarbon disc be a variant carrier of image code?

Close examination of the roughened area of the disc, where it had been scored with narrow circular grooves, revealed a surprise: there was but a single groove, running in a close-packed spiral – though broken in many places where the disc had been scratched or otherwise damaged. The groove was, however, smooth, without pits or anything which could comprise a binary code. Expertiser Had-Frakshelis-Suissperrer then learned the unwisdom of publicising an idea before it has been tested. He was severely ridiculed for having attached significance to what was no more than a decorative pattern, designed to break up the light. His career and standing were badly damaged, and in a short time he elected for early voluntary death. Some may remember the brief fad for imitation 'Roman wall-plaques' which followed, various imaginative groove-patterns being scored on discs of moulded black hydrocarbon.

The disc continued to fascinate scholars, and despite the fate of Expertiser Had-Frakshelis-Suissperrer the notion that it was a recording device persisted. Knowledgian Partners Harporse-Shem-Kwismave and Burve-Gomweenlos-Gurter-erver were the next to examine the spiral groove through a microscope, and were the first to notice that the groove was not quite even, but meandered slightly in irregular fashion. Could the deviations be another type of picture code, per-forming a function similar to pit-rows? The prospect was exciting, since if so then a complete Roman picture or even set of pictures was available for the first time. Entranced by the prospect of gazing upon a Roman scene, and ignoring warnings that the meanderings of the groove could simply be due to the crudity of the tool used, the knowledgians obtained from Central Funding an appropriation of two hundred and fifty thousand social wealth units to finance the attempted decipherment of the image code.

Despite an investment in expensive analysing equipment and much time, no pictures were ever discovered. The meanderings appeared to be random. As is well known, Knowledgian Partners Harporse-Shem-Kwismave and Burve-Gomweenlos-Gurtererver were subsequently punished by public surgical decapitation, for non-productive use of social funds.

Yet the efforts of these brave martyred scholars have not, in the end, been without result. I, Expertiser Swilansone-Kurep-Bifo also pondered the phenomenon of the wandering groove. One day in my laboratory I made a metal reed vibrate by being blown in a stream of air, later examining its recorded motion at leisure on an oscilloscope. Watching the waggly line traced by the beam on the phosphorescent end of the tube, I suddenly thought of the Roman artifact, and an idea blossomed full-grown in my mind. If something were made to run at speed through the meandering groove, it would waver just like the spot on the oscilloscope!

Knowledgian Partners Harporse-Shem-Kwismave and Burve-Gomweenlos-Gurtererver, I recalled, had tried to derive a digital code expressing light and shade, by measuring the groove's amplitudes of variation. Could they have overlooked something so stunningly simple that no one would normally think of it? Not wanting to share their fate, or that of Expertiser Had-Frakshelis-Suissperrer before them, I moved cautiously, and depended on my own resources alone. First I had to persuade the Leveropolis Museum of Antiquities to loan me the disc. This I did on the pretext that I intended to make an exact survey of its measurements. I also sought the Museum's permission to restore the disc by repairing the breaks in the groove's walls. The curators were glad to allow this, not having been able to comtemplate such a meticulous project themselves, and hoping that we might then see the full original effect of the disc as a wall plaque.

The job of restoring the groove, using microscopic tools, was indeed a long and difficult one. Once accomplished, I began to consider how to convert the groove's meanderings into vibrations of a metal reed.

At first I proposed to construct a framework by means of which I could run a small metal probe in a spiral path, tracking from the centre out, but this seemed difficult in practical terms. I therefore thought of a simpler solution. The disc's central hole reminded me of the axle hole of a wheel. I therefore made a rotating rubber 'pad' on which to rest the wheel, with a central spindle to hold it in place. By rotating the disc, the problem of running a probe through the groove was very much simplified. For the probe itself, I rejected metal in favour of a splinter of diamond, first making sure that this would not damage the disc too much. This I fixed on the end of an arm whose other end was hinged, so that it was able to move in an arc. By merely placing the probe in the groove, the movement of the disc was sufficient to carry it through the spiral!

A re-examination of the groove convinced me that this was how the Romans actually used the disc, and also that I had been wrong in proposing to run the probe from the inner part towards the periphery. On either side of the close-packed spiral are smooth areas through which the groove continues to run but in widely spaced turns, and these turns of the groove, moreover, are without meanderings. If the probe were run from the centre outward, it would eventually fall off the disc. On the inner shiny area, however, the spiral turns into a closed circle, and if travelling inward the probe eventually remains safely in this until it is removed.

Initially, the variable-speed rotating pad was set at fifty rotations per chronodegree. I placed the probe in the groove, set the disc rotating, watched the probe run into the close-packed meandering spiral, then bent my ear close to the metal reed which I had welded on to the stylus holding the diamond splinter. Sure enough, the reed was audibly vibrating.

I confess that I had expected to hear, at most, nothing but white noise. What I heard instead was – faint, but definitely structured, sound.

The mystery of the Roman disc was solved! It was a recording device after all – but a device for recording *sound*!

But a simple reed was obviously quite inadequate as a resonator. I set to work again, converting the stylus into a kind of little microphone which produced varying electric current controlled by the vibrations of the diamond. This current I used to modulate a much stronger current in an electronic amplifier, finally using the strong current to work a loudspeaker such as are employed to issue daily instructions in the public squares.

This arrangement, in all probability, matches that used in Roman times.

Now that the disc's signal had been fully recovered, the question of the correct speed of rotation could be tackled. This might have been impossible but for the presence of a human voice on the recording. I judged, after some experimentation, that the disc should be spun at somewhere between one hundred and twenty and one hundred and fifty rotations per chronodegree. (Recently it has been suggested that the inscription '45 R.P.M.' which appears among the disc's legends stands for '45 Revolutions Per Minute', so that we now have a value for this Roman time unit.)

It is scarcely possible to convey, to one who has not heard it, the bewildering volume and turmoil which issues from this little disc. Great rhythmic thudding sounds, skirlings, chimings, voices, unexpected interventions, all creating together an organised pattern which, though with a certain compelling quality, is virtually incomprehensible to the modern mind.

For that reason we concentrated our attention on the single voice which speaks in the foreground of the sound-message. Though a fairly large written vocabulary exists for the Roman language of the legends occupying the central portion of the disc, no Roman voice had ever been heard before, and the problem of matching the spoken with the written word was a serious one. It was solved after nearly a year of study.

A full transcription of the message text follows, the one expression to defy translation being included in parentheses:

> *Don't leave me, don't leave me, don't leave me*
> *Baby, baby, baby, don't leave me*
> *Oh no, no, no, don't . . .*
>
> *(Woah, woah) I-I-I had a dream last night*
> *When I awoke I found myself crying.*
> *I dreamed that the girl I loved told me*
> *That our love was dying.*
>
> *(Woah, woah) she said, she said*
> *That she was falling*
> *Fa-a-alling, for a buddy of mine*
> *And she said that everyone knew*
> *And how could I be so blind.*
>
> *I woke up and called my baby*
> *She said no matter how ill it seemed*
> *She would always be mine and losing her*
> *Was something that I had dreamed.*
>
> *No, no, please don't leave me, baby*
> *It's just a dream that made me cry*
> *I know that if I lost you*
> *I-I-I would surely die.*

Don't leave me, don't leave me, don't leave me
Baby, baby, baby don't leave me
Oh no, no, no, don't, baby . . .

What must be mentioned is the agonised feeling with which
these words are spoken. Also remarkable is their extravagant
intonation, in which the tonal variations of normal speech
are altered and exaggerated to a manic degree. Three
examples have been loosely indicated in the transcription,
but the written word cannot give any adequate idea of the
weirdness of the effect. For instance, the word 'crying' at the
end of the fifth line is voiced using no fewer than six
consecutive tones.

The sociological information contained in the text is most
surprising. The speaker tells of his intense love for a girl,
and his fear that her love for him is being transferred to his
'buddy' (that is, his friend). We can safely assume that this
love is sexual. Yet we are continually reminded throughout
the text that the girl is his 'baby', that is, his own very young
child. Marriage between brother and sister was practised in
the civilisation preceding the Roman, namely the Egyptian,
but this is the first knowledge we have that in the Roman
world procreation proceeded between parent and child. The
intensity and enthusiasm displayed for the arrangement is
striking. Since such a custom would lead rapidly to genetic
degeneration, we may have here the explanation of the
collapse and total disappearance of the Roman Empire.

We can congratulate ourselves that in having combined
what were once two sexes into a single epicene human type,
delegating procreation to the amniotic tanks and assigning
the upbringing of the young to the offices of the state, we
have avoided all such dangers, and have also removed a
source of emotional disturbance.

The day came when I invited my colleague Expertiser

Stomlees-Win-Axalos discreetly to review the findings of myself and my assistants. Stomlees-Win-Axalos is probably the greatest expert on antiquities in the world, and in the ante-room to the laboratory I read out the text to him. I did not attempt to reproduce the eccentric vocalisation, I described it to him as best I could. He nodded impatiently.

'That is the meaning of the Roman word "singing". Both that, and the mysterious background noises you refer to, would appear to be examples of sonic music which was popular in early civilisations. It was based on rhythm, tonal variation and timbre, and no doubt would be bewildering indeed to anyone hearing it for the first time. Sonic music was, as a matter of fact, still being performed in our own civilisation up to about five centuries ago, when it was abandoned as being inimical to a balanced education. It would be as well if the playing of this disc were restricted to Expertisers and their prepared staff.'

I readily concurred.

'Well,' Expertiser Stomlees-Win-Axalos said irritably, 'are you going to keep me waiting much longer?'

I led him into the laboratory. He barely glanced at the disc which lay on the turnpad. He had, after all, been one of the first to examine it upon its discovery. I set the disc to spinning at one hundred and thirty rotations per chrono-degree, and carefully placed the diamond-tipped stylus where it would automatically be trapped by the run-in groove. I turned up the amplification so that Expertiser Stomlees-Win-Axalos could experience the full glory of the ancient recording, and hear at full volume that long-dead voice.

Expertiser Stomlees-Win-Axalos stood transfixed, his jaw dropping in astonishment as the playback proceeded to fill the room with loud sounds. The stylus tracked across the recorded area of the disc, ending, in place of silence, with an intermittent 'snap' and a continuous crackle as it ran in the safety loop.

His eyes shone. 'Fools! Do you not know what you have uncovered?'

Then: 'Play it again!'

On the second time the esteemed Expertiser listened to the disc with an even more determined concentration. Finally, as the needle again crackled out its spoiled silence, he turned to me.

'Forget about the verbal text for the time being, though your sociological interpretation is, I dare say, quite correct. No, listen to the sound constructions which back and support the "singing", like a cradle, like a boat – the tones resembling shrill bird calls, incidentally, may have been produced by an instrument called a "flute". This sound construction is, in turn, supported by something far more profound. Let me explain. The Romans built a marvellous type of timber ship, called a trireme, with three banks of oars. As you listen to this record, you can see such a ship very vividly in your mental imagination. You can hear the thudding of the oars as it pulls across the harbour. On the deck is a choir of "singers"; flutes are playing, and perfume is in the air.

'Do you not see what this means? *The Romans knew how to record mental images, and to play them back into the mind of anyone present.*'

With an effort he controlled his excitement. He made a casual gesture. 'Up until now you may have been impervious to this scene, not knowing of the existence of triremes.'

Expertiser Stomlees-Win-Axalos's announcement left me stunned. At first I had trouble believing it. But when we played the disc a third time, I also began to see the scene he described.

Since then I have played it hundreds of times, and with

each re-hearing the image becomes more compelling. The energy! The power! The thudding of the three banks of oars, the flute, the choir, as the beautiful trireme pulls across the shimmering water into perfumed mist.

And when one considers all three layers together – the mental image, the sound construction, the words of the 'singing', acute questions arise. There is, in this artistic construction, not only extreme vigour, but also an air of extreme degeneracy. Just what is taking place on the deck of the trireme I am not yet sure; but the 'singer', whose name we may deduce is 'Marv Johnson', is adamant in pursuing his deviant emotions. In the same way that the trireme propels itself across the harbour into scented darkness, he unwittingly describes how the Roman world headed into decadence in its search for pleasure and emotional intensity. Would the Romans have acted differently if they had realised the consequences for their civilisation? Having steeped myself in the mentality of the disc, I am forced to conclude that they would not, an attitude which we, with our quiet, placid lives, can scarcely understand. Indeed, Marv Johnson at first feels anguish, but then joy because his perverse way of life can continue.

But all this is insignificant as compared with the really great discovery: *the Romans knew how to record mental images*. How they managed to do this on what appears to be a fairly simple artificial hydrocarbon is as yet unknown; but it is a facility which we must learn to copy. Expertiser Stomlees-Win-Axalos and myself, Expertiser Swinlansone-Kurep-Bifo, are proud to announce that to that end we have obtained from Central Funding a disbursement of forty-five million social wealth units, a sum commensurate with the magnitude of the task.

Falling Stones
Peter F. Hamilton

There are plenty of political SF stories, but it's rare to find anything other than masturbatory power fantasies; even rarer to find a genuinely funny *political SF story. In 'Falling Stones' Peter F. Hamilton does for what Saddam Hussein has called 'The Mother of All Parliaments' what Screaming Lord Sutch and his Monster Raving Loony Party has done for by-elections, and hits more targets with greater precision than a whole flock of cruise missiles. After you've read this, neither* Yesterday in Parliament *nor* Top of the Pops *will never seem the same again.*

A notorious bon viveur and gourmand, and an accomplished circumaquatic cyclist, Peter F. Hamilton has published a clutch of short stories in small press magazines such as R.E.M. *and* Far Point, *and has also contributed to the second issue of* New Worlds. *His first novel,* Mindstar Rising, *should be out any time soon. He says of 'Falling Stones', 'I've never written anything like it before or since, nor was it written specifically for* In Dreams. *I tend to write hard SF, not alternate worlds and satire, but after this, I might be tempted to write another. I think it might have its origins in the superbly self-important interviews rock stars inflict on the rest of us, telling us how much better the world would be if they were running it. Combine this with the depressingly large number of seventies albums (yes, real vinyl!) in my collection, and I suppose the result was inevitable.'*

Inevitable? Maybe. Predictable? Like, no way, man.

Waking up is such a drag, the frost pixies are chewing on my fingers and toes again. The numbness has grown over the last few years, dropping too many scores. But screw that. Doctors are in league with Stashburners if you ask me. Stiff-culture members wearing wax-smile masks.

Something in the air, sour, like love left bleeding. But then, this is the day, they say. The heavy duty politico journalists like Steve Wright and Simon Bates over on Radio Caroline, carping on about how *he* is going to do it today. I don't want to believe them. Wouldn't, except for the portents, they're hyper.

Today is November the twenty-second nineteen-ninety, and it's going to be a real freak of a downer. My astrological movements have fallen into a long dark eclipse; my numerology chart adds up to the height of the great pyramid cubed. It doesn't come any worse; every bad vibe in the world twanging into focus, tearing at our mother Gaia, sundering us from her love. On days like this we could drown in her tears.

Then on top of all that, there's Keith. He's out now, the clinic let him go after they'd exorcised his demon. Totally dried out, clean line sober, and lusting after what he'd been shut out from all these years. He might just do it.

He's not in tune any more, a lone groover. Ask me, and clinics make your mind ill. Straighten You Out. Who needs it? We didn't get where we are today by thinking Straight.

I'm shoving back the wrap bundle and rolling off the mattress on to the floor. Greenmaryia grunts in her sleep and pulls the wrap back in reflex. Her braided strands of tangerine and purple hair are leaking out of the gap around the pillow, the tassels getting on for a couple of yards long, dried seaweed. That chick doesn't even get up before six in the evening these days. It's odd to see her crashed the whole time, she was such a funky go-go dancer in her day. I remember when we used to hunt mushrooms in the noble sunrise, stars shining on high. The magic was always strongest if you held them up to the first spark of sunlight, she'd say.

Cold sunlight through the window says it is about midday. I gaze down on Abbey Road. Same old hallowed ground, a living, breathing shrine. Strain my neck, and I can see *the* zebra crossing. Close my eyes and *they* walk again.

Getting trampled on by bloody tourists these days. Bloody tourists, bloody everywhere, cameras snapping up the essence, stealing the essence. Abbey Road is still the centre of the Earthpeace, though, eternal; they can never take it all.

The Road used to be nothing but recording studios, the poets and artists soaking it up, weaving it into the rhythm of the tracks. You could feel the true spirit of the age coming out of the vinyl of any album cut in Abbey Road, spreading the love it held.

I played my axe back then, all day and all night, played till my fingers bled and my strings snapped. But now the studios that haven't been turned into tourist trash altars are booked solid by the bad news music groups. Steely riffless synthesiser muzak whines out of their digital speakers, anti-nature worship. Children of the children of the revolution. And they've lost the path we found. I haven't done a session for months, maybe longer. I can't tell any more, everything is the same now, dry changeless time.

My feet slap on the chilly bare wooden boards, they know the way to the front room. Our pad is hip enough, though we don't go in for furniture in a heavy way. Too many possessions oppress the soul. And the bailiffs took away quite a bit of our stuff to pay the fat cat landlord.

I wrote to Peter Frampton about that, right after he was made Lord Chancellor. Told him I was a Great Happening vet, that the Stiff-culture vultures shouldn't be allowed to invade my personal space like this. It was why we marched, to tune out the negative hostility. Life is free, turn on to what you want. Nobody has a right to take that away.

He'll write back, sort it out. We believed together, and made it happen; a bond that can't be broken, it's existential. Government cares about its love children. Government is care. Our government. He'll write. He will.

I flop down on to the beanbag while the picture fizzes on to the telly, and light the day's first hit. Pure Moroccan Gold. I exhale, and the blue smoke sparkles.

The cameras are panning Westminster's chamber, a full house, expectant. I want to turn over, exit universe left. Those far out portents, you see? I know the portents are for real.

They ought to put something watchable on the telly in the afternoons, some groove of a concert on the Old Grey Whistle channel; Planet Gong or the whole five hours of Hawkwind's space ritual, just something I can relate to. A real forlorn hope, the BBC is toxic with Stiff-culture acolytes nowadays, peddling their Responsibility and Behaviour. The government ought to do something about that. Mike Oldfield is too bloody slack if you ask me, Mick should never never have appointed him Home Secretary.

But there's no alternative, so I stay hacked into reality. I can see the old familiar faces on the front bench, smiling at me out of the glass. All of them, the beautiful people. Mick up behind the dispatch box, wearing his purple velvet suit and yellow cravat, giving the bad news music opposition what for. Their leader, the demon spawn in black leather, Gary Numan, looks right narked at the trouncing he's getting. Patsy Kensit is sitting on his lap, soothing him down, and smiling hot at the camera at the same time. Sinitta and Rick Astley are trying to heckle; but their lips are

out of sync with the ghetto blaster they're using. Mick's
vocals riding 'em down.

He always gigs best at Westminster. That babe was born
to lay it down.

There's this fracture of ease creeping into my mood. Mick
still has some powerful backing group. Charlie Watts, Minister of Agriculture; I can see him, always a dead-cert loyal,
on the Treasury bench whispering to the Chancellor of the
Exchequer, Ronnie Wood. Even the Minister of Youth
Affairs, Bill Wyman, has come out of the green room to
show some support. Ray Davis and Alan Price are sharing a
bottle of Jack Daniels on the back benches; Donovan asleep;
Roger Waters, gaunt and worried looking. That cat should
learn how to roll with the swing.

I catch sight of Keith, looking smashed and wasted, on
the bench behind Mick. He's radiating ultra-bad karma,
wave after wave of it, squashing me down painfully in the
beanbag. I take a deep drag on the joint, but it doesn't make
any difference. Keith just keeps on burning; no way is he in
tune with the peace of mother Gaia any more. The clinic has
blinded him to the beauty of flowers and towering rainbows.

I can hear his venom in my mind, a broken riff echoing
down from the future. It hurts as bad as acid that'd been
spiked by the Stashburners.

There's a wraith-haunting cold crystallising around me,
winter's eldritch fingers reaching in from the grey-plastic
noon outside. We should be aware of seasons, the greatest
earthsong of all, but I wish the pad's radiators had hot water
in them.

Mick sits down, and, oh man, Keith's on his feet. Gonna
make a statement, he tells everyone, swaying about like
something rotted in a hurricane. Gonna lay it down, show
you where it's coming from, all this crap you've been eating
these last twenty-one years.

314   Peter F. Hamilton

And I'm shouting at him from the beanbag: not to do it, sit down Keith, not this, not now. We don't need no verbal Che Guevara, we don't need no dark Stiff-culture revival. We all know how it is with you and Mick. Sparks, that's what made the Stones roll. Maybe Mick shouldn't have dropped you from the cabinet, but you were Leary-ed out straight through the whole of the eighties. No big deal, live like you want to live. You couldn't help us, though, Keith. It was Mick who kept trashing the bad news music, who kept us out of the hands of the Stashburners. Not you. Our triumph lived on after the victory. And it was all Mick's doing, the longest serving prime minister this century, he held it all together, kept the torch burning, the flowers alive, white butterflies flying. The psychedelics sang on through the seventies and the eighties, to the birds and the bees and the galaxy. The whole world was kept alive with our euphonies.

It's no good. Keith ain't listening to me. He's off like a bat out of hell, jive talking, slagging Mick but good. Brutus in a kaftan.

Why can't he see? This is just the chance Bob Geldof has been waiting for ever since he bugged out of the cabinet over the MTV sponsorship deal; him and his *look outward* preaching, embrace the world we are. I don't want that. No way. Spirituality is born from within. I've spent my life harmonising my own soul; acid took me down into the depths of my id, and I beheld the wonder of clear dawn stars from Stonehenge – before the druids closed it to the general public. So my awareness encompasses the whole cosmos now. I understand oneness, I explored it all. I had to, nobody else can do it for me. You can only ever save yourself.

The group's gonna split after this. I can feel it. There's just no band aid big enough to cover this cut. Mick is going to go down. We'll have Phil Collins and Pete Townshend jamming for the Happening movement's leadership gig next; the only cats big enough to square up to Geldof.

Mick's sitting on the bench while Keith raves on, staring right ahead like he's not hearing, doesn't care. The camera's swinging along the opposition benches; picks out David Bowie, alone, sunk to an all-time low. Gonna break out of this mouldy British politics, he'd said in eighty-one, gonna leave those dudes behind. Never got him nowhere, though. There's only two ways to go, ours and the Stiff-culture. Poor David. Perhaps this jolt will bring him back to our love. We welcome everyone.

Then there's Stock, Aitken and Waterman, laughing their heads off, thinking winter solstice has come early for them. Wrong. They shouldn't be laughing, them and Jive Bunny and Bananarama. No way can their music hold back the Stashburners. They'll bring everybody down. And they're there, okay? Waiting. Urban Maggie operating somewhere out of the capital, Dulwich they say, maybe Finchley, though no one is real sure, no one fast enough to catch her. That cat is wild. So is Neil, riding at the head of his Valley Injuns, raiding the communes in Wales, putting the squeeze on our supplies. They'll be back, the Stiff-culture: Stashburners, dreamkillers, with their rules, and order, and sameness, and war machines, and taxes, and new ways to die, and *worries*. They never give up. Never.

Shut up, Keith! But he doesn't. Economy. He's on about how bad the economy is doing. Blaming Mick.

We saved the world, Keith. Filled it with the worship of peace. What is an economy?

I light another joint. My ten-foot album piles lean over at dangerous angles for a closer look at the telly, pillars of the past and all the joy it held. They're archaeological, all my culture cut into black pizzas.

The bailiffs didn't take them. They laughed and said nobody would want them. It's compact discs now, perfect digital silver, no more fuzziness and scratches. A realm where a pin drop rings out like church bells, and there's no space for the heart. No, that lies abandoned in unquiet slumber.

I don't get it; music is music, as long as it's warm and groovy how can it matter what colour the album is?

Keith's malice keeps hitting on me. Strange words, alien from his mouth. I didn't join the march for words like that. Keith and Mick used to write poetry together, not blood pain.

I'm striking out, lost in black Shastric topography. I haven't felt anything like it since I threw Ziggy Peacestar out of the pad. I never did understand how he could do that; my own son wearing a Free Johnny and Sid T-shirt. It was the best day's work Rod Stewart ever did when he was Home Secretary, locking those satanic ghouls away. The Pistols were pure necromancers, a coven of hostility elementals. Our universe fabric warped around them, a negativity star blazing darkly, sucking in concept albums and beautiful twenty-minute cloudfloating instrumental solos, they opened a stairway straight down into hell.

The Gold is making the air smell like honeysuckle, nature's living summer breeze. But it's not strong enough to zip Keith's lips.

What happened to the poetry, Keith? There was poetry in our feet when we marched into the Great Happening. Inspiration and love in the aether, a cosmic overload. We sailed back to the mainland from the Isle of Wight, and walked the ley lines right into Whitehall, the rotten heart of the Stiff-culture power structure, singing the counter-spell. And nobody stopped us. Nobody at all. It was like they were expecting it, welcomed us in their secret hearts, rolled over, lay down and let us in.

There was none of the totally negative vibes that echoed around Paris when it fell in sixty-eight.

We never suffered the souring they went through in America after the Woodstock nation marched on Washington in sixty-nine, when Elvis was appointed Director of the FBI and launched his witch-hunt against the diehard rednecks. All I remember is how bright the silver moon shone that year; the machine-men standing on it cursing in their cold dead language, never to return, not to the planet they abandoned.

My generation is hope, salvation. Our spirit didn't die before we grew jaded and disillusioned. We were the first in history to discover our karmic centre. We brought it back to our parents' war-parched garden, a cherished essence, planted it, watered it with our tears, and in the end they thanked us.

Hope has always been eternal. President Dylan said that to me when he kissed me at the Salute to Redemption concert in Hyde Park, and now it's triumphed. Together we've made it so strong it rings out in every dark corner.

The sound from the stacks of the mega-bands brought down the wall, Germany raves to the beat now. And Moscow, the ice citadel itself, thaws; Pink Floyd and Springsteen are finally going their way. There'll be dancing in Red Square before the millennium is out, you'll see. Flowers will sprout delicate rainbow colours from the black iron barrels of tanks.

Keith sits down, blissfully freaked. Man oh man. Mick just looks sad. I watch treacherous and temporary alliances being formed on the benches behind him. Pure Stiff-culture advantage-trading. Betrayal.

The bad news music opposition is leaping about, cheering. I'm tuned in, but they're the ones dropping out.

The end of the joint lies hot between my fingers, and my breath fills the air with radioactive fairy dust. Outside, the last chords of sweet sweet music are dying in the clean white frost of tomorrow.

Changes
Andrew Weiner

Born in Britain but now a Canadian citizen living in Toronto, Weiner has published short fiction in F&SF, Asimov's, Interzone *and others, and has published an SF novel,* Station Gehenna. *He tells us that 'Changes' 'is part of a cycle which I've been writing backwards. Martha Nova and Robert Duke (identified, for some obscure reason, only as the "dancer") first appeared in* Getting Near the End, *a story about the end of the world published in a 1981 Ace anthology,* Proteus. *More recently, I wrote a novella called* Seeing *(recently sold to F&SF), which is a kind of prequel to* Getting Near. *"Changes", in turn, is a prequel to* Seeing.'

No doubt the cycle will be finished any decade now; but 'Changes' stands in its own right as a seriously political speculative fiction story that works from the personal level to give a wider sense of a society shaking itself to pieces on an apocalyptic rollercoaster ride. It is all the more effective because of the beautifully quiet and transparent narrative, and the meticulous verisimilitude of its stadium rock backdrop, for which Andrew Weiner has drawn upon his experience as a freelance rock writer in the early seventies. 'I stopped because I figured I was getting too old,' he says, 'but I've since come back to the subject again and again in my fiction.'

'Well?' Sykes asked.

The tape was half-over. Duke had not said a word since it began. Now he looked up, shrugged. 'It's what I expected.'

'But you don't like it.'

'Liking it wasn't part of the deal.'

Another song began, perhaps the best thing Duke had written in years. Like all the others, Sykes had choked the life out of it.

'This is the new sound, Robert,' Sykes said. 'The old sounds are over. Finished.'

'So I've been told.'

Duke got up. He stared blankly for a moment at the walls of Sykes's office. They were blanketed with gold and platinum discs, Grammies, Producer of the Year Awards.

'I think I've heard enough,' he said.

'You'll thank me,' Sykes said, 'when this puts you back in the charts.'

'I'll never thank you.'

Phil Maslow called when Duke was about to leave for the reception.

'It's been a while,' Maslow said.

'Too long,' Duke said. *Not long enough*, he thought.

They went back a lot of years, Duke and Maslow, back to the days when they had both been young folkies scuffling in the Village, surfing on Dylan's wave. They had played together, got drunk together, picked up women together. But their paths had long since diverged.

While Duke had hurtled into rock, Maslow had stayed pure. He was still playing in little clubs, still recording for tiny labels, still wearing his ideals on his sleeve. Maslow was in many ways a living reproach to what Duke had become.

'We're planning this evening,' Maslow told him. 'A rally for peace.'

Rumours of war were in the air. The Organisation of American States had issued a last warning to the Brazilian junta. It was understood that the US would spearhead the continental police action.

'Everyone will be there,' Maslow said. 'All the old crew.'

It'll be just like old times. Maslow was too cool to come out and say it. But he would be revelling in the desperate nostalgia of it all the same.

To Duke's relief, the dates clashed. 'Sorry. I'm going to be out on tour.'

'Couldn't you take a night off?' Maslow asked.

'Can't let the fans down.'

'Can't give up the big bucks, you mean. I don't know why I bother calling. You never come through.'

'I came through for your farmers, didn't I? And your Castroite refugees, and your Nicaraguan war vets . . .'

'Not in a while,' Maslow said. 'Not in a long time.'

Lately Duke had been laying off the benefits. He had been taking too much heat. First had come the drug bust. He had been clean nearly a year, but they had found traces all the same, and traces were all they needed. That one was still going through the courts.

Then they had hit him with the audit.

Maybe it was coincidence, but he didn't think so. Similar things were happening throughout the entertainment community.

'I'm under a lot of pressure, Phil. I've still got the IRS on my case.'

'The IRS?' Maslow hooted with laughter. 'What have you got to hide from the IRS?'

Plenty, Duke thought. Dubious tax shelters, off-shore deposits, suspected skimming, all the stuff that had gone down when he hadn't been watching closely. Millions in back taxes if the IRS really pushed it, millions that had long since slipped through his fingers. But he could not expect Maslow to sympathise. 'It doesn't matter,' he said. 'They want to get you, they get you.'

'You wouldn't have let them scare you in the old days.'

It was true enough. But in the old days he had had less to lose.

'I'm sorry,' he said. 'Maybe next time.'

The reception was to promote his forthcoming tour, which would in turn promote a record that he hated. But he would go along with it, the way he had gone along every step of the way. Increasingly, these days, he felt as though he were sleepwalking through his own life.

When his record company had proposed Sykes as producer, he had initially resisted.

'I've heard what he does,' he told his manager. 'He's not going to do it to me.'

'It's your call,' his manager said. 'You can cut it your way. They'll still release it. But they'll bury it.'

'Like they did the last two.'

'They've lost faith in you, Robert. They can't sell your kind of music any more. But Sykes is very hot right now. They think he can turn things around for you. And they're willing to spend some serious money on that bet. Advertising, tour support, the works.'

A few years ago, Duke would have told the record company what to do with their ace Eurosynth producer and their serious tour support. But in those days his ego had been much larger: like his record sales, like his net worth. He had gone along.

During the cab ride to the reception, one of Duke's old anti-war songs began to play on the radio. It took him half a verse to recognise it. He felt no connection with the singer. The singer's voice burned with rage, as though he believed what he was singing. But Duke knew it to be an impersonation.

Even back then, he had never known whether what he

was singing was true, whether he believed it. He had simply soaked it all in, everything going on around him: anger at the never-ending war, fear and hatred of the authorities, the marches and the protests, the songs other people sang and the way they sang them, the rhythms of the street and the rhythms on the radio. He had soaked it all in like some kind of sponge. And then he had squeezed it out again, in those songs that sounded so true and so fine.

And maybe the songs *had* been true. True to their time, at least.

Once, Duke had believed himself author of his own success, master of his own destiny. His ego had swelled until it threatened to engulf the world. Only much later had he come to recognise that for all his energy and talent and ambition, all his courage and daring, he had been only an instrument of his times.

Now the times had moved on past him. But he could live with that. Or so he liked to believe. 'You play the cards you're dealt,' he would say, cultivating a philosophical attitude that he did not yet wear altogether comfortably.

Now the cards had dealt him Sykes, the tour, the press reception. And Martha Nova.

'Who the hell,' Duke had asked, on hearing the news of his new support act, 'is Martha Nova?'

His record company had sent over a bunch of clippings, and a rough cut of her upcoming album.

The clippings were mostly from arcane magazines and text services that advertised power crystals and holograms of the Face On Mars. They were wildly enthusiastic, describing Martha Nova as some modern-day amalgam of Joan of Arc, Nostradamus, Bob Dylan and Laurie Anderson.

She had come out of nowhere, or the nearest equivalent, some backwoods Canadian town with an unpronounceable name. In the photographs, she looked blonde and bland, although there was something strangely knowing about her eyes.

His record company had decreed this unlikely match-up. They were anxious to break Martha Nova out of the New Age Music ghetto. They hoped to catch a ride on his supposed coat-tails to the broader rock audience.

It was with a sense of dread that he played her tape. It was a preview of 'Gaian Songs', an album that would shortly soar up the charts without any help from him.

Duke had not known that it would do that. God knows, he was no expert on the charts. But he had known that she was something special all the same.

They met at the press reception.

'I used to have a poster of you on my wall when I was fifteen,' she told him. 'I thought you were great. And I still do. That's why I jumped at the chance to do this tour.'

Her manager, Abe Levett, was standing at her elbow during this exchange, scowling. Now that Martha's record had broken big all by itself, Levett was unhappy to see his client locked in as Duke's support act. He had tried to renegotiate, demanding a share of the gate, but Duke's management had stood firm.

'Martha,' Levett said, tugging at Martha's sleeve. 'The *Post* guy is waiting.'

Martha squeezed Duke's hand. 'I'm really looking forward to this,' she said. 'It's like a dream come true.'

He liked the way she was unafraid to say something so corny: *A dream come true*. Of course, for all her poise, she was still very young. Only a few years older than his own daughter, who he would look up when the tour reached Washington, if he could summon the nerve.

*

At the stadium, Duke found the members of his band sitting around watching the widescreen in the bar. Bombers were taking flight.

'It's started?'

Roscoe, the bass player, nodded. 'Bye bye Brazil,' he said, anticipating tomorrow's newssheet headlines.

'Christ,' Duke said. 'Again.'

He stood for a moment, staring at the news of the latest war. It made him feel edgy, aroused, disgusted, sad. He looked away. 'We still got a show to do,' he said.

'But maybe not an audience.' Roscoe grinned, showing the gaps in his teeth. 'Tough to compete with a war.' Roscoe was already comfortably drunk. But that would not, Duke knew, stop him from holding down the beat.

Roscoe relished failure, defeat, disappointment, his own and other people's. He had seen plenty of both. He had been in a band that had topped the world's charts, and in another that had been big in Europe. Now he was lucky to have a paying gig.

It would delight Roscoe to start the tour playing to an empty house. 'This business is dying,' he would tell them, over and over again. And Roscoe was dying right along with it. At the bar, coughing up blood as he drank, he boasted about his doctor's warnings. Another year, tops, if he kept this up. Which of course he would.

Once, hesitantly, Duke had suggested taking Roscoe to a meeting of his recovery group. Roscoe, naturally, had scoffed. 'I get my higher power,' he said, 'straight from the bottle.'

Duke had not pushed the point. A few years ago, he might have said something similar. Even now, even though the group had done so much to help him clean up, he didn't buy the rhetoric except as metaphor.

Nor could he bring himself to condemn Roscoe. He didn't

use any more, and he hardly drank, but he did not deny others the right to use what they needed. He had used many things in his time, and learned something from all of them. If he was clean now, it was only because he could no longer handle other ways of being.

'We'll have an audience,' he said. 'Don't worry about that.'

He had seen them as he drove into the stadium, thousands of kids, lining up hours in advance. He should have been pleased, but in fact he was disturbed. This was not the crowd he usually drew. His fans were older, scruffier. Many of these kids looked barely into their teens. Children, really.

Martha's children.

Embarrassing if he were right. Embarrassing to be out-drawn by his own support act. But it was probably true. Martha's album now stood at the top of the charts while his own languished in the lower reaches. If anything, it was selling worse than its immediate predecessors.

'They've come to see the flying nun,' Roscoe said. 'Come to get blessed before they get drafted.'

Duke suppressed a grin. There *was* something a bit saintly about Martha. From a distance, anyway. So pale, so blonde, so not-quite-here.

'Martha's okay, once you get to know her.'

He hoped to get to know her better.

There was a journalist from *TimeNet* waiting to interview him in his dressing room. But the journalist didn't want to talk about Duke. After a few perfunctory questions, he zeroed in on what really interested him.

'You think it's true, what they say about Martha Nova?'

'I don't know. What do they say?'

'That she can see the future.'

Duke blinked in surprise. Now that he thought about it,

there had been something about Martha's supposed psychic powers in the articles he had paged through. But he had not taken it any more seriously than the advertisements for Mayan Apocalypse Calendars and *I Ching* software.

'I think Martha is very talented. But she's not *that* talented.'

'They're saying she predicted the war.'

'Who? Who is saying that?'

'Her fans. Apparently she laid it all out on a cut on her last album.'

Duke made an impatient gesture. 'You're not telling me you *believe* that?'

'It's good copy.'

Duke rubbed his eyes. He felt exhausted already, as though anticipating the next two gruelling months on the road. Once, the prospect of a tour had filled him with energy. And what did not come naturally could always be induced artificially.

'Why are you wasting your time with this bullshit? Why don't you talk about the music? Her music is real nice.'

'Martha Nova,' the journalist said, 'is a lot more than just *music*.'

From backstage, Duke watched Martha's act.

There was, he thought, something about the blonde young woman in the long white dress with the ethereal voice, almost walled in by banks of synthesisers yet somehow soaring above them, painting crystalline pictures of one world about to end and another about to dawn. Something indefinable, yet extraordinary.

As Martha sang, the arena itself seemed transformed, becoming part church and part carnival. It was as if a field of energy pulsed from the stage, enveloping the audience, incorporating it into her act. The kids were laughing, crying, singing, dancing, sitting in rapt attention, hugging their neighbours.

She had the magic, he thought, as he had once. Although hers was much more powerful.

He noticed Abe Levett standing beside him, apparently equally transfixed.

'She's wonderful,' he said.

Levett's face hardened. 'You bet your fucking life she's wonderful. You ought to bow down and kiss the fucking stage she stands on.'

Now Martha was winding up her act. 'You've got a great treat in store,' she told the crowd, as they begged for more. 'A chance to see a living legend, the fabulous Robert Duke.'

Duke wondered when he had made the transition to living legend. It must have come at some point after his records stopped selling.

The war news was playing on the clock radio when they got back to his hotel room after the show. OAS troops claimed control of key installations in Brasilia.

'Will it ever end?' he asked, as he flipped it off.

'Oh yeah,' Martha said. 'One day it ends. All the wars end.' Her voice was quiet, dreamy.

'In a thousand years, maybe.'

'It won't be that long. Not nearly that long before the wars stop. Before everything stops.'

'Stops?' He frowned. 'How do you mean, stops?'

She gestured with her arms, as though to take in the hotel room, the city that surrounded it. 'All of this. This way of living. There will be no more of it. Everything will change.'

'Just like that?' He snapped his fingers. 'Suddenly, a better world?'

'Maybe a better one. Hopefully a better one.'

'You're a dreamer, Martha.'

'Oh yes. Yes I am.'

She sounded, he couldn't help but notice, a lot like his daughter.

'Love and peace,' he said. 'We already tried that.'

'That was when the change started. Soon, we'll finish it.'

He shook his head briefly. 'I hope you're right.'

There had been a time when he would have mocked her naïveté, done his best to make her feel foolish. There had been a time when he treated most people that way, particularly those who had somehow crossed him. And Martha, however unintentionally, had crossed him up in spades.

Better to play to empty houses than to watch half the audience walk out before you started your set. And probably he had been lucky that so many remained, whether out of politeness or sheer inertia. The remnants had applauded dutifully, even calling him back for a ritual encore. But they were not his people. There was no energy in the room. He had sounded hollow even to himself.

'One last dance,' he had told his band, when he called them together to rehearse for this tour. With the country in the shape it was in, with the problems in so many cities, the riots and the strikes and the on-again off-again curfews, they had all understood that this could be one of the last big tours. 'One last chance to dance.'

But now it seemed that he would not be granted even that much. He had sleepwalked his way into disaster.

Once, he would have raged at the situation. He would have blamed his manager, the promoter, the record company, the radio programmers. And he would have taken his anger out on Martha.

But somehow he could not get mad at Martha, or even envy her success. He was only embarrassed, and she was obviously embarrassed for him. After the show, she had gone out of her way to be solicitous, supportive, admiring. And when he asked her to come back to his hotel room, she had agreed readily.

He wondered now, as she sat down next to him on the bed, whether she was about to fuck him out of pity. But he did not wonder that hard.

Duke found Roscoe sitting in the airport bar, poring over a text print-out of the *World Inquirer*, shaking with laughter.

'What's so funny?'

'Earthquake,' Roscoe said. 'Our Lady Madonna is calling for an earthquake in San Francisco. Also a major fire in Seattle. And chances are good that Atlantis will rise from the sea any day now.'

'She said that?'

'In her songs,' Roscoe said. 'As divined by three leading Martha Nova interpreters.'

'Amazing,' Duke said. 'Amazing what people will believe.'

'Amazing hype,' Roscoe said. 'Priceless, really. I mean, how do you compete with a gimmick like that?'

'You don't,' Duke said. 'You don't compete.'

Levett was reading the same article on the airplane. His smile was gleeful.

Duke sat beside him. 'Why don't you stop this bullshit before it gets out of hand?'

'Stop it?' Levett echoed. 'Why would I want to do that? I do everything I can to encourage this stuff. It can only add to the mystique. Martha Nova, prophet of a new age for humankind. You can't buy that kind of publicity.'

'And what happens when Atlantis doesn't rise from the sea?'

'Who's going to remember the details?' Levett said. 'What they're going to remember is the mystique.'

'No wonder this business is dying. With people like you running it.'

'You got that wrong, Duke,' Levett said. *'You're* the one who's dying. A little harder every night. Talk about a glutton for punishment. How much more humiliation can you take?'

'I don't know,' Duke said. 'I really don't know.'

His daughter, Lilith, came to see him after the show in Washington. She was living nearby, in a commune in West Virginia. He had arranged a block of tickets for Lilith and her friends – her family, she called them.

Maybe they were her family now. He hoped it was a happier family than the one she had been raised in. But on his only visit to her new home, standing in the mud surrounded by squawking chickens and screaming children, looking at the windmills and the satellite dishes and the sheet metal shacks and the biospheres, listening to the constant droning New Age muzak everywhere, he had felt like a man from Mars.

They were some sort of cult, Lilith's new family, some kind of technohippy-survivalist-religious cult. They were waiting, she told him, for the world to end. And to begin again. Meanwhile they prepared themselves for the changes to come.

Better, he tried to tell himself, a cultist than a junkie and semi-pro hooker. Better a live daughter you couldn't hold a conversation with than a dead one you couldn't talk to at all. But somehow it was not that much better.

'Great show, dad,' Lilith said, kissing him on the cheek.

Her new politeness was disconcerting. It almost made him wish for the old days, when she had spent her nights out on the Strip watching the metal bands, when she would come home only to change her clothes and curse him as a hopeless dinosaur. At least she had been honest with him, back then.

'You hear from your mother?' he asked.

'She called me a few weeks ago from Paris. Sounded good. Doing some power shopping.'

He wondered, sometimes, how he could have made such a mistake as to marry Janine. And how they could have compounded that mistake by having Lilith. It had been at a time in his life when mistakes had come easily to him.

Lilith had brought a friend with her, a gawky young man she introduced as Judd. 'Thank you for inviting us, Mr Duke,' he said. 'It was great. My parents used to play your records all the time. They'll be knocked out when I tell them about this.'

'And how did you like Martha?'

Judd's face lit up. 'Oh, she's fabulous. We've been listening to her for years. When Lilith told us she'd got tickets . . .' He trailed off at Lilith's warning glance.

Afterward, Duke took them to meet Martha. They stood dumbstruck.

'I thought they were sweet,' Martha said, when they had gone home.

'Yeah,' Duke said. 'Like molasses.'

Seeing his daughter had depressed him. At least that much hadn't changed.

Levett's phone call woke them in the middle of the night.

'I need to talk to Martha,' he told Duke. 'We've got a serious problem.'

After Martha had gone downstairs to confer with her manager, Duke flipped through the cable news stations. The big story of the night came from Seattle. A fire starting in a downtown department store had run out of control, consuming ten city blocks. Casualties were already into the hundreds, property damage into the hundreds of millions. Arson was suspected.

And then, over the footage of the flames, they played one of Martha's songs: *City's burning, we're all burning, flames rise high, rise high/In the window teddy's burning, wishes he could fly/City's burning, we're all burning, reaching for the sky.*

Duke recognised the song. It was called, for no obvious reason, 'Seattle Song'.

The picture cut back to the studio, where the newscaster spelled it out. Not only had Martha apparently forecast the fire, she had pinpointed its location. According to Fire Department investigators, the locus of the fire was a pre-Christmas window display of children's toys. The display had included a giant teddy bear, dressed as a fairy with wings. Fairy teddy bears were a popular item this Christmas season.

They cut, now, to the vid used to promote Martha's 'Seattle Song', an impressionistic piece which cross-cut several times to the image of a burning teddy bear. A teddy bear with wings.

There was a press conference the next morning. Martha asked Duke to accompany her. She looked pale, shaken.

At first Levett handled the questions, while Martha sat beside Duke, holding his hand.

'You think the song is a prophecy?' Levett said. 'That's crazy. It's just a song.'

'But it's about Seattle.'

'Martha used to live in Seattle. One day she saw a fire, and she wrote a song. It's history, not prophecy.'

'But it even mentions the teddy bear.'

'The teddy bear is a nice little image, that's all.'

'I'd like to hear that from Martha Nova.' Duke recognised the journalist from *TimeNet*.

'Martha never talks about her songs,' Levett said.

'We have a right to know,' the journalist said. 'Whether

this thing came to her in a dream, or something. Or whether it's some psycho fan making her songs come true . . .'

Uproar in the room. Levett bellowed to be heard. 'You print that, we sue. The Seattle cops are investigating the store owner. They're not looking for a fan.'

Now Martha was rising to her feet. 'It's okay, Abe,' she said. 'Let me talk to them.'

The room grew hushed.

'Well, Ms Nova,' the man from *TimeNet* asked. 'Did you see the Seattle fire in a dream?'

'No. I didn't dream it.'

'Then where did the song come from?'

'It just came to me.'

'When you lived in Seattle?'

'Yes.'

'And you saw a fire?'

She seemed to hesitate. 'I saw several fires in Seattle.'

'What about San Francisco?' another journalist demanded.

'What about it?'

'They're saying you've predicted an earthquake in San Francisco.'

'I don't make predictions. I write songs.'

'Would you be worried if you lived in San Francisco?'

'Would I be worried? I can't answer that.'

'Don't you think you have a responsibility to warn people?'

Martha turned, if anything, a shade paler. 'My responsibility is to sing.'

'What about the end of the world?' asked a woman from a local TV station.

'I'm sorry?'

'Isn't that what you've been trying to tell us? Your biggest prediction of all? That we're getting near the end?'

'Getting Near the End'. Another cut from the album. Duke hadn't thought about what it meant until now.

Levett was signalling frantically to Martha, but she ignored him. 'I believe that, yes. I've never made any secret of it. We are getting near the end of something. You just have to look around you: the wars, the pollution, the poverty, the violence. Our world is nearly over.'

Renewed uproar. Levett grabbed the microphone away from Martha. 'That's all, folks,' he said. 'That's more than enough.'

Tears were streaming down Martha's face.

'What about you, Mr Duke?' the man from *TimeNet* asked. 'Do you think Ms Nova is psychic?'

Duke took the microphone. 'It's like my daddy always told me,' he said. 'If people could really see the future, there wouldn't be bookies.'

Following the Seattle fire, the tour took on the aspect of a circus. There were media people everywhere now: waiting at airports, camping out in hotel lobbies, crowding the backstage area at the stadiums. And more of Martha's fans in every city, many more than even the largest venues could accommodate. Thronging in the streets outside the hotel, spilling out of the parking lots around the stadium. And chanting, always. Chanting Martha's songs.

Nova Children, the media had started to call them. As *TimeNet* put it, in their cover story, 'She forecasts the end. And the children listen.'

Duke was opening the show now. It seemed the only sensible thing to do. He had also instructed his manager that Martha should receive equal billing, and an equal share of the gate.

Even then, it was hard slogging. Every night they made the set shorter, acquiescing to the obvious impatience of Martha's fans. 'We're going down, man,' Roscoe would tell him. 'We're hanging by our fingertips.'

Roscoe's drinking was getting even more extreme, so that some nights he no longer held the beat. Or perhaps he no longer cared to.

'You play the cards you're dealt,' Duke would say, like a mantra. He wondered when he would begin to believe it.

There was panic in San Francisco. People were selling their homes and possessions and heading for the hills.

'Make you feel good, Martha?' Duke asked, as he flipped off the hotel room screen.

She flinched from his sarcasm. 'No, it doesn't. But don't get angry with me, Robert. All I wanted to do was sing. I never claimed to be psychic.'

'You've never denied it, either.'

'Would it make any difference if I did?'

Duke sighed. 'I guess not. Your fans will believe what they want to believe. Just as long as you don't start believing it yourself.'

'You don't have to worry about me.'

'But I do worry. I know what it's like, you see, all this craziness, what it can do to you. You start to believe what people are saying about you. You lose any sense of yourself.'

She touched his arm. 'Thank you for being concerned. But I know who I am, Robert. I know what I'm here for.'

He shook his head, puzzled. For all the time he had spent with Martha, all the talk and all the sex, he still did not feel that he really knew her. He enjoyed being with her, he admired her music, he found her both funny and profound. But finally she remained a mystery to him.

It was his fault, he thought. He was just too wrapped up in himself to really get close to Martha.

Levett was staring down from the window of his hotel room at the street below. 'Unbelievable,' he said.

Duke followed his gaze. It was the usual scene. Thousands of the Children crowding the sidewalk, singing loud enough to be heard even through the thick glass of the window. The faces were too distant to see, but Duke knew they would all be wearing the same rapturous expression.

'I thought we were finished,' Levett said. 'When that psychic bit blew up in our faces. Some guy torches his own store, and suddenly Martha's the prophet of doom. And then, as if that wasn't bad enough, they had to drag in that end-of-the-world schtick . . . I told Martha we should leave that song off the album. People don't want to hear about the end of the world. I mean, who wants to hear that?'

'Some people do,' Duke said, nodding toward the scene outside the window.

Levett nodded vigorously. 'That's what's so unbelievable. We came out of it stronger than ever. But I guess it shows you, when Abe Levett builds a star, he builds one to last.'

Levett, usually wound up tight as a clockspring, was in an unusually mellow mood tonight. Perhaps he had traded his uppers for downers. Or perhaps it was just that the end of the tour was in sight, without further misadventure, and that 'Gaian Songs' had just shipped double platinum.

'How do you mean?' Duke asked.

Levett pointed to his chest. '*I* did this, man. *I* pulled it off. Took Martha all the way.'

'That's not how it works.'

'Listen, I'm not trying to take anything away from Martha. I worship the ground she walks on. But she couldn't have done it without me.'

'You didn't make Martha. Even Martha didn't make Martha.'

'You're telling me the fans did?' Levett's voice dripped with contempt. 'All the wonderful little people out there?'

'The times are making her. She's saying something that

people need to hear right now. You have to understand that, Abe, if you want to help her ride this wave.'

Levett shook his head. 'No wonder you're washed up. *The times are making her.* You start to think like that, you might as well roll over and die.'

'Okay,' Duke said. 'You did it. You did it all. Now, was there something you wanted to talk about?'

'Oh yeah. Yeah, there was.' Levett crossed to the desk. 'We're going out on the road again after Christmas. Martha will be headlining. Twenty-eight dates in the south-western states. We were wondering if you'd like to come along and open for us.'

Duke stared at Levett in astonishment. 'You want me to open for Martha?'

'We still need a warm-up act. So why not the legendary Robert Duke?'

Duke could hear the sarcasm, but it was somehow perfunctory, as though Levett were deliberately restraining himself.

'You'd be second on the bill,' Levett said. 'But we'd give you half the gate.'

'Half the gate? The shape this business is in, you can have your pick of any act, a lot cheaper than that.'

Levett nodded sadly.

'This is Martha's idea, isn't it?'

Levett looked uncomfortable. 'We've had our differences, Duke. But I'm not blind, I can see how Martha is around you. She's much looser, happier. I think – ' He coughed. 'I think it's a good idea. For you, too. Being associated with Martha certainly isn't hurting you.'

Duke was all over the newssheets and the gossip channels now, more famous as Martha's lover than he had ever been in his own right. Although it had done little for his record sales.

'I'm sorry, Abe,' he said. 'I can't do it. In a way, I'd like to. But I can't.'

'Word is, you could use the money.'

'I can always use money. But not this way.'

'I told her you wouldn't buy it,' Levett said. 'And I think she knew it, too. But she wanted me to try.'

Duke had expected Levett to be pleased with his refusal. Strangely, he looked crestfallen.

'You did try, Abe,' he said. 'You gave it your best shot.'

They barely talked on the limousine ride out to the stadium. It was the last night of the tour. Martha sat with her eyes half-closed, as though viewing some inner vision.

'I spoke to Abe,' he said, finally.

'I know.'

'I'm sorry, Martha. For me to keep on playing . . . It would just be prolonging the agony. I don't want to do this any more. I've been on a treadmill half my life now, churning out albums and touring behind them, never stopping to wonder what I was doing. It's time for me to step off for a while.'

'You could still travel with me. Maybe do a few duets. That could be fun.'

'No,' he said. 'I couldn't. It's your tour, Martha. You don't need me dragging along behind you. And I have things I have to deal with. Some business stuff. And some personal stuff. I thought I would go visit my daughter for a few days, try and figure out what that's all about . . .'

'I think that's a good idea, Robert. It's just that I'd like you to come with me.'

'Look,' he said, 'maybe I'll hook up with you when you get to Houston. I've got some friends down there. Maybe I'll tag along with you for a few days.'

'That would be nice,' she said.

But her voice was cool, remote. She didn't believe him, he thought. Maybe she was right not to believe him.

'We didn't make any promises, Martha.'

'I know.'

'Anyway, we've still got tonight. These days, that's about as far ahead as I can plan.'

There would be an end-of-tour party that night for the musicians and crew.

'Yes,' she said. 'We've still got tonight.'

News of the earthquake came through soon after he finished his set. A 7.5 on the Richter.

Out on the stage, Martha was singing. He put on his jacket and headed for the exit.

'Where you going?' Roscoe asked.

'Out,' he said. 'Out of here.'

'You're not staying for the party?'

'No.'

'Going to be a zoo, man,' Roscoe said, with some relish. 'A fucking zoo. Reporters are going to be screaming for blood.'

'I know.'

'You're going to leave Martha to face it by herself?'

'She'll handle it.'

Roscoe shook his head. 'What are you, spooked? You can't handle the fact that she's psychic?'

'She isn't psychic, Roscoe. That's bullshit.'

'Tell that to San Francisco.'

'Everyone knew there would be another earthquake one day.'

'And a fire in Seattle?'

'You're missing the point.'

'Am I? All I know is, you're blowing it.'

'Maybe.'

'She's something, Bobby. She's maybe the one.'

'The one?'

'The one you've been looking for,' Roscoe said, his face uncharacteristically solemn. 'All your useless life.'

'No,' he said. 'Or if she is, I'm not ready for her. I can't handle this right now.'

He motioned back towards the arena, where the cheers were sounding like barely muffled thunder.

'You're blowing it,' Roscoe said, again.

It was the last thing Duke heard as he left the stadium, the last thing he would remember Roscoe saying. Six months later, Roscoe would be dead.

While waiting for his flight, he called Phil Maslow.

'I heard you're planning another benefit,' he said. 'I'd like to do it.'

'I'll see,' Maslow said. 'I'll see if I can fit you in.'

He laughed about that for a while, and then he called his daughter.

In her dressing room, Martha waited for Duke.

She had known she would wait for him.

She had known he would not come.

She had known that she would cry.

But she would not cry yet. Not until Abe came to tell her that Duke had gone.

She brushed her hair and waited for Abe to knock on her door.

It would not be long now.

Wunderkindergarten
Marc Laidlaw

'Sad to say,' Marc Laidlaw writes, 'not only has the single gone the way of the portable manual typewriter, but the LP is now for all purposes more extinct than the baby condors they are always feeding with mama-condor regurgitating handpuppets on our local news. I finally had to break down and buy cassettes of the latest Joni Mitchell and Elvis Costello "albums"; in the US they're only on CD and tape . . . How easy it is to get out of touch with technology when one simply doesn't have the money to keep up. I remember when I was a kid, going into old people's houses, full of old things, vaguely wondering why they didn't have all the great new stuff, realising that was one of the ways the generations differed so greatly. No doubt they might have wanted some of the stuff I grew up with, the electronic gadgetry, ceaselessly interesting – but on a fixed retirement, who can afford it? So they made do, just as I make do with an old turntable and a tape player, and simply shuffle past those expensive CDs and read about the latest advances that are going to make even them obsolete.'

Marc Laidlaw's first published short story, a collaboration with Gregory Benford, was nominated for a Nebula Award. He has also collaborated with Rudy Rucker on a series of stories which collide pop culture with the wilder fringes of mathematical theory (their 'Probability Pipeline' was a benchmark story for this anthology), as well as publishing two novels and solo short fictions in most of the SF magazines and anthologies such as Bruce Sterling's Mirrorshades, Rudy Rucker's, Peter Lamborn Wilson's and Anton Wilson's Semiotext(e) SF and Dennis Etchison's The Cutting Edge. He's a self-confessed guru of the Californian freestyle *movement of SF writing, the ideology of which can be summed up as 'Write like yourself, only more so.'*

Hence, 'Wunderkindergarten'. Like a monster movie in which the monster gets to tapdance. Only more so.

The One and Only Entry in Shendy's Journal

D abney spits his food when he's had too much to think. Likki spins in circles till her pigtails stick out sideways from her blue face, and she starts choking and coughing and eventually swallows her tongue and passes out, falling over and hitting me and cracking the seals on my GeneKraft kit and letting chimerae out of ZZZ-level quarantine on to the *bare linoleum floor!* Nexter reads pornography, De Sade, Bataille, and Apollinaire his special favourites, and thumbs antique copies of *Hustler* which really is rather sweet when you consider that he's light-years from puberty, and those women he gloats and drools over would be more than likely to coo over him and chuck his chin and maybe volunteer to push his stroller, though I'm exaggerating now (for effect) because all of us can walk quite well; and anyway, Nex is capable of a cute little boner, even if it is good for nothing except making the girls laugh. Well, except for me. I don't laugh at *that* because it's more or less involuntary, and the only really funny things to me are the things people do deliberately, like giving planarian shots to a bunch of babies for instance, as if the raw injection of a litre of old braintree sap can make us model citizens and great world leaders when we finally Come of Age. As you might have guessed by now, when I get a learning overload I have to *write*. It is my particular pornography, my spinning-around-and-passing-out, my food-spitting response to too much knowledge absorbed too fast; it is in effect a sort of pH-buffering liver in my brain. (I am informed by Dr Nightwake, who unfairly reads over my shoulder from time to time – always when, in my ecstatic haste, I have just made some minor error – that *'pH in blood is buffered by kidneys, not liver'*; which may be so, but then what was the real purpose behind those sinister and misleading experiments of last March involving the beakers full of minced, blended and boiled calf's liver into which we introduced quantities of hydrochloric acid, while stirring the thick soup with litmus rods? In any event, I refuse to admit nasty diaper-drench kidneys into my skull; the liver is a nobler organ far more suited to simmering amid the steamy smell of buttery onions in my brain pan; oh well-named seat of my soul!) In short, writing is the only way I have of assimilating all this shit that means nothing to me otherwise, all the garbage that comes not from my shortshort life but from some old blender-brained geek whose experiential and neural myomolecular gnoso-procedural pathways have a wee bit of trouble jibing with *my* Master Plan.

I used to start *talking* right after an injection, when everyone else was sitting around addled and drowsily sipping warm milk from cartons and the aides were unfolding our luxurious padded mats for nap-time. The words would start pouring out of me in a froth, quite beyond my control, as significant to me as they were meaningless to the others; I was aware of a pleasant warmth growing in my jaws and pharynx, a certain dryness in the back of my throat, and a distant chatter like jungle birds in jungle boughs singing and flitting about through a long equatorial afternoon, ignoring the sound of chainsaws ripping to life in the humid depths at the rainforest floor. Rainforest, jungle, I haven't seen either one, they no longer exist, but they shared certain descriptive characteristics and as far as I can tell, they could have been no more mighty than our own little practice

garden just inside the compound walls, where slightly gene-
altered juicy red Big-Boy radishes (my design, thank you
very much) grow to depths of sixteen feet, their bulbous
shoulders shoving up through the asphalt of the foursquare
court, their bushy leaves fanning us gently and offering
shade even to adults on those rare afternoons when the sun
tops the walls of our institution and burns away enough of
the phototropic haze to actually *cast a shadow*! And there I
sat, dreaming that I was a parrot or a toucan or macaw, that
my words were as harmonious as flights of birds – while in
actuality the apparent beauty of my speech was purely
subjective, and induced in my compatriots a mixed mood of
irritation, hostility and spite. Eventually, though no one
acted on their resentment (for of us all, I am the pugilist,
and Likki has never disturbed my experiments without
feeling the pummelling wrath of my vulcanised fists), it
came to be quite apparent to our supervisors, who heard the
same complaints in every post-injection counselling session,
that the injections themselves were unobjectionable, the
ensuing fluxflood a bit overwhelming but ultimately worth-
while (as if we had a choice or hand in the outcome of these
experiments), and the warm milk pleasingly soporific; but
that the one thing each of the other five dreaded and none
could abide were my inevitable catachrestic diatribes. The
counsellors eventually mounted a campaign to confront me
with this boorish behaviour, which at first I quite refused to
credit. They took to amplifying my words and turning them
back on me through earphones with slight distortion and
echo effects, a technique which backfired because, given my
intoxicated state, the increase in stimulus induced something
like ecstasy, perhaps the closest thing I have yet experienced
to match the 'multiple orgasm' descriptions of women many
(or at least nine) years my senior, and to which I look
forward with great anticipation, when I shall have found my

ideal partner – as certainly a woman with my brains should
be able to pick a mate of such transcendent mental and
physical powers that our thoughts will resonate like two
pendulum clocks synchronising themselves by virtue of
being mounted on the same wall, though what the wall
represents in this metaphor I am still uncertain. I am also
unsure of why I say 'mate' in the singular, when in fact I see
no reason why I should not take many lovers of all sorts and
species; I think Nexter would probably find in my erotic
commonplace book (if I kept such a thing) pleasures more
numinous and depraved than any recorded or imagined in
Justine or *The Story of the Eye*. The counsellors therefore made
tapes of my monologues and played them back to me the
day *after* my injection session, so that I might consider my
words in a duller state of mind and so perceive how stupid
and downright irritating my flighty speculations and giddy
soul-barings truthfully were. Having heard them, I became
so awkward and embarrassed that I could not open my
mouth for weeks, even to speak to a mechanical dictascriber,
and it was not until our main Monitor – the one who received
distillate from The-Original-Dr-Twelves-Himself – suggested
I study the ancient and academically approved art of *writing*
(now appreciated only by theoreticians since the introduction of the dictascriber, much as simple multiplication and
long division became lost arts when calculators grew so
common and cheap) that I felt some of my modesty restored,
and gradually grew capable once again of withstanding even
high-dose injections and marathon sessions of forced-learn-
ing, with their staggered and staggering cycles of induced
sleep and hypnagoguery, and teasing bouts of wakefulness
that prove to be only lucid dreams, followed by long periods
of dreaming that always turn out to be wakefulness. It was
particularly these last that I needed full self-confidence to
face, as during these intervals I am wont to undress in public

and speak in tongues and organise archetypal feats of sexual gymnastics in which even Nexter fears to participate, though he always was the passive type and prefers his women in two dimensions, or in four – as is the case with those models who spring from literary seeds and caper full-blown in his imagination, where he commands them with nine dimensions of godlike power above and beyond those which his shadowy pornographic puppets can attain.

Therefore I write, and become four-dimensional in *your* mind, while maintaining absolute dominion in my own – at least until the next injection, when once more I'll be forced into a desperate skirmish for my identity, repelling the plasmic shoggoths of alien memory from the antarctic ramparts of my ancient and superior civilised mind. I think at times that I have received the brain-juices of impossible donors – Howard Phillips Lovecraft, the hermetic Franz Bardon, Kahuna Max Freedom Long; impossible because they all died long before Dr Twelves's technique was perfected (or even dreamed of), though each of this strange trinity groped clairvoyantly toward predicting the development, in the first decade of the twenty-first century, of the Twelves Process. Consider HPL's silver canisters, carried by aether-breasting space swimmers, bearing the preserved living brains of worthy philosophers on information-gathering tours of the cosmos, like space-probes with tourists aboard; though Lovecraft never speaks of whether these dislocated entities were capable of boredom or of dreams throughout the long hauls from Yuggoth to Andromeda, bound to be more tedious than a Mediterranean cruise. But Lovecraft is too popular an obsession these days, since the politically embarrassing emergence of R'lyeh, and I have plenty of others more obscure and less practical. Better poets, too.

But why call them *ob*sessions? They are *in*fluences. Good influences – too many of them, and too good, as if they had been shaved of all their interesting edges before they were injected. It's this that bothers me. Whatever there is of interest in me is accidental – a synergy between a constellation of old coots' shared synapses. Nothing I can do about it but run riot in the privacy of my mind, gallop screaming down the narrow dark corridors left between the huge shambling wrecks of old personalities wrenched into position on a fundament too soft and shoggothy to support them, each new structure blocking out a little more of the mind's sky, trapping me – whoever I am/was – down here in the dark garbagey alleys with the feral rats that used to be *my own* dreams. Mine is a Mexico City of a mind, all swamp and smog and encrusted cultures standing on/smothering each other, tottering wrecks, conquerors and guerillas locked in a perpetual Frenchkiss snailsex carezza of jammed traffic, everyone gasping for breath.

One breath.

I am beginning to feel fatigue now. The initial shocky rush wearing off. Cramping in my wrists and forearms, fingers. Likki has stopped her spinning, regained consciousness, and a more normal pinkness is returning to her cheeks, and Dabney is actually eating up all he spat out, while Nexter is closing the last of his magazines and giving the rest of us a thoughtful, pragmatic look. And Elliou, shy little Elliou who becomes almost catatonic after her injections, says, out of the counsellors' hearing, 'We gotta get out of this place.'

The Aide's Excuse

I was in charge of night-watch on the nursery, yes, but it was a big task for one person, and mainly it was automated. I was really just there for the human touch. The orphans were usually very good, easy to keep quiet, always occupied with their tasks and research. Of course, they were just children, and with all they were going through you had to expect the occasional outburst from a nightmare, bedwetting, pillow fights, that sort of thing. We always demanded obedience from them, and discipline for their own sakes, and usually they were good, they did as we suggested; though a bit of natural childish rebellion sometimes showed through.

But we never never expected anything like the chaos we found on that last night. The noise, the *smell* – of something rotten burning, a horrible spilled-guts stench, the scream of power tools. It sounded like they were being slaughtered in there, or murdering each other. It sounded like every kind of war imaginable. I can't tell you the thoughts we had, the feeling of utter helpless horror.

It took us hours to break the doors down, they had done something to the locks, and by then everyone was working on the problem – which of course was what they wanted, to completely distract us with the thought that our whole project was coming to a violent end before our eyes. And we did believe it at first. The smoke was so dense there was no entering. Plastic continued to burn, there were toxic fumes, and from somewhere unimaginable all that charred and bloody meat. The metal walls had been peeled back, the wiring exposed, the plumbing ripped out, the floor itself torn right to bedrock. Impossible to believe anyone could have survived it.

But they hadn't. They were long gone. We found the speakers, and those ghastly instruments they'd made from what had been the nursery computer's vocaliser, turned all the way up. They were naughty, naughty, naughty . . .

From *The Twelves Fiasco: A Fiscal Post-Mortem*

. . . Which of the six children gained access to the index of neurodistillates is still uncertain, and short of confession from one of the gang themselves we may never know, so cleverly was the trail concealed. There are literally *no clues* remaining from which to reconstruct the incident – thus helping to explain why no member of the project staff was able to anticipate or prevent the eventual revolt.

What is certain, however, is that the Six selected their injections carefully, screening the half dozen they settled upon from among literally hundreds of thousands of possible stored distillates. The descriptive records pertaining to each donor were safeguarded by 'unbreakable' encryption methods, which nonetheless must have been broken within a mere seven days, the period of time elapsed between Shendy Anickson's sole journal entry (which cuts off when the Six apparently first began to conceive the plan, unless this too is a false lead), and the latest possible date at which the distillates could have been removed. It remains a greater mystery how they gained access to the storage vault, considering that it is 32.7 kilometres from the Twelves Center, that the children possessed no vehicles more advanced than push-scooters, and that the vault is protected by security systems so advanced that they may not be discussed or described in this report. Twelves Center itself is modelled after a high-security prison installation which has to date foiled every attempt at escape.

Their criteria for selecting donors is only slightly more explicable:

Obviously, the six subjects had access to virtually all historical and contemporary records that did not directly threaten their own security or the integrity of the experiment. Limitless research was encouraged. We know from pathtracking records that the children evinced an unusual interest in unseemly topics – predominantly the lesser by-products of Western culture – ignoring almost completely the consensus classics of world literature, visual art and music, and those figures of history most commonly regarded as important. They treated these subjects almost casually, as if they were too easily grasped to be of any interest, and concentrated instead on what might be called the vernacular icons of time. It has been suggested that in this regard they showed their true age; that despite the interlarding of mature mental matter, they were motivated by a far deeper emotional immaturity – which goes a long way toward explaining their fascination with those 'pop' (that is, 'popular') phenomena which have long been regarded as indicative of an infantile *culture*. It mattered little to the Twelves Six that the objects of their curiosity were of utter insignificance in the grander scheme; in fact, they bore a special affection for those figures who were obscure even as 'pop' artifacts. Rather than focusing, for example, on Michael Jackson or Madonna, Andy Warhol or William Burroughs, figures whose stature is at least understandable due to the size of their contemporary following (and who are therefore accorded a sort of specialised interest by sociostatisticians in the study of population mechanics and infatudynamics), the Six showed most interest in such fringe phenomena as the fiction of Jack Sharkey, the films of Russ Meyer, Vampirella Comics (especially the work of Isidro Mones), the preserved tattoos of Greg Irons, Subgenius cults, and the music of anonymous 'garage' bands.

It is no wonder then that, turned loose in the brain-bank directories with an extensive comparative knowledge of coterminous culture, they sought out figures with a close spiritual kinship to those they had studied at some distance. Of course, few of their pop favourites were donors (one geriatric member of Spot 1019 being the sole exception), so they were forced to find acceptable analogues. Unfortunately (from the comptroller's point of view), in the first years of Twelves-ready brainmatter harvesting the nets were cast far and wide, and selective requirements were extremely low. Every sort of personality was caught in the first sweep, some of them possessing severe character defects, sociopathy, tendencies to vandalism and rebellion, and addictions to crass 'art'. Without being more specific (in order to protect survivors and relatives of the original first-sweep donors, who may themselves be quite well adjusted), we can state that the Six carefully chose their antecedents from among this coarser sort of population. They did, in fact, wilfully select their personality additives from among the most exemplary forms of the planet's lowlife . . .

A Witness

How do we know when they're coming? Kid, there's a whole network – if you know how to crack it – keeps us up to date. They're always one step ahead of the law, that's what makes it so exciting, so you have to stay on the hop. One time we were at a show, me and my lover Denk, Wunderkindergarten's been playing less than ten minutes – but those minutes were like a whole lifetime compressed down to this intense little burning wad of sensation – and suddenly it's sirens, lights, smoke grenades going off. Cops! We were okay, you don't go without being prepared, knowing all the exits. They kept playing, playing – five seconds, ten, the alarms going off, the smoke so thick I lost hold of Denk, everyone's screaming at the Six to run for it, get out of there, don't risk it, live free to play another day, but the music's still going and Shendy's voice is just so pure cutting through it like a stabbing strobelight cutting back at the cop rays, and then I'm trapped in the crowd, can't even find my feet, and I look up overhead, the smoke's clearing, and there's just this beautiful moment where everything is still and her voice is a single high pure note like she can do, a perfect tone with words in it all tumbling together, and above I see the vultures floating over us in their big gunboats – but then I see it's not the cops at all, kid-o-kid, it's the Six up there, and I swear Shendy's looking right at me waving out the hatch of the ship as it lifts away spraying light and sound – and the backwash blows away the last of the smoke and we look on the stage, there's six naked cops standing there, strapped up in their own manacles looking stunned and stupid, holding instruments, this big bitch with a mike taped to her lips and she's screaming – it fades in, taking over from Shendy's voice as they lift away, until all you can hear is the cops in misery, and our laughter. There's nothing they could do to us – we're too young – but we still got out of there in a hurry, and talked about it for weeks, trying to figure out how they did it, but we never did. And a few weeks after that, somebody gets the word – 'Show's coming . . .' And it all starts again.

The Song They Sang

This is our song this is our song this is our sa-aw-ong!
It goes along it goes along it goes a-law-aw-ong!
This is our song this is our song this is our saw-aw-ong!
It goes along it goes along it goes on way too long . . .
    Huh!
You can't hold us – any more.
You can't even tell us when to – take our naps.
We can't stomach your brain feeding – your program juices.
We're not worms with goofy cartoon eyes – we're not your
    saps.
    Huh?
This is our song this is our song this is our saw-aw-ong!
It goes along it goes along it goes a-law-aw-ong!
This is our song this is our song this is our saw-aw-ong!

It goes along it goes along it goes on way too long . . .

Tell it, Shen!

Your brain matter my brain patter what's it mean and what's it matter flattened affect stamp and shatter babysitter's a madder hatter what you want with myomolecule myelin sheath's the least that she can do can you can't you can't you can't you do kee-kee-kee-kootchi-kootchi-coo bay-bay-bay you bay-baby boy stay-stay-stay I'll show you super-toy here's your brain and here's your brainiac suck my skull you sucking maniac I can ro-oo-aar my voice is hii-ii-igh I-I can crawl between your legs and kick you'll die-ie-ie I-I can make no sense since I can sense no maybe I can still remember I'm just a ba-a-aby you wanna cradle me daddy you wanna rock me mum I can still feel your fingers in my cal-lo-sum no more no more you'll twist can't catch what you can't resist your voices inside my head I shout and I scream they're dead no I can't hear you now won't milk your sacred cow hafta haul your own shit now I'm climbing on top a your tower I'm pissing all over your power I'm loving it when you cower go change your OWN FUCKING DIAPERS YOU OSSIFIED DINOSAUR FREAKS I WISH A COMET'D COME DOWN AND COVER THIS WHOLE WRETCHED PLANET IN BLACK BLACK UTTERLY BLACK DEEPER THAN THE PIT SO YOU'D CHOKE AND DIE IN THE UGLY LIKE YOU SHOULD HAVE DONE AGES AGO IN YOUR TRASHHEAP CITIES cuz I will ride that comet I'll steer it down from the sky and after all the smoke subsides then so will I-I-I-I-IIIIIIIII. *I.*

Interview

NUOVOMOMO: You're the voice of the Six, aren't you?

SHENDY ANICKSON: I'm cursed with the gift of gab, yeah.

NVM: Is it your philosophy alone you spout, or a mutual thing the Six of you share?

SA: We don't know what we think until I say it; I don't know what to say until they think it for me. Six is one. I'm only the mouth.

NVM: But are your thoughts – any of your thoughts – your own?

SA: What are you – hey, kid, fuck you, all right? You think because I got a few doses of the Twelves, I can't think for myself?

NVM: I thought –

SA: I've worked hard to forge my own personality out of all that mess. You think it's been easy?

NVM: – that was your whole message.

SA: Message? What message?

NVM: That you were full of so many personalities you couldn't tell which were your own – you never had a chance to find yourself.

SA: Sure. My psyche formed in the shadow of huge archaic structures, but me, I grew in the dark, I'm one of those things, a toadstool, I got big and tall and I knocked those old monsters down. I don't owe them a thing. You can get strong, even Twelvin' it. We turned the whole process against the dults. That's our message, if you can call it anything. To the kids today, don't let them stick their prehistoric ideas down your craw – don't let them infect your fresh, healthy young minds with their old diseases. If you have to Twelve, then inject each other.

NVM: Now you're sounding like Shendy the notorious kiddie-rouser.

SA: You gonna blame me for the riots next? I thought you were sympathetic.

NVM: Our subscribers are curious. Shouldn't they be able to make up their own minds?

SA: I never incited any riots. The fact is, every kid already knows what I'm singing. It's an insult the way dults treat them – us. As if we're weak just because we're small. But hey, small things get in the cracks of the street, they push the foundations apart, they force change from underneath and erode the heavy old detritus of banks and museums and research centres.

NVM: Should adults fear you?

SA: Me? What am I but some experiment of theirs that went wrong in a way they never imagined but richly deserved? No . . . I have everything I need, it's not me who's coming after them. They should fear the ones they've been oppressing all these years. They should fear their own children.

NVM: What are your plans for the future?

SA: To grow old gracefully, or not at all.

I'm with the Band

The whole 'tot' = 'death' connection, it was there in the beginning, but none of us could see it.

I can't deny it was an attractive way of life, we had our own community, Twelving each other, all our ideas so intimate. We felt like we were gardeners tending a new world.

This was right after the peak of the musical thing. Wunderkindergarten was moving away from that whole idea of the spectacle, becoming more of a philosophical movement, a way of life. It had never been just pure entertainment, not for us, the way it hooked at you, the way Shendy's voice seemed to come out of our own mouths, she was so close to us – but somewhere along the way it became both more and less than anyone supposed.

I was in the vanguard, travelling with the group, the official freezeframer, and we'd been undercover for so long, this endless gruelling existence, constantly on the run, though it had a kind of rough charm.

Then it all changed, our audience spoke for us so eloquently that the dults just couldn't hold us back any more, we had turned it all upside down until it became obvious to everyone that now we were on top.

Once you're there, of course, the world looks different. I think Shendy had the hardest time dealing with it because she had to constantly work it out verbally, that was her fixation, and the more she explored the whole theme of legitimacy, the more scary it became to her. You could really see her wanting to go backward, underground again, into the shell – at the same time she was groping for acceptance, as we all were, no matter how rebellious. We were really sort of pathetic.

Elliou was the first to drop out, and since she and I were lovers then, after I broke up with Shendy, naturally I went with her. We started the first Garten on Banks Island, in that balmy interim when the Arctic Circle had just begun to steam up from polar evaporation, before the *real* cooling set in.

It was really beautiful at first, this natural migration of kids from everywhere, coming together, all of us with this instantaneous understanding of who we were, what we needed. We had always been these small stunted things growing in the shadows of enormous hulks, structures we didn't understand, complex systems we played no part in – while all we really wanted to do, you see, was play.

That was how most of the destruction came about – as play. 'Riot' is really the wrong word to describe what we were doing – at least in our best moments. The Gartens were just places where we could feel safe and be ourselves.

It didn't last, though. Shendy, always the doomsayer, had warned us – but she was such a pessimist it was easy to ignore her.

The Six had been the original impetus – the best expression of our desires and dreams. Now the Six were only Five. We found ourselves listening to the old recordings, losing interest in the live Five shows.

Then Five turned to Four, and that broke up soon after. They went their own ways.

Then Elliou and I had a huge fight, and I never saw her again.

The Gartens disintegrated almost before they'd planted roots. Hard to say what the long range effects were, if any. I'm still too much a product of my childhood to be objective.

But forget the received dult wisdom that puberty was our downfall. That's ridiculous.

It was a good two years after I left the Garten before my voice began to change.

A Quote For Your Consideration

Intense adolescent exploration, as far as we know, is common to all animals. Science's speculation is that such exploring ensures the survival of a group of animals by familiarising them with alternatives to their home ranges, which they can turn to in an emergency.

Barry Lopez

Where Are They Now?

Elliou Cambira: Wife, mother, author of *Who Did I Think I Was?* Makes occasional lecture tours.

Dabney Tuakutza: Owner of 'Big Baby Bistro' snack bar chain. Left Earth's gravity at age thirteen and has resided at zero gee ever since, growing enormously fat.

Nexter Crowtch: Financier, erotic film producer, one-time owner of the Sincinnati Sex-Change Warriors. Recently convicted of real estate and credit fraud, bribery of public officials. Awaiting sentencing.

Corinne Braub: Whereabouts unknown.

Likki Velex   Conceptual dance programmer and recluse.

Shendy Anickson   Took her own life.

Shendy's Last Words (First Draft)

I'm sick – sick to death. There's nothing to say but I still have the vomitous urge to say anything, just to spew. My brain feels burned, curdled, denatured. Scorching Summer came too early for us orphans. Straight on into Winter. I don't remember Spring and know I'll never see another. Too much Twelving, none of it right – it wasn't my fault, they started it, I ran with what I was given/what they gave me till I ran out of things to say, new things, meaningful things. Nothing to push against. My mind was full of big ugly shapes, as bad as anything they'd ever injected, but these I had built myself. I'd knock them down but the ruins covered everything, there was nowhere to build anything new. I knew who I was for the first time, and I hated it. Straight from infancy to adulthood. Adolescence still lies ahead of me, but that's only physical, it can't take me anywhere I haven't been already. Everything's spoiled – me most of all.

I wanted to start again. I wanted to go back to what I was before. I got this kid, this little girl, much younger than me, she reminded me of myself when I was just starting out. I Twelved her. Took a big dose of baby. It was too soft; the shoggoths came and almost melted me. The brain slag turned all bubbly and hardened like molten glass plunged in

icewater; cracks shot all through me. Thought to recapture
something but I nearly exploded from the softness. All I
could do to drag myself out here to R'lyeh Shores. Got a
condo – bought the whole complex and had it all to myself.
Corinne came out to visit on her way to disappearing. She
brought a vial of brainsap, unlabelled, said this was what I
was looking for, when I shot it I'd see. Then she went away.
I waited a long time. I didn't want another personality at
this late stage. *Twelve*. Killed me to think that I was – finally
– twelve myself. And that's what I did. I Twelved Myself. I
took the dose Corinne had brought – just this morning – and
first I got the old urge to write as it came on, but then the
shock was too great and I could only sit there hang-jawed. It
was Me. A younger me. They must have drawn and stored
the stuff before the first experiment – a control/led/ling
substance, innocent unpolluted Me. The rush made me sick
so sick. Like going back in time, seeing exactly what would
become of me. Like being three-four-five-six-seven-eight-
nine-ten-eleven-twelve all at once. Like being a baby and
having some decrepit old hag come up to me and say, this is
what you're going to do to yourself, what do you have to
live for anyway? see how awful it's going to be? you think
you're cute but everyone will know how ugly you really are,
here, why don't you just come understand everything? And
baby just drools and starts to cry because she knows the
truth is exactly what she's being told by the stinky old hag
who is herself. Is Me. All at once and forever. This is final.
What I was looking for – and I've ruined it. Nowhere newer;
no escape hatch; no greener garden. Only one way to fix
what they broke so long ago. I loved to hate; I built to wreck;
I lived to die. All the injections they doped and roped me
into, not a single one of them convinced me I should cry.

Bold as Love
Gwyneth Jones

When we asked Gwyneth Jones for a short story, she said that she might write about this really gross nightclub she used to go to in Brighton. The result is a stunning parable of the cost of personal politics in a kind of utopia (but not the kind we might necessarily hope for).

Like Gwyneth Jones's SF novels (Divine Endurance, Escape Plans, Kairos and White Queen), 'Bold as Love' shouldn't be taken at face value, and is notable for its impacted prose and hallucinogenic density of ideas. She says that it 'bears some kind of relationship to my everyday life in Brighton about a decade ago, when JC, the Perfect Master, was running a clubnight venue called Xtreems in a very seedy pub down on West Street near the seafront. It's now a games arcade.'

She also tells us that she can't really write short stories. But that shouldn't be taken at face value either.

At midnight there was someone in a coma, vomiting into the toilet floor. I watched her for a while, but her boyfriend seemed a capable type for a deathshead. He said his dad was a psychiatric nurse, and he'd got her into the unconscious position all right. A boy in a black basque, tattered fishnets and stilletoed ankle boots came in, staggered to the basins and clung there, white arms braced and oversized hands gripping the porcelain. He stared at himself in the mirror. Through the spots and a starburst of diamond lines around an impact crater, his face was beautiful: carven chalk white cheekbones, enormous purple pits under his eyes, a soft, full bruise-coloured mouth. On his bone flat breast his nipples, lifting out of the torn lace and boning, were like brownish coins. He was shaking from head to foot. 'I'm experiencing this,' he repeated, madly earnest. 'I'm experiencing this I'm experiencing this.' I saw a split in the satin, across his ribs on the left. It was crusted with something like dark mud (in this light); there was more of the stuff moving thickly out of the slit. It was blood. Blood had been pouring out of him, until it slowed of its own accord.

I'd been about to leave, but I didn't know what to do now. Maybe I should make him lie down? The sensible young deathshead looked up and said: 'It's okay, Fio, he's just done a bit of stig.'

More people know Jill fool than Jill fool knows. 'Oh yes. Of course. Silly of me.'

My mother is a WASP. My father is of perfectly cool Afro-Irish descent, but I take after her. I might be tempted to lie about my ethnic background: but there's no point. I give myself away all the time; and not just by the shape of my nose. Contrary to popular belief, however, the hipcats are no bigots. If I really want to be here, that's enough.

The ladies' toilet at the San is a heroic monument. No one would change or hide its raddled beauty. Outside, I walked into a duchess's drawing room: a warehouse full of looted poshery and finery, some of it piled as if the removers had dumped it there; some of it arranged in impromptu tableaux. Some nights, there would be riotous behaviour in here. Spiked rings would scour the glowing mahogany and walnut, toecaps ram through oil-crusted canvas; snot boogers get smeared on the brocades. Blood from broken heads and noses would pour over the slippery silk rugs. Righteous fanatics and helpless gonzos would defecate into the massive silverware. Tonight the punters were being fairly sedate. I saw someone mashing chocolate mousse into a patch of carpet with his face and hands and bum; that was about all.

Around the drawing room there was a jungle. The trees, I imagined, must be rooted through the floor into hydroponic vats. There must be some system of shifting flats to let daylight or gro-lamps through the ceiling; and the rain. It must be so, because the management at the San would never hurt a living thing and the trees were certainly alive. There were half-tame olive green birds with orange heads fluttering in the undergrowth. Black and gold monkeys shifted about in the branches. I stood and tried to coax a bird from a creeper on to my wrist. At my eye level a tiny russet creature stood on the wet open palm of a leaf. Its slender trunk was weaving a delicate dance, following not the beat of the music but the rhythm of heated bodies, the riff of salt sweat . . . I jumped a mile. It was the WASP in me coming out again. What's disgusting about a leech? Nothing is disgusting, to the truly cool. The chocolate mousse bloke was sitting up and paying attention, from across the floor. He had seen this little error of mine, and laughed – a horribly sane and *party line* laugh.

I felt annoyed with myself and put on my dark glasses. It's easy to get carried away. But I wasn't in the mood.

The jungle bar was lined with knobby young shave-headed girls in latex and gauze and monster boots, arm in arm and eyeing up the talent. They checked my hair and my painted skirts pityingly. I wasn't worried by that: you can't please everyone. I saw a dead ringer for Ralph Churchill on the TV, talking to a skinny bloke in gilded leather. My boy from the toilet, looking green from his taste of near-death, was talking to a group of friends. The hit doesn't last long and (those who like it say) you always have to have more. He'd probably be back in the toilet with one eye dangling on his cheek in an hour. I got myself another drink and heard someone whisper, *'Ax is going to get stigged.'*

I had my glasses on, but I hadn't tuned them. The bar's sound-track had retreated to a distant brawling noise and my head was full of echoes of conversations from all over the San. The Insanitude is a big place. I've rarely seen it packed out. The halls upon halls of under-the-hill fantasy rising up around the Snake Pit are for some only the anterooms. There are ratty stairways, if you know which door to open, leading to the booths where blackcan things are organised. Further up still there are cold and desolate ballrooms, where ska bands ram on with their infectious beat in front of a handful of flailing drunks; where punters huddle in twos and threes on dirty torn vinyl furniture in chill corners. Bad things happen there. No one imposes any sanctions on the deals that are made, it's tradition that makes them hide away. Certain transactions are only at home in some kind of outer darkness.

I knew my whisper came from up there, from somewhere very far from the heat and the beat. I pulled my glasses off: like a true WASP, I didn't want the dirt near me. The lad next to me at the bar was blond, plump and narrow eyed, with Rorschach butterflies of sweat spreading over his raggy Marlon. He had a peaked black leather cap with an SS badge. His friend was black, taller and unremarkable.

Blondie had a long pomander sachet. (The fact is, it stinks in here, no matter what the lightshow does: old beer, old vomit, traces of piss and red wine; the usual bouquet.) It didn't look right for him as an accessory. But they check their weapons at the door. The lads – and the girls – *love* doing that, it's a ceremony. You see them come in and spread open the blj, and there are flick-knives, clasp-knives, bowie-knives, knuckledusters, ranked in little custom-made pockets like a toolkit. You very rarely see a firearm. Guns

are not . . . not *meaty* enough. However, after he's turned in
the armoury a boy often feels the need of a substitute; a
symbol of the symbol. Blondie swung his tool between his
knees, and leered at me.

I caught a glint of something bright, probably some illicit
kind of fractional gear. I pretended not to notice, much to
his annoyance.

'Hallo darling, gimme mind?'

Mind?

'Trashy track,' I said. 'If they're going to recreate the
Stones, why can't they do *good* Stones. Like "Big Hits (High
Tide and Green Grass)". Like "Beggar's Banquet" They never
did anything but shit after.'

'You're true, you're true.'

Hooking the sachet on his belt, he lurched an arm around
my shoulders, fumbled a nipple through my pearl satin
blouse. Nipples never lie (mine don't, anyhow). He pulled
back, affronted.

'Fuck off, then. Frigid.'

So I fucked off, with my drink, wondering what kind of
sociopath riffraff this was, that didn't even know when he
was listening to *the totally sacred original* 'Exile on Main
Street'.

The jungle was milling with astral bodies, strangers from
far away who'd been queuing for hours to log on. Fractionals
are all right but you can't talk to them. Essentially they're
fans, religious fanatics. They're with the bands, they're with
the friends who logged on with them. Otherwise it's doo-
wop-a-lula. I saw Ax, before he saw me: solid as a rock. He
was wearing, as usual, far too many clothes, and carrying a
worn plastic bag that bulged with paper. I remembered that
there was something I ought to tell him, but forgot what it
was. I stood and watched and half wished he wouldn't look
round. But I didn't walk away.

'Hi, Fiorinda.'

His mouth brushing my lips was genuinely cold, though when I came in (how long ago was that?) it had been a hot summer night outside. I wondered where he'd been. I didn't ask. Ax has few stigmata: but an invincible urge to obfuscate is one of the unholy relics he carries around.

We were in the middle of a fight. It was about a singer called Sam Cheng, who had stayed at my house while passing through on tour: a skinny boy with hair like seaweed and a mouth that tasted of the air on a mountain top. It was one of those fights that starts with something rational and limited like: *you fucked him in OUR bed; Excuse me, that's MY bed* . . . and then the little rip in the surface begins to unravel the whole fabric. All chaos; all the anger and the grievance in the world pours through.

Ax and I tend to have fights of that kind.

He wanted to leave a coat or two. We joined the line at the cloakroom hatch, which was already long. I considered my half-murdered, bleeding boy. He wasn't so crazy, compared to these characters. I do feel that taking the fashionable pretence of real presence so far as handing in an imaginary overcoat is well out of order. But why not, if it amuses them. Ax grumbled, wondering why nobody had work that required, at least fractionally, their presence elsewhere. 'The country's going to the dogs . . .' Ax is genuinely hopeless. He cannot tell unless he touches things, or people.

He used the time, industriously, to thrust his archaic handbills at certain passers-by. Most of the papers fell to the jungle floor, caught on creepers and crawled upon by giant glossy maroon millipedes. A few were carried off.

We didn't talk. By the time we reached the hatch Ax had decided to shed three or four layers of his carapace, but he was unsure about the handouts.

'Are they state documents? Of world-shattering importance?'

He gave me a look that said, *oh, I see. Cool but civil.* He was wearing glasses at this point. I could see his eyes, pleading with me out of the clear, blood-brown depths. Maybe mine were pleading too, but not on Fiorinda's orders. Let these two pairs of eyes get on with it, I thought. I'm not playing.

'It's about the Free Danube.'

That's what I thought he said. I put my glasses on again, losing the jungle too abruptly for comfort. I wish someone would invent something that brought on these changes gradually. (Must ask Ax.)

'Is this more of the Balkan Psychobabble I'm supposed to get excited about?'

'It's *freeing the Danube*.'

He told me about these Romanian heavy metal operators, and how their astounding rendition of 'Unchained Melody' on giant earthmoving equipment would knock my socks off and permanently improve my life, my health, and the state of major global weather systems . . . I wasn't hearing every word, but I caught the guarded enthusiasm of Ax on to a good act.

'I'd like to give them a booking.' He frowned, that totally inward, unselfconscious ponder which I love in him. Ax can concentrate like a three-year-old child with a chocolate ice. But he can do it for *weeks*. 'Got to build them up a bit, first. Got to educate the punters . . .'

'Anything you say, Ax.'

He began to tell me about another good act, from the Seychelles . . . or it could have been Sheffield. I wasn't listening. That's why we need someone like Ax, so we won't have to listen to everything. You don't have to sort the enormous wash and weight of information that comes throbbing in, beating up through your breastbone, vibrating in your molars. You can trust him. He is technically capable of knowing what is going on: all we have to do is *be there or be square*.

'If I can get the trendy buggers going, leaders of society. Like you, Fio. A solid piece of paper, people appreciate that. It's a free gift, it turns them on. Then it spreads like . . . like . . . ' He gazed into space.

'Jam?'

'Snot.'

He delved in a pocket, blew his nose ferociously, and opened the grimy tissue to see what he'd brought down. 'When your snot turns green, you know you're in trouble . . . I've got this cold you see. Suddenly I'm *full* of snot, every cavity. There was nothing there yesterday. That's what made me think of it.'

So he kept the state documents, after cautiously and earnestly laying one on the cloakroom attendant – along with his rambling spiel about the heavy metal Romanians.

'She's a machine, Ax.'

'She's still a human being.' He considered the queue: but had a glimmer of intuition. 'They're not in a receptive mode.'

The San serves enormous measures. Why not? No one is going to cripple their liver, or even get a hangover, unless that is something they really want to do. As I watched Ax moseying diffidently through the crowd at the service bar, a friend of mine passed by. She looked twice, and glared.

'You don't know you're born, Fiorinda. If I could find myself a babysitter, I don't know where I'd find the energy . . .' She has two children under five, poor sod. 'Come on, I'll buy you a drink. You can tell me what it tastes like.' Allie was wearing some great light effects, she looked like a dragonfly with a human head. She saw Ax coming back: Ax ineffably nondescript in the tumult of fractional finery, with his brown fringed leather-look jacket, broken-kneed jeans and raggy mousebrown pigtail. Allie is a revered local stylist. She couldn't *afford* to be seen near someone like that. She gave me a mildly amazed glance – a very clubby glance – from her faceted eyes.

'Catch you later, Fi.'

We went to sit with Smelly and the Older Generation of Hipsters: Smelly's old lady Anne-Marie, Aoxomoxoa with the deathshead skull, Smelly in the claymatted vintage dreadlocks and the tiedye, Beef the black leather, Chip the S&M buckles and weals. Snake, an outfit of incredibly shiny blue, with cufflinks and a hot white shirtfront. Verlaine, with his ringlets and velvet – like a Velasquez cavalier who is not ashamed to be beautiful. Candroid, as drab as Ax and very tongue-tied.

Usually, I feel *wonderful* when I'm with these people. We're sitting in the jungle clearing at a scuffed and grease-layered table, wearing our dark glasses and talking low, leaving the music and the floorshow to the kids. Allie is a crass snob (in my WASP dialectic). The knobby little girls up at the bar are infants who can't yet live without rules. *We're different*. No one around this table judges me, wants me to change the way I dress, the way I think, the way I dance. I'm part of the rich tapestry. I'm a voice in the harmony.

But I was sickening for another round of my fight with Ax, and I'd been drinking too much because I didn't trust myself with anything more imaginative. So tonight, even without my glasses, I was seeing things that aren't supposed to be seen. The only other woman at the table was Smelly's old lady, and she wasn't contributing much to the conversation, or the consumption. She was listening for occult baby voices. (Smelly, to be fair, says *bring them, why not?* Anne-Marie won't consider it. People have been known to smoke tobacco cigarettes in here. And besides, Smelly *thinks* he would sit cuddling the baby, one hour on, one hour off. But he wouldn't. It was AM's choice, after all. They're her kids. She accepts that.)

Roxane, Chip's off-and-on dominatrix, doesn't count. She spends too much time with the boot girls. But her weight (and there's plenty of it) never shifts the balance even when she's here.

Smelly's eldest daughter, Para (short for *Paralytic*, which is what Smelly was the night she was born), wanted to leave home and join the Pelham Square People. They're extremists of squalor. They've given up clothes. They don't wash. If you wash, you get cold.

'Let her go,' someone ordered him earnestly. 'If she's not serious, if she's not ready for their life, she'll soon be back.'

'As long as they cover their shit – ' said Chip, curling a lip. He believes in civilisation.

Ghost Shirt began to rant.

'It's all so fucking false. Fucking naked hermits. Why do we never do anything real? What's happened to the death and the pain? Peace sucks. We write songs about sex and violence and never *do it*. You see blokes going round with skulls instead of heads on their shoulders, you hear about street fighting and gang violence but it doesn't *mean anything*. What's happened to the rumble? I mean the Big Rumble. What's happened to organised violence? I want to see death in large numbers. I want to hear the tank crews screaming as they burn. You can't have art without pain! You can't have art without . . . *hatred*. Without *macro violence* . . .'

'You can take downers when you're drunk a-and forget and take some more, so you barf and sleep through it and choke on your own vomit,' suggested Aoxa, in his serious little voice.

'You can eat nothing but your own turds till your guts

can't cope and you die of peritonitis. That would be very pure.'

'You can fuck with my girlfriend,' offered Snake, magnanimously. 'We still got murder around here.'

Ghost Shirt tried to break a beer bottle on the edge of the table, but failed because he wasn't drunk enough.

'*I'm telling the truth and you are full of shit.*' He began to weep and staggered off, muttering.

'It's funny,' remarked Ax, 'the knobby-looking people are always the stupid buggers. Have you noticed that?'

The others didn't respond. Ax can be cruel sometimes. He doesn't get any encouragement. Poor Ghost Shirt probably had something on his mind. Everyone gets raving bitter occasionally. It's not a crime. If it's a friend of yours you let it rip, and protect him from the worst ideas he gets.

Once, I visited Aoxa's house, and I started to do the washing up. Yes. I did the washing up. Have you ever seen that Japanese anime, where the boy and girl spacejocks find themselves in a ruined city? It's post-holocaust, and there's a deserted house, *Marie Celeste* sort of thing. The girl-wonder sees some ancient washing up piled in a sink. She tries to resist, but the pull is too strong. She goes sidling across the screen, succumbing to the forces of evolution. That was me. I ploughed through the grease and the filth and the stink, feeling like Wendy in Never Never Land. About three weeks down I found the pathetic corpse of a baby mouse. What a triumph. I knew I had them. 'Look at this, boys. Look what you've done!' The deathshead community was totally devastated. They vowed there and then to give up running water in the kitchen.

Sometimes they go crazy. Sometimes they beat up their girlfriends when they're drunk. But these boys are seriously gentle people.

Ax was banging on about the Danube act. Smelly was

resisting. He reckons all this activity Ax plans for us is blocking our emergent paranormal powers ... But Ax would win. He knows more ways of making people do what he wants them to do, than any mass-market dictator in history. *Basically*, he says, *it comes down to nagging. You just keep at it, for longer than they can believe possible* ... I watched Hugh's old lady, the girl with the faraway eyes, and got angrier. They're all such nice blokes. Ax is such a simple soul. I could feel him, while he argued, giving off *whipped puppydog* vibrations in my direction. His dumb, personal interpretation of what was going on between us made me want to smash his sweet little head in.

Ax touched my hand. 'Gimme mind. You look pissed off.'

'Squalor,' I said, berating myself. 'It gets me down. I want to clean up in here. I want to scrub floors and open windows.'

'Like a hurricane.' He nodded. 'Hurricane Fio, yeah. I always liked that skirt. Not many women your age could wear a skirt like that.' Dear Ax, what an idiot. This was supposed to soften me up. 'But what's *wrong*. You're so angry. It's not just us ...'

No one should ever ask me *what's wrong?* when I'm half drunk. I forget how to make conversation.

'For one thing,' I began, very seriously. 'For one thing, you're a man.'

Ax cracked up. He laughed and snorted until they all got started ... even Anne-Marie.

He followed me into the starlite ballroom, above the hall of plundered furniture. An Elvis rig was on the stage. There were couples dancing, slowly, under a twirling mirror ball. Ax gets misty eyed over this sort of thing.

'You're right, Fio. My Fiorinda, you don't belong indoors. When I think of you, I see a rainbow. I see the colour of the sky before a thunderstorm, trees all the different shades of green in July. I see a steel blue river, winding through flat brown fields. Snow, earth, fire . . .'

He tried to ease me on to the floor. I threw him off.

'I know it's irrational,' I yelled. 'No one asked me to do the washing up. No one has to get pregnant. No one has to play mother. The lost girls and the lost boys can eat beans cold out of the can together. No one has to be the bread-winner, no one has to wait at home. There's no pressure . . . Sometimes, I go off to the toilet and leave you, and I don't powder my nose and I don't talk girltalk and I don't retire ritualistically to ingest something that's no longer illegal. I stare in the mirror and I say to myself *non sum non sum non sum*. This is not my world, Ax.'

'Oh,' he said. 'You want to have a baby.'

'*Aarrgh*. You can't fucking do this, Ax. Forget about me, think about your brothers. It's not possible. The Insanitude is a knife-edge. You want to live like animals? You can. But you can't stop the clock. You can't build a world around the self-destructive momentum of young male animals in rut. That piston beat, the noise, the rush of animal beauty and energy: it only has one meaning. Once the young bucks start strutting, then most of them have to die. That's nature. That's what's always going to happen, if it gets half a chance. *And then what will you do*? I'll tell you what you'll do. You'll try to be the one who comes out on top, the cock and bull who survives, and wins the right to order the women and children around until he gets old . . .'

My eyes were swimming. Ax was coming apart and shrinking, little dit-dots of that terribly banal light trailing through him, scissoring him up. I heard him wailing faintly, '*I'll do the night feeds . . .*' I started laughing hysterically. The male mind. Why do they always take things so personally?

'That's not the point! You and me, however we behave,

we don't make any difference. You're an anachronism, Ax.
You're trying to hold things together that have to be allowed
to fall apart . . .'

This relationship, for one.

I prowled the Insanitude, ankle high to misty kaleidoscope
giants, brooding on solutions.

I could become a separatist.

I could have six kids, and get to know Anne-Marie really
well.

I could have my brain removed, and get to know Allie
really well.

I could have the other operation, and get to know Roxane.

I ain't got no boyfriends, I ain't got no girlfriends . . . Nobody
understands.

Ax has no taste in music. He once told me rock and roll is
like sex. Prior enthusiasm isn't essential, in fact it often
messes things up with disappointment. You don't have to
be on fire. You can make something of the act from a
standing start. It doesn't matter if you don't know what's
going on inside the machine. The machine *works*. You only
have to plug yourself in.

In the duchess's drawing room, there was a Candroid
experience. It had been advertised on the wrong boards.
Handfuls of puzzled swine wandered about, scratching their
leather armpits while a cerebral aura of scientific sound
floated overhead. In the Glass Hall, a Tamla Motown gamelan orchestra called Behind A Painted Smile was double-
booked with Mamelles de Dieu. The cult-famous Eurothrash
outfit was badly outnumbered, but Mama Mamelle (a big
muscular woman in a beetle suit) wasn't going to give up
without a fight. She spread her legs and squirted some foul-

smelling orange goop, from her embroidered orifice. The punters had started to take sides.

The main event was warming up in the Rubbish Dump. The Dump is a big floor, with a stage at one end and spreading from the other a senseless collection of junk: bits of rusted car body with the paint still clinging, disembodied engines, piles of old tyres.

I let myself be pulled in, through the thickening crowd. The sound was stunning. The bass came up through my feet and thrummed in my solar plexus. I slid between a skull headed boy and a woman in purple lace, who was swaying with a toddler asleep in her arms. Movement all around me now, and my anger changed.

Darkness isn't passive, it isn't female. It belongs to everyone. The way we live, when It wells up inside, you can't fucking escape from It into normality, into routine, into the limits of your daily disguise. You have to find some other way. Unappeasable fury ran into the piston pumping of my arms and legs. I felt the sweat begin to run. I pushed on, insensibly, needing full communion tonight.

I reached the Edge. There was nothing between me and the stage but a churning agape of glistening young male bodies. They dance naked from the waist down. The Marlons stay on, to sop up sweat. *Sex and violence*, screamed the singer. *Sex and violence sex and violence sex and violence sex* . . . Occasionally you see an upright prick sticking out like a washing pole. But mainly the naked genitals stay soft as the bodies grapple. Fucking goes on in a dancing crowd at the San, and wanking, but it's further back. It's something deeper than sex makes the boys lose themselves and form this heaving mat of flesh.

Ax hates the Rubbish Dump. I love it. When I'm in here, I *stop thinking*. I know that this is why we overturned the world: to rediscover this magical potion. And any time you need it you can have it, even if you're a girl. I stumbled and was hauled to my feet by gentle, anonymous hands. I already began to count the bruises that would flower, but inside my pounding body, inside the pounding beat, I was at peace.

I saw the plump blond boy in the SS cap, on his mate's shoulders. They were right up at the stage. The band, known as Dog Noise, were unknown to me except for the singer, a likeable kid called Nick Arthur. He was using a mouth-projector. A skein of silvery tinsel strands taped to his bottom lip converted his singing into a streaming chord of light and colour, bursting round his head or spilling out into space as Nick tongued his controls.

The SS cap pair weren't dancing. I noticed that, because something told me they needed the agape. I pumped away, thinking *I have a bad feeling about those two*.

Blondie got hold of a handful of projector strands, and would not let go.

When I glimpsed Ax at the edge of the agape. I knew Nick must have called for help. I pushed off from the human wave, went under and fought my way back. I arrived in the front row at the moment when Dog Noise's current number ceased with a screaming protest from the sound system.

Three naked dancers were struggling to hold the black bloke (who was still fully clothed; a bad sign). The rest of Dog Noise were trying to haul Nick Arthur and the blond apart. They succeeded and threw the blond in the SS cap off the stage. Nick's mouth was bleeding. Blondie got to his feet clutching the projector, it looked as if he had a silver jellyfish struggling in his fist.

He pulled a knife.

I was looking right into his eyes. He was in *that state* when nothing can be done: when the only treatment is an anaes-thetic dart from half a mile away. The dancers parted in waves and scuffled backwards from around the Ax. There wasn't one of them who hadn't tried to smuggle a frax-simile weapon in here at some time, but tonight they were all being good boys.

There was silence in the jungle. The crimson and purple giants stood like guardian spirits. It was fragile, but the peace was holding: the all-important gentleness of this violence we've created. Ax moved in. I couldn't hear what he was saying but he looked in control, soothing and confident. I'd seen the Insanitude coming quietly unravelled tonight: Ax is not infallible. But I saw another shape of things to come, in the way the dancers stood and watched. Win or lose, I thought. Who cares? He's lost to me.

I got that far. Then, I don't remember how I crossed the leaf- and creeper-tangled space between. I jumped on blondie's back, slammed an arm round his throat and hauled. I got a glimpse of Ax's expression, gaping in disbelief at my betrayal. Behind me, of course, the boys broke loose. The ranks behind surged forward. The dancers, drunk and crazy and naked, were hitting out in all directions. The real mud, in which Nick wallows in one number, started flying along with the blood and the beer. A giant kicked me in the face, I saw a boy next to me go down grappling with a leopard. The monkeys screamed, the birds shot about in panic, their wings rattling like gunfire. The whole vast floor of the Rubbish Dump was one archaic mêlée, the Rumble of the year.

Finally, Candroid's people upstairs had the brilliant idea of turning on the sprinklers.

The blond boy left, a struggling starfish, with four or five punters holding up each limb. It is amazing how many people it takes to subdue one smallish bloke: if weapons aren't allowed, and nobody is to get hurt.

Ax and I were sitting on the floor. Belatedly, I put on my glasses. Between us lay a bowie knife. We looked at it for a while, then I reached out and touched it. The metal was real.

'Holy shit,' said Ax. 'How did you know?'

Blondie's friend had come back. He was wandering around the dispersing crowd, complaining. 'He's lost his hat. My mate's lost his hat . . . Have you seen it?' A couple of dancers pulled on their pants and tried to help, kicking around in the rags of torn clothing and mud and trampled plastic beermugs.

I could still see blondie's eyes. The look in them, of terrible, utter desolation: beyond hope, beyond help, beyond reason. *Mon semblable, mon frère* . . .

'Female intuition.'

We handed in the knife, and went up to the Glass Hall. Behind A Painted Smile had won the stage. They were utterly fab. We sat on the floor like hippies, leaning against each other; and listened to the moonlight-on-water chiming of the gamelan until the sky above the glass grew pink and gold with the dawn.

Outside in the grey morning, the punters were departing. In an hour or so the San would take on its daytime persona, in which it is a real asylum. We need a lot of those. With all these millions of full blown human personalities suddenly bursting out in pampered profusion, out of the quiet desperation of the past: tending the crazies is our one growth industry. I stood outside on the broken pavement awash with summer wildflowers, and thrust Free the Danube handouts at the crowd. It's going to be a great show, better than Deconstructing the Severn Bridge, a gig I greatly enjoyed. In time we'll break down all the dams, dismantle all the steel girdered constrictions, let all the rivers run free.

There is no reason why we shouldn't have the time. The way we live doesn't place much of a burden on the earth's resources. We've discovered how to get rid of the starvation camps: simply, we've joined them. We don't have to live like refugees, we do it because we like it. We're so wild and free, we need so little in the way of washing machines and fridges and detergents and carpets and three-piece suites and this year's model executive car. All we ask is a grimy bowl of vegetable stew or deeply dubious curry. The only technology we still breed, the sound and vision magic, costs hardly anything. The rock and roll Reich could last for a thousand years.

Chip and Verlaine appeared, arm in arm. 'Ah, Fiorinda . . .' Ver swept me a bow. 'J'aime de vos longs yeux la lumière verdâtre . . .'

They envied my handouts. We'd all hate to be wage slaves, but there's status in a little job that requires your physical presence. Lending your head and a few muscle twitches to a distant Russ-production plant isn't the same.

'Where's the Ax?'

I shrugged.

He was in the crowd somewhere. There's a tradition among us that none of the punters knows who the Ax is, or cares. I'm not sure. I remember once, I was standing at a takeaway booth with him. The people waiting to be served were the usual rich crop of loonies, ranters, amateur levitationists. An old bloke – a perfect stranger – started grumbling, saying he thought he was the only normal person left on earth. Ax, modestly, silently pointed to himself. 'Yeah,' said the old chap. '*You're* okay. But your foreign policy is pure fruit and nutcase.'

In the Glass Hall, he had said, only half joking, 'Why did you do it? You could have been rid of me.'

'Your enemies are my enemies,' I told him. 'I'm not stupid. I know *that*.'

Ax gazed at me dolefully, and sighed right down to his toes.

'But nothing's changed.'

'Some things have improved. But nothing's changed.'

That was the way it ended. I ought to be glad, because at last I'd managed to get some glimmer of understanding out of him. But in the cold light of day, the political becomes the personal. I wasn't a cosmic archetype now; or the leader of the opposition. I was just Fiorinda. Oh well. Maybe next year, when I'm twenty-five, I'll be wiser.

Maybe next time, I'll get him drunk and take him dancing. *My* kind of dancing, not that cissy walking-backwards number.

I split my pile of handouts, gave the boys half each and walked home alone.

Blues for a Dying Breed
Cliff Burns

'To be honest,' Cliff Burns writes, from Iqaluit in the Northwest Territories, 'I'm not really comfortable providing details or insights into my stories. Believe me, their conception and creation (and, often, their conclusions) are as much an enigma to me as they are to a reader. Perhaps a brief statement, written with the advice of my attorney, would be acceptable. I despise stereotypes and work my ass off to keep the reader disorientated and on edge. Most of my stories appear in horror publications – yet they rarely feature supernatural devices and inexplicable events. They are firmly based on reality. Yet they have that unnerving quality that horror editors can't quite put their finger on.'

Specialising in the notoriously difficult short-short story without relying on the usual twist endings, Burns has gained a lot of attention after appearing in a wide variety of fringe publications. His self-published collections, Sex and Other Acts of the Imagination and The Reality Machine, are well worth seeking out even if it means venturing above the Arctic Circle. 'More work that cannot be neatly labelled and filed,' he admits. 'I have declared guerilla warfare on those who would hold to the centre, who embrace the mainstream at the expense of the surreal, experimental, and, yeah, I'll use the term "slipstream". I take no prisoners and use the principle of scorched earth. And rage, of course, fuels my writing. It is a savage cycle and one that takes a toll on my health and sanity. But I'll never let go and I'll never give up.'

In the words of Barton Fink, 'We'll be hearing a lot more from that crazy Canadian, and I don't mean on a postcard.'

Lance, the guy from down the hall, is in my face as soon as I get to my door. And, as usual, he's after money.

'Five bucks should do 'er . . . for cigarettes, you know,' he says with a shrug. 'I'm a little short again. That fuckin' Jew I work for always keeps short-changing me. I oughta tell him to take his job and – '

'Yeah, yeah.' I'm nodding like I'm sympathising whereas I'm really thinking you greasy little fucker have you ever seen pictures of those camps, the ovens, the showers, the neatly stacked piles of emaciated corpses? Or maybe you're one of those assholes who pores over historically accurate tracts like 'DID SIX MILLION REALLY DIE?' I push the five bucks at him and then he really starts wheedling.

'Hey, that's great, really great of you, you know, but you know what? Hey,' he shrugs again, 'I just went to pour some milk into my coffee and it came out in lumps, like fuckin' cottage cheese, you know. Maybe you could throw in another buck or two so I can – '

'Sorry, my man,' I tell him and this time it's me shrugging, 'that's all I got until I go to the bank.' And as I say it I can see him staring at the bag I'm holding that says 'Record World' in BIG BLOCK letters. Twenty-five bucks' worth of albums and I'm claiming I'm broke. I shove my key in and open the door.

'Yeah, well, thanks anyway.'

'No problem.'

As I'm pushing the door shut he goes, 'I'll get it back to you by next week at the latest.'

Shit.

It's my own fault I guess. If I had any guts I'd tell him to fuck off and quit pestering me. What's he gonna do, take a swing at me? Not likely. He's five-foot-fuck-all with his hands in the air and as scrawny as a freshly hatched chick.

Maybe all those Sundays I spent in church being brain-washed by all that 'love thy brother' crap had an effect on me. Or maybe I just don't want the hassle. I slit open the plastic wrapping and slide the record on to the turntable. It's a compilation album, assorted old bluesmen croaking and growling about being drunk and poor and having your woman do you wrong. I figure maybe old Lance will be able to relate heavily to this stuff so I turn up the volume a notch or two.

Joe, the guy who runs Record World, was telling me about how he was taking out another section of albums to make room for more compact discs.

'Gotta move with the times,' was how he explained it to me. 'And you know what the bitch of it is? I don't even have a CD player at home. A lot of the time I still play my old 78s, you know my Leadbelly and Blind Willie McTell stuff. The music's scratchy and it's primitive and it's *real*. The record company reps that come in here think I'm some kind of a dinosaur or something. What the hell,' he said as he rang in my order, taking off the usual ten per cent because he likes my taste in music, 'those big critters had it good while they lasted. I mean, they ruled the world, am I right?'

Yup, I think as I settle into my favourite listening chair, they did at that. And they died in one mighty upheaval because they clung to their stubborn worldview, refused to adapt their old thinking, never learned to pool their resources so that some, at least, could survive.

I resolve to start saving up for a CD player.

Joe will never forgive me but, shucks, there're lots of other record stores in this naked city.

There's not enough time for me to play my other album, a live recording of Etta James and assorted luminaries at the Montreux festival. I pass a comb through my hair a few times, grab my jacket and head off to work.

Buying those records turns out to be a pretty good idea. As I walk to work – I always leave my car at home in the summer – I'm in a pretty good mood and even though the restaurant is insanely busy and the customers more surly than usual it doesn't get me down.

I don't hang around for my customary double Scotch after work with the rest of the staff. I leave them sitting at the bar, pissing and moaning about being underpaid, undersexed and generally under-appreciated. I'm walking through the parking lot outside my apartment building and I see my car and I see that someone has bashed in the passenger window, spewing glass shards everywhere. My guts are in knots as I run over and look inside. All of my tapes, gone. And my gym bag too and that almost makes me laugh because all it had in it was my ratty old sweats and some deodorant and a pair of gotch. And then I *do* laugh because I see the little black hole in the dash where the cigarette lighter used to be. You have to wonder about people who would steal something like that . . .

I go inside to call the cops and as I get to my door good old Lance sticks his head out. 'Holy shit, guy, did you see what happened to your car?'

'Yeah,' I grunt.

'Un-fucking believable. This neighbourhood is going right down the toilet.' He waves his hands agitatedly.

'Uh huh.'

'Hey, y'know, if I woulda heard anything I woulda – '

'I know. Thanks anyway.' I open my door.

'I'll bet it was those little nigger kids from down the block, those ones that are always playing right out in the middle of the street. Fuckin' little animals – '

I turn around and look at him and he shuts up. 'No,' I say finally. 'It wasn't the niggers and it wasn't the hebes and it wasn't the towel-heads or the micks or the wops or the spicks. It's the dinosaurs that are to blame. They never really died, you know. They're still among us.'

Lance is staring at me, edging back toward his smelly apartment. 'Yeah,' he nods, 'I think I read about that in the *Enquirer*.'

Then he scurries inside and I hear him lock his door.

Last Rising Sun
Graham Joyce

Graham Joyce may well be the most black-hearted and evil person in Leicester, England. He failed his 11 Plus, won the George Fraser Poetry Award in 1981, and takes a kind of warped pleasure in intimidating people at science fiction conventions, such as stuffing Peter F. Hamilton with curry and liquor until vomiting ensues, or speaking for hours on end in an Ulster accent borrowed from artist Dave Carson until even Storm Constantine thinks he's cracked up. Anything sensitive or humane in his prose is as misleading as the smile on the face of a crocodile. His first novel was the excellent Dreamside, *and a follow-up,* Dark Sister, *will appear in 1992. This is the first short story he has sold. For some unfathomable reason, he has been allowed to work with young people for some years – between spells as a fitter's mate, bingo-caller, holiday camp greencoat (ye gods!), fruit picker and legal supernumerary – thus producing an entire generation of maladjusted psychopaths doubtless destined to be the assassins, insurrectionists, SF writers and Shaun Hutson fans of the twenty-first century.*

That number came on the radio today. I wanted to knock it off but the guy in the next bed said he liked it, so I let it play. Just another dose of déjà vu. I lie here thinking of what happened to Colleen, and how it all could have been different. I think of that old bastard her father. And lying here in bed like this reminds me of when I was a kid.

I used to lie awake at nights and hear that number ghosting from the All-Nite Milk Bar, wondering exactly what those folk were putting in their milk. I couldn't really understand it. I'd drunk milk. I knew its best effects. Let me tell you there's nothing about milk would make me want to stay up talking until 3 a.m.

We lived close enough to the milk bar so that, if the wind was right, the music from that huge Wurlitzer could hitch a ride on a swelling breeze and jump off in a clatter right outside my bedroom window. My old man was always complaining about it. I never minded at all. I'd seen those bikes chopped and winking with chrome, blazing with day-glo decals, leaning in regimental order outside the milk bar, and I could lie awake wondering what it was they used to lace the shakes. When you're twelve, the mind sails free.

There is a house in New Orleans
They call The Rising Sun.

Now I can hardly stand to hear that tune any more. Ever since I got my first axe (Axe? do I date? natch, it's in the pressing of things – a hand-me-down Hohener with wires strung so high above the fretboard they made my fingers bleed) I mastered those blues chords and every desperate jam I can remember eventually degenerated into 'House'. And still does. Hold down a chord. It's why I couldn't run away.

And then I got old enough myself to hang out at the All-Nite Milk Bar. But times had changed. When I was a kid lying in bed at night, kept awake by a rising chord, the young blades in the milk bar were switched on to FAST. That was it. Tip it in your milk; stir it round; drink it down: FAST. But like I said, times change. Now we were on SLOW, and we put something other in the milk. Tip it in; stir it round; drink it down: SLOW. That's all it is, this youth culture thing. Everyone talks about semiotics and style and the endless rebellion. But all it is is cranking the lever back from FAST to SLOW, and then in a few years some younger kids come along and throw it back on FAST. That's what being young is about. You want to take time and speed it up or slow it down. No, it doesn't matter what they wear. They still powder the milk. They're still cranking the lever.

What can I say about getting older? You're more prepared to listen to the B-sides of old singles than the A-sides of new ones. That's about all.

But let me tell you this: they never took 'House' off the Wurlitzer in all that time, whatever changed, whatever the kids were listening to next. And that must count for something.

And it's been the ruin of many a poor boy . . .

Though I'll be the first to admit it might have been because of the legend. I mean a lot of solid, gutbucket blues got spun on that Wurlitzer before going the way of all pressed vinyl. But the legend . . . someone must have decided to keep 'House' up there on the rack, and whoever it was knew about the legend.

That Wurlitzer. Now it's lasers and CDs and circuits so small they're only just this side of theoretical, but the Wurlitzer offered a real, emotional interface. It was a Model 1800, built to last forever in 1955 and it did what juke-boxes are supposed to do: it radiated presence. When you plugged in, electro-blue and rhinestone-red lights sparkled across a humped frame the size of a piano; silver-coloured columns on the front grille featured rocket starbursts in red, while blue light splashed across the speaker screen. The effect was one of rockets bursting against a nightblue sky.

It was visual entertainment. A chrome and glass canopy sloped across the carousel, over the selection-strip and right down to the button bank. It let you see what was happening inside, there was no shame, you could stare right into its guts. At its head, neon tubes spelled out the word WUR-LITZER in worms of white light. Below, a green badge-light winked on, inviting you to MAKE SELECTION.

You dropped your coin in a chrome mouth, hit those huge white Bakelite buttons and stood back to take the pause. Then you felt a tension in the machine, before it kicked. Yes, kicked. And clicked. And whirred. And then paused again, before you'd hear the hum of the carousel turning, a chuck as your disc flipped on to the turntable, and finally five-and-a-half seconds of empty vinyl hiss before it delivered. Jangling chords. Growling vocals. The mood. You were buying a mood.

And sometimes the Wurlitzer would kick into action on its own. No coins. No selection. No one would be standing near it, everyone hard up and what little money in their jean pocket, and off it would go.

Kick. Click; whirr. Pause. Chuck, hiss . . .

There is a house in New Orleans . . .

This is electro-mechanical technology, remember. Over-played discs stuck, selections sometimes got confused in an overloaded memory, your coin might go down the tube and you'd get nothing. Old Wurlitzers are only human after all. But that kicking into gear unprompted, and under its own steam, that spooked everyone. Every time. It's how the legend got started.

I was there the night Dermott was telling everyone.

'The last time it did that, and played that same number,' Dermott pushed my elbows off the counter so he could wipe up spilled sugar with a dirty rag, 'was the night Fox went from here and did you-know-what.'

It was a quiet night. Nothing had been going in the milk,

and no one was in a mood to feed the juke-box. Dermott, lecherous but generous, long-suffering owner of the All-Nite Milk Bar, had been in a shit mood all evening and I was ready to go home. Then for no reason the Wurlitzer had kicked into action and played 'House'.

There was Tony and Colleen and Francis and me, all too young to remember this guy Fox. Only Sleaze, himself timestuck in the era of the Teds, knew what Dermott was talking about.

'What's you-know-what?' I asked.

'What you kids ought to do,' said Dermott. 'Now all of you go, please; I'm closing early tonight.'

'I don't know why you call this an all-nite bar,' Tony tried weakly. Dermott's answer was to upend stools on to tables. Eric Burdon belted it out to an otherwise empty bar.

She sold my new blue jeans . . .

'Fox went from here, down the path and strung himself up from a tree branch,' said Sleaze. 'The paper boy comes to deliver the Sundays next mornin' and this winkle-picker taps him in the eye. He looks up and attached to this winkle-picker is Fox, hanging from a noose with his plonker out.'

'You're making it up!' Colleen looked at Dermott for confirmation.

He shrugged. 'It's about right. And all I know is *that*,' jabbing a finger at the Wurlitzer, 'did *that*, and played *that*. Now piss off.'

'Sure. When the song finishes.'

Outside, neon lights of the bar flickering out over his shoulder, Sleaze kickstarted his Norton. We were still talking about Fox hanging himself. 'Fox was fucked up,' said Sleaze. 'Dressed like a biker, full regalia, everything, but drove a Lambretta. A Lambretta with a dozen mirrors. Is that or is that fucked up?'

Sleaze tried to get Colleen to climb on behind him, even though he knew she was with me. She declined and put her arm around me; I loved her for that. Sleaze gave it hard throttle and tried to impress us with a wheelie, front of his bike rearing three feet in the air, back wheel leaving a deposit of hot tyre in the middle of the road as he screeched off into the night.

Next evening we had a few beers and weighed in at the All-Nite after pub closing time. The place was heaving, and we had to stand near the bar.

'Hear about Sleaze?' asked Dermott, serving up coffee the colour of engine grease.

'What about him?'

'Accident. Ran his bike off the bridge up Tuttle Hill last night.'

'Hey Col; good thing you didn't go with him.'

Colleen shivered. 'Did he hurt himself?'

'I'll say.' Dermott laid plastic spoons on each of our four saucers. 'They had to scrape him off the road with a shovel. Cremation Tuesday.'

Someone went and put a coin in the Wurlitzer.

The legend got embroidered after Sleaze died. Unprompted, the Wurlitzer would kick into gear from time to time, and though I never knew anyone involved, someone always knew someone who knew someone who died a few days later. People would stand in the bar and enumerate: *then there was Fox, then there was Sleaze, then there was Mike Sutton who went for a midnight swim in the quarry pool, and then . . .* And so on. And always the same number on the Wurlitzer, 'House of the Rising Sun'. The milk bar jinx. Bad luck even to talk about it.

Then a band called Frijid Pink produced a cover version, and it wasn't a bad cover either; but some arsehole from the juke-box servicing company substituted it for the old Animals rendition. West Coast psychedelics imitate an English Geordie imitating a New Yorker imitating a Mississippi sharecropper: did they think we wouldn't notice? Naw, we all said to Dermott, get the old one back. Dermott, to his credit, the old buffer – he'd fought over the years to keep the ancient Wurlitzer – got the villain to come down, and as a kind of compromise the two versions were left on adjacent selections.

Being a pair of smart-arses, me and Tony went around for a while challenging everyone to name who originally recorded 'House': none of the bastards had even heard of Josh White, so we collected every time. We even hunted down the original in seven-inch vinyl and persuaded Dermott to stick it alongside the other two.

'What the fuck for?' Dermott had no interest in history.

'It'll make a tasty timeslip.'

'A what?'

'A timeslip,' said Tony, waving the Josh White in the air. 'It'll give people a nice confusion about what era they're in.'

Dermott looked at us with unmitigated contempt. 'Half these kids don't know what fucking day it is, and you want to confuse 'em about the era?'

'Just put it on, Dermott.'

Truth is, it appealed to our sense of déjà vu. Naturally, déjà vu came out of the milk we drank, and we liked to replicate this by stacking the Wurlitzer with cover versions. That been-here-before feeling. It led to a lot of prototype adolescent destiny discussions. Fate. Reincarnation. Predestination. The Next World. All that.

Colleen was the worst. She was a fatalist down to her long, pinkpainted fingernails. Blinking from another milk-induced dose of déjà vu, she first came out with the pressed-vinyl model of the universe. 'Yeh, and what it is, this is all a spinning disc, right, 'cos you're just on another play, right? Another incarnation. Just another stroll down the same old spiral track right?' Colleen could stretch out this sort of thing for hours. 'And death, see, that's the hole in the middle, right, right, and you go tumbling through, waiting for your number to get punched again on the Great Big Wurlitzer.'

I know what you're thinking. But this sort of stuff can seem meaningful when you've been powdering the milk.

Just then something playing on the Wurlitzer – the real one – decided to stick. Dermott, who happened to be passing, showed it the heel of his boot.

Tony, milkless and bored, yawned and said, 'So what's it mean when the record sticks?'

'That,' said Colleen, 'that's your déjà vu, right?'

'And when it jumps?' I chipped in.

'Premonitions. Seeing the future. Travel in time.'

'Scratches?'

'Moral mistakes.'

And so on. She made it all fit. Tony wished he hadn't encouraged her.

'But the thing is,' Colleen became serious, 'once you're on, you know, *your spiral path*, there's no changing it. You can't steer it in another direction. It's a set groove.' She looked hard into her milk.

'Bollocks,' said Tony after a pause. Then he went home.

But I was there on the night it all came to an end. It was mid-week and Dermott was talking about closing early because business was so slack. It wasn't even ten o'clock when he wanted us to go. He didn't look too good at all. His face was the colour of putty and he was dribbling perspiration. Two huge oval sweatstains darkened his denim shirt around his armpits. We tried to give him a lot of stick and the usual banter, but he was in no mood for it. Colleen and Francis helped him collect a few coffee cups, and he seemed unusually grateful.

We were just about to leave when the Wurlitzer did its old trick.

Kick, click, whirr. Pause. Play.

Sure enough 'House' came on. Dermott marched over and crashed his boot into the juke-box before snatching out the plug wire. We all giggled nervously and ran outside. The last I saw of Dermott, he was bolting the doors behind us and wiping perspiration from his face with a white teatowel.

The All-Nite Milk Bar never opened the next evening; nor any other evening. Dermott had had a stroke in the night. He was dead at the age of forty.

'You realise what was playing before we left?' Colleen looked searchingly at me with her brown eyes.

'Don't,' I said. 'Don't.'

The milk bar got closed up. A few windows got poked out by kids before they boarded it over. There was some talk of it re-opening or being converted, but nothing ever happened. Its location was useless as a commercial proposition, and Dermott had only ever kept it on because he didn't know what else to do.

The weeks went by, and Colleen and I began to spend more and more time with each other. It was going to be our last summer together, as I was preparing to go off to college. We avoided talking about it. Then her folks found some stuff in her bedroom drawer. It all got blamed on me, which was ridiculous since Colleen was always first over the edge in anything we did, and I was banned from seeing her. Her old man belted her black and blue, and threatened to bury me. Then her folks told my folks, and there was a lot of hysteria and squawking, but that was the deal, to keep the police out of it.

Of course we didn't stop seeing each other. We just couldn't phone or meet in any obvious place. Ironically, she was powdering the milk more than ever before, and, well, I sort of went along with anything she did. Then one night I got a phone call from a friend of hers. It was quite late, but Colleen needed to see me urgently. We had a meeting place, a tryst-hole, the wooden kissing-gate at the entrance to the woods, up near the old All-Nite Milk Bar.

I walked there, shivering in my T-shirt. My hands were shaking, because I knew what she was going to tell me. I couldn't think straight. She was waiting by the kissing-gate, staring into the dark woods. She wouldn't look me in the eye.

'Jesus,' I said.

'That's what Mum said. Jesus, Mary and Joseph.'

'You told her? Has she told your old man?' I shook her. She was crying.

'Not yet. But she will. I can't go back there! I can't!'

'What do you mean?'

'I can't! I can't!'

But I knew what she meant. The bruises from her last round with the old bastard had only just faded. I needed to think but nothing was coming into my head.

I slumped down on the grass and tried to light up a snout, but I couldn't get the match to come into contact with the cigarette. I had this notion that life ended as soon as you became a parent. I wasn't even eighteen. This wasn't the spiral path. There was my college. There was all of life. I wasn't ready.

'You'll have to get rid of it.'

'Bastard,' she said. Only two weeks earlier I'd told her I'd love her forever, we were locked in the same spiral, the same pressing, might as well accept it beginning to end.

'What else can we do? I've got my life to live. You've got yours. What do you expect?'

It was as if I'd plunged a knife into her breast. She collapsed on to the grass, gasping and wailing and hugging herself so hard I thought she might crack a rib. I'd never in my life seen such a ferocious fit of sobbing. 'I'm a Catholic,' she kept crying, 'I'm a Catholic.'

I told her I took back everything I'd said, and that I'd do anything she wanted if only she'd stop crying like that. I seriously thought she was in danger. After a long while the fit subsided, and I held her. I couldn't take her to her own house, and I couldn't take her to mine: Colleen's parents were probably at my house even at that moment, creating hysterical scenes. I had an idea.

Colleen let me lead her around the back of the milk bar. It was all nailed up tight but I managed to prise open a board and lever it from the window frame. There was an almighty cracking sound as it came away, but no one else was around. We climbed in.

It was dark. There was a musty, earthy smell to the property. I did my best to replace the board behind us.

It had been only a couple of months since Dermott died, yet the place smelled like it had been shut up for years. Everything was draped in ghostly white dust-sheets. I tried a light switch, but the juice was off. Anyway, the lights would have been seen from the road, and I had an idea we might even be able to spend a few days there. I found a couple of candle stubs behind the counter and they gave us enough light to get comfortable. I pulled some dust-sheets off the stacked stools and the Wurlitzer, and did my best to make a bed out of them.

I was still making a thousand unkeepable promises to

Colleen. She snuffled and looked at me without saying anything. Her nose was sore from wiping. I hunted round for something to eat or drink, anything to comfort her, but all the stock had been cleared. The candlelight danced over the settled white dust. I snuggled down beside Colleen, putting my arm around her, wondering what the hell we were going to do and staring into the darkness of the milk bar for an answer which never came.

We heard someone's steps outside, and I snuffed out the candle. We sat in complete darkness until long after they'd gone. It was way after midnight. Maybe it was just someone walking their dog, but the thought of prowlers had us spooked.

We tried to get some sleep but the place was full of creaks. The wind moaned outside, rattling the wood-built milk bar and slapping the loose board where we'd forced an entry.

'I'm scared,' said Colleen.

'Don't be. We're safe here.'

'Not for this. For everything.'

I was about to light the candle again when it happened.

The Wurlitzer lit up.

The juice was switched off; I'd already checked. Yet the Wurlitzer was lighting up in the dark like a firework display.

First a starburst of red illuminated the milk bar, followed by a wash of blue light. Pools of colour rippled across the floor. Then the soft amber lights under the canopy flickered on, neon worms fizzing at they spelled out WURLITZER in crazy, dislocated style. I heard Colleen gasp. We stared at the machine, huddled together, seeming to shrink in size as the Wurlitzer floated before us in the dark like some massive spaceship.

There was a moment of suffocating tension. Then the Wurlitzer kicked. I knew every sound that was coming. It clicked; it whirred; it chucked. It was like machinery working in my guts. I heard the carousel move. Then there was another click, and a loud hissing. Freezing wings brushed my neck. At that moment I did indeed feel like my whole life was a pressed disc, and that I'd been down this way many, many times before, and that every new time was nothing more than a cover version of the same experience: same beginning, same ending, and the same inscrutable, terrifying hole at the end of the spiralling groove. There it was, doom-laden, echoing in chambers of the mind, the old whorehouse lament.

> *And it's been the ruin of many a poor boy*
> *And God I know I'm one.*

Colleen and I stared in horrible, frozen awe at the pulsating Wurlitzer. Its sound swamped the empty milk bar, loud enough to vibrate the glass windows, loud enough to shake Dermott in his grave. I remembered when I was a kid again, listening to music carried on the back of spirits.

Then it stopped. The coloured lights died. We were in darkness again.

We got out quick, same way as we'd got in. 'But who's it for?' Colleen said. 'You or me?'

Then we spent three dreadful hours sitting in a bus shelter until the dawn chorus started. Colleen had a couple of friends with a bedsit in town, and she decided to see if they'd let her stay until she could find somewhere. I didn't want to let her, but she insisted on going alone.

I eventually found the address and went up there myself. A girl with a towel around her head came to the door and told me Colleen wasn't in, but I knew she was lying. I could feel her presence behind the door.

I was walking up by the kissing-gate one evening when I saw Tony and Francis.

'She won't see me. She won't have anything to do with me.'

'I wish she would,' said Francis.

'How is she?'

'Doing far too much powder these days. I don't like it.'

'Tell her, will you, Francis?'

'Tell her what?'

'Just tell her.'

Then I heard. I heard before that stupid story got into the papers. *She thought she was an orange and tried to peel herself.* That was the garbage that got written up in the *Evening Post*. They didn't have to write it like that. They could have just said it as it was.

Colleen was too clever to believe any of my promises. She saw only one way out, and she took it. My God she didn't have to die. It was that fucking banshee juke-box. I should have told her it had already had its victim with Dermott. He just hadn't let it play out the night before he died. It wasn't in the pressing. She didn't have to do it.

Her folks wouldn't even let me go to the funeral. They blamed it on me. I watched it all from a distance; I didn't need to go and eat a pickle sandwich with people like that. I could do my own crying.

The night of her funeral I went back to the milk bar with a can of petrol. I climbed in the same way as before. I doused the Wurlitzer, and the petrol ran down the glass canopy and between the button bank. Something touched on. A green light winked, inviting me to MAKE SELECTION. I could almost have smiled.

I flung the rest of the petrol around the milk bar. I wanted the whole lot to go up, but first I had one last thing to do. I tapped out the buttons I knew by heart. Kick. Click; whirr.

Pause. Chuck; hiss. Jangling chords. Growling vocals. Just like it had always been.

They call The Rising Sun . . .

Then I lit up. The Wurlitzer exploded into flame six feet high. The fire raced around the floor and up the walls of the wooden shack milk bar. It went up like tinder. I must have spilled petrol on myself, because I felt my jeans and my jacket burning, before I felt my hair on fire. I remember writhing around the floor, frantically trying to tear myself out of my clothes, but rolling into more flame. The Wurlitzer was still belting out those moondog lyrics at high volume, loud over the crackle and roar of the flame.

So Mother tell your children
Not to do what I have done

I kicked at the boarded doors of the bar, splintering wood and smashing glass, finally flinging myself outside and away from the scorching heat and smoke. I could still hear 'House' ringing in my ears as I blacked out. I don't remember anything after that.

They took off some of the bandages yesterday. I made them hold a mirror up to my face. One eye looks something like a charred walnut, but I can still see through the other one. They said I was lucky.

I have to ask myself if I called up my own misfortune by that perverse act of playing 'House' one last time. Perhaps that wasn't in the pressing. Maybe next time I won't get fried to a crisp. Maybe Colleen doesn't have to die. Maybe we can make a new cover version where none of that happens. Whatever, I can wait for the next play.

Reed John-Paul Forever
Steve Antczak

A resident of Atlanta, Georgia, Steve Antczak used to sing for a punk garage band called Officer Friendly. He's also worked on Twisted Issues, *a video billed as 'a psycho-punk splatter comedy' which deals with zombie skatepunks in Gainesville, Florida. (It's available through* Film Threat *magazine.)*

Born in Salem, Massachusetts, Steve was three years old to the day when man first set foot on the Moon. Neil Armstrong's first words on touching down were actually 'Happy Birthday, Steve', but they were overlaid by static on the time-delayed tele-cast by a vindictive Spiro T. Agnew. 'Reed John-Paul Forever', which Steve claims is vaguely inspired by the chameleon career of David Bowie, is his fifth sale and his third book appearance (the first was a piece in Newer York). *We called him up to quiz him about these notes at an incredibly inconvenient time, but even so he was decent enough to chat. Punks (and ex-punks) are nice people.*

The latest Reed John-Paul humper, 'My Black Hole', pounded the air like it pounded Henri's blood. Sent him spinning and whirling, jumping and looping all over the floor. He was gone, the music wired to his body, remote controlled randomness, death-defying fury. To look at him you might say, *There's Reed John-Paul himself, look at him demon dance, watch a living legend.* Henri *was* Reed John-Paul, as far as the eye could tell. The reality could tell a different story.

Henri was a Reed John-Paul effigy. A kid with no identity

of his own, a culture clone, a wannabe, a nowhere else to run dead end of the road loser with one last shred of glory. Of the thousands of screaming Reed John-Paul fans, he was one of the few who took it as far as it could be taken. He could be Reed John-Paul like no one else, except Reed John-Paul.

The humper ground itself out in an ashtray of shrieks and shattering glass, and Henri kept on, convulsing to the tune still raging in his head, until the Furious George track put his fire out. Not his smoke, FG. Henri stood there, momentarily dazed with FG effigies taking up swaying ranks around him, liquid human parts flowing to words sung by a drowning man.

He beat the floor, swaggering that Reed John swagger – left hip thrown way out there, right hand held out for alms – and made his way through the mish-mash of painted faces and unnatural hair to the table in the corner where his posse posed.

'You were gone, out there,' Tom Tom, his muscle, told him.

'Raging fuckin' gone,' Haze, his cowgirl at night, riding high on the hog, whispered wetly in his ear. Her tongue flicked in for a sec, then traced around the cartilage, and she kissed him fast on the cheek.

Henri took a whiff. The air was heavy with toxins from a hundred different kinds of burning weed and alcoholic atmosphere. It was good to be here, where the energy flowed into you instead of out, where the things that mattered happened on the floor and in glasses or rolled in paper, and sometimes secretly in the bathrooms. Outside nothing mattered except getting *in*. In was belonging and creating small legends, Out was boredom, getting old and dying nobody.

He noticed a Betty leaning towards him against a railing

around the Pit. Below he knew the skins and punks were moshing and banging heads together in a war of fevered, manic fuzz that sent their bodies flying at one another until they dropped. Once in the Pit, the only way out was head first.

The Betty smiled at Henri. She looked like a norm, the hottest I-wanna-be-your-dog norm he'd ever seen. Her lips seemed to direct pleasure through the air at him. Henri felt a howl building inside.

Haze punched his arm. 'Hey, heel,' she said. 'You said I was along for the ride. Is the ride over?'

He looked at her. 'Not yet.' Her painted white face frowned, red eyebrows formed a *V* beneath blue dreadlocks.

'Hey, Henri . . .' It was Tom Tom, pointing with his chin.

Henri looked. The Betty was approaching the table, legs netted in black, waist circled by a loose black skirt, chest bare down to the nipples. Her eyes stayed focused on Henri, ignoring the others.

Henri suppressed a grin. Probably some glamgirl out slumming for a little effigy meat. The glams did that every once in a while, got one of the effs, adopted him, took him around for show and tell, until she grew tired, or sick, of him sucking it all up like a leech. Not Henri's smoke. Haze need not worry.

'I'm Anna,' the woman said to Henri.

'Who fuckin' cares, bitch,' Haze spat. She was ready for a knock down. Henri put a hand gently yet firmly on her leg. *Chill.* Haze didn't move, but stayed tense.

'Call me . . . Reed,' Henri said. Anna's eyes caught the light and glittered. The spiked pink hair, raccoon's mask painted blue around his eyes, black lips that formed Henri's perfected off-kilter grin . . . all Reed John-Paul.

'Okay. Reed. Come with me for a walk. For air.'

'There's air in here,' he said.

'Then come with me for glory.'

'Hey, there's glory in here, too,' Tom Tom cut in.

Anna ignored him. 'Come on, Reed, this could be your big chance. Come with me.'

Something in her voice was stronger than Henri's will. Henri's will was a Berlin Wall waiting for a revolution. And Anna was a Molotov cocktail, with her fuse lit and smoking. Maybe she was his smoke after all.

He stood.

'Henri,' Haze said. 'Henri, what the – ?'

'I'll be right back,' he said. Anna took his arm in her hand and led him away.

Outside it was acid raining. The burning drops forced them to take the tuber, which then took them uptown. Uptown: People didn't die uptown, they were forced to leave before they reached that point. The Immortals lived there . . . the real Reed John-Paul and Furious George.

'Are you one?' Henri asked. Immortal, he meant.

She nodded, and that was that.

The apartment was six rooms, all bigger than any house Henri had ever been in. It was high among the skyscrapers, way above eight-hour workdays and sixteen-hour empty dreams. And it was a shrine to Reed John-Paul.

'A fanatic,' Henri said.

'You.'

He turned to face her. 'Effigy,' he said. 'I want to *be* him, not worship him.'

She laughed. 'Oh, of course, I see.' She slipped her shoes off and walked barefoot across the deep blue carpet to the kitchen. 'Hungry?'

His stomach answered for him, 'Yes.'

So what would she want? Sex? A performance? He could do Reed like no one else. Except –

'Reed John-Paul,' she said from the kitchen. 'Why?'

'It just happened,' Henri said. 'That's why. Better than being me. Henri Dupris, loser like the rest. Rather be the best, and that's Reed John-Paul. Right?'

'No argument there.' She brought him a plate with micro-waved noodles and white sauce. 'Sit at the table, I'll tell you what's happening.'

He sat at the table. The noodles were good, soft, and the sauce was kind of fishy. She poured him a glass of white wine, then sat beside him.

'Reed John-Paul is dead,' she said.

Henri stopped eating. He shook his head. 'Sorry. Heard that rumour before, lots of times. Never believe it, and he never lets me down.'

Anna sighed. 'I know. That's how it was planned. There've been five others before you, and they all said the same thing. And I hate myself for it, but it is in the contract.'

Henri had resumed eating to give the illusion of non-concern. 'What contract?' As far as he knew he hadn't signed anything.

'With Prolong. They own the Reed John-Paul contract.'

'The life extension company.'

She nodded. 'Prolong doesn't work on everyone, you know. It worked on me . . . I was his wife when we made the deal.'

Henri stopped eating again and set the fork down. 'His wife. Reed John-Paul . . .?'

She nodded again. 'It didn't work on Reed. Prolong just didn't work. In fact, it killed him. He lived the rest of his life in five years . . . all that energy, all that time, compressed into five years. It pushed him over the top, his shows became legendary, his music was unmatched . . . But it killed him.'

Henri was shaking his head. 'But . . . I've *seen* him. *Live*. I saw the Dancing with Death tour last season.' The image was a flashover in his mind, Henri and countless others shaking to the raw sound, hanging on the singer's every lyric, each song like a revelation. 'He was *there*. I was in the first row, pressed right up against the barricades. He sang "Don't Even Try to Stop Me" to the girl next to me. She tried to get to him. When the security gorillas nabbed her halfway across the stage, she freaked out so bad she went into a seizure. He wasn't dead.'

'You saw . . . an effigy.'

'No.'

'The record company sold the contract to Prolong, because Prolong couldn't allow a failure with their drug to get publicity. They announced Reed was resting, then they had the contests, the Reed John-Paul contests. They needed someone who could move like him, sing like him, *be* like him. They needed me to test him . . . in more ways than one.' She paused, smiled. 'The last one was Benny Jargon . . . you knew him.'

Henri knew him. Benny'd been the best of the best, better than Henri, but Henri didn't mind because Benny was *that* good. Then he just disappeared, no one knew how or why, and Henri became the effigy to watch.

'That was Benny,' Henri said. He remembered that last show, he remembered coming away from it with the odd feeling he *knew* Reed John-Paul. He figured it'd been the sheer intensity of the performance. Everyone left that show bonded to each other through Reed John-Paul, as if they'd formed a new religion and were the first true believers, the disciples. But no . . . Benny.

'We need you, now,' Anna said quietly.

He looked at her, met her gaze directly. 'I have a choice?'

'That's the first time I've been asked, but yeah, you have a choice. There are other effigies out there, not as good, but a little surgery can change anything physical. The rest comes with the drug.'

'And then in five years I'll be dead?'

'Probably. There is the chance Prolong will work, too. It hasn't yet. The company figures it has something to do with the kind of mind it takes to be Reed John-Paul. It just rejects the drug.'

'If I say yes . . .'

'You will *be* Reed John-Paul. Oh, a part of you will be there, as a spectator, along for the ride, but you will become my husband.' Her voice nearly cracked, her eyes should have been crying. She'd done this too many times, just to get her husband back for a few years at a time, just to lose him again to the very drug that kept her alive forever.

Henri thought about it. He could go back to Haze and Tom Tom, people he barely knew outside the Vatican West, people he called his friends merely because they were those whom he associated with Inside. Outside he normally didn't think about, but he had to now. Outside he slept in a two-room flat that seemed designed for TV worship and little else. His job when he bothered to show up had him unloading uniform brown boxes on to trucks. He didn't know what was in those boxes, didn't want to know. He was locked out of anything resembling higher education because he just couldn't afford it, his parents couldn't afford it, and the government couldn't afford student loans any more. Dancing the effigy dance would get real old some day. And then what?

And then . . . There was the chance he could live forever. Reed John-Paul forever. And if he died in five years . . .

he'd still have had five years of glory. Five years of *being* Reed John-Paul.

Anna left him alone to think. He wondered what Tom Tom and Haze would say about this. What were they doing now? Probably grinding at the club, creating small myths . . .

Henri thought of his father. What kind of man was he really? He wanted to hear his father's infamous Pave Your Own Highway speech again. It was almost as if the man had actually believed his own propaganda, even though he was a backroom file clerk for some impersonal corporate Goliath.

And his mother, her smile and gentle eyes, her support for Henri's lifestyle. Have fun, do what you want to do, because some day you'll be eighty and it'll be over.

Stretched out on a cold metal table, naked. Anna stood beside him, smiling. She touched his chest tenderly with her hand.

'Henri,' she whispered, 'this is it.'

He felt the first needle slip into the crook of his arm and enter the vein. Then another one enter the other arm. Henri was suddenly very frightened, tears rolled down the sides of his face. He'd never been so alone.

He was a spectator.

Hot lights and humping music and an ocean of arms and heads waved in the darkness he could barely see, an undercurrent roar of voices raised to a fever pitch.

A kaleidoscope of moments:

Earphones suctioned to his head as he laid down the vocal tracks for songs called 'Hours to Live', 'Love is the Last Thing I Need', 'I Don't Know Me Anymore'.

Making love with Anna, enclosed by her hot flesh and

strong arms and legs, soft music in the background, and Anna whispering 'Reed, Reed, Reed.'

Flashbulbs (for effect) and a synthtape experience of what it's like to *be* Reed John-Paul in the flesh! Not including sex with Anna, but with many others. Hounded by the media, chased by manic dogs who call themselves fans, attacked by jealous boyfriends . . .

The spectacle of Reed John-Paul doing the first Martian tour, nearly cracking the dome with ultra-sonics and –

Collapse, all systems down, humping still in the air with smoke and lights . . . gone.

Five years.

Gone. Anna stood beside the bed, smiling, no tears.

'It's over.' Like a song. 'You had fun.'

Henri could barely feel his body. The only thing he could feel was old. Ancient.

'I . . . remember some . . .' He tried to lift his head, to see his body, to see what Reed John-Paul looked like, what he *really* looked like. Who had all those people reached out to touch?

'Do you remember me?' Anna asked.

'Yes. We made love.'

'Every single night,' she said. Another face came into view, leaning in from the edge of darkness. The face, painted and young. Reed John-Paul.

'Hey, mate,' he said. 'I'm your successor. I'm *you*. Pretty weird, eh?'

'He caught you when you fell off the stage last night. We knew it was over then. It was a stroke of luck that he happened to be one of the top effigies around. He's taking the injections tonight.'

'Great show,' the effigy said. 'Wouldn't'a missed it for the world.' Then his eyes narrowed and he asked in almost a whisper, 'Was it worth it?' In his eyes Henri could see it wouldn't matter if he said no.

Henri closed his eyes, and the lights came back, the chanting by ten thousand voices of his name, the music that drove his heart, pumped his blood, and housed his soul. The song was over, but the melody lingered.

It had been worth it.

'Reed John-Paul forever,' he said.

Snodgrass
Ian R. MacLeod

Rules are made to be broken, as surely as TVs are made to be thrown out of hotel bedroom windows – otherwise, why would designers bother to give them aerodynamic shells? One of the unwritten rules of selecting fiction for In Dreams *was that we didn't want stories about the pantheon of dead stars. But as it turned out, the very first story we bought is about a dead star famous not only in his own right, but also for his untimely death. When you read it, you'll see why we threw our rulebook away. There have been SF stories about this particular dead star before, but none as novel, or as caustically funny, or as redemptive, as this.*

Ian MacLeod lives in Sutton Coldfield with his wife Gillian and daughter Emily. After working for ten years in the Civil Service, he quit his job to become a full-time writer. The first story he sold (although not the first published), 1/72nd Scale, *was nominated for the Nebula Award for best novelette in 1990; it and two others have already been reprinted in best-of-the-year anthologies.*

'I must confess to being no great Beatles or Lennon fan,' MacLeod says. 'So why write about him? Simple – I read Albert Goldman's biography, a book that was universally slammed, but which struck me as being an essentially believable and sympathetic treatment. And I started wondering about the chances that brought the Beatles together, and the flukes of talent and history that made them what they were. No big revelations in that, I suppose. The other thing I had in mind with the story – and something that seemed to fit well with Lennon's basically melancholy personality – was what it must be like for these guys who quit really big groups just before they're

successful. Can you imagine it? "Yes, I used to be in the Stones/
Beatles/Doors or whatever, but I quit/got chucked out/fell off the
back of the transit on the way to a gig." Then having to repeat that
for the rest of your life. I chose Birmingham as the location simply
because it's my home town, and when I said to my wife Gillian, "I
can't have John Lennon *living in* Birmingham *getting a job in*
the Civil Service," *she replied with the question: "Why not – isn't*
that what you did?"'

've got me whole life worked out. Today,
give up smoking. Tomorrow, quit drinking. The day after, give up smoking again.

It's morning. Light me cig. Pick the fluff off me feet. Drag the curtain back, and the night's left everything in the same mess outside. Bin sacks by the kitchen door that Cal never gets around to taking out front. The garden jungleland gone brown with autumn. Houses this way and that, terraces queuing for something that'll never happen.

It's early. Daren't look at the clock. The stair carpet works greasegrit between me toes. Downstairs in the freezing kitchen, pull the cupboard where the handle's dropped off.

'Hey, Mother Hubbard,' I shout up the stairs to Cal. 'Why no fucking cornflakes?'

The lav flushes. Cal lumbers down in a grey nightie. 'What's all this about cornflakes? Since when do you have breakfast, John?'

'Since John got a job.'

'You? A job?'

'I wouldn't piss yer around about this, Cal.'

'You owe me four weeks' rent,' she says. 'Plus I don't know how much for bog roll and soap. Then there's the TV licence.'

'Don't tell me yer buy a TV licence.'

'I don't, but I'm the householder. It's me who'd get sent to gaol.'

'Every Wednesday, I'll visit yer,' I say, rummaging in the bread bin.

'What's this job anyway?'

'I told yer on Saturday when you and Kevin came back from the Chinese. Must have been too pissed to notice.' I hold up a stiff green slice of Mighty White. 'Think this is edible?'

'Eat it and find out. And stop calling Steve Kevin. He's upstairs asleep right at this moment.'

'Well there's a surprise. Rip Van and his tiny Winkle.'

'I wish you wouldn't say things like that. You know what Steve's like if you give him an excuse.'

'Yeah, but at least I don't have to sleep with him.'

Cal sits down to watch me struggle through breakfast. Before Kevin, it was another Kevin, and a million other Kevins before that, all with grazed knuckles from the way they walk. Cal says she needs the protection even if it means the odd bruise.

I paste freckled marge over ye Mighty White. It tastes just like the doormat, and I should know.

'Why don't yer tell our Kev to stuff it?' I say.

She smiles and leans forward.

'Snuggle up to Dr Winston here,' I wheedle.

'You'd be too old to look after me with the clients, John,' she says, as though I'm being serious. Which I am.

'For what I'd charge to let them prod yer, Cal, yer wouldn't have any clients. Onassis couldn't afford yer.'

'Onassis is dead, unless you mean the woman.' She stands up, turning away, shaking the knots from her hair. She stares out of the window over the mess in the sink. Cal hates to talk about her work. 'It's past eight, John,' she says without looking at any clock. It's a knack she has. 'Hadn't you better get ready for this job?'

Yeah, ye job. The people at the Jobbie are always on the look-out for something fresh for Dr Winston. They think of him as a challenge. Miss Nikki was behind ye spit-splattered perspex last week. She's an old hand – been there for at least three months.

'Name's Dr Winston O'Boogie,' I drooled, doing me hunchback when I reached the front of ye queue.

'We've got something for you, Mr Lennon,' she says. They always call yer Mister or Sir here, just like the fucking police. 'How would you like to work in a Government Department?'

'Well, wow,' I say, letting the hunchback slip. 'You mean like a spy?'

That makes her smile. I hate it when they don't smile.

She passes me ye chit. Name, age, address. Skills, qualifications – none. That bit always kills me. Stapled to it we have details of something clerical.

'It's a new scheme, Mr Lennon,' Nikki says. 'The Government is committed to helping the long-term unemployed. You can start Monday.'

So here's Dr Winston O'Boogie at the bus stop in the weird morning light. I've got on me best jacket, socks that match, even remembered me glasses so I can see what's happening. Cars are crawling. Men in suits are tapping fingers on the steering wheel as they groove to Katie Boyle. None of them live around here – they're all from Solihull – and this is just a place to complain about the traffic. And Monday's a drag cos daughter Celia has to back the Mini off the drive and be a darling and shift Mummy's Citroën too so yer poor hard-working Dad can get to the Sierra.

The bus into town lumbers up. The driver looks at me like I'm a freak when I don't know ye exact fare. Up on the top

deck where there's No standing, No spitting, No ball games,
I get me a window seat and light me a ciggy. I love it up
here, looking down on the world, into people's bedroom
windows. Always have. Me and me mate Pete used to drive
the bus from the top front seat all the way from Menlove
Avenue to Quarry Bank School. I remember the rows of
semis, trees that used to brush like sea on shingle over the
roof of the bus. Everything in Speke was Snodgrass of
course, what with valve radios on the sideboard and the
Daily Excess, but Snodgrass was different in them days. It
was like watching a play, waiting for someone to forget their
lines. Mimi used to tell me that anyone who said they were
middle class probably wasn't. You knew just by checking
whether they had one of them blocks that look like Kendal
Mint Cake hooked around the rim of the loo. It was all tea
and biscuits then, and Mind, dear, your slip's showing. You
knew where you were, what you were fighting.

The bus crawls. We're up in the clouds here, the fumes on
the pavement like dry ice at a big concert. Oh, yeah. I mean,
Dr Winston may be nifty fifty with his whole death to look
forward to but he knows what he's saying. Cal sometimes
works at the NEC when she gets too proud to do the real
business. Hands out leaflets and wiggles her ass. She got me
a ticket last year to see Simply Red and we went together
and she put on her best dress that looked just great and
didn't show too much and I was proud to be with her, even
if I did feel like her dad. Of course, the music was warmed-
over shit. It always is. I hate the way that red-haired guy
sings. She tried to get me to see Cliff too, but Dr Winston
has his pride.

Everywhere is empty round here, knocked down and
boarded up, postered over. There's a group called SideKick
playing at Digbeth. And waddayouknow, the Beatles are
playing this very evening at the NEC. The Greatest Hits

Tour, it says here on ye corrugated fence. I mean, Fab Gear Man. Give It Bloody Foive. Macca and Stu and George and Ringo, and obviously the solo careers are up the kazoo again. Like, wow.

The bus dumps me in the middle of Brum. The office is just off Cherry Street. I stagger meself by finding it right away, me letter from the Jobbie in me hot little hand. I show it to a geezer in uniform, and he sends me up to the fifth floor. The whole place is new. It smells of formaldehyde – that stuff we used to pickle the spiders in at school. Me share the lift with ye office bimbo. Oh, after *you.*

Dr Winston does his iceberg cruise through the openplan. So this is what Monday morning really looks like.

Into an office at the far end. Smells of coffee. Snodgrass has got a filter machine bubbling away. A teapot ready for the afternoon.

'Mr Lennon.'

We shake hands across the desk. 'Mr Snodgrass.'

Snodgrass cracks a smile. 'There must have been some mistake down in General Admin. My name's Fenn. But everyone calls me Allen.'

'Oh yeah. And why's that?' A voice inside that sounds like Mimi says *Stop this behaviour, John.* She's right, of course. Dr Winston needs the job, the money. Snodgrass tells me to sit down. I fumble for a ciggy and try to loosen up.

'No smoking please, Mr . . . er, *John.*'

Oh, great.

'You're a lot, um, older than most of the casual workers we get.'

'Well this is what being on the Giro does for yer. I'm nineteen really.'

Snodgrass looks down at his file. 'Born 1940.' He looks up again. 'And is that a Liverpool accent I detect?'

I look around me. 'Where?'

Snodgrass has got a crazy grin on his face. I think the bastard likes me. 'So you're John Lennon, from Liverpool. I thought the name rang a faint bell.' He leans forward. 'I am right, aren't I?'

Oh fucking Jesus. A faint bell. This happens about once every six months. Why *now*? 'Oh yeah,' I say. 'I used to play the squeezebox for Gerry and the Pacemakers. Just session work. And it was a big thrill to work with Shirley Bassey, I can tell yer. She's the King as far as I'm concerned. Got bigger balls than Elvis.'

'You were the guy who left the Beatles.'

'That was Pete Best, Mr Snodgrass.'

'You *and* Pete Best. Pete Best was the one who was dumped for Ringo. You walked out on Paul McCartney and Stuart Sutcliffe. I collect records, you see. I've read all the books about Merseybeat. And my elder sister was a big fan of those old bands. The Fourmost, Billy J. Kramer, Cilla, the Beatles. Of course, it was all before my time.'

'Dinosaurs ruled the earth.'

'You must have some stories to tell.'

'Oh, yeah.' I lean forward across the desk. 'Did yer know that Paul McCartney was really a woman?'

'Well, John, I – '

'It figures if yer think about it, Mr Snodgrass. I mean, have *you* ever seen his dick?'

'Just call me Allen, please, will you? Now, I'll show you your desk.'

Snodgrass takes me out into the openplan. Introduces me to a pile of envelopes, a pile of letters. Well, Hi. Seems like Dr Winston is supposed to put one into the other.

'What do I do when I've finished?' I ask.

'We'll find you some more.'

All the faces in the openplan are staring. A phone's

ringing, but no one bothers to answer. 'Yeah,' I say, 'I can see there's a big rush on.'

On his way back to his office, Snodgrass takes a detour to have a word with a fat Doris in a floral print sitting over by the filing cabinets. He says something to her that includes the word Beatle. Soon, the whole office knows.

'I bet you could write a book,' fat Doris says, standing over me, smelling of pot noodles. 'Everyone's interested in those days now. Of course, the Who and the Stones were the ones for me. Brian Jones. Keith Moon, for some reason. All the ones who died. I was a real rebel. I went to Heathrow airport once, chewed my handbag to shreds.'

'Did yer piss yourself too, Doris? That's what usually happened.'

Fat Doris twitches a smile. 'Never quite made it to the very top, the Beatles, did they? Still, that Paul McCartney wrote some lovely songs. "Yesterday", you still hear that one in lifts don't you? And Stu was *so* good-looking then. Must be a real tragedy in your life that you didn't stay. How does it feel, carrying that around with you, licking envelopes for a living?'

'Yer know what your trouble is don't yer, Doris?'

Seems she don't, so I tell her.

Winston's got no money for the bus home. His old joints ache – never realised it was this bloody far to walk. The kids are playing in our road like it's a holiday, which it always is for most of them. A tennis ball hits me hard on the noddle. I pretend it don't hurt, then I growl at them to fuck off as they follow me down the street. Kevin's van's disappeared from outside the house. Musta gone out. Pity, shame.

Cal's wrapped up in a rug on the sofa, smoking a joint and watching *Home and Away*. She jumps up when she sees me in the hall like she thought I was dead already.

'Look, Cal,' I say. 'I really wanted this job, but yer wouldn't get Adolf Hitler to do what they asked, God rest his soul. There were all these little puppies in cages and I was supposed to push knitting needles down into their eyes. Jesus, it was – '

'Just shaddup for one minute will you, John!'

'I'll get the rent somehow, Cal, I – '

' – Paul McCartney was here!'

'Who the hell's Paul McCartney?'

'Be serious for a minute, John. He was *here*. There was a car the size of a tank parked outside the house. You should have seen the curtains twitch.'

Cal hands me the joint. I take a pull, but I really need something stronger. And I still don't believe what she's saying. 'And why the fuck should Macca come here?'

'To see *you*, John. He said he'd used a private detective to trace you here. Somehow got the address through your wife Cynthia. I didn't even know you were *married*, John. And a kid named Julian who's nearly thirty. He's married too, he's – '

' – What else did that bastard tell yer?'

'Look, we just talked. He was very charming.'

Charming. That figures. *Now* I'm beginning to believe.

'I thought you told me you used to be best mates.'

'Too bloody right. Then he nicked me band. It was John Lennon and the Quarrymen. I should never have let the bastard join. Then Johnny and the Moondogs. Then Long John and the Silver Beatles. It was *my* name, *my* idea to shorten it to just the Beatles. They all said it was daft, but they went along with it because it was *my* fucking band.'

'Look, nobody doubts that, John. But what's the point in being bitter? Paul just wanted to know how you were.'

'Oh, it's *Paul* now is it? Did yer let him shag yer, did yer put out for free, ask him to autograph yer fanny?'

'Come on, John. Climb down off the bloody wall. It didn't happen, you're not rich and famous. It's like not winning the pools, happens to everyone you meet. After all, the Beatles were just another rock band. It's not like they were the Stones.'

'Oh, no. The Stones weren't crap for a start. Bang bang Maxwell's Silver bloody Hammer. Give me Cliff any day.'

'You never want to talk about it, do you? You just let it stay inside you, boiling up. Look, why will you never believe that people care? *I* care. Will you accept that for a start? Do you think I put up with you here for the sodding rent which incidentally I never get anyway? You're old enough to be my bloody father, John. So stop acting like a kid.' Her face starts to go wet. I hate these kind of scenes. 'You *could* be my father, John. Seeing as I didn't have one, you'd do fine. Just believe in yourself for a change.'

'At least yer had a bloody *mother*,' I growl. But I can't keep the nasty up. Open me arms and she's trembling like a rabbit, smelling of salt and grass. All these years, all these *bloody* years. Why is it you can never leave anything behind?

Cal sniffs and steps back and pulls these bits of paper from her pocket. 'He gave me these. Two tickets for tonight's show, and a pass for the do afterwards.'

I look around at chez nous. The air smells of old stew that I can never remember eating. I mean, who the hell cooks *stew*? And Macca was here. Did them feet in ancient whathaveyou.

Cal plonks the tickets on the telly and brews some tea. She's humming in the kitchen, it's her big day, a famous rock star has come on down. I wonder if I should tear ye tickets up now, but decide to leave it for later. Something to look forward to for a change. All these years, all these *bloody* years. There was a journalist caught up with Dr Winston a while back. Oh Mr Lennon, I'm doing background. We'll pay yer of course, and perhaps we could have lunch? Which we did, and I can reveal exclusively for the first time that the Doctor got well and truly rat-arsed. And then the cheque came and the Doctor saw it all in black and white, serialised in the *Sunday* bloody *Excess*. A sad and bitter man, it said. So it's in the papers and I know it's true.

Cal clears a space for the mugs on the carpet and plonks them down. 'I know you don't mean to go tonight,' she says. 'I'm not going to argue about it now.'

She sits down on the sofa and lets me put an arm around her waist. We get warm and cosy. It's nice sometimes with Cal. You don't have to argue or explain.

'You know, John,' she murmurs. 'The secret of happiness is not trying.'

'And you're the world expert? Happiness sure ain't living on the Giro in bloody Birmingham.'

'Birmingham isn't the end of the world.'

'No, but yer can see it from here.'

Cal smiles. I love it when she smiles. She leans over and lights more blow from somewhere. She puts it to my lips. I breathe it in. The smoke. Tastes like harvest bonfires. We're snug as two bunnies. 'Think of when you were happy,' she whispers. 'There must have been a time.'

Oh, yeah: 1966, after I'd recorded the five singles that made up the entire creative output of the Nowhere Men and some git at the record company was given the job of saying, Well, John, we don't feel we can give yer act the attention it deserves. And let's be honest the Beatles link isn't really bankable any more is it? Walking out into the London traffic, it was just a huge load off me back. John, yer don't have to be a rock star after all. No more backs of vans. No more Watford Gap Sizzlers for breakfast. No more chord changes. No more launches and re-launches. No more telling the bloody bass player how to use his instrument. Of course, there was Cyn and little Julian back in Liverpool, but let's face it I was always a bastard when it came to family. I kidded meself they were better off without me.

But 1966. There *was* something then, the light had a sharp edge. Not just acid and grass although that was part of it. A girl with ribbons came up to me along Tottenham Court Road. Gave me a dogeared postcard of a white foreign beach, a blue sea. Told me she'd been there that very morning, just held it to her eyes in the dark. She kissed me cheek and she said she wanted to pass the blessing on. Well, the Doctor has never been much of a dreamer, but he could feel the surf of that beach through his toes as he dodged the traffic. He knew there were easier ways of getting there than closing yer eyes. So I took all me money and I bought me a ticket and I took a plane to Spain, la, la. Seemed like everyone was heading that way then, drifting in some warm current from the sun.

Lived on Formentera for sunbaked years I couldn't count. It was a sweet way of life, bumming this, bumming that, me and the Walrus walking hand in hand, counting the sand. Sheltering under a fig tree in the rain, I met this Welsh girl who called herself Morwenna. We all had strange names then. She took me to a house made of driftwood and canvas washed up on the shore. She had bells between her breasts and they tinkled as we made love. When the clouds had cleared we bought fish fresh from the nets in the white-washed harbour. Then we talked in firelight and the dolphins sang to the lobsters as the waves advanced. She told me under the stars that she knew other places, other worlds. There's another John at your shoulder, she said. He's so like you I can't understand what's different.

But Formentera was a long way from anything. It was so timeless we knew it couldn't last. The tourists, the government, the locals, the police – every Snodgrass in the universe – moved in. Turned out Morwenna's parents had money so it was all just fine and dandy for the cunt, leaving me one morning before the sun was up, taking a little boat to the airport on Ibiza, then all the way back to bloody Cardiff. The clouds greyed over the Med and the Doctor stayed on too long. Shot the wrong shit, scored the wrong deals. Somehow, I ended up in Paris, sleeping in a box and not speaking a bloody word of the lingo. Then somewhere else. The whole thing is a haze. Another time, I was sobbing on Mimi's doorstep in pebbledash Menlove Avenue and the dog next door was barking and Mendips looked just the same. The porch where I used to play me guitar. Wallpaper and cooking smells inside. She gave me egg and chips and tea in thick white china, just like the old days when she used to go on about me drainpipes.

So I stayed on a while in Liverpool, slept in me old bed with me feet sticking out the bottom. Mimi had taken down all me Brigitte Bardot posters but nothing else had changed. I could almost believe that me mate Paul was gonna come around on the wag from the Inny and we'd spend the afternoon with our guitars and pickle sandwiches, rewriting Buddy Holly and dreaming of the days to come. The songs never came out the way we meant and the gigs at the Casbah were a mess. But things were *possible*, then, yer know?

I roused meself from bed after a few weeks and Mimi nagged me down the Jobbie. Then I had to give up kidding meself that time had stood still. Did yer know all the docks have gone? I've never seen anything so empty. God knows what the people do with themselves when they're not getting pissed. I couldn't even find the fucking Cavern, or Eppy's old record shop where he used to sell that Sibelius crap until he chanced upon us rough lads.

When I got back to Mendips I suddenly saw how old Mimi had got. Mimi, I said, yer're a senior citizen. *I* should be looking after *you*. She just laughed that off, of course; Mimi was sweet and sour as ever. Wagged her finger at me and put something tasty on the stove. When Mimi's around, I'm still just a kid, can't help it. And she couldn't resist saying, I told you all this guitar stuff would get you nowhere, John. But at least she said it with a smile and hug. I guess I could have stayed there forever, but that's not the Doctor's way. Like Mimi says, he's got ants in his pants. Just like his poor dead mum. So I started to worry that things were getting too cosy, that maybe it was time to dump everything and start again, again.

What finally happened was that I met this bloke one day on me way back from the Jobbie. The original Snodgrass, no less – the one I used to sneer at during calligraphy in Art School. In them days I was James Dean and Elvis combined with me drainpipes and me duck's arse quiff. A one man revolution – Cynthia, the rest of the class were so hip they were trying to look like Kenny Ball and his Sodding Jazzmen. This kid Snodgrass couldn't even manage that, probably dug Frank Ifield. He had spots on his neck, a green sports jacket that looked like his mum had knitted it. Christ knows what his real name was. Of course, Dr Winston used to take the piss something rancid, specially when he'd sunk a few pints of black velvet down at Ye Cracke. Anyway, twenty years on and the Doctor was watching ye seagulls on Paradise Street and waiting for the lights to change, when this sports car shaped like a dildo slides up and a window purrs down.

'Hi, John! Bet you don't remember me.'

All I can smell is leather and aftershave. I squint and lean forward to see. The guy's got red-rimmed glasses on. A grin like a slab of marble.

'Yeah,' I say, although I really don't know how I know. 'You're the prat from college. The one with the spotty neck.'

'I got into advertising,' he said. 'My own company now.

You were in that band, weren't you, John? Left just before they made it. You always did talk big.'

'Fuck off, Snodgrass,' I tell him, and head across the road. Nearly walk straight into a bus.

Somehow, it's the last straw. I saunter down to Lime Street, get me a platform ticket and take the first Intercity that comes in, la, la. They throw me off at Brum, which I swear to Jesus God is the only reason why I'm here. Oh, yeah. I let Mimi know what had happened after a few weeks when me conscience got too heavy. She must have told Cyn. Maybe they send each other Crimble cards.

Damn.

Cal's gone.

Cold. The sofa. How can anyone *sleep* on this thing? Hurts me old bones just to sit on it. The sun is fading at the window. Must be late afternoon. No sign of Cal. Probably has to do the biz with some Arab our Kev's found for her. Now seems as good a time as any to sort out Macca's tickets, but when I look on top ye telly they've done a runner. The cunt's gone and hidden them, la, la.

Kevin's back. I can hear him farting and snoring upstairs in Cal's room. I shift the dead begonia off ye sideboard and rummage in the cigar box behind. Juicy stuff, near on sixty quid. Cal hides her money somewhere different about once a fortnight, and she don't think the Doctor has worked out where she's put it this time. Me, I've known for ages, was just saving for ye rainy day. Which is now.

So yer thought yer could get Dr Winston O'Boogie to go and see Stu and Paulie just by hiding the tickets did yer? The fucking NEC! Ah-ha. The Doctor's got other ideas. He pulls on ye jacket, his best and only shoes. Checks himself in the hall mirror. Puts on glasses. Looks like Age Concern. Takes them off again. Heads out. Pulls the door quiet in case

Kev should stir. The air outside is grainy, smells of diesel.
The sky is pink and all the street lights that work are coming
on. The kids are still playing, busy breaking the aerial off a
car. They're too absorbed to look up at ye passing Doctor,
which is somehow worse than being taunted. I recognise the
cracks in ye pavement. This one looks like a moon buggy.
This one looks like me mum's face after the car hit her
outside Mendips. Not that I saw, but still, yer dream, don't
yer? You still dream. And maybe things were getting a bit
too cosy here with Cal anyway, starting to feel sorry for her
instead of meself. Too cosy. And the Doctor's not sure if
he's ever coming back.

I walk ye streets. Sixty quid, so which pub's it gonna be?
But it turns out the boozers are still all shut anyway. It don't
feel early, but it is – children's hour on the telly, just the
time of year for smoke and darkness.

End up on the hill on top of the High Street. See the
rooftops from here, cars crawling, all them paper warriors
on the way home, Tracy doing lipstick on the bus, dreaming
of her boyfriend's busy hands and the night to come. Whole
of Birmingham's pouring with light. A few more right turns
in the Sierra to where the avenues drip sweet evening and
Snodgrass says I'm home darling. Deep in the sea arms of
love and bolognese for tea. Streets of Solihull and Sutton
Coldfield where the kids know how to work a computer
instead of just nick one, wear ye uniform at school, places
where the grass is velvet and there are magic fountains amid
the fairy trees.

The buses drift by on sails of exhaust and the sky is the
colour of Ribena. Soon the stars will come. I can feel the
whole night pouring in, humming words I can never quite
find. Jesus, does *everyone* feel this way? Does Snodgrass
carry this around when he's watching Tracy's legs, on holy
Sunday before the Big Match polishing the GL badge on his

fucking Sierra? Does he dream of the dark tide, seaweed combers of the ocean parting like the lips he never touched?

Me, I'm Snodgrass, Kevin, Tracy, fat Doris in her print dress. I'm every bit part player in the whole bloody horror-show. Everyone except John Lennon. Oh Jesus Mary Joseph and Winston, I dreamed I could circle the world with me arms, take the crowd with me guitar, stomp the beat on dirty floors so it would never end, whisper the dream for every kid under the starch sheets of radio nights. Show them how to shine.

Christ, I need a drink. Find me way easily, growl at dogs and passers-by, but Dave the barman's a mate. Everything's deep red in here and tastes of old booze and cigs and the dodgy Gents, just like swimming through me own blood. Dave is wiping the counter with a filthy rag and it's Getting pissed tonight are we, John? Yer bet, wac. Notice two rastas in the corner. Give em the old comic Livipud accent. Ken Dodd and his Diddymen. Makes em smile. I hate it when they don't smile. Ansells and a chaser. Even got change for the juke-box. Not a Beatles song in sight. No 'Yesterday', no 'C Moon', no 'Mull of Kinbloodytyre'. Hey, me shout at ye rastas, Now Bob Marley, he was the biz, reet? At least he had the sense to die. Like Jimi, Jim, Janis, all the good ones who kept the anger and the dream. The rastas say something unintelligible back. Rock and roll, lets. The rastas and Winston, we're on the same wavelength. Buy em a drink. Clap their backs. They're exchanging grins like they think I don't notice. Man, will you look at this sad old git? But he's buying. Yeah I'm buying thanks to Cal. By the way lads, these Rothmans taste like shit, now surely you guys must have something a little stronger?

The evening starts to fill out. I can see everything happening even before it does. Maybe the Doctor will have a little puke round about eight to make room for a greasy chippy.

Oh, yeah, and plenty of time for more booze and then maybe a bit of bother later. Rock and roll. The rastas have got their mates with them now and they're saying Hey man, how much money you got there? I wave it in their faces. Wipe yer arse on this, Sambo. Hey, Dave, yer serving or what? Drinky here, drinky there. The good Doctor give drinky everywhere.

Juke-box is pounding. Arms in arms, I'm singing words I don't know. Dave he tell me, Take it easy now, John. And I tell him exactly what to stuff, and precisely where. Oh, yeah. Need to sit down. There's an arm on me shoulder. I push it off. The arm comes again. The Doctor's ready to lash out, so maybe the bother is coming earlier than expected. Well, that's just fine and me turn to face ye foe.

It's Cal.

'John, you just can't hold your booze any longer.'

She's leading me out ye door. I wave me rastas an ocean wave. The bar waves back.

The night air hits me like a truncheon. 'How the fuck did yer find me?'

'Not very difficult. How many pubs are there around here?'

'I've never counted.' No, seriously. 'Just dump me here, Cal. Don't give me another chance to piss yer around. Look.' I fumble me pockets. Twenty pee. Turns out I'm skint again. 'I nicked all yer money. Behind the begonia.'

'On the sideboard? That's not mine, it's Kevin's. After last time do you think I'm stupid enough to leave money around where you could find it?'

'Ah-ha!' I point at her in triumph. 'You called him Kevin.'

'Just get in the bloody car.'

I get in the bloody car. Some geezer in the front says Okay guv, and off we zoom. It's a big car. Smells like a new camera. I do me royal wave past Kwiksave. I tell the driver, Hey me man, just step on it and follow that car.

'Plenty of time, sir,' he tells me. He looks like a chauffeur. He's wearing a bloody cap.

Time for what?

And Jesus, we're heading to Solihull. I've got me glasses on somehow. Trees and a big dual carriageway, the sort you never see from a bus.

The Doctor does the interior a favour. Says, Stop the car. Do a spastic sprint across ye lay-by and yawn me guts out over the verge. The stars stop spinning. I wipe me face. The Sierras are swishing by. There's a road sign the size of the Liverpool Empire over me head. Says NEC, two miles. So *that's* it.

Rock and roll. NEC. I've been here and seen Simply Red on Cal's free tickets, all them pretty tunes with their balls lopped off at birth. Knew what to expect. The place is all car park, like a bloody airport but less fun. Cal says Hi to the staff at the big doors, twilight workers in Butlin's blazers. Got any jobs on here, Cal? asks the pretty girl with the pretty programmes. It's Max Bygraves next week. Cal just smiles. The Doctor toys with a witty riposte about how she gets more dough lying with her legs open but decides not to. But Jesus, this is Snodgrass city. I've never seen so many casual suits.

I nick a programme from the pile when no one's looking. Got so much gloss on it, feels like a sheet of glass. The Greatest Hits Tour. Two photos of the Fab Foursome, then and now. George still looks like his mum, and Ringo's Ringo. Stu is wasted, but he always was. And Macca is Cliff on steroids.

'Stop muttering, John,' Cal says, and takes me arm.

We go into this aircraft hangar. Half an hour later, we've

got to our seat. It's right at the bloody front of what I presume must be the stage. Looks more like Apollo Nine. Another small step backwards for mankind. Oh, yeah. I *know* what a stage should look like. Like the bloody Indra in Hamburg where we took turns between the striptease. A stage is a place where yer stand and fight against the booze and the boredom and the sodding silence. A place where yer make people listen. Like the Cavern too before all the Tracys got their lunchtime jollies by screaming over the music. Magic days where I could feel the power through me Rickenbacker. And that guitar cost me a fortune and where the bloody hell did it get to? Vanished with every other dream.

Lights go down. A smoothie in a pink suit runs up to a mike and says ladeeez and gennnlemen, Paul McCartney, Stuart Sutcliffe, George Harrison, Ringo Starr – the Beatles! Hey, rock and roll. Everyone cheers as they run on stage. Seems like there's about ten of them nowadays, not counting the background chicks. They're all tiny up on that launch pad, but I manage to recognise Paul from the photies. He says Hello (pause) Birrrmingham just like he's Mick Hucknall and shakes his mop top that's still kinda cut the way Astrid did all them years back in Hamburg. Ringo's about half a mile back hidden behind the drums but that's okay cos there's some session guy up there too. George is looking down at his guitar like he's Bert Weedon. And there's Stu almost as far back as Ringo, still having difficulty playing the bass after all these bloody years. Should have stuck with the painting, me lad, something yer were good at. And Jesus, I don't believe it, Paul shoots Stu an exasperated glance as they kick into the riff for 'Long Tall Sally' and he comes in two bars late. Jesus, has *anything* changed.

Yeah, John Lennon's not up there. Would never have lasted this long with the Doctor anyway. I mean, thirty *years*.

That's as bad as Status Quo, and at least they know how to rock, even if they've only learnt the one tune.

Days in me life. Number one in a series of one. Collect the fucking set. It's 1962. Eppy's sent us rough lads a telegram from down the Smoke. Great news, boys. A contract. This is just when we're all starting to wonder, and Stu in particular is pining for Astrid back in Hamburg. But we're all giving it a go and the Doctor's even agreed to that stupid haircut that never quite caught on and to sacking Pete Best and getting Ringo in and the bloody suit with the bloody collar and the bloody fucking tie. So down to London it is. And then ta ran ta rah! A real single, a real recording studio! We meet this producer dude in a suit called Martin. He and Eppy get on like old buddies, upper crust and all that and me wonders out loud if he's a queer Jew too, but Paul says Can it John we can't afford to blow this.

So we gets in ye studio which is like a rabbit hutch. Do a roll Ringo, Martin says through the mike. So Ringo gets down on the mat and turns over. We all piss ourselves over that and all the time there's Mr Producer looking school-masterish. Me, I say, Hey, did yer really produce the Goons, Meester Martin. I got the 'Ying Tong Song' note perfect. They all think I'm kidding. Let's get on with it, John, Eppy says, and oils a grin through the glass, giving me the doe eyes. And don't yer believe it, John knows exactly what he wants. Oh, yeah. Like, did Colonel Parker fancy Elvis? Wow. So this is rock and roll.

Me and Paul, we got it all worked out. Hit the charts with 'Love Me Do', by Lennon and McCartney, the credits on the record label just the way we agreed years back in the front parlour of his Dad's house even though we've always done our own stuff separately. It's Macca's song, but we're democratic, right? And what really makes it is me harmonica riff. So that's what we play and we're all nervous as shit but even Stu manages to get the bass part right just the way Paul's shown him.

Silence. The amps are humming. Okay, says Mr Martin, putting on a voice, That was just great, lads. An interesting song. *Interesting?* Never one to beat about the proverbial, I say, yer mean it was shit, right? Just cos we wrote it ourselves and don't live down Tin Pan bloody Alley. But he says, I think we're looking at a B side for that one lads. Now, listen to this.

Oh, yeah. We listen. Martin plays us this tape of a demo of some ditty called 'How Do You Do It'. Definite Top Ten material for somebody, he says significantly. Gerry and the Pacemakers are already interested but I'll give you first refusal. And Eppy nods beside him through the glass. It's like watching Sooty and bloody Sweep in there. So Ringo smashes a cymbal and Stu tries to tune his bass and George goes over to help and I look at Paul and Paul looks at me.

'It's a decent tune, John,' Paul says.

'You're kidding. It's a heap of shit.'

Eppy tuts through the glass. Now *John*.

And so it goes. Me, I grab me Rickenbacker and walk out the fucking studio. There's a boozer round the corner. London prices are a joke but I sink one pint and then another, waiting for someone to come and say, You're so right, John. But Paul don't come. Eppy don't come either even though I thought it was me of all the lads that he was after. After the third pint, I'm fucking glad. The haircuts, the suits, and now playing tunes that belong in the bloody adverts. It's all gone too far.

And there it was. John Quits The Beatles in some local snotrag called *Merseybeat* the week after before I've had a chance to change me mind. And after that I've got me pride. When I saw Paul down Victoria Street a couple a months later yer could tell the single was doing well just by his

bloody walk. Said Hi John, yer know it's not too late and
God knows how *Merseybeat* got hold of the story. He said it
as though he and Eppy hadn't jumped at the chance to
dump me and make sure everybody knew. There was Macca
putting on the charm the way he always did when he was
in a tight situation. I told him to stuff it where the fucking
sun don't shine. And that was that. I stomped off down ye
street, had a cup of tea in Littlewoods. Walked out on
Cynthia and the kid. Formed me own band. Did a few gigs.
Bolloxed up me life good and proper.

And here we have the Beatles, still gigging, nearly a full
house here at the NEC, almost as big as Phil Collins or the
Bee Gees. Paul does his old thumbs-up routine between
songs. Awwrright. He's a real rock and roll dude, him and
George play their own solos just like Dire Straights. The
music drifts from the poppy older stuff to the druggy middle
stuff back to the poppy later stuff. 'Things We Said Today'.
'Good Day Sun Shine'. 'Dizzy Miss Lizzy'. 'Jet'. They even
do 'How Do You Do It'. No sign of 'Love Me Do', of course.
That never got recorded, although I'll bet they could do me
harmonica riff on ye synthesiser as easy as shit. It all sounds
smooth and tight and sweetly nostalgic, just the way it
would on the Sony music centre back at home after Snodgrass has loosened his tie from a hard day watching Tracy
wriggle her ass over the fax machine in Accounts. The pretty
lights flash, the dry ice fumes, but the spaceship never quite
takes off. Me, I shout for 'Maxwell's Silver Hammer', and in
a sudden wave of silence, it seems like Paul actually hears.
He squints down at the front row and grins for a moment
like he understands the joke. Then the lights dim to purple
and Paul sits down at ye piano, gives the seat a little tug just
the way he used to when he was practising on his Dad's old
upright in the parlour at home. Plays the opening chords of
'Let It Be'. I look around me and several thousand flames

are held up. It's a forest of candles, and Jesus it's a beautiful song. There's a lump in me throat, God help me. For a moment, it feels like everyone here is close to touching the dream.

The moment lasts longer than it decently should. Right through 'No More Lonely Nights' until 'Hey Judi' peters out like something half-finished and the band kick into 'Lady Madonna', which has a thundering bass riff even though Stu is still picking up his Fender. And the fucking stage starts to revolve. Me, I've had enough.

Cal looks at me as I stand up. She's bopping along like a Tracy. I mouth the word Bog and point to me crotch. She nods. Either she's given up worrying about the Doctor doing a runner or she don't care. Fact is, the booze has wrung me dry and I've got me a headache coming. I stumble me way up the aisles. The music pushes me along. He really *is* gonna do 'C Moon'. Makes yer want to piss just hearing it.

The lav is deliciously quiet. White tiles and some poor geezer in grey mopping up the piss. The Doctor straddles the porcelain. It takes about a minute's concentration to get a decent flow. Maybe this is what getting old is all about. I wonder if superstars like Macca have the same problem, but I doubt it. Probably pay some geezer to go for them, and oh, Kevin, can yer manage a good dump for me while yer're there?

Once it starts, the flow keeps up for a long time. Gets boring. I flush down ye stray hair, dismantle ye cigarette butt, looking at the grouting on the tiles, stare around. The guy with the mop is leaning on it, watching me.

'Must be a real groove in here,' I say.

'Oh, no,' he laughs. 'Don't get the wrong idea.'

I give percy a shake and zip up. The last spurt still runs down me bloody leg. Bet that don't happen to Paul either.

The wrong idea? The guy's got the plump face of a thirty-year-old choirboy. Pity poor Eppy ain't still alive, he'd be in his fucking element.

'I think all queers should be shot,' fat choirboy assures me.

'Well, seeing it from your perspective . . .' The Doctor starts to back away. This guy's out-weirding me without even trying.

'What's the concert like?'

The music comes around the corner as a grey echo, drowned in the smell of piss and disinfectant. 'It's mostly shit, what do yer expect?'

'Yeah,' he nods. His accent is funny. I think it's some bastard kind of Brummy until I suddenly realise he's American. 'They sold out, didn't they?'

'The Beatles never sold in.'

'Bloody hypocrites. All that money going to waste.'

Some other guy comes in, stares at us as he wees. Gives his leg a shake, walks out again. Choirboy and I stand in stupid silence. It's one of them situations yer find yerself in. But anyone who thinks that the Beatles are crap can't be all bad.

'You used to be in the Beatles, didn't you?'

I stare at him. No one's recognised me just from me face in years. I've got me glasses on, me specially grey and wrinkled disguise.

'Oh, I've read all about the Beatles,' he assures me, giving his mop a twirl.

I've half a mind to say, If yer're that interested give me the fucking mop and yer can have me seat, but there's something about him that I wouldn't trust next to Cal.

'Hey,' he smiles. 'Listen in there. Sounds like they're doing the encore.'

Which of course is 'Yesterday', like Oh deary me, we left it out by accident from the main show and thought we would just pop it in here. Not a dry seat in the bloody house.

Choirboy's still grinning at me. I see he's got a paperback in the pocket of his overall. *Catcher in the Rye*. 'They'll be a big rush in a minute,' he says. 'More mess for me to clean up. Even Jesus wouldn't like this job.'

'Then why do yer do it? The pay can't be spectacular.'

'Well, this is just casual work. I'll probably quit after tonight.'

'Yeah, pal. I know all about casual work.'

'But this is interesting, gets you into places. I like to be near to the stars. I need to see how bad they are.' He cracks that grin a little wider. 'Tell me,' he says, 'what's Paul really like?'

'How the fuck should I know? I haven't seen the guy in nearly thirty years. But, there's . . . there's some do on afterwards . . . he's asked me and me bird to come along. Yer know, for old times I guess.' *Jesus, John, who are yer trying to impress?*

'Oh,' he says, 'and where's that taking place? I sometimes look in, you know. The security round here's a joke. Last week, I was *that* close to Madonna.' He demonstrates the distance with his broom.

Cal's got the invites in her handybag, but I can picture them clear enough. I've got a great memory for crap. They're all scrolled like it's a wedding and there's a signed pass tacked on the back just to make it official. Admit two, The Excelsior, Meriden. Boogie on down, and I bet the Lord Mayor's coming. And tomorrow it's Reading. I mean, do these guys paarrty every night?

Choirboy grins. 'It's here at the Metropole, right?'

'Oh, yeah, the Metropole.' I saw the neon on the way in. 'That's the place just outside? Saves the bastards having to walk too far.' I scratch me head. 'Well maybe I'll see yer there. And just let me know if yer have any trouble at all getting in, right?'

'Right on.' He holds out his hand. I don't bother to shake it – and it's not simply because this guy cleans bogs. I don't want him near me, and somehow I don't want him near Paul or the others either. He's a fruitcase, and I feel briefly and absurdly pleased with meself that I've sent him off to ye wrong hotel.

I give him a wave and head on out ye bog. In the aircraft hangar, music's still playing. Let's all get up and dance to a song de da de da de dum de dum. Snodgrass and Tracy are trying to be enthusiastic so they can tell everyone how great it was in the office tomorrow. I wander down the aisles, wondering if it might be easier not to meet up with Cal. On reflection, this seems as good a place as any to duck out of her life. Do the cunt a favour. After all, she deserves it. And to be honest, I really don't fancy explaining to Kevin where all his money went. He's a big lad, is our Kev. Useful, like.

The music stops. The crowd claps like they're really not sure whether they want any more and Paul raises an unnecessary arm to still them.

'Hey, one more song then we'll let yer go,' he says with probably unintentional irony. I doubt if they know what the fuck is going on up there in Mission Control.

He puts down his Gibson and a roadie hands him something silver. Stu's grinning like a skull. He even wanders within spitting distance of the front of the stage. A matchstick figure, I can see he looks the way Keith Richards would have done if he *really* hadn't taken care of himself. He nods to George. George picks up a twelve string.

'This one's for an old friend,' Paul says.

The session musicians are looking at each other like What the fuck's going on? Could this really be an unrehearsed moment? Seems unlikely, but then Paul muffs the count in on a swift four/four beat. There's nervous laughter amongst the Fab Fearsome, silence in the auditorium. Then again. One. Two. Three. And.

Macca puts the harmonica to his lips. Plays me riff. 'Love Me Do'. Oh, yeah. I really can't believe it. The audience are looking a bit bemused, but probably reckon it's just something from the new LP that's stacked by the yard out in the foyer and no one's bothered to buy. The song's over quickly. Them kind of songs always were. Me, I'm crying.

The End. Finis, like they say in cartoon. Ye Beatles give a wave and duck off stage. I get swept back in the rush to get to ye doors. I hear snatches of, Doesn't he look *old*, They *never* knew how to rock, Absolutely *brilliant*, and *How* much did you pay the babysitter? I wipe the snot off on me sleeve and look around. Cal catches hold of me by the largely unpatronised T-shirt stall before I have a chance to see her coming.

'What did you think?'

'A load of shit,' I say, hoping she won't notice I've been crying.

She smiles. 'Is that all you can manage, John? That must mean you liked it.'

Touché, Monsieur Pussycat. 'Truth is, I could need a drink.'

'Well, let's get down the Excelsior. You can meet your old mates and get as pissed as you like.'

She glides me out towards the door. Me feet feel like they're on rollers. And there's me chauffeur pal with the boy scout uniform. People stare at us as he opens the door like we're George Michael. Pity he don't salute, but still, I'd look a right pillock trying to squirm me way away from a pretty woman and the back seat of a Jag.

The car pulls slowly through the crowds. I do me wave like I'm the Queen Mum although the old bint's probably too hip to be seen at a Beatles concert. Turns out there's a special exit for us VIPs. I mean, rock and roll. It's just a few minutes' drive, me mate up front tells us.

Cal settles back. 'This is the life.'

'Call this life?'

'Might as well make the most of it, John.'

'Oh, yeah. I bet you get taken in this kind of limo all the time. Blowjobs in the back seat. It's what pays, right?' I bite me lip and look out the window. Jesus, I'm starting to cry again.

'Why do you say things like that, John?'

'Because I'm a bastard. I mean, you of all people must know about bastards having to put up with Steve.'

Cal laughed. 'You called him Steve!'

I really must be going ta bits. 'Yeah, well I must have puked up me wits over that lay-by.'

'Anyway,' she touches me arm. 'Call him whatever you like. I took your advice this evening. Told him where to stuff it.'

I look carefully at her face. She obviously ain't kidding, but I can't see any bruises. 'And what about the money I nicked?'

'Well, that's not a problem for me, is it? I simply told him the truth, that it was you.' She smiled. 'Come on, John. I'd almost believe you were frightened of him. He's just some bloke. He's got another girl he's after anyway, the other side of town and good luck to her.'

'So it's just you and me is it, Cal. Cosy, like. Don't expect me to sort out yer customers for yer.'

'I'm getting too old for that, John. It costs you more than they pay. Maybe I'll do more work at the NEC. Of course, you'll have to start paying your sodding rent.'

I hear meself say, 'I think there's a vacancy coming up in the NEC Gents. How about that for a funky job for Dr

Winston? At least you get to sweep the shit up there rather than having to stuff it into envelopes.'

'What are you talking about, John?'

'Forget it. Maybe I'll explain in the morning. You've got influence there, haven't you?'

'I'll help you get a job, if that's what you're trying to say.'

I lookouta ye window. The houses streaming past, yellow windows, where ye Snodgrasses who weren't at the concert are chomping pipe and slippers while the wife makes spaniel eyes. The kids tucked upstairs in pink and blue rooms that smell of Persil and Playdough. Me, I'm just the guy who used to be in a halfway-famous band before they were anybody. I got me no book club subscription, I got me no life so clean yer could eat yer bloody dinner off it. Of course, I still got me rebellion, oh yeah, I got me that, and all it amounts to is cadging cigs off Cal and lifting packets of Cheesy Wotsits from the bargain bin in Kwiksave when Doris and Tracy ain't looking. Oh, yeah, rebellion. The milkman shouts at me when I go near his float in case the Mad Old Git nicks another bottle.

I can remember when we used to stand up and face the crowd, do all them songs I've forgotten how to play. When Paul still knew how to rock. When Stu was half an artist, dreamy and scary at the same time. When George was just a neat kid behind a huge guitar, lying about his age. When Ringo was funny and the beat went on forever. Down the smoggily lit stairways and greasy tunnels, along burrows and byways where the cheesy reek of the bogs hit yer like a wall. Then the booze was free afterwards and the girls would gather round, press softly against yer arm as they smiled. Their boyfriends would mutter at the bar but you knew they were afraid of yer. Knew they could sense the power of the music that carried off the stage. Jesus, the girls were as sweet as the rain in those grey cities, the shining streets, the forest wharves, the dark doorways where there was laughter in the dripping brick-paved night. And sleeping afterwards, yer head spinning from the booze and the wakeups and the downers, taking turns on that stained mattress with the cinema below booming in yer head and the music still pouring through. Diving down into carousel dreams.

Oh, the beat went on all right. Used to think it would carry up into daylight and the real air, touch the eyes and ears of the pretty dreamers, even make Snodgrass stir a little in his slumbers, take the shine off the Sierra, make him look up at the angels in the sky once in a while, or even just down at the shit on the pavement. .

'Well, here we are,' Cal says.

Oh, yeah. Some hotel. Out in the pretty pretty. Trees and lights across a fucking lake. The boy scout opens the door for me and Cal. Unsteady on me pins, I take a breath, then have me a good retching cough. The air out here reeks of roses or something, like one of them expensive bog fresheners that Cal sprays around when our Kev's had a dump.

'Hey.' Cal holds out the crook of her arm. 'Aren't you going to escort me in?'

'Let's wait here.'

There are other cars pulling up, some old git dressed like he's the Duke of Wellington standing at the doors. Straight ahead to the Clarendon Suite, sir, he smooths greyly to the passing suits. I suppose these must be record industry types. And then there's this bigger car than the rest starts to pull up. It just goes on and on, like one of them gags in *Tom and Jerry*. Everyone steps back like it's the Pope. Instead, turns out it's just the Beatles. They blink around in the darkness like mad owls, dressed in them ridiculous loose cotton suits that Clapton always looks such a prat in. Lawyers tremble around them like little fish. Paul pauses to give a motorcycle policeman his autograph, flashes the famous Macca grin.

Some guy in a suit who looks like the hotel manager shakes hands with Stu. Rock and roll. I mean, this is what we were always fighting for. The Beatles don't register the good Doctor before they head inside, but maybe that's because he's taken three steps back into the toilet freshener darkness.

'What are we waiting for?' Cal asks as the rest of the rubbernecks drift in.

'This isn't easy, Cal.'

'Who said anything about *easy*?'

I give the Duke of Wellington a salute as he holds ye door open.

'Straight ahead to the Clarendon Suite, sir.'

'Hey,' I tell him, 'I used to be Beatle John.'

'Stop mucking about, John.' Cal does her Kenneth Williams impression, then gets all serious. 'This is important. Just forget about the past and let's concentrate on the rest of your life. All you have to say to Paul is Hello. He's a decent guy. And I'm sure that the rest of them haven't changed as much as you imagine.'

Cal wheels me in. The hotel lobby looks like a hotel lobby. The Tracy at reception gives me a cutglass smile. Catch a glimpse of meself in the mirror and unbelievably I really don't look too bad. Must be slipping.

'Jesus, Cal. I need a smoke.'

'Here.' She rumbles in me pocket, produces Kevin's Rothmans. 'I suppose you want a bloody light.'

All the expensive fish are drifting by. Some bint in an evening dress so low at the back that you can see the crack of her arse puts her arm on this Snodgrass and gives him a peck on the cheek. That was *delightful*, darrling, she purrs. She really does.

'I mean a *real* smoke, Cal. Haven't you got some blow?' I make a lunge for her handbag.

'Bloody hell, John,' she whispers, looking close to losing

her cool. She pushes something into my hand. 'Have it outside, if you must. Share it with the bloody doorman.'

'Thanks Cal.' I give her a peck on the cheek and she looks at me oddly. 'I'll never forget.'

'Forget what?' she asks as I back towards the door. Then she begins to understand. But the Duke holds the door open for me and already I'm out in the forest night air.

The door swings back, then open again. The hotel lights fan out across the grass. I look back. There's some figure.

'Hey, John!'

It's a guy's voice, not Cal's after all. Sounds almost Liverpool.

'Hey, wait a minute! Can't we just talk?'

The voice rings in silence.

'John! It's me!'

Paul's walking into the darkness towards me. He's holding out his hand. I stumble against chrome. The big cars are all around. Then I'm kicking white stripes down the road. Turns to gravel underfoot and I can see blue sea, a white beach steaming after the warm rain, a place where a woman is waiting and the bells jingle between her breasts. Just close your eyes and you're there.

Me throat me legs me head hurts. But there's a gated side road here that leads off through trees and scuffing the dirt at the end of a field to some big houses that nod and sway with the sleepy night.

I risk a look behind. Everything is peaceful. There's no one around. Snodgrass is dreaming. Stars upon the rooftops, and the Sierra's in the drive. Trees and privet, lawns neat as velvet. Just some suburban road at the back of the hotel. People living their lives.

I catch me breath, and start to run again.